GRAVITATIONAL FIELDS

a novel of peacetime and war

by HARRY RAJCHGOT

COPYRIGHT

This is a work of fiction, but is based on true events and modelled on individuals who lived through them. Any resemblance to individuals now either living or dead other than as composites is largely but not entirely coincidental.

Cover design by Cheryl Everett Rajchgot.

Library and Archives Canada Cataloguing in Publication

Rajchgot, Harry, author
    Gravitational fields : a novel of peacetime and war / by Harry Rajchgot.

ISBN 978-0-9950435-1-0 (paperback)

    1. Holocaust survivors--Fiction. I. Title.

PS8635.A45548G73 2016   C813'.6   C2016-901285-9

Never again.

Marching Naked to Jerusalem

I walk the silken
road of joy
Naked and radiant
with delight
Towards the loins
of my patient lover
Towards the city
Jerusalem

The sacred city
is a woman
She longs for me
to enter her
Her stone-ranged keep,
her golden gate
Shudders with
her wet desire

Submerged in the sweet
spring of Shiloah
By the water tunnel hewn
from Gihon's source
I enter the citadel through
her secret grotto
Anointed before her
with fragrant oils

I stand below you
wanton and shameless
Mother Eve before eating
the fruit of knowledge
Beguiled by the promise
of the tree of life
Transformed by the touch
of the hand of God

From Ur towards Zion
I sang Your name
Was transformed by the

vigour of Your words
From Sinai's smoke,
the great mountain trembling
My loins thrust outwards
that fateful day

My breast is dripping
the milk of passion
Feeding your thirst
O my Jerusalem
Speaking the poetry
of your song
Singing the music
in your embrace

When Abram marched
to God's great mandate
Towards where Isaac
would lie upon the rock
Amazed by the splendour
of his one son's submission
Abram held his breath
and dreamt of hope

Walking the sweet path
towards the stone of sacrifice
I expose my soul
to your desire
I give myself to
the grace that guides you
I march naked
Towards Jerusalem

Abraham, son of Terach, stands exhausted and downcast. It has been a long struggle to climb up into the mountains. He has just sacrificed his son, as God had commanded him to do. He now turns to God in despair and cries out.

"Turn back the sun, Lord, the tides and the wind, take night away from day, begin again at the advent of time. Give me back my boy."

God replies: "I cannot."

Abraham questions. "Are you not God?"

There is only quiet, the wind blowing across sand, the crying of a silenced heart.

We are fortunate not to live in that universe.

Too Late

For a moment, there was no sound. Duvid stood hidden below the bridge crossing into his village, waist-deep in cold river water. Above him there was a brief exchange in harsh German, followed by a laugh. A whiff of tobacco smoke reached his nostrils. Someone leant over the side of the bridge and spit. A splash near the reeds. A lit cigarette followed, then a quick hiss. A whistle shrilled, and in an instant, an insistent thud of boots on wood, soon becoming a quieter crunch on dirt and stone. The voices moved off. The birds sang again. The soldiers had gone.

Duvid released his breath, and allowed himself to gasp. His legs swung out of the autumn-cold water. He was intent on only one thing, now that he had returned to his home, and so hardly felt the cold. He slipped forward, grasping the algae-slicked stones along the bridge's side, then burrowed through the mass of reeds bordering the river. The low rooftops along the town's edge came into view. Crouching down, he ran towards the wood thicket near Yankel's shop. No one had spotted him.

He hesitated at the edge of the brush. A rush of human voices startled him and he pulled back deeper into the shadows. The howls and cries rose from a multitude of yellow stars, each of its souls orbiting in a turbulent miniature galaxy, gathered in the bright air beyond Duvid's vegetative darkness.

At the centre of the spiral towered a golden-haired military officer. He raised his arms and time stopped. All eyes gazed towards him. Pupils narrowed, eyelids tightened in foreboding. The sky's fiercely knowledgeable light was restrained by human shadows.

From all sides, the same timbre of the voices he had heard on the bridge shouted out now. The crowd pulsated, trying to dash this way or that. Women clutched their children. Men tore at their chests, raising their arms to the holy sky, vomiting in dread and horror. The sky looked back, unblinking, neutral, giving no evidence of its sentient nature.

Duvid dropped down into the ground, and again stopped breathing. His chest heaved silently, pleading for him to release it to do its work. Slowly he exhaled, a faint hiss. More shouts from beyond the shade were followed by the mutter and grunt of truck engines, the smell of burning petrol. After a few minutes, only silence remained. Duvid still hid, trying to blend into the soil, mutate his form into grass and stone and tree root.

Night came. Crickets rasped out their leggy music, a sphere of life around Duvid's dark silence. He dared move now. His thoughts were a cauldron of emotions, fear and revulsion, blackened shadows sliding one across the other. The now-vacant voices muttered in his ears.

He began to sob. Too late. He had come too late.

The future is truly and mercifully hidden. By ourselves, by others, by the nature of the world itself.

Yet how else do we continue our dance into the future? Our blindness is a blessing—it allows us to believe in tomorrow. We are all caught in a web of events which grows, thread on thread, ravelling from the past into the far tomorrow. Our worlds—my world, your world, this multitude of universes that belong individually to each one of us—conceal their mystery. In every generation, a series of cataracts collapse abruptly into rivers of belief and doubt, whirlpools of menace, maelstroms of dismay, a cascade through the unmapped wetlands of time.

What are the many aspects of the deep unknowable face of this endlessly finite space-time we inhabit? Between us are suspended strings of being and event, dimensions binding the past and the present. Do they float in the air like a spider's flimsy silk thread, to carry us off on winds of random chance? Can we know these wisps and filaments, divine their tenuous being?

Can we change the outcome?

PART I – PEACE and PEACE AGAIN

1 Wonders

Simon dragged himself wearily out of his sleeping bag and rose in the dark. Outside the tent, in the middle of the night, the soft earth sucked at him, threatening to swallow him whole. Beneath his toes, in the overhang of branches, in the blind suffocating air, in the humid soil, in all these places were a myriad of unseen slimy creatures, thousands of jointed legs, palps, suckers, and gossamer wings, warring silently for dominion among themselves. His skin came alive with the touch of fluttering wings. Despite his disgust and terror, the palpable stillness drew his eyes upward to the myriad wavering points in the sky above his head. The sea of light was dazzling. The unnumbered stars frightened him, as he looked up and realized how truly alone he was in this open universe soaring above him. Simon shut his eyes tightly, escaping the world of menace around him. He fingered the canvas of the tent, anchoring himself.

"Camping is a wonderful thing for a young boy," Simon's father had insisted, "clear, fresh air, nature all around. Better than those comic books of yours." Simon had sighed and wanted to complain, but knew better. He was no zealot of nature; he preferred his comic books. Yet it was his father's stubborn conviction that his two sons should in summer be as close to nature as possible. Here, in these menacing woods, in wild unrepentant night, his father's will prevailed.

The wet air that breathed into Simon was pungent with its intrusive odours, with the piercing sounds of centipede night. It was late summer in these Laurentian woods. The frenzy of black flies was long gone, but the persistent mosquitoes still hung on, not yet killed off by the cold of the last August nights still to come. A few always managed to get into the tent during the night, when he or his brother woke up and went outside to pee against the bushes, and then he would wish for sleep to silence their buzz next to his ear. While the mosquitoes' wings irritated the froth of misted air, at a slower pace the attributes of the seasons were changing, gliding from the thick, dark nights of high summer into the betraying evenings of autumn.

Looking up, he felt that he was floating beneath a vast star field, a faint luminous ocean. He could almost touch individual incandescent whispers suspended in their measureless perfect blackness. Duvid had described to his twin sons how the universe trembled. Each point of light above had a slight flicker, like the shaking of his grandfather's hands as he had intently concentrated on threading a needle so long ago in Poland. Each star was a reflection off the head of a needle, shaking in the hand of a master tailor, always working at sewing the universe together. Except Simon knew that it was not so, despite what his Jewish school teachers told him. The needle was without thread, and shaky nevertheless.

Tonight, the Northern Lights were displaying their rare splendour, writhing sheets of colour flashing across the sky, throbbing to the pulse of the earth's magnetic field, his planet a jewel lit by the sun's rays. He was overwhelmed, not sure what he felt—a measure of dread mixed with delight at the beauty revealed above his gaze.

Metal clicked, a faint orange glow burst out, and Simon turned. His father was also awake. Meters away, his father's drooping form bent into itself, a black shadow framing the light that stretched from its source in his hand, speeding off into the forever of the universe. Simon disliked the smell of tobacco smoke and turned away.

His father quietly came up behind him, fully knowing that his son knew he was there, fully knowing that Simon wouldn't be startled by the sudden, solid touch of his father's hand on the back of his head, before it became soft against his cheek. His hand carried the odour of tobacco, deeply worked into the skin, permeated into each crease and pore, held there despite the washing of hands again and again.

"Come away from the tent. You will wake your sleepy brother. Here, sit on this rock." Simon reluctantly released his grip on the tent flap and balanced his way across the darkness.

"Exquisite. How else to describe it, this magnificent sky? You don't see a bit of this in the city. The air is so clear here."

"Ta, if you want clear air, why do you smoke?"

"Some things are difficult to explain. Something I need. Like food."

"So when I'm older, I'll smoke too?"

"Ach, no. Don't start. It's a terrible thing."

"Except if you do it?"

"Another question, Simon?"

"Ta, Ma says to ask is no sin."

"Yes, it's true. We are alive. To ask is what we must do. God demands it of us. You know, Simon, I sometimes forget how young you are when I hear these questions of yours."

Simon bristled invisibly in the dark. "I'm not so young, I'm already ten."

"Yes, I know this, Simon. I don't forget your age. I just mean that sometimes you act older."

"Sometimes? When?"

"Yes, sometimes. When I was ten, I asked many questions too, but to question was not always such a favoured thing. Many of the answers I could not accept. The *heder* teacher in my town in Poland tried to beat the skepticism out of me. His leather strap was long as my leg."

"He beat you?"

Simon's father paused and sucked smoke into his lungs, then exhaled slowly. "I told my father that I was never going back to school. He answered that it was my own fault I was beaten. It wasn't my fault. I was there because of God, so it was God's fault. That's what I told my teacher. For saying that, he beat me again."

The wooden ruler across the hand, that was the favourite of Simon's teachers. His hand tingled now, a memory of pain flowing into the cool rock he straddled. Simon found it tedious to go to *heder* after school, with its stiff, self-righteous teachers, fierce and ugly, their suits shabby and shiny-seated, their long beards flecked with particles of kosher food, nose hairs exuberant, and crumbling wax curds guarding their deaf ears. Quick to punish, slow to hear. Repulsive. They were God's advocates, His explicators. If it was God's fault, then it was their fault too.

"Do your teachers hit you? No, of course not, this is not permitted, and they would have to answer to me. The world has changed in this aspect. Yet much is the same."

"Like what, Ta?"

"The world is still a fearful place."

"Like for Ma?"

"Yes, she is always afraid."

Simon waited for an explanation but nothing came.

"Ta, are you afraid?"

"When I was young like you, I was, yes, but no longer. Fear has passed me by. I have seen too much. I fear no stars, nor teachers. They look down and do nothing to me or for me. I know you don't like being here. You complain enough. But it is good for the soul to touch nature like this. That is why I bring you here. When I was young, I always played and explored in woods."

"You lived there during the war, didn't you?"

"You should not listen in when grownups talk."

Simon waited for more but it didn't come. He swam into the silence that was his father's response to such questions. He shuddered. His hands slid along the rock, searching for some handhold, then pulled back from the unknown creatures that shared its surface.

"I'm afraid now, Ta."

"Of what? A few insects?"

"Ta. Forget it."

"Ach, my so sensitive son. Being like this will bring you no good in life, Simon."

"So can I ask another question?"

"I didn't succeed to stop them yet? What?"

"Some of my friends at school have many cousins and uncles and aunts. I have hardly any."

Simon's father hesitated. The tip of his cigarette flared momentarily.

"We came out from Europe after the war."

"What do you mean?"

"Simon, leave it."

"But why?"

"I said leave it, Simon.

"No, tell me. They died?"

The cigarette brightened again.

"Yes. Many died."

"In the war? People you knew?"

"Yes, people I knew. Now no more questions." His father stood up and tramped away. The tactile darkness surrounding them instantly swallowed his father. All sound stopped. Simon was left alone, paralyzed by fear.

"Ta," he whispered desperately. His voice didn't work anymore. The woods came alive again with a flutter of wings, the staccato of crickets signaling, the worried crack of snapping branches, then a sudden dead silence. Fear lashed him to his seat on the rock. How many footsteps was he away from the tent? Crashing sounds now exploded out of the woods. Was this still his father or a large animal? Before Simon could summon the courage to rise and run, he heard rather than saw that his father stood next to him again.

"Ta? Where did you go?" Simon whimpered.

"You're afraid? Really?"

"Not really."

"So now you are brave? Now that I'm next to you?"

"Yes, Ta."

When I say to stop asking, you stop. Do you understand now?"

"Yes, Ta."

His father crouched.

"You could disappear in the woods, Ta. Maybe die."

"Really? Out among the trees? From what, being attacked by moths? Such nonsense."

The two went silent again.

"What happens after we die, Ta?"

"Do I look like such a genius to you, to answer such a question? Simon, it is better not to think about that. You should more be afraid of what happens while you live. No one knows about death. Even someone who says he knows is ignorant. Do not trust the rabbis, or, God forbid, the priests, Simon. They above all others know nothing. They will tell you their stories, many stories. Empty superstitions. They all mean nothing. You must decide for yourself, Simon. No one can give you the answers except you."

"Ta, do you believe in God?"

Duvid, Simon's father, stared at the dark form of his son. Simon really was growing up. Duvid retrieved a small stick from the ground and twirled it between his fingers.

"Such a big question. You are growing up. No. Yes. It doesn't make sense. Ah, but some things one must believe, just to make sense in our own heads. Even things that make no sense."

"Like what?"

"Like God. Like the stars in the sky."

Simon remained silent momentarily, perplexed. He sensed he needed to ask a simpler question.

"Was the sky always like this?"

"Like what?"

"So full of stars. When you were a boy."

Duvid gave Simon a querying look. "Ach, such a question. You must think I am as old as the sky itself." His father sniggered. "When I was young, yes, it was exactly the same. Even deep in the woods of Poland. But the world I knew was not the one I know now, the one you know. I spoke a different language, had different ideas, believed things that I no longer can. We Jews, we have certain beliefs, or once did—one God, Who, it is said made a pact, a bargain, with us, that if we followed His laws, He would protect us. When I looked up at the sky when I was young, I believed something of that." Duvid settled to his knees. In a distracted frenzy, he dug through the layers of fir needles with his stick. "No, the sky and the earth are not the same for me. There are just as many stars."

"So what is different? Not the stars."

"No, not the stars."

"Who, the people?"

"The people. Yes, our people."

It was time to speak. Duvid took a deep breath.

"I don't need to tell you that I lost my whole family during the war, some in the *shtetl*, others in the ghettos, most in the concentration camps. You know this already from hearing us talk when you should have been asleep. We Jews lost more than all the stars you can see, far more in lives and traditions and meaning than most people can imagine or believe. Some say that we even lost God."

Simon had already blundered into this territory. He knew too much about it already. Never before by Duvid's direct recounting. Simon's imagination had been filled with the knowledge of these whos by his father's reluctant yet florid stories overheard from behind doors and darkened bedrooms, traded to visiting relatives and friends, that always started out hesitant and then plunged into the terrible retelling of one or another person's story, always one more someone who was dead. Dead in the war.

A deep chanting voice was reawakening now within Simon. It knew the time was now right for it to moan its hollow tone. It came every night when he thought about death and what might possibly follow it. It was a voice from out of a vacuum, its intonations neither rising nor falling, echoing dully in an empty place inside him. It clutched at his guts and tore through his skin. He shuddered at its approach. He wanted to run but the voice held him motionless. His eyes glazed, fixed on the stars above, holding to them like to a pier in a lake.

Gaze into me, Simon, look into my terrible darkness, so deep you drown.

... *look up... look up... look up...*, it droned onward. Simon felt around for something to grasp. The rock slid away. He was dizzy.

As he peered upwards into the infinitely deep darkness, he was aware that a chasm was again opening silently all around his feet. It was the dread of the abyss that surrounded him always, only felt and realized when he was in this state, which now came over him. His father's silence ordinarily guarded Simon's balance, a wall that kept him back from this edge. It was when he spoke that his words released these vertiginous forces, leaving Simon to hang on this precipice. If he looked up for only that one second, Simon sensed, the spirit which owned the voice would seize him, drag his quaking soul into the liquid depths. The chant continued.

... look up... look up... look up...

The monotone trailed off to silence. Simon's belly churned. It hurt. He stared at the seemingly numberless lights above him.

... look up ... look up ... look up ...

Stop talking. STOP. Make it stop.

"Ta, who cares?"

"Who cares? WHO CARES? Simon, such a horrible thing to say, like an evil child." His father grabbed at a stone and launched it into the night. It thudded against a tree somewhere in the dark. Another followed, then another. Duvid took a deep breath, paused, and lit another cigarette.

"You only say such a thing, Simon, because you are a little fool, confused and afraid."

Simon watched the man stiffen. Shame flooded him suddenly and thoroughly. His father sucked on the cigarette.

"Can I smoke?"

"You really want to smoke? To be a hero? Sure, so here, smoke, smoke. Kill yourself! Here, take, take!" Duvid pushed the cigarette towards his son's hand. Simon took a single puff and was instantly woozy. He coughed. His insides were on fire. He tried to take another puff. Duvid began to laugh.

"So, you like? No, but I see you want to like."

"Ta, am I really a fool?"

"Yes, only a fool doesn't care."

"I don't want to care, Ta."

"I know. But they would have been your family, Simon. Cousins, aunts, uncles. Your grandparents."

"Only they're not."

"Simon, they lived once. You can't erase them like the Germans did. They were my life and they're all dead. My whole family, dead. Do you understand what this means? My mother and father, my three sisters, Hinda, Chaya, Henna, my four brothers, Moishe, Avrum, Itzele, Hersh." Then a pause, almost an afterthought. "Miriam."

Simon's eyes glistened with interest.

"Who was Miriam? Another sister?" Simon wondered if he had miscounted.

"My girlfriend."

"You had a girlfriend before Ma?"

"Simon, I met your mother after the war."

"Did Miriam die in the war?"

"I do not know." Duvid paused, exposed, weighing what he should say next. "The war came, like a storm, and it was too late. I ran to the woods."

"What did you do there?"

"I hid."

"That's it? You hid?"

"I cannot speak of it, Simon."

"But what happened to Miriam?"

"She disappeared."

"How?"

"I've said too much already."

Simon pulled back. From inside his tent, his brother Adam's voice howled out in his sleep. Simon stared ahead, frozen, afraid to cry too.

"Simon, it was a hard time, one I would rather forget. And I cannot."

Simon, angry now, saw his father deflating.

"Ta, why did you run away? Why didn't you fight?" Duvid stared at Simon as if he were observing an alien from another planet. It was a newly frightening world for the boy.

"Were you a coward?"

A long pause. "It wasn't like on television, Simon."

The boy gave a furtive look at his father's face.

"So what about Miriam?"

A faint light flickered in Duvid's eyes. "I told you I don't know. There were a thousand rumours after the war. I never saw her again. Who could know which were true, or even half-true?

"She left for Israel. She was in Argentina. A Russian prison camp, maybe. A teacher in Siberia. She had a son. She had a daughter. She died of typhus, or pneumonia, or by firing squad. Or froze to death in a blizzard.

"I tried to write to her in all these places where she might be. I never heard anything back. Not a word, ever. So I stopped thinking of her. Until now."

Simon's father's face disappeared in the darkness. Simon waited for more to come. And waited.

"Does Ma know this story?"

"She knows that I lost everyone I once knew. It is more than she wants to know, to know that alone. She is not strong, not anymore. Your mother, she lost also, maybe not everybody, but enough. Too many. She also is lost, as I am. We can never forget all this. I wish only that we could leave it and walk away, but it follows us everywhere, always, as if it was my fault."

"Whose fault is it?"

"The whole world's. Everyone's. No one's. God's."

"God's?" This blaming was a revelation to Simon. A new thing in the world.

"But can a man question God? Yes. No. For me it is not possible. Belief, my upbringing–I cannot so easily put them aside. My mind is too slow for such changes."

"What if she is alive now?"

"Impossible! What change would that make for me if she was? Now, nothing. Nothing. I am a father. I have a family to take care of. It would make no difference. No difference at all." Duvid took a puff of his cigarette, held it deep, and slowly exhaled. "Don't say anything to your mother about any of this. It will only distress her."

Simon's father's eyes seemed moist as the glow of his cigarette illuminated them. Then they were obscured by darkness.

"I have two sons, both of you miracles, like from God, even if you are sometimes fools. I never expected while the war was going on that such a thing could ever happen. You and your brother, when you were born, we hoped maybe it would replace for us some of those who died." He sighed. "But you cannot replace anyone. People are not parts from a sewing machine."

"Ta, you don't even believe in God. How can you talk like you do?"

"Simon, it is not that I do or do not believe, I swear to God, I do not know which I really feel. See, there I go contradicting myself again. No, it is that I am angry at God, and if I do not allow myself to believe in Him, how can there be someone for me to be angry with?"

Simon thought about this paradox for a moment. "You're angry because He let your family die?"

"No, Simon. No. That was His right. We cannot know His reasons. Why He allowed this to happen, we cannot ask. If He exists."

The man stopped speaking. He had allowed the cigarette to burn short. He inhaled, then waited for the smoke to do its slow damage in his lungs before expelling it again. He coughed lightly. The smoke and his breath mixed, lit only by the stars above and the glow of the ashen cigarette below. Simon turned his attention to the mosquitoes buzzing past his ears. He swung at them awkwardly in the darkness. For a few seconds, the sounds of their wings stopped. All was silence, all around them. The two were at the centre of a great silent sphere extending beyond the edges of the world.

"He was not required to save them. God needs to follow no law, not even His own." He pulled smoke into his lungs again. He spoke as he exhaled.

"The reason I am angry," he stopped, then repeated, more poison in the words, "the reason I am angry," he took a very deep breath, "is that He let me live."

Duvid stopped speaking, shocked that Simon was suddenly shaking with cold.

"Simon, it's too cold for you. Go back to the tent now. You should sleep." Duvid stared up at the ancient stars above. He had said the wrong things again. A shiver passed through his spine.

As Simon looked back for a moment while zipping the tent shut, he saw the flash of the lighter once more firing up. He lay down, closed his eyes, and imagined death striving to get into the sleeping bag. Its weight forced down on his chest, reached around his heart and squeezed, while Simon fought for air.

Then he heard his father's footfall pass heavily just outside the tent and for an enigmatic moment he felt safe. His mind became murky and he was immediately asleep. Simon's dreams, filled with stars and dead uncles and cousins, and traces of smoke, the odour of the burning of cigarettes and other unknown fuels, passed through his sleeping mind, leaving little trace when he woke. There was that cool, damp, dewy air on his back and in his nose when his eyes opened, that early morning cold outdoor feeling that he disliked so much.

He could smell the biting odour of wood smoke drifting in. His father was cooking breakfast. He heard Adam's voice outside. Simon turned and saw that Adam had left the tent flap open. He scratched at an itching ear.

2 Rain

For weeks now, days of oppressive heat had ended in evenings of coursing rain. Hannah jumped at every jolt of thunder, each time excusing herself to Rachel's mother, Dora, who gave her an indulgent smile. They sipped on cups of hot tea and waited for the storm to pass. The cabin was dark, except for the feeble light of the Sabbath candles, which had by now burned down half their heights.

"I hate the sound of a storm. It makes me so afraid."

"Oh, it's all right. It's natural to be afraid like that." A bright flare of lightning knifed through the kitchen again, and Hannah cringed, anticipating the thunder roll that would follow. Hannah's husband sat alone in a chair next to the screen door, staring silently at the rampage outside.

Duvid had arrived by bus just hours earlier. He had imagined that he could escape the stupefying city heat in the fresh country air. It was Friday. The weekend was about to begin. He had had work to finish, but the heat and humidity in Montreal had been unbearable. When his wife had called from the village store's pay telephone the previous night, he had almost told her that he couldn't come, but the weather had been more than he could bear.

Each morning of the week, the women's wear contractor delivered more piecework before Duvid left the flat for his regular job in a lady's wear factory on Mayer Street downtown. As the man left, Duvid looked up. The sky overhead churned with thick, dark clouds. From day to day, he expected rain, but it didn't come and didn't come. The heaviness of the air increased daily. On his way home, he decided to spend a few scarce dollars on a small electric fan at a hardware store on St. Lawrence Street. He would do without something else. It didn't help much, though. The fan clattered so he couldn't to doze off. He paced up and down the apartment hallway, trying to tire enough to at least nap.

By Friday, the work was still unfinished. He had hardly slept. He had awoken that morning spread awkwardly over the sewing machine, his hand wrapped around the needle, his neck stiff, wondering at a dream of heat that had come back to him again. He decided to breathe country air that weekend.

The days of summer were still long in mid-August, and when he had arrived the Sabbath would not begin for several hours still. He sat outside on the patch of grass in his wooden lawn chair, reading the Friday paper. The heat filtered into him through his pores, his arms sagging from the weight of the newspaper and his eyes slowly closing. A fly dopplered past through the air above his head, the sound of its wings quickly rising in pitch and then falling off as rapidly. His eyes were about to close completely when another sound, a woman's screams, ripped them open.

His wife was the source of those cries. He tried to break through the cobwebs woven across the entrances to his mind. His arms and legs were entangled lethargically, slowly breaking free. He turned his eyes toward the scream and saw his wife with her hands coming up to her mouth. In the direction she stared, blocked from his view by the clothes she was hanging on the clothesline, was the small river that flowed by in front of the cottage.

Duvid ran towards her, breaking through the line of bed sheets dangling in the still heat. His sons were there in the stream, bobbing up and down, their heads and hands visible. The water was slowly creeping up their necks to their chins. They were visibly moving downstream, sliding in some terrible parallax across his field of vision as he charged down towards the water.

He flew forward into the cool flow. His arms cut the water into blocks of liquid, his legs beating it into foam as they forced him forward. The first boy, he couldn't tell which, because their heads were starting to disappear below the surface, came within reach. He pulled him towards himself with all his strength.

He tried to reach both boys at once, but Adam, the one he realized he had in his hands, began to slip away as his father turned and tried to catch Simon, just out of reach. Simon's eyes filled with terror, the river already lapping into his mouth. Duvid dragged Adam to the bank, where Hannah stood, and threw him into her arms. He turned immediately and was back with Simon before water could cover his nose. He had brought him halfway back to his wife when Duvid saw Rachel.

The top of her head was just visible, her hands flailing weakly while her billowing long black hair plotted the turbulence of the water's flow. By this time, Dora was also standing on the bank, screaming wildly. Duvid looked at her and then back at Rachel, almost gone below the water's surface. Where he now stood the water was not very deep. He knew that Simon was strong and that the boy's height could keep him above the water's grasp for some moments more. There was only one decision possible. He let Simon go, dropping him back into the water's hold, and pushed off again. Behind him, he could hear Hannah's tortured wail. Within a few seconds he had reached Rachel and dragged her back to the bank where her mother squatted. Rachel's mother reached down for her and pulled her out. The girl sputtered and gasped, crying quietly. Duvid was already away, this time to recover Simon before it was too late. Simon clung tightly to Duvid on the way back, not making a sound. After he helped push him up onto the riverbank, Duvid finally climbed out. Rachel was holding her mother tightly, looking up at him. Simon's mother stepped forward, her face a tight mask. She said not a word, she simply pulled her arm back and slapped his face hard, then turned back to drag the boys toward the house and dry clothes.

Dora came up to Duvid, who stood uncomprehending, staring at his wife disappearing into the house. "She's a mother, Duvid. Let her be. She almost lost her boys." She said this as if somehow this would explain anything to Duvid. She took one of his hands and held it in both of hers.

"Thank you," she said, then she too turned and pulled Rachel back to the cottage. The girl was still whimpering quietly, clinging tightly to her mother's waist, forcing her mother to twist as she walked. Duvid stood there another few minutes, still wondering at his wife's reaction. Then he finally returned to the cottage to change his wet clothes. He would return to his newspaper tomorrow.

"Mother love", he thought to himself, bewildered by its narrowness, as he pulled off his wet socks. As if he had had a choice to save only his own. His right hand hurt. He looked down at it and saw that he had somehow cut it. There was a wide gash along the band of skin connecting his thumb and the other fingers. It was very red. He found a dry rag and wrapped it around his hand tightly, until the bleeding had stopped. Despite the heat, he felt suddenly chill, and very hungry. Duvid changed into fresh dry clothes and went into the kitchen to warm himself in front of the wood stove.

At the table Adam and Rachel sat eagerly shovelling blueberry pie into their mouths. Simon was huddled in a large frayed towel that his mother had bought at a thrift store on the Main, in front of the cast iron stove where the Sabbath supper was cooking. The heat of the stove projected onto Simon's face where it poked through the folds of material.

To Simon, the emotion generated by the rescue seemed to have heated him internally, so that he felt it was he who was the source of heat. He was glowing, the towel serving to protect the room from the molten energy boiling within him. He looked up at his father, standing there so quietly. He seemed so remote. Simon's corrupted rescue had left him in shock, confused and angry. In succession powerless and saved, betrayed and condemned, then triumphant–the contradictions now blazed in his furnace.

For the first time Simon wondered who this stranger could be. Father–this was such an abstract role. Its archetypal character revealed nothing to Simon. Except when he was saving Simon's life. But in a way, Simon vaguely saw that this was his everyday role, that Duvid was daily saving his life, from moment to moment. Saving him from some terrible thing that he knew little about, but for the bits of its character that Duvid had described, but whose menacing existence was so very clear. He had known of it all his life, it having inseminated his soul from the first times he could remember, somehow placed there by Duvid's metaphorically towering presence.

Duvid stood there in his undershirt and pants, near the stove, for a few minutes, warming himself, before continuing to dress in a white, long-sleeved shirt. His shoulders drooped, the skin of his face was lax from exhaustion. For a fragile moment, he seemed vulnerable, in need of something that Simon might be able to provide. Then he straightened up and walked away, over to the screen door, to observe nature's frenzy. The soft moment had burnt away, leaving no residue in Simon's mind.

Duvid somehow defined Simon, made him who he was to be, without any need for praise, just as the original Adam of the Book of Genesis, in naming the animals, had defined their future roles outside the Garden. Duvid had himself gone through this same transformation as a boy, and his own father, also named Simon, before him, and so on backwards down the rungs of generations. How could Duvid reward that which was assumed to be natural and normal? That which required no effort, no deviation from the accepted road, which without a doubt followed the path of least energy. It was surely modelled on the fall of a body through the curves of space-time, around some massive object that mimicked the presence of God.

That afternoon, just after the rescue, the weather had changed for the worse. The sky was still clouded over with its great pillows of white and grey, arched high into the fading light. Angry lightning and thunder accompanied a violent rain.

On the lawn chair outside, Duvid's newspaper dissolved away. After the rain, the air chilled considerably. The weekend turned cool, a foretaste of the autumn coming.

3 Doctoring

Adam called out. "Simon, where are you?"

Where was he? He couldn't have gotten so far ahead of him. The woods weren't very thick. He should be able to see him if he was nearby. The forest was sparse, mostly spruce. A few poplar and maple shoots reached up here and there in a small clearing created by fire years before. He could hear the twitter of a bird off to his left, then a flutter as it flew off. Adam heard something light tap its way through the branches on its way to the ground. A little ahead, the sound solidified into a pine cone rolling gently across the dead litter covering the earth.

The boys had gone into the forest together to pick blueberries, at their mother's request. She had promised them she would bake a pie and pastries in the cabin's wood stove if they collected enough fruit.

This was the third year that Simon could distinctly remember that the family had stayed in the country for the summer, but unlike his father's vivid recall, Simon knew that there were other memories hidden in his own mind that he could not find. After all, he was only ten years old–so young. That's what his mother said–what do you expect of him, he's so young? –when his father criticized him for this or that. His memories didn't stretch back very far, but neither did his experiences. He knew there were things back there, vaguely remembered, dismembered, disconnected without reference, that might make some sense if he could only find them, somewhere inside his head.

Adam slapped reflexively at a mosquito near his ear. Where was Simon? He felt somehow responsible, older, even though the two were twins. Born within minutes of each other, they had once been held equally in their mother's surprised arms, snuggling in, struggling for a breast for milk and comfort. Where was his brother? He turned in a circle, searching through the trees and the low bushes, making sure not to get too far from the path they usually followed.

"Ha, ha, ha! Fooled you!" Simon was rushing up behind him suddenly, leaves whirling around, brittle dry twigs cracking under his feet, his arms waving, looming suddenly as large as the sky.

"You dumb-head. Where were you? I'm going to tell Ma. She'll let you have it. You know she said to stay together. There's wolves and bears in these woods."

"No, there aren't."

"Yes, there are. Ma said so. She knows."

"No, Adam, she doesn't. Ma doesn't know anything. Not about these woods, for sure. There are no bears within two hundred miles of us. And no wolves within a thousand miles."

"You'll see. I'm going to tell Ma, and she'll tell Ta. You're in trouble. You'll see."

"Tell. Who cares. I don't."

"You're bad, Simon."

"You're too good, Adam. You're a goody guy. Goody guy! Goody guy!" Simon did a manic dance in a circle around Adam as he repeated the last two words.

Simon always did this when Adam reproached him. Adam didn't know what to do about it. Except tell his parents. That didn't seem to help much either.

"Hey, Simon, you're wasting time, while I'm here picking blueberries. I'm going to tell Ma not to let you eat the pie she's going to bake."

"Tell her. She won't listen to you just because you want her to. She'll give me a piece just like you."

"No, she won't."

"Yes, she will. She's not a dough head like you. Anyway, she's really baking for Ta, you know. He's coming again tomorrow from the city and you know how he likes blueberry pie so much."

"He didn't pick any either."

"So? He has to work."

"Yeah, I know." Adam mulled something in his head, then let it go.

"Did you see any full bushes?"

"Yeah, there's a bunch that way, off the path." Simon pointed ahead of them and off to the right.

"Show me where."

"That way, Adam. Behind you." Simon scurried away now. "Goody guy!"

"Stop that!"

Adam wanted to punch at Simon, but when he turned, his troublesome brother had again disappeared.

A wooden fence strung with wire lay a little ahead in the direction that Simon had pointed, with a clearing on the other side. Simon reappeared on the fence, and from there he pointed to the blueberry bushes beyond the edge of the trees. There the wood's shadows dominated a dry soil sparsely populated with low plants. The ground was littered with spruce needles. The limestone and granite that this area was built on poked through here and there, patches of grey and green lichens troubling their exposed surfaces, while thick soft moss filled depressions where water accumulated in hollows in the underlying rock, before it could find its route into fissures or evaporate into the air.

Further to the left, near the fence, grew thorny canes of raspberry and blackberry, a few still hanging with ripe fruit. Their brambles would snatch at their clothes and scratch their young skin. The boys had often crawled in among them, and Adam was now caught by the crackling leafy poles, unable to move forward or back. By contrast, Simon slipped forward effortlessly. "Stay still, I'll get Ma," he whispered, responding to his brother's whimpers. Then he laughed and crawled away.

Stinging rivulets of sweat washed down Adam's dirty forehead into his eyes. He was now almost blind, sweeping his moist forehead with one hand, rubbing his eyes with the other. The air was thick with insects energized by the dry dusty heat. Absently, he swatted at what seemed to be a fly buzzing past his ear. It was a mistake quickly regretted. Sharp jabs of pain were a quick education. Without knowing how, he broke out of the trap of brush, and was soon running back to the cabin, swatting erratically at his clothes. Under his shirt and pants, a colony of honeybees was attacking him in a frenzy.

The jabbing pains on his abdomen and between his legs hobbled his steps. It was a good thing he could run well. His mother was in the country house, as was Rachel. Simon hadn't yet bothered to come back. The girl's mother was out at the village, buying some essentials for supper. The screen door's spring creaked open, and a loud bang followed as Adam tore into the house. Rachel and Adam's mother Hannah converged on him, following the traverse of his screams.

While he lay moaning on the old dingy couch in the cabin's dimly lit salon, Hannah, her eyes wet, carefully pulled back his pants and then his shirt and underwear. Adam writhed in pain, while Rachel, who was almost the same age as Adam, stared at him while his mother gently pulled each dying bee away from him and applied the warm water and baking soda paste that she had instructed Rachel to mix up.

"You'll be my little nurse, Rachel. Go fetch me a towel and some warm water from the stove. Just be careful not to burn yourself."

Adam was in too much pain to care that Rachel was staring at his little protrusion, which was now swollen to twice its usual size by the bees' stings. The fingers of Rachel's left hand stroked her long straight hair. Her right hand she held lightly to her lips. Hannah considered Rachel's fascinated gaze.

"Rachel, you're a big girl now. You don't have to be embarrassed because this is doctoring you're doing, and that's something God approves of. Now hand me that wet towel, please." She took a moment to dab her forehead with her handkerchief.

Rachel took a satisfied breath when Adam's mother went back to the bathroom to retrieve a towel. She found doctoring pleasing. Especially since God Himself approved.

Simon galloped through the front door moments later. He gaped at the scene. His brother was on the couch, his pants down. Rachel sat next to him, her face full with concentration. She was dabbing at Adam's penis with a wet face cloth.

Rachel, her face illuminated by a satisfied smile, turned towards Simon. "I'm his nurse," she declared.

4 Eli's Journal

My Journal:

My name is Eli. I live in the city of Chelmek in the southwest of Poland, in this orphanage, but the word orphanage is wrong. The children here were taken away from living parents. My own mother has vanished, long ago.

My mother, my love, I miss you so much. This book began as her record. I am continuing from where she stopped, when I was removed from her.

Chelmek was part of Germany before the war. It sits not far from the Polish town of Oswiecim. I hear whispers of terrible things done there during the war that no one later spoke about aloud. It was a shared silence—I will not speak and neither will you. I sensed that there was some evil there. One of the teachers did say what he believed—that the Jews lived in the camp in Oswiecim for a time until trains could take them somewhere far away to live separately, that it was all their own fault they were taken away, because they caused the war. Where did they go, I asked? I got no answer. Perhaps it was just a story. That's what I was told: it was just a story. My mother told me her own stories of that time and wrote them in this book. She describes the terrible smells and the rail cars arriving each day for the week that she was able to observe from the woods outside. So many people go in. Where do they all go? Many come out each day in work crews then back at night. The guards yell. And every minute, that awful smell, biting and sweet all at once. When a wind blows it is carried for kilometres in all directions. At night, sparks fly up from the tall chimneys. Perhaps it was the industry of the camp.

My mother used to sing to me every night, and some nights, when she was not well, I sang the same songs to her. That's how I learned them. My mother made those songs, and they were all so beautiful. She showed me that she had everything written down—her life before the camp, her songs. The war, before the war. All of it.

I read her words when the guards are eating their meals or asleep. The writing is tight and very small, written with a stick from the fire or a pencil tip she somehow rescued from the guards after they wrote their reports, on paper from confiscated old books that some of the inmates had brought with them, torn apart and discarded, scattered in the woods, or used at the latrines.

My name is Eli. I don't know more than that. I remember my mother, when I was with her long ago. We were in the woods, in a village where there were guards who told us what to do, where to go, when to wake up, when to eat. There was little to eat, but we were told when to eat it. We were told when to sleep, even though I couldn't because it was so cold that my legs and hands shook during the night. My mother covered me with her thin coat and shivered for me, but I was still cold. My mother worked cutting logs every day. The logs were put on trucks and taken away to build something, but I never knew what. I wasn't allowed to ask questions.

Another boy, Marcin, about my age, was also there with his mother. He asked until the guards beat him. He still asked, but when they beat his mother he stopped. He's dead now. Because of the cold he became very sick. My mother told me not to stay near him, because I could also get sick. I heard the word cholera muttered among the others watching, and when I looked to my mother to tell me what it was, she covered her eyes and then pulled me away. A few days later they dragged Marcin away with his bed sheet tied tightly around him and took him into a field where they burned his body. We all watched from far away, except for Marcin's mother, who tried to run to him. The guards stopped her. She screamed and yelled, and at the end, when the fire had burnt out, the guards gave up, and she ran in circles around the ashes, late into that night, screaming, screaming, screaming his name. Marcin! Marcin! Over and over again. The guards yelled at her to stop. They wanted to sleep.

Late at night, when we were all very tired of the noise she was making, one of the guards banged the door of his hut very loudly and walked into the clearing. Then we heard a loud noise, like the crack a tree makes when it falls. Everyone was too frightened to say anything, or even to look out. I cried and cried and shook. My mother sang me a song while I shook. After a time, I fell asleep. In the morning Marcin's mother could not be found. We didn't ask where she had gone. We never asked anything.

I remember my mother's songs with their lovely tunes, even now that I haven't seen her for many years. When I was ten, they took me away and brought me here, to this place they call Josef Poniatowski Orphanage. I remember sitting in one truck after another, for many days. I had no idea where I was going, and still don't know where I was when I was last with her, but it was very far away in the mountains. And now I am alone here and my mother perhaps is dead. I brought my mother's journal with me, in the small sack they allowed me. They inspected my things, but allowed a few mementos, as they called them. Perhaps there was a little bit of good left in them. For whatever reasons they had, I came from there with my mother's writings.

I feel always to cry. I would cry for her every night, but I am watched by the others. They always look for my weakness. I sometimes cry in the showers, when the soap is in my eyes. My father is surely dead. I never knew him, but my mother told me about him, how he fought in the war and was captured near the end. He was a Jew, and so am I, my mother tells me, because she is too. What is a Jew? I asked her when we were alone together, but she never said. She just sang me another song. She said she hoped I would never find out, because all that the Jews ever feel is pain.

They may call this place an orphanage, but no one here is an orphan. No one! The other boys, like me, have all been taken from our homes, from our parents. No one ever says anything about it.

I am beginning to understand about being a Jew. I know now why my mother didn't want me to find out, but whether I want to be one or not, it isn't a choice I can make. She was right, though. All I ever feel is pain. They know, and that's all that matters. No one ever speaks to me except with insults. I have no friends. They all hate me and I am alone. At first the others whispered the word–Jew– like quiet mice, but Biszhinskiy, the teacher, didn't hesitate–he has said this loudly in class, and now they all do the same. I feel torn from the walls I hide within, condemned. When I am allowed outside, at least there I can wander alone. Sweet solitude. The trees pretend that I am not there and I am happy. The birds look away to the sky, and I smile. They do not want to see me, they do not sing their tunes for me, but they do not hurl ugly names at me either.

Each day here is like every other, the food always the same. Today I wanted to eat alone again, but I couldn't. The other boys sat next to me, laughing, telling their stupid jokes. They taunted me. "Hey, Jew, why do you stink like that even after you wash?" "Is something wrong with your prick? A piece is missing. Did one of the Jewish girls eat it? No, it wouldn't be kosher." Then they all laughed again. They kicked my shins under the table, jerked my food tray so my drink spilled. They tripped me when I was trying to clean the table so I wouldn't get into trouble. I was blamed anyway. And then they laughed again. They always laugh. I hate them. I hate them all.

On the beds in the dormitory, the sheets and pillow cases become greyer with each washing. The paint on the walls is peeling off in large strips and the plaster is broken in places. At night mice hop around, sneaking in through the holes in the walls. All the beds are in one large room. I sleep in the far corner. Pavel, who sleeps below me in the bunk bed, is like a wall between me and the others. They whisper and giggle after the lights go out. They throw things. The air is filled with the odours of sweat and farting. There are more complaints in the dark, before it is finally quiet. I smell Pavel peeing in his sleep, then I dream.

Pavel never asks any questions either, but he once did. Not any more. He listens to the teacher, who says not to ask. Sometimes it is better not to know the answer, either. Pavel used to answer the teacher's questions to the class. He would eagerly put up his hand. The teacher liked him for that. The other boys didn't like him, but they didn't hate him like they do me. He's lucky, because he's not a Jew, at least. Last week, Pavel volunteered to bring a paper to the school office from our teacher. The teacher chose him as a reward, because he was such a good student. Pavel must have been thinking about something, because he took too long getting there. For this the director hit him on the palms of his hands. When he returned, delayed, the teacher hit him again, hard, with a ruler this time across the back of his head. It bled, a lot. Now Pavel looks away whenever Biszhinskiy asks for a messenger. He has stopped putting his hand up in class.

I miss my mother. It must be my fault I was taken from her. Maybe I did something very bad, something I can't understand. Or maybe I have made it all up. Maybe she ran from me and I only imagine her being dragged off crying fiercely as the truck I was in drove away. I hate her for letting me go. I hate myself. I hate thinking. My brain becomes as thick as the dormitory air. I need clear air. They have told me that on Sunday I can ride a bicycle to the country. The empty sky and needles of cold air in my throat will do me good, they say. I will visit the empty camp at the end of the farmers' fields. The camp that everyone is silent about. They're all afraid of the ghosts that might be there. I'll show them that ghosts don't exist and then they will respect me. I'm not superstitious like they are. My mother taught me not to believe that nonsense.

And then I'll come back here. I wish I could escape, but in truth, there is nowhere else for me to go. Nowhere in this whole world.

5 Soup

Outside the small cottage, a summer storm at first only obscured the sun, but soon the afternoon darkened, the wind picked up, and the rains started pelting down on the corrugated metal roof. Lightning tore the sky. Hannah tried to concentrate on the task of cooking, but each explosion of thunder drew her eyes toward the windows. The three children, Adam, Simon and Rachel, had gone for another walk along the river in the afternoon and still hadn't returned, despite their mother's warnings about avoiding the water. They were not to attempt the river again. It was midweek. Duvid wasn't there. They solemnly agreed, and then Simon smirked on their way down to the water. He gave Adam a mock push and retreated only when Hannah, who was watching from the cottage door, yelled out.

"You will give your mother a heart attack!"

An hour or more later, there was no sign of the children. The power had gone out a little while ago, and the first drops of rain fell against the windows. For light, Hannah had lit an array of Sabbath candles and placed them strategically around the kitchen.

"Dora, are the children coming soon, you think? It is raining already."

"Hannah, don't worry so much. Your sons are safe. The children will be back soon and they'll be hungry. Is the soup almost ready?"

Hannah stirred the soup devotedly on the wood-fired country stove. Perhaps by making this effort, she could speed their return.

"Come here. Taste, give me your opinion."

Dora bent forward, took the spoon in one hand, and blew gently across the surface of the liquid to cool it.

"Delicious, Dora. You are a masterful cook. You used to share your cooking with us when you were renting the room. No more since you moved out, what is it now, yes, almost a whole year. Ah, I miss your food, and your family too, of course." A pause. "Your new place on Esplanade Street must be better for your boys than a single room, but it costs a lot more, no?"

Hannah was hesitant to speak. Words could only lead to offence and anger. It was always so among Europeans: feud growing from anger, anger from small failings of the tongue. Lifelong quarrels could come of such small slights. She had seen it between brothers who had not spoken for ten years.

"What, you don't speak to me anymore, Hannah?"

"It was not a place for the boys. Nowhere for them to play. You wouldn't let them into the kitchen, so they had to do their homework on their beds."

"They were reckless. You remember your boy running into my icebox with his wagon? A house is no place to ride."

"You're still angry about this? I paid you for the repair."

"Since you left, we bought a new frigidaire instead."

"Very nice. Use it in good health. It must have cost you plenty, this frigidaire."

"The old ice box leaking water, the iceman clomping in with big dirty boots. Who needed it? Old piece of junk. Morris wanted to keep it for his schnapps bottle, but he never made any sense. Hardwood, he said, oak. Who cares? The new ones are enameled metal, easy to keep clean. The junk man gave me a few pennies, so good riddance."

Hannah remembered that it was Rachel who had pushed Simon. "You don't remember when Rachel rode in your parlour with her roller skates and scratched your new coffee table?"

"Rachel? Never!"

"Dora, she told you herself."

"My Rachel? Hannah, it was your Simon's fault. He dared her to skate off the top of the table onto the floor. She could have broken her neck. You know very well that your sons are never so innocent."

"Boys can be trouble, but when girls get into trouble, it can be worse than with boys. And your Rachel is not such an angel."

"What are you saying? This is more than a scratch on a table you speak of. Be careful what you say about my Rachel. You'll give her a reputation."

Hannah paused and took a small breath. Rachel already had a reputation, she thought, Hannah didn't need to invent one.

"His fault, her fault, such a discussion! Children are children."

"Children, sure. But you also are like a child. Too proud to stay with me, but the apartment building you moved to isn't so great, from what I hear. Broken walls. Rats. I hear this new flat is expensive. Paying plenty for not much. You immigrants are pushovers. You should try for better."

"Dora, you think we're stupid? We live where we can afford. We had a better life in Israel, except for the wars, always the wars. Here, we only have to work hard and make a living, not battle. One day, I hope, it will be easier. Maybe for my sons." Hannah stirred the soup more briskly. Thunder again rolled outside.

"Oh, such a storm I never saw."

"Hannah, I'm sure you've seen worse."

Hannah responded with silence. She continued her stirring.

"Hannah, you never talk much."

"Maybe it's you who doesn't listen. Dora, when Duvid and I were first married in Israel, we lived in a city of tents on the beach. Then right away, war with the Arabs. After it was over we were able to settle on a farm and Duvid built us a house there with his own hands. And then came another war. After it was over, Duvid could not stay any more. Too much fighting for him to bear. So we came here. And now we are in a cramped flat only big enough for a man and his wife and two boys, and you call us proud. Dora, I am not proud. We pay for what we have with our sweat. It is small but it is very clean. It is like a paradise for us here in Canada.

"Before Israel, in Germany, we stayed in a camp–they called us displaced persons–people without a country. The war was just over. It was much worse there. Never enough food, not enough beds. No medicine. Fighting among ourselves. Frightening stories of a nurse killing Jewish babies–who knows if it can be true. I was in the American sector, at least. And I will not even talk what conditions were in Russia. It was worse during that war, the real war."

Dora responded with her own history lesson. "It's never easy to come to a new country. My father came here from Lithuania. He also had his troubles."

Hannah wasn't listening. She expected her two boys would barge through the door at any moment. The sky was darkening with ever more clouds and she could hear the rumble of faraway thunder rolling in from the hills to the north.

"Lithuanian Jews had a hard life. My father was inducted into the Russian Navy. Ten years throwing coal into boilers, their fires turning the propellers. The Russians were fighting Japan. His ship was hit and sank, but he had been sent up on deck to fetch food for the crewmen below, and he escaped on the wreckage."

The children were suddenly back. The screen door's spring made its tortured stretching sound, then the door banged shut. Rachel stood there out of breath and the two boys displayed bouquets of wildflowers they had picked along the river. Their faces were streaked with mud. Dora looked up. "Take your shoes off. So much mud."

"What pretty flowers. They will look nice on the kitchen table." Hannah, relief on her face, reached for a large empty jar from behind the stove and took it to the sink to fill it. "You young adventurers were caught by the rain, I see. I was afraid you would get sick."

"You worry too much, Hannah." Dora turned her attention back to the three youngsters. "Are you hungry, children? Yes? So go wash your faces and hands. Change into dry clothing. Then come to the table. Ah, youth with their wild ideas. When I was young, we couldn't afford to rebel. We had to help the family. Not like these lazy ones today, who only make work for their parents. We can never rest. Children bring more trouble than joy."

"They make us suffer, but we need our children."

Dora looked at Hannah, disbelieving. "Like a hole in the head. *As a loch in kop*, my father always said." Such a foreigner, this Hannah. She had a lot to learn before she started to think like a Canadian.

Soon the three children were back at the table. The boys slurped soup into their mouths as if starving. Dora brought a big bottle of Kik Nectar to the table. She asked the boys what they had been doing.

"Nothing. Picking flowers."

"Very good. Fresh air is good for children. Do you know about poison ivy?"

Rachel had led them to a girls' camp she knew of, further along the river. Despite their recent near-drowning, Simon, Adam and Rachel had shucked their clothing and waded in their underwear upriver to the reeds edging the camp. From behind the bushes, they had watched as the girls and their counsellors skinny-dipped in the water. The boys had stared excitedly as the first shafts of lightning broke the sky and the counsellors rushed naked out of the water. Afterwards, Rachel pointed out the translucent wetness of her underwear and laughed. The boys turned away uneasily and waited for body heat to dry their own before dressing.

"Rachel, you eat so slowly," Dora continued. "What are you thinking so much about? Flies will jump into your soup. In Africa, they fight each other for soup like this. It's such a delight to watch these boys eat with gusto."

The boys, their minds still elsewhere, looked up, embarrassed. "What, these young men treat a compliment like a curse. So, talk to me a little. Are you shy to speak in English? In this country, boys, you can't afford to be shy. And you can't afford to not speak English." She turned to Hannah. "It will be better for them if they do. I can hear when they talk to each other, it's always in Yiddish."

"Dora, if my boys need advice I will give it to them myself."

"Oh, Hannah, Hannah. No arguments between us, but you have to adjust. You can't afford to have people thinking that you're different. The world is bad enough already. They call you immigrants *greeners*, green people, newcomers, behind your backs, you know. Is this what you want to stay forever? Foreigners? This is not the old country. This is Canada. They have to stop speaking Yiddish. It was the same for my family, when my father first arrived, but now look at us. We are Canadians."

"It's the same thing their teachers tell us, to make them stop with the Yiddish."

Simon was squirming in his chair. Adam had his mouth open but said nothing. Hannah continued. "And how will they talk to us, if they forget their *mame-loshen*, their mother tongue?"

"They will teach you and Duvid, you'll see. Soon you will all be like us."

"*Oy.*" Hannah put her hand to her mouth and chuckled.

"Don't laugh, Hannah. It isn't funny. A little piece of blueberry pie, children?" Dora served them. "So, boys, do you think about what you'll do when you're older?"

Adam answered with pie juice slipping out the side of his mouth. "I want to be a doctor."

Hannah quickly wet a rag at the sink and set about vigorously wiping Adam's face. He winced and tried to pull away. She held him firmly by the cheek.

Dora continued. "Listen to Mr. Big Shot. You want to be a doctor? See, for this you have to speak a good English."

Adam stared at Hannah.

Dora rambled on. "They say it's a good profession, but for me it's dirty. To have to look in a person's *tuches*, I find it disgusting. Maybe you should try for something else. An accountant, maybe. Or an optician? Now those are clean occupations."

Adam twisted uneasily. Hannah came to his defence. "He will do what he wants the most. To be a doctor is a good profession. It is blessed to save lives. And he is smart. He will be a very good doctor, if only God lets for him to be accepted."

"A Jew can't get into medical school, Hannah. There's a quota. And if you're an immigrant with an accent, it's even harder than that."

"He will just have to work harder. If he is the best in the school, they will have to take him. And he will know English, a perfect English. They both will."

"And you, Simon, do you also want to be a doctor?"

"No, I want to be a journalist."

"A what?"

"A journalist. A newspaper reporter."

"Ah, you see. Another profession where you need to know the language of the country. Do you understand now why it's so important? Do you know what I'm saying?"

Simon said nothing. Hannah was also silent. A pink blush spread up her neck and across her cheeks.

"Another dirty profession, but one where you look at the ugliness of life. It must be a hard job to get, and to keep, too. And dangerous. Why not choose something easier, more practical, like my Rachel. She'll be a teacher. There will always be children to teach."

"Ma, you know I don't want to be a teacher. I want to be an artist."

"Shush, Rachel. I will hear no such a thing. Children have no practical sense any more. They are all so spoiled."

Rachel glared at her mother, then went back to sipping her soup.

Hannah took a deep sip of tea and sighed. "Adam and Simon, maybe Dora is right. Why don't you go to your room and read a little? You don't want to forget everything you learned in school. I will bring candles but don't touch them to start a fire."

The boys sidled off to their tasks. Rachel remained at the table, eating slowly.

"Your soup must be cold by now. You're such a slowpoke. Hannah will be insulted that you don't like her cooking."

"M-A-A-A!!" Rachel threw her spoon down, jumped up, and rushed out the door. The screen door banged loudly. Dora watched her go, then got up to clear the table.

"My daughter's such a hothead."

"It is raining hard outside. Maybe you should go after her. She will get sick."

"I know my daughter well. She's very strong-willed. Don't worry, Hannah, she's like a cat, she doesn't like to be wet. She's very impulsive, my Rachel. She'll come back soon. You'll see."

Dora placed the dirty dishes in the sink, then she was fidgeting with a rag, and wiping the table.

"Dora, rest a little bit. You can't stay still a minute? After all, it's *shabbos*."

"*Shabbos, shmabbos*. Does a mother ever have time to rest? You have two. It must be even harder for you."

"One or twelve, it's never easy with children. But it's better for them to have a brother or a sister. It's better for children not to grow up alone."

"I had five brothers and sisters, but they all died as children, either of influenza or consumption. My father worked at an iron foundry. He made iron gravemarkers for them, by himself. My parents and I would visit their graves once a year."

Hannah stared at her pot of soup, simmering quietly. "Yes, in Poland before the war, we also visited the dead. After the war, the dead had no graves. We could not visit."

Dora continued, ignoring her. "The graves were at the edge of the cemetery next to a cow pasture. They used to stand along the fence, mooing at the graves. After my parents died, I didn't go back there for a long time. I visited my parents' graves recently, after the funeral for a cousin. I placed small stones on their graves. No one uses iron now, only stone. I couldn't find the gravemarkers of my brothers and sisters."

"Maybe they rusted away," Hannah volunteered.

"That's not possible. They were stolen away. Who would be so base as to steal from the dead?"

Hannah didn't say anything.

"Maybe they are under the stone wall that was built in place of the fence. I don't know. People now live where those pastures were. Can you imagine living next to a graveyard?"

"During the war, my Duvid lived inside a graveyard. He carried the dead."

Dora had heard too much already of these stories told by these European Jews. She refused to believe half of the stories that Duvid told. "The country road that led to the graveyard is now a city street. The wall around is sturdy, but where are my family's graves? Nobody knows any more. It's terrible." Dora sipped at a tea, her eyes clouding, momentarily quiet.

Hannah was quiet too. She wondered at the graves of her brother Chaim and his family, and those of her parents. All lost during the war. Where were they? She could never know, never place a stone on their monuments. If she ever went back. They were just earth and ashes, washed loose in the rain. Rain such as was falling tonight, the rain of the dead.

"Maybe another tea, Hannah?"

Hannah quietly got up to brew more tea, while Dora sat and stared out the window at the dark clouds in the early evening sky.

"Dora, Rachel is not back." It was getting dark now. Rain streaked the screens in the windows.

"You'll see. Even with all that rain and wind, Rachel will be fine. I know her. You should worry for your own boys, not my daughter."

The candles were burning low, their flickers sending quivering shadows scurrying across the walls. The candle flames wavered as the door opened. Rachel walked back into the house. The rain was pouring down in wild sheets outside. It was fully dark now. Rachel stood inside by the doorway while water pooled on the floor around her. Her clothes were glued to her. Strands of her long dark hair had coalesced into ropes and hung straight down, framing her wet face. Hannah saw her first, then Dora. Neither spoke, struck by the sight of the apparition. Dora's cup was shaking so hard that tea splashed out into the saucer.

"Where have you been? You frighten the life out of me. Do you hate your mother so much?"

"I went for a swim. The water was warmer than the air."

"A swim? In your clothes? In this storm? You could die from lightning. You will drown one day."

"Oh, mother."

"And you lost your socks again?"

Rachel had stared straight up into the dark, watery sky. It was close to dusk, the sun making a feeble attempt at the horizon to sow its final weak glow over an indifferent landscape. The interface of water and air was alive with countless eruptions as raindrops collided exuberantly with its flow. Rachel opened her mouth wide, capturing the rain. A jagged thrust of light surged madly through the dark billows above her. She smiled, excited by the danger.

The river steamed. Its flow was slow and gentle, in succession cool then warm, then cool again. Her toes teased the mud along the bottom. It was thick and soothing, wholly sensuous. She opened and closed her legs rhythmically. The coolness of the water flowed into her, tickled, then slipped out again. Her head went down, mouth open, and she tasted the water, its chemical composition perfect, reflecting the balance within her, a kindred fluid.

There were delicate nibbles on her foot. A tadpole, perhaps. Then another thought. Bloodsuckers. Revulsion seized her. Rachel succumbed to momentary panic and lost her balance. She fell, inhaling a small amount of water. Coughing and blinded, she struggled for a moment, then quickly recovered and pulled herself out of the river. She was almost ashore now, inspecting her skin. Nothing. Relief followed.

Rachel kicked her feet in the water to clear them of mud. Her mother had just bought her the camisole and yellow flowered panties she had on. They were tight, and clingy with moisture. She peeled them off and tossed them awkwardly into the river, and watched the leisurely flow of the current carry them away. She stood there naked for a minute, tasting what it must be like to be free.

She thought about her mother. Enough time had passed that her mother must be worried by now. Good. Time to go back. She pulled her water-logged dress out of the bushes and slipped it over her head. She slid her feet into her sodden shoes and headed back to the house. She was smiling. Her mother would be quite angry.

6 Eli's Journal

This spring day begins bitterly cold. I have the day off. This is Sunday, and as it is the anniversary of the finish of the Great Patriotic War, it is not a day I can easily forget. Also it is my birthday. Today I am sixteen. As my way of celebration, I take a bicycle ride in the countryside. I woke up very early and even now the sun has only just cleared the horizon. Soon it will lift itself into the low cloud cover and the day will lose its golden lustre.

It is a sullen day, but pink and orange blend along the illuminated edges of the low clouds. A promising start, but a brisk wind blows too quickly. I shiver despite my effort. A crow barks from the top of a tree, and wrens war with song while they steal nesting territory from each other. The light is strange today, thick and heavy. It seems to take up more space than it should as it passes through the clear air. It comes at me horizontally, broken in its flight by the smallest objects, a leaf, a twig, a mosquito in flight. They barter their darkness with the light, their long shadows cutting through the air like needles.

Besides the infrequent cackles of the birds and the whuff of the wind, the bicycle chain makes the only sound as it passes from pedal to back wheel and around. Everyone still sleeps. No one shares the transient beauty of the young day with me. This is no different than always. I now believe I am condemned to be lonely forever.

Once again I visit the camp. Yes, again, though I don't understand what draws me here. I feel compelled to visit this abandoned place. I am curious, but also, I feel something pulling me inwards to its core.

The first time I approached I felt ill, my legs rubbery, my head was hot, my hands quaking. I could not make myself go past the front gate. I would have to return another time and walk through that gate, with its German wrought iron slogan above its entrance. "*Arbeit Macht Frei*," it said. Beyond that gate, I glimpsed brick huts, rank after rank, so many, and all around them, the double fence of rusting barbed wire.

As I left that first time, I looked down and noticed a patch of crumbling cloth. I reached for it and held it up to the sky. Sunlight glowed through, sparkling and fragmented. As I walked away, I picked the cloth apart, thread by thread, and released each into the wind. They blew away, until there was nothing left but a smudge of dirt between my fingers.

This is not a pleasant place, surrounded by the wire that stops everyone else. It feels dead, haunted. It strikes fear in me every time I sneak under the wire fence. While I am there, my skin crawls and the hair on my neck lifts. I feel watched by something or someone, some horrific entity, and yet I know that no one, nothing, is there. I have been to this place several times now, but each time has been difficult. Yet I have come back.

At the orphanage they rarely speak about this place, even though it is so close by. This is a secret spot, hidden, shunned, like an abandoned graveyard. I think they are afraid of it, afraid of its ghosts. They are all so stupidly superstitious. Not like me. I do not allow myself to believe such nonsense. Yet, now, the fear fills me. It is a real presence.

Some teachers say this is a place where all the Jews died during the war. Saliva drips from the corners of their mouths when they say the word 'Jew'. I protest. I am a Jew. They smile, amused. I am alive, I argue. They smile more. I hear them think: "For how long?"

I am alive. And why am I alive? Perhaps something in that place will give me a reason that I can know. This is what draws me, this need to understand.

It is very cold. I shiver as I walk through the gate. I slip past the rusty barbed wire that covers the two layers of fence. Its concrete posts curve inwards at their tops, much like the crook of a shepherd's staff. Large rectangular huts loom ahead in long rows and columns, in a frightful grid. I walk towards them. Today will be a new step for me. Even though I have been here many times, I have never before dared to enter any of these buildings and walk into their shadows.

A wide depression interrupts the level path. It is thick with dead vegetation and bare branches. I feel lost. Instead of going around, as I have in the past, I decide to walk through the drop in the ground. The surface is uneven and rough, covered in low brush. A mist drifts across. This low place is still in deep shadow. Roots grow out of the soil in sinuous knotted cables towards the edges of the depression, and they weave together like a blanket. I pick my way carefully so I won't stumble.

Bushes become steadily thicker and taller, blocking the wind. The air becomes warmer. Because of these obstacles, the slope is much longer than what it had appeared from the outside. When I reach the centre, I have to rest. A tiny clearing no wider than a man's height encompasses this middle ground. There is a bowl-shaped depression here, a depression within a depression, like a hill inverted. I lay down to rest on the edge of this second drop, my feet dangling in the hollow, and take a swig from my water bottle.

A few stones dig into my back. I pick them up and roll them in my fingers. They are smooth and round, each no larger than a wren's egg. Their shapes are pleasing, and I slip them into my jacket pocket, then lay back down.

From this vantage, the rest of the world is blocked from view. The bird songs have stopped. Above my head, the clouds still glow pink. To either side is rough green grass. Summer seems to have advanced itself here. The odd wildflower pokes through, orange or purple. On one sits a honeybee. Its busy grinding buzz sings to me, until it flies off with its cargo of pollen and sap, taking its melody with it. With the departure of the bee, a sudden silence wraps itself thickly around me.

It is so quiet. I can hear the faint pulsing of blood in my ears. Above me, I imagine the sound of the faint rubbing of cloud against sky. Then, beyond that, there is a hint of the vibrato of the earth, weaving its way, plucking the strings of space to its celestial tune.

I am overcome with a feeling of contact with everything around me. Then, in an instant, there is again sound. A blast of air blows across the treetops. Blades of grass lift, dancing elegantly in currents of soft air that try to escape and join wilder air flying free just inches above my head. By watching the grass ballet, I can see that the wind has begun to form itself, to acquire discipline and rotate in a cyclone within the outline of the drop in the ground.

I stand up and look around over the edge of the depression. I notice long, white objects. I touch one gingerly and it falls away from the sandy earth. I recognize it now–it is a bone, and after it come a number of other smaller bones - someone's dead hand. I pull my own fingers back. I hear myself scream. In a panic, I fall backwards, crawling up and out of the hollow. I turn and run to the closest brick building. I don't dare look back.

To one side are heaped large piles of blackened brick rubble. The cold wind sends a chill through my bones. I stare at my hands. They are covered in a thin gloving of dry clay. I clutch myself against the thieving wind.

A door hangs open ahead of me, swinging with the wind. It bangs lightly. As I enter, the sun breaks through the clouds. The hair bristles on the back of my neck, but I open the door wide and walk in. It is bright inside. Part of the roof has collapsed inwards. A tangle of wooden boards hangs suspended above my head, defying gravity. In the area enclosed by the collapse, the sun shines on the bare wooden interior. Beyond this roughly circular zone, all is dark. Dust motes swirl thickly in the glowing air, a galaxy of tiny stars against the darkness behind. All around are large wooden shelves.

I hear muffled voices in the shadows behind me, but when I turn, the space is as empty as before. The floor creaks with my footsteps, joining with the phantom sounds, hanging in the air, muted, like the voices of the dead. They echo from wall to wall, the waves of an ocean reflecting off its many shores.

I fight back fear. I force myself to bend down, to look below the bed boards, not knowing what I am searching for. All I see is dust and spider webs, shadows hiding nothing. In the wood of several of the bunks, I see groups of scratches. Do they signify anything? All detail is lost in the past, disintegrated by the passage of time into small mounds of fine dust, their origins in the acts of living obscured. Here and there are other marks, initials and words, written in various scripts and languages. Perhaps they are the names of persons, towns, or slogans and dates. None carry any meaning for me.

I have found nothing. I turn for the swaying door. The air moves. My hair rises in response, dancing lightly above my head. I see something embedded between the bed boards ahead. In the half-dark, my eyes adjust slowly and then I see that it is a haftless rusty blade, a thin sliver of rusted metal, partly wrapped in a piece of fabric. Several threads wave in the air as the wind catches them. A few taps from my canteen are enough to dislodge the blade, and the rust crumbles, freeing the cloth covering it. The yellowed scrap is captured by the wind. It cartwheels in a zigzag path through the air and then falls into a bunk two rows away.

I walk over to where it has fallen. I pick it up carefully but there is not enough light for me to examine it properly. I place it in my jacket pocket. There are scratches in the wood here also. Another name. I squint to read it. ...*Duv*... *Gr*...*zt*... I reach out and run my fingers lightly over the letters. Someone's father, or son, or cousin scratched these marks in the wood. Duvid, I think, someone named Duvid. And the family name? r...zt... What could this name be? A dark empty feeling fills me suddenly. It could be my father's name.

"It cannot be him." I say the words aloud, as if I am speaking to someone next to me. I try to dismiss the thought. There must have been a multitude of men with such letters in their name, or with similar names. It is impossible. A new and deeper terror grips me. I want only to escape. I break and run through the door, before slowing, ashamed at my ridiculous terror. I reach into my pocket for the patch of crumbling cloth and hold it up to the sky. The wind catches its threads and dashes it away. I watch it come to pieces as it flies, and then, with a long breath, turn and make my way out of the camp.

That night, I remember, when I was about to be taken from her, my mother telling me the name of my father. She wrote it in her book for me. She told me he could still be living, that he was strong and resourceful. Now I knew this idea to be imaginary. Her folklore, invented for me. Something to sustain me in my loneliness after she was gone from my life.

Perhaps. Perhaps. But no, I cannot accept this either. Can I allow myself to believe such a thing, such an unlikely thing, that these scratches could belong to my father? They would not mean that he died there in that camp, but that he could have survived was so unlikely. Impossible, even. The truth descended on me, like a cold fog rushing in from the sea. He did die, there, in this terrible place, and then, in that terrible time. I had no one left.

In my bed, I stare up at the darkened ceiling, and through it. I continue to look farther and farther into the imagined sky above me. That distant sky holds clouds and aurorae and distant nebulae beyond perception. Does it hold anything else? Does it reach for me like the gentle hand of a father blessing the head of his child, or is it a sky filled with menace?

The night after I visit the camp, I dream. I have difficulty walking. Bones fall out of the dark sky to the ground, pointing in one direction. My clothing is vertically striped, in black and in white, but in other colours too. Its edges crumble to a tasselled fringe, blowing off in the wind.

I must leave this place. It is death, like the camp. I must find a way.

7 Reflections

Duvid stood in front of his bathroom mirror. The slight fog left after his bath obscured his reflection. Deftly holding a Gillette razor like an artist's palette knife, he felt the razor handle rub the scar between thumb and forefinger, formed where he had cut his hand saving his sons from the river some years before. It itched slightly. He put the razor down on the side of the sink and rubbed the dense rope of tissue with the fingers of his left hand. It was another suture placed by his own body to stitch itself together. Shaving foam slipped up to his right eye and he brought his left hand with its numbered tattoo up from behind his back to quickly wipe it away. His right eye stung.

There were other ropes, the deep-set scars, the ones that he could touch. A cauliflower of discoloured skin spread on his left shoulder, a reminder when he bathed or made love to Hannah. He fleetingly brushed the spot where stray piano wire had impaled him during the war. He had been trying to set the wire across the wooden bridge, but it had slipped. He had cowered under the bridge then, writhing silently, while German trucks rumbled above his head. He now sat on the covered toilet, staring in front of him, wondering. Just inches and his fate would have been the same as that of the enemy captain, whose head had been separated from his neck by a similar length of wire on another road a few kilometres away. Duvid had watched from his perch on a tree branch.

Duvid's skin displayed a map of his history. A scar marked the front of his thigh where an axe had sliced through his skin into bone, when he had cut wood as a child. Along one cheek ran a horizontal fine straight line, almost invisible except in a certain light. It was the impression of the hot bullet that had grazed his face, then struck his friend Pinny's skull in one of many battles during the young days of Israel. The scar on his hand had joined the others, a youngster welcomed grudgingly into a pantheon of dark moments. He rarely allowed himself to visit this temple.

Yet the past hovered always in his mind, despite Duvid wanting it to be gone. It would always remain like that. Whether he should be keeping pieces of that past was something he struggled with every day. He still had the documents and written recollections from the time of the war. From time to time, when Hannah wasn't watching, he pulled them from the hidden place in his workroom where he kept them, and stared at them, again and again wishing he could destroy them, wanting to erase the past, and yet, following each of these struggles, he decided he had to guard them. Another sort of scar that tore apart his nights and weakened his days.

The past. It was gone, and yet it lived on, so powerful. It was filled with regret, and guilt, and grief, and the burden of failure.

His family gone. He had been unable to save them. He had come too late, because of a momentary indecision one day, a hesitation the day before that, a sideways movement that carried him off the path the day before that day before.

Too late. Too late.

The idea echoed in his head. In truth, the journey here had been long and difficult. His devotion and belief had been hardened by its rigours. But it was not enough. It could never have been enough. Why had he ever thought to begin such a hopeless task? He had known they would not listen. They had their thousand reasons not to come away. To his every word, there would have been a dissent. His words would have been only unconvincing noises. Words without any meaning.

His brothers, his sisters, each had responsibilities. They had children to care for—how could they be expected to endure such a journey? And the old people, frail and confused? They had only small shops, not enough silver, not enough gold, to pay their passage through the coming wilderness. They were only leather workers, or tailors, or bakers. They were settled, not nomads. They had no knowledge of the road. How would they find food, or shelter? They would reply with another voice, a different language than his. They would be right. They would be wrong. Both. They could never accept. They could not follow him. But he had been unable to test the truth of these certainties. There would have been a chance, if he could have been there earlier. But he had failed. And from this ground, guilt grew luxuriantly.

Deep inside his soul, against reason, he knew that he had abandoned his family, wilfully or not. The power wasn't within him. His failure had made certain what was before only apprehended destruction. Yet despite knowing, he could not then allow himself to dismiss the possibility of their survival. He had to hope that he might one day see them again—he had hoped for hope, really—but, no, neither could he truly believe such to be possible, because to do so would, in the end, when the truth crashed upon him, bring him to wish his own end, his inner demolition.

Duvid stared through the steam at his reflection in the mirror. It was the morning of the first day of Rosh Hashanah. Soon Duvid would take his sons to synagogue. There they would stand in awe before the Ark as the cantor captured the dark spaces with the power of his voice. Life was sliding along too quickly. Soon the twins would be preparing for bar mitzvah.

He blinked. The start of a new year was the wrong day to think such regressive thoughts. He released them. They flowed down the drain with the shaving foam. Duvid looked away from the past, straight ahead at the family he now was raising, his great accomplishment, the two growing sons who left him proud every time they won an argument with him.

The seasons ran on. And the years, one, then two. The days passed invisibly. Then one day it was winter. Simon trudged along gloomily, his father trailing slightly behind him in the Sunday snow. Adam wasn't with them. He had remained behind at Hannah's insistence he stay in bed because of a fever, wrapped thickly in blankets, Vicks VapoRub spread across his chest. Since the time an infection had left him with a perforated eardrum, his mother had never allowed him out of the house when his forehead felt too warm to her. Hannah had tried to protect Simon too, but Duvid had ignored her pleas about the dangers of the weather. So Adam was reading the boys' shared treasury of Superman and Uncle Scrooge comic books, while Simon was out here in this insane winter.

Father and son left a drift of vapour condensing in the air. They puffed their way over to the outdoor ice rink, a ten minute slow walk from home across the street in Fletcher's Field, the park which ran along the west side of Esplanade. Ice filled the potholes in the street, snow was heaped between the leafless poplars that lined the tenement courtyard. The wind whistled and moaned without pity.

"Ta, why do I have to go skating and not Adam? He's not really sick at all." His father's face wrestled with him.

"You are lucky, Simon. Otherwise, where could you get any exercise in the winter?" Duvid answered the question himself. "Nowhere. It is important to exercise. And to be responsible for yourself. When I was your age, I was already considered a man. Not so long from now, you will be told that you are a man, though this is not so. You are far from ready for that status yet. Back in Poland, I would strap some boards on the bottom of my boots, and that was what I skated on. No one helped me to go to the ice rink. There was none. We skated on the frozen river."

"Sure, Ta. Boards on your feet?"

"Why do you talk like this? Do you think you know something, with all that they teach you in school, do you know how to do anything practical?"

"Ta?"

"What now?"

"What if the war hadn't happened in Poland? Would I have been born anyway?"

"My smart son thinks too much. He asks questions I can't answer. I would still be living in Poland, a tailor like my father, with who knows how many children. Maybe I would be happier, how can I know? A man can never go back through time and change the course of his life. The world is like a river, flowing forever down a hill, always faster. The currents of the world are too powerful for us to ever change them once we have passed through them."

"Ta, do you remember when we almost drowned? Why did you pull Adam from the water, first, why not me?"

"You are angry at me for that still? I saved your life. He was closer. It was lucky for you both I was there that day."

"And then you let me go. To get Rachel. Instead of me, your son. Ma was right. What kind of father are you? You don't try hard enough to save your own family."

"But I did. You're alive."

"You didn't try hard in Poland. You ran away to the forest. You told me that."

"Yes, I told you that. But I didn't tell you everything. Come along. Quickly, we'll freeze before you get a chance to skate."

"So would I have been born anyway?"

"Simon, Simon. You are like a dog that bites and never lets go, but this is a question only a man much smarter than me could answer. I was once very smart, when I was a youngster, like you are now, but growing up, it melts the brains away. Even our Einstein thought up his great ideas when he was young, so complicated they are that I never understood even a piece of them. But I am not an educated man, just a tailor like my own father was.

"And you, ach, would you be here? Only God can know, Simon. Him you cannot ask a question. Even if He is truly there at all. But you are here in the only world that we know. You are your mother Hannah's child, not someone else's."

"Like Miriam?"

"No. Things happened this way and no other. Maybe this is the only way they could have happened. You are not replaceable; this world is not changeable. It is the only one we can know."

"Maybe it would have been better if I was never born. Then maybe all these people you tell me about would not have died."

"Life is not an equation, Simon, like a bookkeeper's ledger. Don't waste your thoughts on the past, especially my past. It is enough that I have to. It is over long ago."

"What if the war happened to me? Would I know what to do?"

"There is only one way to learn life, and that is to live it. One can only hope to survive the examinations. A boy becomes a man by learning to control his impulses. One has to learn what to do, but also what not to do. Truly, you are not ready. You have had a soft life."

"You know what, Ta? You talk too much."

"Maybe you're right that I should stop talking. But you should not answer your own father back like this. You show no respect. You act like a shiftless, insolent boy."

"Ta, did you learn those words in your *Reader's Digests*?"

"So, I see you have learned how to fight me. But it shouldn't be your father you fight with. You get nothing but kindness from me and your mother. Things would not be such a pleasure for you in Poland."

"Stupid Poland again! I could never have lived in Poland, Ta. If there wouldn't have been a war, you would have stayed in Poland and I wouldn't have been born. You would have twelve other children by now, and none of them would be me." In his mind, Duvid was now back in Poland in the first days of the war, trying to save his family, aware that some terrible thing was about to happen to them all if they stayed.

There had been war nearby and far away for the two previous weeks as the German blitzkrieg decimated and then eliminated the Polish cavalry-led army. Now any remaining resistance in the small towns was being mopped up.

He was an impulsive seventeen years old when the Germans rolled into their small town on the Friday, the second day of Rosh Hashanah, September 1939. The supper was on the stove, simmering slowly. The men had just returned from their prayers at the town synagogue. The Jewish families were ordered out of their houses. Several men were pointed out by local Poles, and dragged away. There were shots further back on the road into the town. A house was burning. The synagogue was being looted.

Duvid had stood in shock next to his fourteen-year-old sister Chaya. She was ordered to remove her dress and show that she had no valuables secreted away in her clothing. Young, shy, steeped in rules of female propriety, she hesitated. A soldier had come forward and ordered her to continue, his rifle pointed at her. She was about to receive a blow from his rifle butt for her delay, when her mother intervened, tearing the girl's dress away herself and showing how there was nothing of value to be had there. It had been almost more than Duvid could bear, but he knew better than to react.

Later, there were dead bodies to bury. He knew he would have to leave. It was logical. Also logical was that his family would know to come with him. At the end of that day, with the Germans gone on to the next town, he saw that he had been wrong. They would not go. He had to run off alone to the forest.

A thick guilt now swept through Duvid, like the wind gathering strength in the turbulent air around them. Cold and silence, guilt and anger, filled the father and his son, while Duvid laced up Simon's skates at the outdoor ice rink, making sure they were 'good and tight', as he put it. He stopped and watched for a few minutes as his son glided around the rink. He could see that Simon was making progress in both skill and strength. Despite the invective a few minutes earlier, Duvid allowed himself to feel pride in his contentious son, and his feelings of betrayal softened. Now he would return to finish the factory work he had brought home with him.

Before they left the flat, Hannah had told Duvid to bring Simon's boots home and not leave them for a thief to steal. He lifted them and walked home, leaving Simon on the ice rink. Simon's dead uncle Burach, Hannah's brother, had owned a pair of leather boots in Russia during the war. At night, while in Odessa, he guarded them by placing them under his head as a pillow. He had woken up to find them gone. Such fine boots, made of soft yet strong leather, warm in winter, always dry. It had taken him all of the remaining summer to save enough rubles to buy an inferior pair on the black market, probably removed from the feet of a dead soldier. Hannah had many times told Duvid and their sons the story of her brother's boots. So now Simon's boots were gone home with Duvid, and the boy was left with only his skates.

Simon's boots were only made of rubber, of course, but who knew, somewhere close by was another thief who wanted just such a pair of rubber boots, in just such a size, so he had to be careful. So after Simon had spent a long hour skating around and around as the winter afternoon got colder and the wind stoked its bitter howl, he had to hobble home in his skates. He could hardly feel his toes. His ankles felt like they were breaking sideways. The weak winter sun was beginning to set in a jaundiced sky. The long block and a half home the wind whispered frightfully into his ears, and when he arrived, his cheeks were red with white centres, his earlobes insensible.

Hannah was horrified when she saw Simon's frostbitten cheeks. Without putting on her coat, she scurried outside with a metal pot to scoop up snow and carried it quickly inside to the kitchen. There she rubbed the snow vigorously on the patches of white.

"Simon, stop squirming so much. Let me warm your frozen cheeks. Duvid, you can be a little more careful with your son, no? You don't know it's today winter outside? It's not enough Adam is sick; I now need two boys with a fever?"

But Duvid didn't respond. He was looking down at the scar on his hand, no longer in the same room as Hannah.

8 Sons

A week remained before the boys' *bar mitzvahs*. They would share a part of the reading of the Torah that Saturday morning, along with others called up for the reading that day. Honours at synagogue were distributed by rank. They were ancient ranks, first a Cohen, from the obsolete priestly class, then the Levites, who once had looked after the Temple in Jerusalem before its destruction. The last reader was traditionally a member of *klal yisroel*, all of Israel, from among the surviving remnants of the Twelve Tribes, many long extinct, carried off or expelled by this or that conquering army. It was a long history of loss, long remembered and long mourned.

There would be the *kiddish* afterwards, and his sons would be men, adults among other Jewish men, at least for matters of ritual.

At breakfast, while Duvid grilled Adam about his portion of the reading to come, Simon was silent. When Duvid got to him, Simon refused to answer.

"What is wrong today?"

"I don't want a *bar mitzvah*."

"Now you say. Now?"

"I did before. You just wouldn't listen."

"You can't refuse. It's all arranged."

"I don't want to do it."

"You won't be a man if you don't."

"A man? Do you think I'll be a man if I do?"

"Well, maybe not completely a man, Simon. I don't see you with the girls yet. But in synagogue, you will be one."

"I don't care about synagogue."

"What, you're not a Jew?"

"I don't know."

At this point, Hannah came away from the stove and wiped her hands on a dish towel.

"He's as much a Jew as you, Duvid. Do I see you go to pray three times a day? He'll be fine. Leave the boy alone. All he needs is to be circumcised, and that happened long before he could talk."

"Thank God for that, that I didn't have to argue with him over that too."

"So you'll have one son who becomes bar mitzvah on Saturday. Your money for the kiddish won't be wasted. You'll see, Simon will live. And so will we."

The school year was over for now. Saturday came, and only Adam read from the Torah. Besides his parents, only the few family and friends noticed Simon not being there. Adam would have appeared somewhat betrayed up on the *bima*, standing next to the old hairy rabbi, if anyone but his mother really cared what he looked like. The men were all too busy intermittently praying and arguing business in between the words of the rabbi's sermon and the cantor's singing. Hannah smiled warmly at the back of the synagogue, behind the *mehitza*, the women's barrier. Duvid smiled stiffly and a little grimly next to his Adam. Simon spent the morning at home, listening to music on the kitchen radio. "*One Fine Day*" by The Chiffons, "*It's My Party*" by Lesley Gore. Simon knew Adam would try to get his revenge later, but for now, he was pleased with getting away with his refusal.

Hannah was right. Simon lived. So did the others in his family. The boys' rivalry continued as it had before.

And so it went. Summer once more. A season of stories and dreams. Of the two boys, Simon was the dreamer, his head always in the clouds or in a book. His haunt was the scrubby park that lay across the street from where he lived. Here he would tell his stories to the small group of boys who clustered around him, a modern Aristotle and his peripatetic band of followers. He described to them another universe below their feet, where the ants lived in intricate mazes below the ground, listening to the thunder of these children as they walked about. Simon frightened the boys with eerie tales of the park's trees. They came alive and wandered about during the night. The trees visited the children's windows in the darkness and scratched at the panes of glass to rouse them. They would wait for the boys to startle awake, unable to move or speak, frozen with terror. The tree branches would reach in and drag the boys away into these subterranean tunnels where the ants could feed on their paralyzed bodies.

Simon's sleep was filled with his own dreams, midnight struggles that left him awake and listless when the dawn's early light touched the dark eastern horizon with its paint, the morning birds chirping earnestly. Simon dreamt of ghosts, the wandering souls of people he could not identify, men with long thinning beards, women with dark dresses and scarves over wig-covered heads. Men and women living much like his ants, in underground passages, running at the sounds of the thunder in the streets above them. Men and women wandering like leafless trees in a burnt forest, looking for their stolen children, searching for a pane of unbroken glass.

Simon and Adam slept in the same room. It was not a large apartment. The two had never minded sharing this space at night, but it also meant sharing other intimacies, glimpses at each other's terrors and growing urges.

Such a night of dream Simon had known before. The dreams repeated, over and over, with different actors and locations, telling him their same story. A shadow moved toward his sleeping shape on the bed, a dark form undefined yet human. A hand reached out of this darkness, an old gnarled hand, blue thick veins twisting like jagged vines across its frail yellowing skin, an old hand shaking with a coarse tremor, its joints thick and ugly. A man, an old bent man, emerged from its indefinite darkness, reaching out to touch Simon on the cheek. He sat heavily on the edge of Simon's bed, easing himself down roughly, painful hemorrhoids and arthritic spine defeating any semblance of grace.

The bedspring creaked, in concert with the old man's joints. Adam stirred at the sound, then opened his eyes and stared. Simon was rising, bending from the waist, his head turning slowly towards the face of the old man, the eyes open and yet unseeing, still asleep. Simon's mouth opened and started a low howl. Adam did not see the old man, only his brother attempting to escape from his dream.

Held in the dream, Simon saw the old man reach for his cheek, felt the cold fingers, his bare cracked bones, passing through him, while the old man's mouth attempted to speak in a language which Adam heard in Simon's voice, which he only vaguely understood now, the language he had first heard when he was younger but had since mostly forgotten. The bedsprings creaked again, the old man departing the dream.

Adam stared at Simon, who was mouthing the Yiddish words: "*Kleine kindt, mein kleine kindt!*" Then Simon was screaming, the strength of his voice abruptly regained. Adam, terrified beyond thinking, now added his shrieks to those of his brother. Hannah rushed in to find out what the disturbance was about this time, but saw no one but her sons, both howling in fear. She had heard some of the Yiddish words in Simon's voice. She was jarred by a recollection of her own strange dreams. Old dreams, long forgotten.

Hannah slipped back into bed, trying not to disturb Duvid, always a light sleeper.

"What was that?" he muttered.

"Just a bad dream."

"Again?"

"Children always have bad dreams."

"And you."

"Me?"

"You toss around sometimes. Sometimes it even wakes me up."

"I'm sorry, my Duvid. You too have them."

"Yes. Yes, I do. Well, they're dreams. There's nothing to be done, they come when they want."

"Let's try and get some sleep tonight."

At that, Duvid went silent, and after a short interval, he was snoring lightly until Hannah nudged him over onto his side. Shards of dreams came back to her. It was impossible to forget all those things that had happened during the war. It was especially at night that the memories came. During the day, thank God, she was too busy looking after her little men, and the big man, their father. She smiled at this snatch of a thought, and the moment of peace allowed her eyes to close and she too was again asleep.

The tree, tall and massive, crashes down, smashing through the surrounding branches. A scream and a rush of bodies, cries of people trying to help, but to no avail.

Then Hannah was awake again. Duvid, when she turned, was not in bed. She heard the toilet flush. She waited, but he didn't return.

"Duvid?"

There was no response. Doubly shaken by the dream and Duvid's absence, Hannah rose to look for him. The hallway was flooded by light from his workroom, where she found him hunched over, his head in the closet.

"Duvid, what are you doing?"

Duvid straightened up and turned.

"I thought you were asleep."

"And so, what? What are you doing?"

"Looking for something."

"Like?"

"Poems, Nothing important. Something I just remembered."

"Poems? In the middle of the night?"

"Yes, in the middle of the night. You know that your husband can sometimes do something crazy."

"Yes, Duvid." Hannah smiled and shook her head. She was still not satisfied, but it was evident that questioning more would lead nowhere. She thought of his long ago poems to her. She grabbed his hand and tugged him along back to the bedroom, allowing him to pause only long enough to shut the light.

"So, let's be a little crazy now, poet." And with that she kissed him and pulled him to her side of the bed. "Don't complain. It will help us sleep better."

"I won't ever complain, Hannah."

9 Men's Talk

Leibel Perelman and his wife, Rivka, Duvid's cousin, came often on Sundays to visit. When first arrived from Israel, the two families had economized by sharing an apartment. One day every week, they still shared time together. Visiting the park on late Sunday mornings in summer had become a ritual. They would sit around the gazebo on the grassy slope below the woods, along with many other Jewish families in similar circumstances, survivors of the European conflagration. Some weeks, if they stayed late enough, a band played sweet nostalgic music for them. They would share a picnic lunch, drinking in the sultry day as if it were the champagne they could never afford. Other weeks they would converge on the Perelman's' flat for the midday meal, which they called dinner. It was an anarchic meal, of braised beef and chicken, boiled beets, salads of finely chopped fresh vegetables, mashed potatoes doused with beet or spinach borscht. Each reached simultaneously for the food served up in large bowls at the centre of the table, and the wives piled their children's plates high, and insisted that all be eaten. To waste food was sinful. Who knew what famines tomorrow would bring? The men sipped on tiny glasses of schnapps, telling stories and jokes. After the meal, the boys, still amused by the way their urine turned red after drinking beet borscht, were off to the toilet for a communal pee.

Did you hear the one about Schwartz when he was in Florida? He's out at the pool relaxing and the lifeguard, a very pretty girl with long blonde hair and beautiful big knockers, she walks up to him. 'Mr. Schwartz, there's a sign right there that says NO PISSING IN THE POOL. Can't you read?' So Schwartz answers her: 'So why me? Everybody pees in the pool.' And the lifeguard, she answers 'Yes, Mr. Schwartz, but NOT FROM THE DIVING BOARD!'

Toilet humour of one sort or another ruled the day. It always seemed to be the same joke. Each time the wives tsk-tsked at the word knockers, and cupped their outraged hands over their children's ears, while the men chortled with laughter. Since the women had fewer hands than there were ears, they covered one ear of each child, hoping this would protect them from filth, at least partially. The children ignored their boring parents, guzzled large glasses of Coca Cola, then had a belching contest. Mrs. Perelman guarded the newly bought cotton tablecloth. Heaven help the one who dared to spill so much as a drop.

"Leibel, look at the boy, he's going to spill his glass again, so, nu, say something! Leib!"

Leibel feigned not knowing his Rivka. The glasses they all drank from were only used when company was over. They had been imported directly from Czechoslovakia, bought at a small hard-goods store on the Main, not far from the big fruit store. The fruit store owner's wife was known to keep an eagle eye on the store's clerks. Sometimes she manned the cash herself. At times, she might look the other way when she weighed the bag of bananas, and let one or other of the Jewish ladies get away with the occasional bargain. They would talk to their friends, who would come looking to save a few pennies. It was good for business, as long as it was limited. Other times she would lean a finger on the scale when the woman was someone else.

Mrs. Perelman had been careful to preserve the oval silvery paper labels on the glasses when she washed them, so that anyone who drank from them would respect their origin and her good taste in buying them.

The children listened with both curiosity and boredom. Their parents shared stories about their devastated families. They had each lost someone. They remembered the deprivations of the last war.

"The people of Russia suffered much more than the soft Americans during that war. And nobody in America knows. They only know of John Wayne. Like the war was between cowboys and Indians."

"Ah, these Americans cared more about a few communists than an army of Nazis. Why else did it take them so long to start to fight? Why, because they were afraid to help Stalin. They hoped Hitler would finish him off first. They got a good lesson from Pearl Harbour. It served them right. Such a soft people the world never saw."

"Stalin too was a terrible anti-Semite."

"No. It was Stalin who saved the Jews from the Nazis by taking them in."

"He was an anti-Semite, anyway. After the war was done, he wanted to continue what Hitler had started. Look what he did to the Jewish doctors."

"What nonsense is this? What are you talking, you who don't know as much as a small child?"

"It doesn't matter if you agree with me about Stalin. You are a communist and that's all there is to that. Everyone is an anti-Semite, even this President Eisenhower. And here in Canada, the whole government, the whole country. No question. Or else they would have let in a few Jews before the war."

"These American Jews brought the troubles they had with Senator Joseph McCarthy on themselves. They voted for Eisenhower, after all."

"But President Eisenhower was good for the Jews. And who else was there to vote for? The Democrats never wanted to help Israel."

"What are you talking? Truman was the one who recognized Israel in 1948. Without him, no one else would have. Eisenhower was not good for the Jews. It was he who was an anti-Semite. Look at who he took as a vice-president, this crook Nixon, the dog-lover. He only helped Israel because the Russians helped the Arabs. Look at what he did during the Sinai campaign. Didn't he force Israel to give back the Sinai to Egypt? This was a friend of the Jews?"

Hannah piped in. "It is a shame on the whole world what troubles the Jews of Israel are still suffering through, after all we had to go through during the war. And still war and war again."

With her input, the men's discussion crumbled. This was men's talk. What was becoming of the world, when women started to have political opinions?

10 Patterns

The boys were hunched over on the floor in the parlour, doing their homework, and this pleased Hannah, but the newly acquired television was on. She had had her doubts about this device, but Duvid had been determined to have a small piece of what he called American luxury in his house. Being able to afford it gave him a feeling of accomplishment.

Voyage to the Bottom of the Sea was on. Fast-paced music, bubbles, and a giant multi-armed squid filled the TV screen.

"How can you study with such noise, such loud sound—can I call that music? You don't do your homework in your room? Why do you think you have desks? Your backs will break if you sit like this. You'll walk like hunchbacks before you even grow up."

"Oh, Ma."

"You worry me. How can you concentrate on your homework with one eye and one ear on these television shows? So much fighting. It's not a good example for young boys."

"Ma."

"Go," she ordered, switching off the program, and to soothe them, "you're such smart boys."

"I was finished anyways, Ma." Adam flashed her a defiant smile.

"Well, you don't need such nonsense. Don't you have anything else to do for school?"

"I need to make a sign for a science project, but I need a piece of thick paper for that."

"Your father is not home yet, but I'm sure he would want to help you. He can give you a piece of his pattern paper. Go look in his workroom, but don't disturb anything he's working on."

Adam walked into what looked to him like chaos. Large and small scissors, a wooden yardstick, a box full of white or dark waxy rectangles for tracing patterns on cloth. Bolts of cloth rolled and stacked up in one corner, coloured threads on cone-shaped forms on the window sill, curved paper patterns hanging by clothes pegs from a line of cord that passed from the picture rail of one wall across to the other. Where would his father keep his pattern paper? Adam looked under the table. He saw only cardboard boxes, each filled with cloth. No blank paper.

The closet. Its door was partly closed, blocked by another box filled with parts for the sewing machine which stood against the wall next to it. Adam pushed the box aside with one foot and pulled the closet door open. It was a narrow space. He was startled by a mannequin on one side. On the other was the roll of Kraft paper he wanted, but at its bottom end it was wedged against the wall by an old suitcase.

Adam pulled the suitcase forward to free the paper roll just as his father entered the room.

Duvid was livid. "What are you doing there? What! Did I ever tell you you could touch anything in this closet? Get out! Now!" Duvid had grabbed Adam by both wrists by now and was dragging him from behind out of the workroom. "DON'T YOU EVER COME IN HERE WITHOUT MY PERMISSION!"

Hannah came running. "What are you screaming for? The boy didn't do anything. I told him to come in here to find some paper for a school project. What is wrong with you, all of a sudden?"

"I have things here that should not be touched!"

"What do you have, Duvid, that you should yell so much? The boy has done nothing wrong. I have never heard you like this before."

"Something I don't want to talk about."

"A secret?"

"How can I have secrets? You always have your eyes on me. Just my old patterns I keep there. Nothing."

"Duvid?"

"Leave it, please."

It stopped. Hannah went back to the kitchen, and Adam to his bedroom. At supper, only Simon spoke. He looked puzzled when no one answered.

11 Growth

The sun sets. The sun rises. Between the two we dream. Unlikely shapes appear in the darkness, try to disappear with the glow of the aural dawn. They persist as vague apparitions, to puzzle us all day. All our days. The cycle repeats forever, endless.

Dora, Rachel's mother, passed by her daughter's room as she slept. Dora sighed along with the soft breathing drifting out of her daughter's bed. A deep sadness plunged through her. She felt unfulfilled and betrayed by this unruly defiant child, now growing ever more rebellious. Dora wondered if she herself had perhaps been too pampered as a child, and had knowingly or not passed this condition on to her daughter. Rachel had never wanted for anything. Although they lived frugally, for Dora and Morris it was a choice turned into a habit. They had the means to live much better, but not the taste for it, not any more. Of course, that constraint was for themselves only. It didn't include their daughter. Not in her mother's mind, at least.

And not in Rachel's.

Rachel was an only child, a limitation which Dora and her husband Morris hadn't planned as such. It was just that physiology hadn't cooperated, despite the fire Dora had still felt within. Morris had died only last year, when the girl was fourteen. The memory of that day now flooded through Dora, with its bitterness still sharp. Dora sighed another deep sigh. Rachel now was left as her single focus. Despite the pain she often brought Dora, Rachel was still that, her daughter, the centre of her life.

Morris would have been happy to have had a son, someone to carry his name together with his genes into another generation, but it had not been. The energy that would have gone into his business had instead been diverted into sex and into bickering. Dora wondered if that was what had killed him. Now it was too late. Their double bed was useful now only for piling up pillows. Dora sighed again.

Both their sexual couplings and their arguments had invariably been loud. They had scandalized the widow Pfeffer, an older woman who lived in the attached triplex next door to theirs. Mrs. Pfeffer cherished the complaints she could make to her Mah Jongg friends about the late night noise. She would fix her ear to a glass held against the wall adjoining their bedroom.

She had been a widow for many years. She and her husband had never had any children, so she had bought herself a small dog to keep her company. It was her delight, but it yapped at strangers and urinated each time someone came to the door. She had despaired that it was too stupid to ever be house-trained. To her annoyance it barked jealously whenever she eavesdropped.

The dog's hearing was much better than hers. The walls were thin. No amount of shushing on her part could shut the dog up. Sometimes she would hear Morris imitating the animal's loud howling while he was *shtupping* Dora. It would become doubly agitated. It hopped up onto the widow's bed, biting excitedly into the pillows and wetting the bed covers. Mrs. Pfeffer pounded on the intervening wall in protest. The activity on the other side of the wall would break down into a cacophony of laughter, while Mrs. Pfeffer hauled the sheets off her bed and carried them to her new Inglis washing machine.

Often when she walked her dog in the late afternoons, Morris would be sitting out on his balcony next door, sipping his hot, very sweet tea. A broad smile greeted her as she passed. He took a vicious delight in imitating the yelping of her dog. The animal answered with a frenzied crescendo of high-pitched howls. These would continue uncontrollably long after she had carried the dog inside. When this happened on her way out, the poodle would spray her shoes and feet as it eagerly tried to defend her. Morris broke into loud guffaws, sputtering tea out in front of him. He only stopped when Dora came out and pulled him indoors. Dora sighed again as she remembered this too. Now she too was a widow.

Her Rachel had spent another school year growing rounder breasts and longer legs, slowly losing the baby fat that rounded her cheeks and waist and her still-clumsy limbs. Her rich black hair kept her in the bathroom for hours, tending to its needs. Dora hesitated to wake Rachel for school, relishing this benign moment.

She turned in a circle, taking in the minutiae of Rachel's teenaged life, the photos of rock and roll heartthrobs, the stuffed bear that guarded the door, the frilly pink bathrobe and slippers. She turned to the dresser mirror in her daughter's room and noticed the lipstick sitting there. Where had Rachel gotten this? With what money? She had an allowance, but not enough to pay for such an indulgence. And, besides, what did she need lipstick for? At her age, yet. Dora picked up the lipstick tube and lifted the top. Red. Bright red. Dora was appalled. This is a grown woman's colour. Even on my lips, it would be a scandal.

She was a recent widow. She couldn't wear such a shade, not so soon after her husband's death. Dora scrutinized herself in the mirror, the woman she was now. Her face was still unlined, her lips firm, her breasts still round and high, still desirable. She patted her hair and smiled. 'Not too bad,' she thought. 'I'll try it.' She was carefully applying the colour to her lips when she heard Rachel stir, start to yell. It was never easy.

"That's mine."

"And where did you get it? Such a bright red. Only the *shikse* prostitutes on Saint Lawrence wear this, not a young lady."

"So why are you putting it on?"

"This is not your business. I'm your mother."

"I didn't give you permission. It's mine. And it makes you look ugly."

Again the insults, Dora thought.

"So where did you get it. Answer me!"

"My friend Betty let me share it."

"Your friend Betty? Didn't I tell you shouldn't see this girl? I'm telling you, Rachel, your friends will be the end of you. You'll get a reputation. Aren't there any nice Jewish girls at your school?"

"They're all so boring. You can't keep me from my friends, Ma."

"We'll see. Remember we're moving away soon. It'll be a new neighbourhood, with new friends, a new school."

"You can't make me go with you. I'll run away."

"You're too spoiled to run away. Where will you find all the little things I give you?"

"Mother!"

"Get dressed. It's time for school. Come eat your breakfast."

"I hate you!"

"I'm sure you do, but come eat your breakfast anyway. That way, you'll be strong enough to really hate me."

April had barely begun. The Grynsztyns wouldn't share a country house with them this coming summer. The families had lost touch with each other. The Grynsztyns were also moving to another neighbourhood. Just as well, Dora decided. Those two boys were a bad influence. Good riddance.

Dora had sold the brown brick triplex on Fairmount Avenue that she and Morris had bought such a long time ago.

"It's worth nothing now and never will be. Too much upkeep. Morris worked so hard at this, but what do I know about hot water and radiators, or shovelling snow from the steps to the third floor? Too much work for a widowed woman," she mumbled to herself in self-justification. "Soon no one will want to live in such a neighbourhood of poor people running from every catastrophe in the world. It's turning into a slum."

Cote des Neiges, where they were moving in a few weeks, was an area that held promise. She had friends who had bought duplexes on Van Horne, Victoria, Kent. These new names sounded fresh and civilized. Clean English names, not the Saint this and Saint that which were attached to every other street around here. The rents her friends took in paid the mortgages they had taken out, not like the pittance she could charge here. She had settled on a house on de la Peltrie. Not so fancy, maybe, not so English-sounding, but easier to afford. The new area was becoming largely Jewish. Her Rachel would be safe.

Dora prepared Rachel's breakfast while her daughter spent the next half hour in the bathroom. The girl had only just started to wear a little lipstick. She put it on before she left and wiped it off at the door to the school. The rules didn't allow it. On her way home, she and her girlfriends would again adorn their lips. They giggled as rowdy groups of upper grade boys hurried by them, always jostling, and sometimes grabbing her by the waist. Rachel's mother had yet to agree to buy her a training bra. The bolder ones pushed each other forwards, groping against the girls' incipient breasts, and most often hers. Rachel secretly enjoyed when they did that, regretting that the hands couldn't stay in place longer, more languorously.

Rachel inspected her skin closely in the bathroom mirror. There was no knowing when her face would break out, to her own and her friends' horror. The day in front of her was a huge blank, more slow agony until classes were done, when she could tease the boys. She and her friends threw mock kisses at them. Rachel imagined that they could become real. Then she and the other girls would peel away and rush home. She half-hoped that the boys could not sense that she was interested, while half-hoping that they could.

"Ma, why are we moving?" Rachel wondered. What was wrong with where they lived now? Her friends Helen and Lena weren't moving. Why did she have to?

"It's a better neighbourhood. All the Jewish families are moving away from here. There's a shopping centre nearby. A Chinese restaurant close to us on Van Horne." Rachel wasn't impressed.

Dora had gotten used to being picked up by her friends on Sundays for a get-together at the Yangtze Restaurant. She habitually kept kosher in her home, but she now allowed herself to transgress when she went out. She had taken to the oddly exotic but strangely inviting flavours of the (pork) garlic spare ribs and the won ton soup. Recently she even ventured into ordering an all-dressed pizza for her daughter and her friends when they came by after school. Mrs. Pfeffer would have been scandalized.

Dora noticed her daughter's lips were a ripe scarlet, gaudily obvious.

"Rachel, you're wearing that lipstick? I told you I don't like this. Go take it off. You'll catch a disease sharing like this. And your friend's mother allows this?"

"Ma, you're too old-fashioned. Besides, it's not your business. I'm old enough to do what I want."

"So, listen to Miss Independent, will you? Next you'll be bringing boys into the house when I'm not here."

Rachel was not far from that stage, but she still hadn't been totally alone with a boy. There was the odd occasion, in the darkroom at school, where she was the only girl in the camera club, but the boys were short, or unattractive, and she didn't usually encourage them, except for the divine Michael. He was a possibility, if only he would notice her, but so far, his only interest was the chemistry of light, not of desire.

When Rachel's father was still alive, she too had held her ear to the bedroom wall and wondered at her parents' activities. She dared to slip into their bedroom before they went to bed, where she hid behind the massive free-standing European armoire that functioned as their closet. From there, she observed as her parents went through stages of pachydermal lovemaking, until her father achieved an orgasmic state and dissolved into a soft pool of fatness. From where she was, crouching in the dark, she observed his heavy gasping, his huge naked body spread prone on the bed. She stared at his swollen dark penis, lying there deflated between his fat legs, bedded on the wide pillow of his scrotum. His fingers were clustered on the middle of his chest, as if he had been trying to gather up his sick heart and comfort it. She hoped he was dying. After a few minutes, though, the gasping subsided. Moments later, he was snoring, fast asleep.

All this was a mystery that intrigued Rachel, one that she wanted to explore.

Rachel started into her eggs and toast. For a brief moment, she thought about telling her mother how she got the lipstick, but only because she wanted so desperately to shock her. In her mother's bubble world, her beautiful but dutiful daughter still lived in a puffy cloud of comfortable thoughts. Shoplifting was hardly one of those.

Stealing a small item like the lipstick from the Kresge's store on Mount Royal was hardly a difficult thing. Her friends all had done it. It was like a game. A competition. The middle-aged salesladies who worked at the cash like old cows were mostly thinking of other things as the girls drifted through the cosmetics area of the store after school, adjusting their hair in the small mirror on the counter. Two asked excitedly to see this comb or that hair clip. The third would slip something into her tunic blouse. The manager would never dare to ask to look there, not with their fathers ready to come down to the store and break a few teeth, nor with their mothers prepared for a boycott.

In the school library, she had been affected by the pictures in the National Geographic, but for her it was the exotic landscapes and faces that raised her interest. The world around her was nothing like these other places, where men and women stood unconcerned in strange-looking costume in strange-looking habitats. And naked. It made her mouth water, this appetite for the alien. The interplay of light and shape hid at the back of her mind, waiting to act.

There had been plenty of family photos, momentary smiles frozen into photo-reactive chemicals by the clicking shutter. The family snapshots were nothing like National Geographic. She, in an unflattering swimsuit at the beach on the back river, smiling. She and her parents, at her tenth birthday party, smiling. Her parents, at their wedding so many years before, their faces giving every indication of exhaustion, but, oddly, smiling. Smiles and smiles and smiles, not a hint of rancour, tragedy, or effort anywhere. Joy everywhere. The one time she had dared to show them, Rachel's *goyishe* friends had referred to these as Natural Jewographic, for them a closer-to-home sort of exoticism. Rachel's mother winced when her daughter told her about this.

"What kind of company do you keep, Rachel. They will lead you into shame."

"Mother, stop it!"

"So no more 'Ma'? Now it's Mother? You're becoming a real little shiksele. I don't like this. I don't like it at all."

She had asked, begged, demanded, that her parents buy her a camera. Her father had only laughed.

"What do you need it for? Will it bring you something good? A job?" It was the way he always disarmed her.

"Tata."

"No."

She hated him. She hated his smirk of satisfaction when he refused her something. Something deep, something essential, had now been taken from her. By him, this stupid, puffy, fat man who pretended to be her father. With his fat belly, his flaccid prick with its ugly circumcision. Not at all like how she imagined Michael's to be. No, not like the penis of a god. She couldn't be related to this disappointment of a parent. Not at all. Never had been. There. She had delegitimized him. He wasn't really her father at all.

Yes, she wanted him dead.

She would get back at him some day. And her mother, well, Dora was no use either. She had a willing heart, true, but she had no money, not more than the small amount of grocery money Morris gave her. That she already squeezed so that she could buy the little things that might keep her contentious daughter pacified. Rachel recognized she had hit a wall for now. She would just make her own door in it. It was as simple as that.

So Rachel stole the camera. The audacious idea fired up her wild imaginings instantly. It was only a small step farther than stealing lipsticks. It would be easy. And so it was. She hid it in her tunic, simply dropping it in. Her winter coat provided enough bulk to disguise it. The squirm was practiced. She had tried it several times at home in her room, pushing a small box of tissues in there while bent over, as if looking into a glass display case. Mildly uncomfortable, but effective.

Getting film was so easy. Everyone in the camera club at school, except for her, were all boys. The activity was supposed to be supervised by Mrs. Jankow, but this teacher spent much of her time arguing on the phone with her mother. The students provided their own film. Rachel determined to get an extra roll or two from the others. Most of the boys, the ugly ones, were too scrupulous, so it had to be Michael. She asked for his help in the darkroom, and this time, when he agreed, she brushed against his back as she leaned behind him while he showed her how he fanned his hand across the exposing plate to soften the focus on one area of the photo. She reached one hand on his shoulder, pressing herself against him from behind. She whispered next to his ear how she was learning so much from him. Afterwards, he was more than happy to give her some of his film. He couldn't say no. Rachel was enjoying this. It was all becoming child's play for her.

Rachel remembered the day very well. That day. She was watching from her vantage point, again exploring her parents' strange activity. Her father had, as usual, rolled onto his back and was making the same heavy gasping sounds, but they had continued into heaving wheezes. Her mother, quickly pulling on a pink quilted housecoat, had rushed out of the bedroom in distress.

From her vantage point behind her mother's dresser, Rachel could hear Dora alternately blubbering and yelling into the black dial telephone. Rachel slipped out of the bedroom, but was blocked in the hall by her mother's bulk. Dora hung up and tried again. She stabbed her fingers into the rotary dial. They kept bumping and slipping out prematurely. She alternated between bawling and shrieking. Already confused enough, Dora distractedly ordered Rachel to go to her room, then went back to negotiating with the handset. Her face was flabby and white, her cheeks streaked with tears running through rouge and powder. At that moment Rachel's father walked out of the bedroom wearing only his briefs. Rachel, appalled, retreated back into her bedroom next door to hide. She saw her camera and grabbed it. This was a National Geographic moment.

"What are you doing, woman?"

"I'm calling an ambulance."

"What for? I look dead to you?"

"No, but I thought you were..."

"Don't think such a thing. It's like wishing it on me. I'm full of life. Look." He pointed downwards. "Besides, do you know what they charge for an ambulance? It's an outrage. Come on, let's go back to bed."

Dora grabbed Morris and gave him a hug. In a wave of emotion, she pushed her head against his chest, her hands on his shoulders. Rachel slipped past her distracted parents into the darkness of their bedroom. The window shades were pulled down. She stood waiting behind the armoire. She could hear her mother laughing in the corridor, before becoming silent. Her parents walked back in and climbed into bed together. Rachel pointed her camera. The flash was already installed. The bulb flared three times before her parents began to scream in one voice. Next door, Mrs. Pfeffer's dog howled in concert. Rachel quickly ran to her room and slammed the door. Seconds later, there was a loud banging on the door and the outraged roar of her father, but Rachel didn't obey and open the door, and after a while, she heard his feet padding back to bed.

When Rachel woke up the next morning, she heard her mother bawling. Rachel's father was dead. Rachel was surprised to find herself crying too.

12 Ovens

Duvid reached into the closet of his workroom and pulled out his old suitcase, where he kept the paper patterns for his tailoring. He was still rattled by Adam's scrounging around in this refuge he had created to hide his secrets. Inside this valise at the bottom of the closet, which he had stuffed behind the linings and leather samples and bolts of cloth, behind the small padded ironing board for ironing sleeves and belts, was the heavy yellow envelope holding a bulge of papers he had brought with him to Israel and then to this country. He patted the little mound, reassured. Hannah would never look here, he was sure. His secrets would always be safe. He opened the suitcase and selected the pattern he needed. The suitcase went back into the closet. Sliding the pattern onto his cutting table, he returned to his sewing stool and shook his head.

Maybe he should just take these old things and throw them away. This was not the first time he had thought this. They would be gone, no longer there to oppress him. He would be a free man. A man without a past.

No, he decided again, no. He had to keep them. He could not lose all those years of pain. He needed them for justification for leaving. Leaving over and over again, until now, at last, they were arriving. Leaving was done with. Canada had been good to him and his family. This was a peaceful country. They were not rich by any measure, but there was security here. He had even managed to save a few thousand dollars. He had suggested to Hannah that they might buy a duplex, something some of the other Jewish families were doing now. The rent would pay the mortgage. Hannah's response, as always, was fear.

"I don't like this idea of yours, Duvid. You will lose your money. The bank will take the house and everything you have worked for will be gone." It would take some more time to convince her. And more hard work, but he was used to that.

"Duvid, I need a few things from the bakery." Duvid looked up from his sewing machine, where he was just finishing off the last of the dress samples he had been working on that week. It was Sunday. The smells of roasting chicken and brisket mingled in the air.

"Hannah, can't you see that I am very busy?"

"Duvid, the Perelmans are coming for dinner."

Duvid sighed loudly enough for his wife to hear. "What is it that you need, Hannah?"

"Can you go to the delicatessen too? I need a few slices of stuffed chicken, and some spinach borsht."

Duvid protested. "But this you always make yourself."

"So I didn't have time to make it. I too can be busy. You go to the bakery for me on the way back. I need a rye bread. And a *challah*, not one left over from Friday, either, like last time. A dozen rolls for the dinner. And a few Danish for after, to eat with the tea."

"My arms are not strong enough for such a load." he responded half-jokingly.

"You can take the boys with you. Otherwise they will sit inside all day. No snacks. It will spoil their appetites. They are skinny enough already."

"So why should they be interested in coming with me if there is nothing for them."

"You can let them choose the pastries, but remember, they are only for after the dinner."

Duvid rose from his bench by the sewing machine and went to the parlour to collect his two teenagers. They were sprawled on the bare floor, reading comic books and staring out of one eye at the television set. Duvid shook his head in disapproval.

"Such laziness. Comics, television, always looking at such worthless stuff. And you, Adam, with your outer space nonsense, do you expect we will all be doing the waltz on the moon in a few years? It's all so ridiculous, this huge expense, money thrown away when there is so much need here on our planet. Why are you not out playing ball in the park? You need some fresh air, not rockets flying into the sky. Come, boys, your mother needs us to go to the bakery."

Simon protested. "Ah, Ta, why do we have to?"

"Don't argue. Come right away. I need your strong young arms."

The boys rose painfully and slowly, each push upwards against gravity an apparent groaning agony. They twisted in silence out of this domain of sloth because protest would be futile. Duvid watched as they fought their stockinged feet into their shoes, dumbfounded by their preference for inactivity.

The delicatessen was a few blocks away, on St. Lawrence. Once out on their street, they turned right, past the tall Lombardy poplars that stood like sentinels along Esplanade, filtering the morning sun. Their father marched them past the Jewish Public Library at the corner of Mount Royal Avenue. A streetcar screeched in front of them on its steel tracks, a shower of sparks bursting out at every juncture of the overhead wires that its pole touched. A flock of sparrows, startled, erupted from the mostly deserted street and flew in a wide circle, chittering in the air, before they landed in the same spot again after the trolley had passed.

The three now turned right, about to traverse St. Urban. A few Sunday drivers cautiously manoeuvred their cars through the intersection. Duvid marshalled his sons across the street. Outside the Arena Bakery, a flock of pigeons milled around for the crumbs thrown out onto the sidewalk every morning. Duvid led, with Adam a few steps behind, staring into the store windows, while Simon came last, after having taken a few exploratory kicks at the pigeons on the edge of the flock. The aroma from Moishe's Steakhouse down the street on the Main made Simon and Adam hungry. Duvid bought them each a piece of sausage at the delicatessen close to the Warshaw grocery store. Hannah admonished him inside his head. He ignored her. They were growing boys.

The twins jostled each other as they walked to the bakery on the way back. The irresistible aroma of bread baking filled the air. Once inside the door, they stood in line for their turn at the counter. Bracketing the bare wood floor where the customers elbowed each other for position, glass-fronted cases held Danish pastries, sugar cookies, coffee cakes, and apple strudels. Against the wall behind the cash, breads of different shades, rolls, and *challahs* were piled in large bins. The room was lit mainly by light from the outside. A few bare incandescent bulbs with a yellowed coating dangled on cords from the ceiling. A fine dusting of white flower seemed to cover all the surfaces and float in the air of the room. Hanging from the ceiling light fixtures were long spiral strips of light brown fly paper, clogged with their prey. Flies flew around anyway, coming in off the street whenever the door opened.

A wasp whirred past the boys' faces as they waited with their father. Adam and Simon cringed, but the few wasps in the bakery were more intent on crawling over the sticky sweet rolls in the counter display. Others banged their bodies compulsively against the plate glass windows, trying to return to their hives.

Duvid's turn came slowly. There were many others waiting to be served on a Sunday morning. The boys stood next to the open displays in the windows, watching the angry wasps try to pass out of the bakery through the glass. Duvid kept an eye on his sons, hoping they could stay out of trouble. To distract them, he asked them to choose from the danish pastries. When his turn finally came, he gave the saleslady at the cash his order and waited for her to slice the kimmel bread. While she was gathering the pastries from the display case, he glanced sideways at a tall man staring at the sweet rolls. There was something familiar about the man's rugged-looking face. His complexion was pale, the head topped with red hair. He seemed engrossed. A flash of some thought sparkled on the man's face, sat there fleetingly, and melted into a detached smile. The man seemed to be recalling a joke.

After a moment, Duvid's confusion was replaced by a surge of fear. The man was staring at Duvid's bare arm. The tattooed numerals were clearly visible.

"I know you. From where, though?" Duvid's voice was reedy.

"I don't know who you are. Maybe you hallucinate on such a hot day. I doubt that we have ever met."

Duvid's mind began to race. He shook his head, puzzled. The woman behind the counter was trying to get his attention. Behind her, Mrs. Belner, the owner's wife, was pulling a kimmel bread out of its stack and sliding it into the slicing machine, trying to keep up with the demands of the customers. There were others in line behind him. He turned to pay. An image flew through his mind: the man at the window, younger, wearing a grey German uniform. He recalled the smile of the officer, snakelike. Duvid glanced down at his sons, anxious to see that they were still there. Duvid struggled to form a few words. The barren look on his face must have been obvious. "You?" was all he managed. All the man gave back was a wavering smile. Mrs. Belner, ignoring the dispute, was waving her hands towards herself to urge her customers forward to the counter.

She almost bellowed. "Come along, come. Don't wait until tomorrow. Buy the bread while it is still fresh from this morning."

The saleswoman, a concerned look on her face, was placing several bags into Duvid's arms and urging him to move on. He took the bags automatically. The boys, who had been hovering at a distance, came closer. Their hands reached out to take the extra bags.

"So, you have two boys. Sweet little men. You must be very proud." The man held Simon's chin with one hand, stroking his forehead lightly with the other. Duvid's sons turned their faces towards their father, uncertain about what was going on.

"How dare you touch my children! You have found me again. Leave us in peace. You didn't do enough during the war?"

The boys looked at the man, then looked back at their father's face. His eyes bulging, he gripped his sons' shoulders, projecting them out towards the door.

"You are mistaken with your old memories. A man can become confused. Leave me alone."

"Your change, mister." The saleswoman was holding out a handful of coins. She looked annoyed, unsure about what she was witnessing.

Mrs. Belner interjected. "I don't know what your discussion is about, but can't you see that I have a line of customers here. They need bread just like you. Take your dispute outside. I don't want it in here."

Heart racing, Duvid turned to take the money. When he turned back the man was outside the front door of the bakery. Duvid rushed to follow, the other man far ahead of him by now.

"Boys, take these home. Tell your mother I will be there soon. Be careful crossing the street." Then he was rushing away. Simon stared after his father's shrinking figure, Adam at the wasps in the window. The insects were gorging themselves myopically on their last meal.

"Duvid, where were you?" Hannah was shaking. "I have been so afraid since the boys came back without you. It's been two hours already. Rivka and Leib just arrived a few minutes ago." Hannah had been about to load a large metal platter with rolls from a large paper bag that stood on the table. It dangled from her hands now as she gaped at Duvid.

"I saw a man from the war, Hannah. A German officer. The one who sent me to the death camp before the war's end."

The platter clattered loudly on the floor, scattering Vienna rolls across the dining room rug. Rivka bent reflexively to pick it all up.

"I followed him home, Hannah. He walked fast, like he had the legs of the devil. He doesn't live far from here, on Marianne. It is unimaginable, such a thing, that he should follow me here to this country, to this city."

Leibel Perelman reached for the bottle of schnapps and poured two glasses, his hands shaking. He had barely survived the Majdanek death camp.

"Here. This you should drink. Make a *lechaim*, Duvid."

Duvid ignored him and continued speaking.

"I went to the police station to report him. I know now where he lives, after all. I walked into the station and went up to the desk. The policeman at the front desk asked why I was there."

I told him: "I live not far from here. I saw someone."

"Someone?" he asked.

"Yes."

"Doing what?"

"Doing nothing. The crime didn't happen here."

"It's no crime to be someone. We don't investigate crimes from another country. You're an immigrant, aren't you?"

"So you see I have an accent. Yes, I came to Canada a few years ago."

"There are a lot of you in this district. Look, what crime are you reporting?"

"Murder."

"Murder? Really? In what country?"

"Poland."

"You'll have to report that to your consulate."

"My consulate? I'm a Canadian citizen now."

"Wait here a minute. I have to speak to someone else."

"The policeman turned and walked over to someone at another desk. They both looked up at me and one of them must have made a joke, because I could see the two of them laughing together. The desk officer came back and told me I'd have to wait to speak to a Sergeant Michaud."

"Where?" I asked.

"Down that hallway. Wait outside room 24."

"Will it be long?"

"It's Sunday morning. Do you have to go to confession?"

"My wife is waiting for me."

"Lots of wives are waiting for their husbands. Priests too."

So I waited outside Room 24 for over an hour before Sergeant Michaud came out.

"What did he do, this murderer you're reporting?"

"He was a German officer during the war. Sub-commander in a death camp."

"In Poland?"

"Yes."

"During that war, you said?"

"Yes."

"Did he do anything to you here in Canada?"

"I don't know. No. What I know about is what I already told you."

"Listen, Mr. Gry..., geez, that's a hard name to pronounce."

"Yes, the other officer already told me that."

"I'm just trying to be clear about your facts. As far as I can see, this man did nothing that we are able to charge him with. It was no crime in Canada. And wartime is wartime. It's your word against his, anyway. He can't be charged. That's the law."

"You won't do anything? A murderer can walk the streets a free man? This is justice?"

"The police don't dispense justice; we follow the law. Mr. G., forget about this guy. Don't ask for trouble, just go home. And don't try to do anything yourself. You'll be the one breaking the law."

"This is Canadian justice? It's a joke. It's a terrible outrage!"

"I'll escort you to the door."

"I'm not stupid. I can find the way myself. That's what I told him."

Leib held out a glass of schnapps for Duvid. Duvid glared, then downed the glass. "No crime here in Canada. No crime in Canada! Can you believe it?"

His face was ashen. Leibel tipped his own glass, swallowing hard, and dropped heavily onto the chesterfield.

Hannah's eyes opened to the darkness of the bedroom. A dream, an old dream, had come to her during the night. Its power had shaken her awake, but now, staring into blackness, she remembered nothing, only a feeling of dread. Next to her she expected to hear her husband's soft snoring, but there was silence. She turned, alarmed. Duvid's side of the bed was empty. She felt deserted.

Hannah rose and groped her way down the hall to the kitchen. Duvid sat at the kitchen table, gripping the bottle of schnapps. Hannah approached, glaring. Duvid was not normally a drinker.

"Hannah, I must have woken you. I am sorry."

"Duvid, drinking like this–it is not like you." Hannah cradled his face in her hands. "My poor sad husband, you should be sleeping. You will have to get up to work soon."

"I could not sleep. I keep seeing the face of that lizard. It is not right. They did such evil things to us, and now, to walk free, here, on the next street? It is not right."

"Duvid, you must put it away from your head. It must be gone. Over."

"Hannah, I lost my family to these monsters, every one of them. There were no survivors besides me. And you too, you lost. And the Frankels. And the Axts. So many others. This I can leave? For this I fought so hard for our people, for Israel? And now to have this man smiling at me with his reptile grin when he sees me in the street. Or imagining doing terrible things to our sons? And he believes I cannot touch him. This is something I can let go, you think? And he cannot be the only one. There must be others like him who have brought their poison with them."

"Duvid, what do you think? What else can you do? You already tried the police. There is nothing else. Let it go. No matter what you imagine doing, it can only bring us trouble."

"Hannah, I do not want to bring us trouble, but I must let this pass through me. Please leave me here and go back to bed. Don't worry for me, I will be there soon."

Hannah, hesitating, turned for the bedroom, then turned back. "Maybe you are mistaken, Duvid. Maybe it is not him." Her face pleaded with him to change back into someone else, someone he had been not long ago.

"Maybe."

Hannah smiled slightly and patted the side of his head. His admission allowed her to return to bed.

Duvid watched in the dark as Hannah's form padded back to bed. He was quite certain of the man's identity. How could he ever forget? He rose and walked into his workroom, past the industrial sewing machine. He bent and reached into the pouch at the back of the closet. Yes, they were still there. They had been there only this morning, it was true, but now he just had to touch them again, to make sure they were where he had left them, know that if he needed to have them, that this testament to evil still existed. These few scraps of cloth on which he had scratched out his memories, and the documents he had managed to take with him from the concentration camp lay there on his lap. He had found them in those last days, when he had some moments of free movement in the commandant's office. They felt warm to the touch, as if they could resurrect something in the past. Duvid shut his eyes tightly and resealed the bag.

As much as possible, he had to keep these from Hannah. He knew she suspected something. This was too dangerous for her. Hannah had her own demons. She too often tossed wildly in her sleep, transported to evil times in her dreams. Her past would never go away either. Duvid returned to the kitchen and swallowed the rest of the glass of liquor. It burnt his throat pleasantly. After what seemed a long time had passed, Duvid rose shakily from his chair and followed after his wife's trail. When he pulled himself under the covers and against her body, she was asleep. She started momentarily as he passed his hand around her waist, then settled back to breathing softly. Duvid's eyes stayed open until dawn. By morning he felt like a broken man.

Duvid heard Hannah let a long sigh slip out of her as she lit the shabbos candles on the sideboard. The difficult week was at an end. Duvid had only had fitful sleep, but he felt himself gradually returning to normal. Yet at supper he ate in silence, picking at his food, not questioning the twins about the week's schoolwork as he usually did. Afterwards, while Hannah washed the dishes, Duvid sat at the kitchen table, reading his newspaper, while the boys escaped to the parlour to watch television.

Duvid eyed the newspaper, scanning the pages. The words he read echoed in his head, but he was oblivious to them. The page was hypnotic. After a few minutes, he slowly eased his head down towards the tabletop. The week's insomnia had had its effects. He stirred momentarily when Hannah, turning from the sink, touched him lightly on the head before going off to shoo the boys to bed. He drifted back into deep sleep.

Duvid woke to the sound of sputtering. His neck was sore. The Sabbath candles were burning low, their glow almost gone. He rose and stared into the shallow pools of molten wax feeding the dying wicks. One burning wick hissed. Its flame guttered and went out. A troubled puff of smoke rose, dissipating in the low light. Then the second candle went out. The smoke of its dying went untraced in the darkness. Duvid felt defeated. He turned towards the bedroom.

A few weeks passed uneventfully. Life was settling back to normal. Hannah no longer awoke at night. Duvid slept and his energy seemed to come back. He returned to his avid questioning of the boys about their studies while they ate. They chattered together about what they had seen on the news about the latest exploits in the space race between the Russians and America.

"Imagine, he said, how far the world has come from when I was young and lived without even an electric light."

The boys blinked uncomprehendingly. Duvid's appetite improved. Hannah was relieved.

The front doorbell rang in the late afternoon while Hannah was washing the pots she had just used to cook supper. She wondered who it could be. She was alone and afraid. The boys were working on a school project at a friend's home a few blocks away on St. Joseph. They would not be back for another hour. Neither would Duvid, who had gone by bus to pick up some bolts of cloth.

The bell again rang insistently as Hannah wiped her hands on a dish towel and walked the long hallway to the front door. She peered out through the glass in the door and saw Duvid standing there with a policeman on either side of him. Her heart sank. She quickly unlocked the door.

"Mme. Grynsztyn?"

"Yes?"

"Your husband here was taken into custody a little while ago. No charges laid yet, so we're just making sure that he comes straight home and doesn't cause any more trouble."

Hannah assured the policemen that he would keep the peace. She thanked them copiously, wanting only that they go away, and pulled Duvid in. Leaning hard against it, she shut the door.

"Duvid, what did you do?"

"I did nothing, Hannah."

"Nothing? The police, not one but two, bring you home from doing nothing?"

"I went to his house, Hannah. I could not stand it anymore."

"You mean the German?"

"Yes." Duvid closed his eyes. He didn't explain himself, but turned and walked to the kitchen, sat down and poured himself a drink. Hannah followed.

"This is a bad thing, this drinking, Duvid. It has to stop."

Duvid downed the drink, then stood up and went to the sink.

"Yes, Hannah, I know. I am sorry." He upended the half-empty bottle and its contents flowed down the drain. Hannah grimaced at the reek of alcohol.

"What were you doing at the German's house, Duvid?"

"I went there to talk to him, to tell him that I had evidence against him. I wanted him to go away, but he started to tell me that he had friends and if he wanted, they could do things to us. To you and our boys, Hannah."

"So you called the police?"

"No, I started to scream at him. He shut his door. I banged on it."

"For this came the police? You did more than bang on the door, Duvid."

"Yes, I did more. I broke the door off its hinges. That was when he called the police."

"Oy."

"He had a little boy with him too. His son, I suppose. The boy was crying."

"Oy."

"The police arrested me while he smiled. They brought me to the police station, but after, they let me go. He didn't want to sign a complaint against me. He was afraid I would tell the world about him and his bunch of bloodsuckers, I am sure of that. He didn't want his name on a document. But he will not push me around. Never!"

"Duvid, please. What evidence?"

"I lied to him, Hannah, to scare him. I have no evidence. No documents. Only what is burned into my mind. I swear to you."

"Promise me that you will not go back there again. Promise me. No more. I am afraid for our sons. And he has a child also. The war is over. It is over, Duvid."

Duvid nodded, in some sort of agreement. He glanced back at the bottle he had just emptied.

Hannah went to the door to greet her sons after their day at school. They marched in, each holding a chocolate bar in his hand. The man with them stood in the doorway, blocking the light, his angular face accentuated by shadows. Holding his hand was a small boy. His son, it seemed. He was much younger than Hannah's boys.

"Ah, the wife." he said, "Please tell your good husband something for me. I saw him standing on the street outside my apartment yesterday. Maybe he will listen to you better than to me." The man gave her a wide firm smile.

"After all, I know where you live. Tell him that. And no more police, please. I do not want to call them again. Do this and I will not return. I have a son also, a family, like you. Leave me in peace and I will do the same for you. And just one more thing. He must return my documents. Tell him this also."

The man's son looked frightened. He tugged at his father's arm.

"Papa. Can we go home, please?" Looking down at his boy, the man seemed to hesitate. Hannah pushed the door closed.

"Go away or I will scream. It is I who will call the police," Hannah yelled through the door. When Duvid came home from work later, he found her in the kitchen, tears staining her face as she cooked. She gave him the message. He listened quietly, giving no hint of emotion, then went off to see that the boys were busy with their homework.

Later, after supper, Duvid remarked to Hannah: "We have to move away."

"Move?"

"We'll find a house in another part of town. Disappear from this man. Maybe Cote des Neiges or N.D.G. Others are starting to move out also. We have already talked about buying a house, a double duplex. You have to agree now. We can buy with my cousin Abram together, one side for each."

"He will still find us. He has only to look in the telephone book."

"I will change our family name, maybe. Like that, it will also be easier for the *goyim* to say it. Everyone is doing it now."

"Duvid, you trouble me."

13 Moving

Adam won a prize for writing a short story in his English class. All the children in the school had written stories for Arbour Day. One in each class had been selected a winner. Adam's story was about a tree that ate people in the night. The prize was a tiny tree. It was a black ash only a few inches tall, just a sprout. Simon complained to his parents that it was really his story, but Adam held the prize in his fingers. It was his, then. If it was Simon's, he would have written it, no? Simon could only sulk.

Adam decided to plant the tree in the earth next to the courtyard cement, past the tubular cast-iron fence. Duvid dug the hole and showed him how to tamp the earth down. "Adam, in Israel where you were born, we once had a farm with trees. I grew oranges, and lemons too. Do you remember?"

Adam looked on, confused. He had only a very faded memory of a farm. It made him wonder what else he didn't remember. The next morning, Adam had another fever and Hannah had to keep him at home for a few days. That's why he didn't find out that his teacher had announced to the class that the winners would be planting their trees at the school.

When Adam returned to school a few days later, he found that the other winners had already planted their trees at a special ceremony. They were placed in a straight line in the schoolyard, also near the fence, where the asphalt edged into earth. One of his classmates called him a loner, and then everyone was saying the word. Adam just looked on, repentant about his choice of site for his own tree.

At supper his father told him that to be a loner was not such a bad thing. He was independent, his own man. Adam felt better.

Duvid had stayed out of trouble, as he had promised. The other man had been true to his word too, and not returned. For Simon and Adam, the chronology of events was by now becoming a blur. The old neighbourhood would soon be left behind. They would be in a new school, with new classmates. Things were happening too quickly.

By this time, Duvid and Hannah had decided to move. They didn't tell the boys why, only that they had bought a house far away. One Sunday afternoon, Duvid had, with a lift from his cousin Shimshe, taken the family with him to show them their new home.

Each of the boys would have his own bedroom. There was a small garden in the back of the house, and a patch of grass and bushes in the front. There was even a garage in the back for the car that Duvid said he planned to buy soon. He had hoped that his sons would be impressed, but one look told him that his two boys were not happy about the changes to come.

The boys had lived in their courtyard apartment house on Esplanade since before the time that they had started school. Simon was now in grade ten. The flat held memories of familiar sounds and smells, of mice running and scratching inside the bulging walls, whose plaster key-holds between the wooden laths had given way long ago, of silverfish on the floor of the bathroom, of the odours of cooking cabbage and boiling chicken passing everywhere.

The neighbours were packed tightly together. The sounds of their laughter, their gossip, and their arguments had carried in amplified echoes up and down the skylight wells that connected the small vent windows of the stacked bathrooms, and across the short distances between balconies during heated summer nights.

Simon worried about losing friends. He wondered how things would be different in the new neighbourhood. What was happening to his family was not isolated, though. Several of his friends had gone away in the last two years. Others would be leaving soon. Simon's parents had told him and his brother that they would have a better life in the new neighbourhood.

Simon crossed the street to the park and looked back. He suddenly knew the definition of the place where he had lived so long. It was clear to him that it was a slum. The apartment building on Esplanade Street was below some standard that he had now set for himself. If his family were to continue to live here, he knew they would ever remain poor, uncultured, and undereducated. He had no knowledge of where he had picked up these ideas. He stared across the street from the vantage of the park, and the word had formed in his mind again: slum. It seemed such an ugly word, full of slime, decay, and crumbling failure. He had heard his parents use it about their *goyishe* neighbours who lived on other blocks in the neighbourhood. Places they would never live in, they claimed, they were so dirty and decrepit, even though, when Simon had sometimes visited these schoolmates, their flats were no different than his own, with the same mice, the same silverfish, the same noises and the same smells. He also knew that he could never use the word slum about his family apartment without hurting his parents terribly.

This insight still didn't make it any easier on moving day when it was time to walk away from the empty apartment, its walls hollowly echoing every step. The cracks in the plaster, produced by the years of use and neglect, showed through the paint. The hard wooden floors creaked as he crept out into the light. The balls of dust in the corners, behind where the larger pieces of furniture had rested, fluttered lightly back and forth as he passed, as if waving goodbye to him.

Suddenly he was outside, cut off from what was no longer his home, feeling once again some sense of the refugee-immigrants he and his parents had been when they had first arrived in this country. He looked back once more. He promised himself that he would come back one day to see who was living here. Some child would be living in this slum, not caring that Simon had been here before him. That child would visit old Mr. and Mrs. Tabackman's shop on Mount Royal Avenue, to buy Tootsie Rolls for five cents and chocolate milkshakes for a quarter. The streetcar rails that snaked up the mountain would still lead to adventure. Simon shook the brooding nostalgia away, a tired dog shaking water from its coat. The raw emotion made him shudder.

He walked past the spot where Adam had planted the tree just a few weeks earlier. It looked lonely without its brothers, fragile and exposed. He bent next to it, and with his fingers dug it out of the ground. Simon tenderly wrapped a few leaves off a nearby poplar tree around the soil and the roots of the baby tree, then ran to join his parents and Adam, who waited at the curb for him.

"My tree! You're stealing it!"

"I'm saving it," Simon insisted. "It's really mine," he added.

Duvid tried to take the tree from Simon's hands and return it to its hole. "It will die if you bring it," he advised Simon, but Simon struggled and Duvid finally gave up. He shrugged at Adam, who stood next to the car, glaring.

Adam stared at the tree in Simon's hands and at his father, and punched his grinning brother in the stomach. Hannah pulled the boys apart and hustled them, bickering loudly, into Shimshe's car.

"Hey, don't drop dirt in my nice new Pontiac, boys. And stay quiet. I don't need to have an accident." The arguing continued. The brothers only shushed when Shimshe, finally fed up, yelled at them to shut up.

The moving truck that had been parked on the street in front creaked through the agonized sounds of shifting gears and lurched off heavily. Shimshe started the engine of his car, ready to drive the family to their new home in what was still a suburb. The boys stared through the rear window as their home dwindled and soon disappeared, as the car climbed its way onto the mountain road, which would take them towards the western end of the city.

Notre Dame de Grace. NDG. EnDeeGee. The name sounded so foreign to Simon now. Over the next few short years it would become familiar to him, its name slide off his tongue easily whenever he spoke of it. It would eventually become home. As time nourished it, the city would grow and sweep past and beyond, into the quiet territories of hummingbirds and chipmunks, of cows and corn.

14 Entry

The day sparkled, the sky a deep sapphire, parallel cirrus cloudlets decorating its stratospheric limits. The trees that stood across the street from Simon's school rippled with new leaves basking in the brightness flooding down, and silently churned oxygen into the hungry air. Oblivious to the chemistry going on just above his head, Simon breathed in the generated gases and gave back lungsful of carbon dioxide for the trees to work on. The earth that fed the trees grumbled as it was processed through the long slow bellies of pink earthworms digging through its loamy thickness. Hidden under sails of grass flattered by the passing wind, ranks of worker ants followed the potent signal trails of their fellows.

Simon usually waited next to the chain link fence surrounding the asphalted yard of Monklands High School. Melvin was the only friend he had made since the Gryns, their family name newly truncated, had moved into the neighbourhood. The two habitually met after school and plodded home along Terrebonne. The street pulsed with traffic at this time of day.

Today, Melvin was serving an after-school detention for arriving late, so Simon walked home alone. The knot of students at the corner jostled to get onto the city bus. They studiously ignored Simon. He clutched at his briefcase, afraid that one of them would try to snatch it again, like last time, when they had thrown it out of the bus window a block further down the road. Nothing happened this time. Simon crossed the street and walked past the small brick and stone duplexes, with their sloping driveways and never-used balconies, lining the grandly named Cavendish Boulevard. At the next corner, Simon dropped by the Woolworth's lunch counter for a chocolate milkshake and bought himself a small bag of chips. This was freedom time. No one checked on Simon now.

Adam was on the volleyball team and practiced after school two days a week. Two other afternoons, he was getting help with his science fair project from Mrs. Stacy, the chemistry teacher. The year previous, Adam had won second prize, causing his mother to brag about her acclaimed son to her friends for a few days, and his father to grudgingly congratulate him, before asking who had gotten first prize.

Simon walked directly home now. In his right hand he carried his father's old leather briefcase, near to bursting with textbooks and notebooks. Frayed at the corners, badly scuffed from that trip aboard the bus, its patinated brass fittings scraped, it was still a source of both pride and grief for Simon, who often imagined himself a young spy carrying important papers for a special mission, yet winced when other students remarked on its dinginess.

Simon would have time to himself once he got home. His mother had started work recently for a furrier and worked overtime quite a lot. It was the high season and the boss needed to fill the orders. His father wouldn't arrive home from his clothing factory job until five, almost an hour from now. For now, Simon was on his own, master of the house, lord of his solitude. This was his time to laze, time also to imagine himself an adventurer, a hero, a government agent abroad. All too soon his brother would arrive and compulsively down a large bag of potato chips while chattering about the school team, using pillows to simulate the volleyballs.

Walking to the front door, Simon stopped when he noticed that the tree he had rescued at the time of the move had been trampled flat. Its short trunk, a mere sliver, was cracked, its leaves mashed and shredded.

Simon got down on his knees and lifted his tree back into an upright position. When he let go, it fell back, limp and scrawny. How could someone just do this? His tree, even if Adam claimed it too. Outraged, he looked up and down the street. No one. Who would walk through his front lawn? The mailman?

Nobody but Simon really cared, either. His mother would later only give him a quick smile, he was sure. His father would ignore him and go to his workroom in the basement. His brother, well, he had been jealous. He hadn't wanted him to have the tree in the first place. He would probably laugh when he found out. Simon seethed in his impotence.

Simon, distressed now, let himself in with his own key. The key under the front doormat was only for emergencies. He didn't lift the mat to see if it was still there. There was no question about that. It always was. Looking might alert a thief, his mother had said. So he didn't look.

He headed to the kitchen at the back of the house for a glass of chocolate milk. On the table his mother had left a freshly baked cake and a knife. Chocolate, his favourite. He was thirsty, as usual, especially after the bag of chips he had finished on his way home, but he ignored the cake for now. The milk was filling enough. He finally settled in the parlour in front of the television set to do his homework. He had to have it done before his father arrived, when the usual questioning would begin at supper.

The Rocky and Bullwinkle Show was on. Simon's eyes glazed and he forgot about his assignments for the moment. Boris Batanov had just been tracked down to his lair below the streets of the city, where he and Natasha had hidden a stolen super energy beam. When the commercial break finally came, Simon rushed to the kitchen to refill his empty glass. The show would be over soon. He didn't want to miss *The Man from U.N.C.L.E.* episode that would be starting soon. His mother's cake looked appealing, now that he was hungry again, and Simon lifted the knife. As he was about to slice into the cake, he heard heavy stomping footsteps on the stairs from the basement that lay off the hallway between the kitchen and the front door. His arm stopped moving in mid-air and he stared at the knife hovering in front of him. He listened closely. The sound couldn't have come from the Keitelmans, who rented the top level of the duplex. Wrong direction. The sound came again, this time the fall of footsteps on the creaky wooden floors in the hallway behind him. There really was someone else in the house. His mother? No. His father? Also no. They would never miss work to come home early.

Simon froze. The tip of the knife was shaking in front of him. The footsteps continued. He couldn't tell if they were getting closer or moving away. The creaking became suddenly louder–someone was charging down the hallway in the direction of the front door. The sounds Simon heard next were, first, the front door thud against the wall as Adam exuberantly threw it open and then slammed it shut, second, Adam's voice yell loudly that Simon was going to pay for breaking his tree, and third, a noisy collision near the front door, and Adam's scream mixing with a man's loud grunting. Instinctively, Simon turned and made for the cacophony as fast as he could. Some tribal drive gelled his scattering thoughts into one: he had to help his brother.

Simon tore down the hallway. He saw hands on Adam's shoulders. His own heart drummed inside his ears as he threw himself forward, driving his frame into the mix of bodies, and the knife fell away. The three collapsed to the floor, flailing. Simon dragged himself out of the heap and grabbed the knife. The man twisted back and forth on his belly like a fish flopping out of water, his face wedged into the corner by Adam's weight. Adam, grabbing both of the man's upper arms just above the elbows from behind, wriggled his body down flat against the floor. Adam forced his arms under the other's, and finally slipped into a full nelson hold.

The man was breathing hard, his chest quivering with effort. His legs moved erratically. Simon pressed his weight onto the man's legs and in a moment of clarity, realized that he could press the point of the knife against the small of the invader's back, as he had seen so many times on so many television shows. The man stopped moving almost immediately. His body seized up, his arms and legs stiff, and slowly, his muscles relaxed and he began to groan and complain. His accent was not local, but somewhat like that of the boys' father.

"Let me go or I will complain to the police. Look, boys, I am here by mistake. I thought this was my cousin's house. If you let me up, I will show you where he lives."

The boys looked at each other, suddenly confused, trying to decide what their next move should be.

"Could he be telling the truth, Simon?"

"This is no mistake. He's a liar. He was here when I came home. Why didn't he say something then? He could have just walked out. And how did he get in?"

"With our key?"

"Yes, yes, boys, I found it under the mat, where my friend said it would be. Everyone puts a key under the mat. And all the houses on this street look the same, you know."

"Maybe it's true what he says, Simon."

"Don't believe him. Don't believe him!"

Their father should be home soon, but what would they do with this man until then, he worried? Were they strong enough to hold him?

"What do you want? Why are you in our house?"

Adam continued with his own question. "What's your cousin's name and address?"

"Let my arm go and I'll show you. It's written on a piece of paper in my jacket pocket."

"Don't let go, Adam."

"Come on, boys. There's no harm done."

The two brothers were beginning to hesitate. "I'll reach into his pocket, Adam. You hang on to him."

"Hurry up. I'm getting tired."

Simon reached into the pocket and extracted his wallet. There was a paper, all right. The address on it was their own. What he also found in the pocket was the extra front door key.

"This is our address, not his cousin's. And look, our key."

"Crook! Why did you keep the key in your pocket? Were you planning to use it again?"

Simon yelled. "Maybe his wallet has a paper with his name on it
."

Adam held on tightly. Simon sat upright on the man's legs now, digging the tip of the knife into the man's back without cutting through his shirt, just deep enough to stimulate the imagination. With the other hand, Simon was checking through the wallet for anything that might identify the trespasser. At this point the front door opened quickly and thunked decisively against the man's head. His eyes closed and his forehead dropped hard against the ceramic floor tiles of the entranceway. Simon stared up into his father's surprised and weary eyes.

"What's going on here? Who is this?" Duvid queried his sons, "I come home to find my sons fighting a man next to the front door."

Adam looked back at his father, mystified. He had no idea. All he knew was that from the second he had marched in the front door, he had been in this inexplicable tug of war, all his efforts disrupted by his brother's clumsy and interfering scurrying.

Simon gave his opinion. "He's a crook, Ta."

"Simon, how did this crook of yours get in here?"

"He had the key to our door. It was in his pocket." He held the key up as proof. "He was here when I got home."

"Did he take the key from in front?"

"Yes."

"Now he's as senseless as a wooden bench."

"Maybe we should call the police?"

"Let's turn him over and see if he's still breathing. Adam, let go. It's okay, he's still unconscious."

Duvid tugged the man onto his back and recognized him immediately. The German.

"Do you know this man, boys?"

The brothers looked into each other's faces, neither wanting to admit stupidity, searching for memory in the reflected light of the other's eyes. Those eyes remained blank.

"This is a bad man. I'm going to bring him to the police station, but we'll have to tie him up first." Suddenly overcome, Duvid slid down against the wall until he was seated on the floor. His eyes closed.

"Why don't we just call the police and have them come here and arrest him?"

Duvid opened his eyes and stared at Simon with a grave look on his face. "Do you remember when Mrs. Kostelios next door had the thief in her house one morning and she called the police? How long before they came?"

"It was late in the afternoon. You see. I must make it easy for them. For immigrants like us, they come slowly. We are not like the rich men of Westmount, the English, who can give them more than their salaries. I will better take this bad man to them when he wakes up and is able to stand. Now go get me something to tie him with. Let me think. We need cloth, strong cloth. Bring me the canvas in the big box in my workroom. And my scissors. Quickly, before he wakes up."

Simon came charging back with the material and a length of leather.

"Ah, this leather is useful. Smart boy." Simon backed away, looking both proud and curious. What was his father going to do?

Duvid cut and tore the canvas into long narrow strips and tied the wrists in front. He set the arms tightly against the man's sides by wrapping a long section of leather around the man's arms and chest. Finally, he tied a short length of cloth tightly over his mouth.

"Boys, I know you cannot understand what this is about, but one thing is very important. You must not tell your mother this happened. It will only frighten her. You know how she is. Every little thing makes her jump. And don't tell anyone else, ever. They will be only too happy to ask your mother about it, and then where will we be? So stay silent."

Duvid had no reason to doubt that the boys would follow his instructions. They always were careful when their parents warned them in this way. This would be no different, especially that they would not want to upset their mother.

"Keep him here while I drive the car around into the garage in back." Duvid scooped up the intruder's wallet. "The police will want this."

One minute later, Duvid walked in through the back door. "Okay, boys, remember, not a word to your mother. I may be a long time talking to the police, so I won't be back soon. Just tell your mother that you saw me, but I had to go back to work. A sudden rush order came that I have to go pick up and I expect there will be a lot of traffic. Now go do your homework."

Duvid pulled the just-conscious man to his feet and forced him down the back steps into the garage that stood just behind the kitchen. The boys stared at him as he tripped and trundled past them, curious at the man's frantic expression. They stood there staring at each other. After a few minutes of silence, they returned to their books in front of the television set.

Duvid had taken the knife from Simon. He would need it when he got the man to his destination. Once Duvid got him into the garage, he popped open the trunk and tipped the man into it, to a stream of angry, mumbled protests. The gag covering the man's mouth darkened with saliva. Duvid pulled it away from the man's mouth.

"How did you find me? Why did you come here?"

"So, the Jew answers back now. You found me. I would have been happy now if I hadn't gone to buy bread that day. So now my wife has left me, thanks to you. She won't even allow me to see my son. You wouldn't stop. Every few days I saw you watching. You smart Jew, with your new car and your new licence plates. I saw you. I saw your car. Finding someone is never difficult. You made it so easy. I also noticed that you changed your name. I must have really frightened you."

"I have my family to look out for."

"You also have my documents."

"I am happy that at least one person, this wife of yours, has some sense in this world. It appears I succeeded in frightening you, too. I also made a fool of you. I have no documents. I said it to scare you away. Instead you came here. So I am as big a fool as you are." Duvid replaced the gag. He had heard enough. He slammed down the trunk hatch and got into the driver's seat.

It was a full hour's ride in the new Pontiac up to Val Morin, in the cottage country in the Laurentians to the north of Montreal. Duvid knew the area well. He had bought the car, his first, only six months earlier, despite Hannah's protests that the money could be put to better uses. Now its utility would prove itself. Duvid turned off the main highway and took a narrow road into the woods. There were no cottages here, just a route through to the next small town.

After twenty minutes, Duvid took the bend and switched onto an almost invisible lumber track into the deeper woods. There was a sign offering lots for sale with a Montreal telephone number, but the area was as yet far from developed.

Finally, Duvid stopped the car and got out, pulled the man from the trunk and leaned him against the car. Mosquitos and black flies buzzed around his ears. He had the urge to leave quickly. He held the knife in one hand.

"I will finish you here." The man was visibly shaking now, his steps away from the car broken and slow. Duvid pushed him forward down a gentle slope towards a few large trees. This would be a good place for it. He pressed the man heavily against a tree trunk and raised the knife. The man's eyes displayed his terror.

Duvid squeezed the haft of the knife and slashed it down next to the man's head. It embedded itself heavily into the trunk of the tree. Duvid's elbow hurt from the force of the impact.

"That's what I'd like to do, but I'm not an animal like you are. You come into my house and frighten my sons. This is unforgivable. You and I have only one thing in common. We are both fathers, and for that reason alone I cannot kill you. Maybe I am a kinder man than you, or maybe just stupid. I will leave this knife here. You can use it to free yourself. But never come near us again, or the next time, I will not remember that I am more civilized than you. The documents you want don't exist. You have no more reason to bother us." Duvid turned and walked off. Without any hesitation he got into his car and drove away, not even looking back at the man.

The German struggled to his feet and turned towards the tree. His wrists were tied tightly. Reaching up as much as he was able to, despite the leather strap holding his upper arms against his sides, he just managed to take hold of the knife between both hands and leaned back, working it up and down. His weight loosened it slightly, but it held in the wood. He lost his balance and fell, knocking his head against a rock in the process. If his mouth hadn't been covered firmly with cloth, he would have screamed. A trickle of warm blood gushed out of a wound on his forehead and down between his right eye and his nose. The bleeding alarmed him, but it didn't last very long before subsiding. Again he got to his feet. He tried once more. This time the knife came away more easily. He inserted it, point upwards, between his chest and the material binding him, and began to saw up and down. His neck was itching madly from the black flies eagerly feeding on his blood. He tried to ignore them.

The knife was sharp, but the leather was tough. It separated slowly. A loud crack sound echoed through the woods. The man recognized it as the report of a rifle. A hunter. The man lifted his head and saw a figure in an opening between the leaves, a man holding a rifle at the crest of a hill some hundred yards away. The hunter disappeared silently.

Help had arrived! The German man loped forward up the slope.

Duvid stopped along the road at a country store and bought a pack of cigarettes. It had been years since he had smoked, but now he desperately wanted one. He drove to where an old wooden bridge traversed what was now, this especially dry summer, a stream, from which he had plucked his sons years before. He got out and looked through the man's wallet. He slowly tore the cards he found. Bits of paper fell like confetti into the water that burbled below him. The wallet had been stuffed thick with paper money. This he kept.

"Why not? Look how much he took from me!"

Duvid hefted the empty wallet in among the trees.

He put a cigarette between his lips and lit the tip. He had smoked half the pack before he crumpled it up and threw it too into the water. He had had enough. Duvid climbed back into his car and headed home.

He had better change where he kept the extra front door key from now on. He fervently hoped that the man would not return to haunt their lives. Maybe he had frightened the man enough that he would stay away forever. But still, he felt very unsettled. He wished that his two curious sons could one day forget what had happened today, but he knew they wouldn't, but at least they would never tell Hannah. On that he trusted them completely. She must never have to see that man at their door again. He now had a good reason to hang on to his pathetic scraps of cloth and bits of paper, in case he needed them if that dreadful man ever did come back.

Duvid shuddered at the idea. He could only hope for the best. Maybe it would have been better if he had killed the man, but inside himself he felt the truth. His days as a killer were over. He had neither head nor heart nor stomach for it any more.

The bound man struggled forward through the deep green of the Laurentian forest, spittle soaking his gag as he tried to yell out for attention, one eye blinded by the blood that had caked over the lid. The knife was still in his hands, still pointing upwards, positioned under the leather restraint.

The German could see the hunter closer now through the trees. Maybe he could attract his attention. He would be saved. Gratitude filled his heart; he had never been so happy to be alive. Then the sharp incomprehensible pain in his right side.

A tree root knotted up above the forest floor. He tripped and fell forward, thudding into an upended tree trunk that had fallen recently. As he rolled under it, the handle of the knife struck the wood and travelled through his skin and into his chest. He started to gasp as one lung collapsed.

The muscles of his legs convulsed a few times before stopping. There he lay, under the tree trunk, hidden from sight, his chest filling with blood, asphyxiating. His fading mind, wondering suddenly at what was happening to him, veered through the facts of who he was and how he might be discovered. The hunter hadn't seen him. His wallet was gone. He had had no work, just a secret monthly pension arriving from somewhere in South America. It would continue to arrive in his mail slot for a few months, then stop after the man who rented him a room returned them to the post office. No, that man would continue to cash them. Who would ever check the signature?

His wife, after she had thrown him out, could have no idea where he had gone, nor would she care. She never wanted to see him again. Now she would have her wish. His young son would even forget that he had ever had a father. The man was an unknown, disconnected from all that there was or had ever been. He might as well be one of the vast numbers of unidentified skeletal remains that still littered the great funereal fields of Europe.

15 Eli's Journal

We stand for the brotherhood of the children of former enemies. For unity in the universal logic of Marx and Engels. These ideas our teachers drum into our empty heads. Blah, blah, blah, be-blah. I am left skeptical, and I am not the only one, but we have all memorized our lessons well. We adjust our smiles and we hide our thoughts. It is all so dreary. How can anyone possibly believe this is the answer to mankind's needs?

Last month, for the cause of International Socialism, I travelled to The Democratic Republic of Germany as the representative of my technical school. I don't say I am a Jew to anyone. My mother has taught me well.

I had never been to Germany before, but I hate the Germans and I know very well that they hate me. As a Pole, as a Jew, as an outsider. Even so, I make a few contacts. Maybe these people will be useful, despite the venom between us.

I am nineteen today, on the verge of graduation. I must get out of this place.

I have been assigned to work in an East German chemical plant. Who can understand why? I only know that I must go. I can only hope that it will be better than the orphanage. I tell myself: how can it be worse?

I stay at a workers' hostel, where I share a room with another young man, Anton. We work together at the same factory, the only one in the town, and we often go out drinking together after we have our pay, with others from the plant. There is not much else to spend our money on.

His friends derive from many parts of the German Democratic Republic. For some reason Anton seems to prefer my company to theirs. He tells me his secrets, his plans, his desires. I listen. He seems to trust me. I tell him a few things about myself too, but my mother long ago warned me not to become too close to others, and there are certain things he can never learn about me. For my part, I do not trust anyone.

Anton tells me he was born in a small town only a few kilometres away from the border between the Russian and Western zones. He wishes he were born a little bit further west, in the Federal

Republic, where men are free and wealthy, where the stores are full of an abundance of goods, where the women are sexy and would lure him into their beds. He loves the West, he declares. I advise him to stay quiet, that speaking like this to anyone else will lead to his arrest. He knows, he says. He is only talking to me because I am reliable. He wouldn't say such things to anyone else. He tells me he is an only child; that he misses his mother. He wants to have a girlfriend, but thinks he is too ugly. I agree without saying it. He asks for my advice about girls. I wish I knew what to answer, but the little I know seems to satisfy him.

When we go drinking, Anton is the first to become drunk, and the first to complain. The food at the hostel is terrible. Not as good as his mother's. After all the young women in the beer hall reject his crude advances, he complains that there aren't any worthy girls in the town. His pay isn't high enough, he says. I ask him what he would spend more money on, since the girls aren't good enough for him, and the food isn't worth what it costs already. Anton replies that in the West, such a situation can't happen. There, if you have money, you can spend it all, to the last penny. Here the only use for money is to give bribes, so you can get something which would otherwise be kept from you. Anton dreams to escape to the West. This part he whispers. He knows he talks too much, especially when he drinks, and he also knows that there are ears everywhere.

As for myself, I have bought an old guitar and spend my spare time learning to play. I find some of my mother's songs in her notebooks. They are full of yearning, romance and breaking hearts, the tragedies of war overcome by the joys of love. They seem strange as I read them. My mother speaks to me across the years, and perhaps across the distance too. How can I ever know if she still lives, somewhere in the frigid steppes of Asia, or the mountains of the Caucasus? I only hope, but there is the dread in me that she has been dead a long time and that I will never see her again. The worst is that I will never know. The songs fill me with longing, a deep loneliness. Yet they are beautiful, and if she is dead I swear I will make her songs live for her.

End-of-year holiday comes and we have a few days off. Anton has invited me to visit his family. They still live in the same flat where Anton was raised. Anton's father and mother greet us at the door, and invite us in. With a rather formal warmth, his father keeps his hand back when I extend mine, after firmly clasping his son's. His mother's smile is stiff. I see they are tense and suspicious.

We are in time for dinner. Anton's sister Marta and her husband Erich are also here, and so is his uncle Gregor. So many Germans. My skin crawls. I feel surrounded. At the same time, I savour the intoxicating smells of the bratwurst and the *kartofflen* roasting and my stomach's desires overpower me. My harsh judgments come apart after the first glass of pilsener.

At the table, Anton's father talks about the war, how he was an infantry captain on the Western Front.

"What about you?" he asks.

"Me?"

"Your father, I mean. You are Polish, no? Was he not a soldier defending his country?"

I hesitate. I lie. "He fought at the beginning, but was killed. In the blitzkrieg."

"Ah," he says, "but I did not kill him. I was not there."

No sympathy at all from this man, just an 'ah'. I churn inside again, even though I told him a lie.

"Where did you fight?" I ask.

"In France and Holland, finally Berlin, before I was captured, but I did not fight. I never killed anyone."

"Never?" I ask. I am being too bold, I imagine. They may throw me out.

"It was a heady time for a young soldier," he says, "until things turned. If I had to shoot, I would shoot wildly, never take aim." His eyes sparkle as he says these things. He stares vacantly at some point in the air. I don't believe a word. He became a captain without killing anyone?

"Not possible," I say.

"What do you know about it? Were you there? You young men know nothing. You never endured hardship, you are soft."

He was never in the East, he says, didn't suffer like his two brothers, who froze to death at Stalingrad, but there were many moments of terror, ugly things seen and done. Done by others, not him.

"What about when the Russians came?" I ask.

"They were terrible, those Tatars and Khazaks, all barbarians. Imagine, led by Jewish officers." He becomes agitated. "If only we had been able to..."

I listen intently, waiting for his next words, but they stop. Gregor cuts him off and tries to calm him.

"They raped my sister!" Anton's father yells.

I say nothing more. I have raised a sheet of ice between us as a defence.

"The past is the past." Gregor declares, "Let it lie where it was and not come forward to poison our lives." We raise a glass of schnapps and toast family.

He would never have been shooting at my mother, I realize, but I see him as an old Nazi anyway.

He brings out a few medals, decorated with swastikas.

"These are illegal to own, but after all, they are my memories."

Anton's uncle stands in a rush, his hands gripping the edge of the table.

"What are you saying? This is a stranger. He may report you."

Everyone stares at me. Anton looks doubtful. "Did I make a mistake inviting my friend?" he asks.

It is certainly time to neutralize their suspicions.

"I was born and grew up in a Russian labour camp. Those communists arrested my mother and kept her there. I hate them too. My mother was a poet. I have my guitar. Let me sing you some of her songs." They seem less hostile, even mollified, after I tell them this.

Anton's uncle Erich is a Communist Party member.

"What are you talking about? There are no labour camps." he declares. "The Party is just." He glares but says nothing more. He turns away and stares at the wall, as if wishing I was not there.

This is bad. I am caught between the two sides of trouble.

"What of your mother?" Anton's mother asks.

"I don't know. We were separated years ago. I don't know anything about politics." The questions stop awkwardly. I mention nothing about being Jewish.

After we finish eating, I sing my mother's songs. The songs are in Polish, and no one understands a word, yet they seem moved. Anton's mother dabs a handkerchief on her eyes. His sister hugs her husband. Despite his earlier antagonism, Erich smiles. The songs seem to be doing their work.

When I am finished, they toast to my mother. I am unable to respond except to drink the *schnapps*. It burns in my throat and I cough furiously. Everyone laughs. I seem to have broken through their reserve. I am quite emotional now. I am crying. One drink leads to another, and soon we are all very drunk. Anton talks about his desire to escape. His uncle Gregor warns him to shut his mouth. The walls have ears, he says, as Anton's excited voice rises a bit too high. I think it but do not say it: the chairs around this table have ears too.

Erich stares ahead and still says nothing. After a short time has passed, he gets up to leave and bids everyone but me a good night. I feel like a fish in a tank of hot water. I have stumbled onto the road to trouble.

There is a knock on the door. Anton's parents rush to open it. I read the fear on their faces. I too am afraid now. We are due to be returning to our work town in a few days, if we are not arrested first. I have longed for the end of this long night, expecting the secret police to come banging at the door at any time.

It is Anton's brother-in-law at the door. Anton's mother blubbers some German sounds, too quick for me to understand, but he says to remain calm. I am puzzled. Is this a trick before the police arrive? Erich tells Anton and me in a hushed voice to prepare ourselves to leave.

Anton asks if we are to be arrested.

"No, you are going west."

"What?"

"West."

"Now?"

"Yes, now."

"What about Eli?"

"He can't stay. He knows too much. He's going with you. Both of you, give me all your documents. Nothing must lead back to us. To me. Just in case."

"In case what?" asks Anton's mother. She knows only too well: in case we die, in case we are captured. She mumbles something, running a finger up and down then sideways across her chest.

We empty our pockets quickly. I keep only the journal of my mother in my knapsack, but it bears no name, no dates, no address. Do I have a reason to stay, close ties of any kind? No.

Anton's mother is worried, afraid for her son's safety. "You will take care of my son," she orders.

She prepares us a bundle of food—bread, cheese, and sausage—and gives Anton a package of dry underwear and socks. She also pushes a bundle of West German marks into his hand. Where she got them, no one tries to guess. Finally, she slips Anton an envelope on which the return address is that of her brother Willy, who lives in Frankfurt. She has not seen him since soon after the war ended.

I decide to leave my guitar behind. If I drop it or knock it against something, it will make too much noise and give us away. "No," Anton's mother insists, "you will get us into trouble if it is found here. Take it away."

It is after midnight and raining lightly when we leave. Erich drives us to a secluded spot along the fence near the border with West Germany, somewhere out in the countryside. This area is poorly watched, he says. Another couple broke through the wire while trying to escape just a few days before. They were captured, but the bureaucracy has not yet caught up, and the fence is still to be repaired. He points us in the right direction. I see nothing out there. It is quite dark, a moonless night, covered in clouds. The rain and fog obscure everything.

We slip away. Anton's brother-in-law doesn't wait to see how far we get. He immediately drives off into the darkness, his headlights off until he is a safe distance away. His car engine provides the only sound, and this soon dwindles away to nothing. In moments there is little to hear except for the wind. Anton eagerly rushes forward in the direction Erich indicated, and I follow close behind. My pants get caught in the ragged ends of the torn barbed wire, and I stagger and fall. My guitar resonates like a drum in the darkness as it hits the ground. Anton turns and shushes me, and as he does so, steps on a mine a few footsteps past the fence. My guitar protects me from small fragments of metal. I am just far enough from Anton not to be caught by the power of the blast. I am spattered, but unhurt.

I lift myself away from the guitar and inch forward towards Anton on my hands and knees. He isn't moving. He is sitting upright. When I get to him, I see that he is dead. Part of him is gone—only his upper body remains, his eyes wide open, a look of surprise on his face. The ground around him is very wet, more than could be caused by the soft rain now falling. I close his eyes so he will stop staring at me. I am in shock. I breathe too quickly, gasping for air. I slow myself down. Slow, I think, slow. I want to cry, but I brush the horror and grief away. I wipe my eyes.

I will be caught if I don't leave immediately. I force myself to think, to think of my next step, and the one after that. I grab the package of marks Anton carried. It has broken open, but is mostly intact. It all looks so terrible, but I pull myself away. I go on, stumbling, running. The noise of the explosion will soon bring the border guards riding up on their motorcycles.

I keep turning to look behind me. I struggle to walk quickly, and after a few minutes I see a sign partly in what I think is English. I do not understand what it says, but know I am past the real border, which is a hundred metres beyond the fence. I am in the West.

How quickly things can change. I am filled with something like fear, but that is the wrong word. It is larger than that. It is dread. I have just passed between worlds, from the world of humans to that of demons. From the rational to the world of magic. I am surrounded by soldiers who speak to me in loud words that run together in nonsense sounds. Some are white, but a few have black skins. Strange. They laugh between themselves. Are they taking me back? I hear the words. I know them to be English, although I don't know what they mean. An officer shouts at them to shut up, then calls to someone farther off behind him.

One soldier who speaks German comes forward and translates the questions the officer asks. He has a strange accent. Is this an American? I understand, but ask if anyone speaks Polish. No, he says.

Who am I? Where do I come from? Where did I intend to go? Do I work for Russian intelligence? One of the soldiers passes me a cigarette and lights it for me. I don't smoke but I take it anyway. It wouldn't do to offend. The smoke is sweet, different from what I know from the work hostel. I relax.

The air has a fresh scent, moist after the recent rain. I am transported to a police post, a large box made of cement, where I am seated on a wooden bench and questioned again. They give me fresh clothing. I am allowed to rest.

I fall asleep and am awakened to be escorted into an army vehicle. I am driven through a town to an army barracks, where I am given a small room with a bed and a reading lamp. There is a toilet, one I can sit on, with toilet paper soft as lamb's wool. I am given a towel and soap, sweet-smelling and smooth, and shown to the shower. The next morning, more questions. My name? My date of birth? Where was I born? I guess at the answers to some of the questions. I am amazed when they return the package of money.

After a few days, which seem like a century, I am released with a new identity card, a hero of the West as I have courageously escaped the dreaded Communists. But really, I am more lucky than brave. Still, I receive a lot of attention. News reporters question me. It is all very hectic and too full of detail for me to describe it all clearly. There is a party at the town's college, where I am for some reason the guest of honour. Two young women take me to their home, an apartment near the centre of town. We sit on the couch in the parlour and we smoke marijuana cigarettes. It is my first time and I feel uncomfortable and confused. I feel suddenly hungry.

They feed me. They make love to me for what seems hours before I finally beg off with tiredness. They are amused by my circumcision. They laugh at some charmingly funny thing I say, although I am mystified at what it might be. They cover me with kisses before allowing me to sleep. I dream of the border, of Anton's half-body. His eyes look through me as he attempts to get up from the ground. He asks me to help him. In the distance I hear dogs barking, soldiers yelling orders, and I run. Anton calls after me to help him. I look back and he is dead again, his eyes still open. I come awake screaming. The girls surround me, they cuddle me, cooing softly.

I wake up in one of their beds the next day. The beds are mattresses on the floor, but are softer than any I have ever slept in before. The two young women have both gone. The clothing they wore the previous night is still scattered across the hallway and the floor of the bedroom. There are posters on the walls. They are labelled. Che Guevara. Mick Jagger. Peter Fonda, on a motorbike. On a wooden shelf supported by cement blocks, a record player, and a mass of recordings in cardboard sleeves. Next to the machine, a large candle, not lit. The ceiling is painted black. I hear the sounds of children playing in the street outside the window.

I wait for the girls but finally give up. They don't appear to be coming back soon. I find my things, even my money. I walk into the bathroom. The girls' towels are soft, fluffy, large and pink. On a shelf next to the sink sit a multitude of lipsticks and small bottles of various forms of makeup. This all seems like in a fairy tale, a place of mystery and magic. The bathroom smells of perfume.

I see the bathtub and can't resist. The bath is surrounded by all sorts of lotions, creams, soaps, and rinses. I peer at the tiny labels, partly in German and what I take to be English. I can see that I would be better to know this language of the Americans. I study the words and try to learn the ones that correspond to the German I already know.

I spend an hour in the luxury of the tub, refilling it again and again with hot water as the bath cools. Hunger finally drives me out. I dress, find little to feed myself with in the refrigerator. I step into the brightness of day.

I stop at a small cafe and order a coffee and pastry. I hand over a bank note and the girl behind the counter has a look of astonishment. She opens the cash and hands me back a large pile of coins that I quickly slip into my pocket without trying to count my change. I eat the puff pastry and sip the aromatic coffee with delight. I concentrate on the flavours, savouring each morsel. I go to the counter and order another, different this time. I can't stop myself. The tastes are astonishing.

I notice a poster in the entrance for a youth hostel and ask about it. Go there, they tell me, it's where all the young travellers from out of town stay.

There, no one knows who I am, although some recognize my accent. They are full of helpful advice. The location of the laundromat. The nearest bank. A café with excellent pastries. The closest Catholic church is just up Lindenstrasse, past the monument.

"Thank you, but I won't need it."

"Ah, a Communist atheist?'

"Perhaps, but also I am a Jew." For some reason I feel I can now speak honestly. They wonder at my answer.

"How can that be? There was not even one left in this town. Where are you from?" they ask.

"Auschwitz," I respond, not knowing the effect of this word. Their faces twist and they pull away to mutter to one another.

"Is this a joke?" they ask.

I chuckle, as if I had meant it to be one. They relax again. I see that I have much to learn.

16　Urges

Each of us is a universe. It is only through our own eyes that the world lives. Without us, once we are gone, our abandoned universe will also cease to be. So we think. The world of man is a world of a multitude of individual universes, blinking on and then off, like so many fireflies in a misty forest in the late summer evening. Rarely we bridge into the world of another being, feel for them, care for who they are. Such we call love. These hesitant contacts can be direct and open, or convoluted and dark. We rarely understand which.

Towards the end of his first year at McGill, Simon was quickly immersed in the goings-on of a world undergoing seismic change, Adam not so much.

Adam was a hard worker, disciplined and ambitious, set on the goal of medical school. He didn't go out, spending much of his time at the upper campus medical library. Simon was enrolled towards a degree in science, namely biology, but after classes was soon involved with the music scene and the political changes visible all around him. At the student union, he drank coffee and talked politics with the Maoists and Trotskyites and sundry left-leaning students, arguing about weaknesses of western democracy and the superiority of the dictatorship of the proletariat. They sifted a sea of words about the bourgeois basis of romantic love. They focused on the true definitions of the First, Second, and Third Worlds. They debated the next great change, whether it would be the spread of wealth, the triumph of sexual liberation, or pursuit of violence as fashion. Simon drifted into the offices of the McGill Daily, writing the odd article, interviewing a genetics professor about eugenics, a political science lecturer on the role of the individual and the collective in the society to come. There were opinions about radical change, and of course, the changing roles of men and women.

And then there was sex. Girls began to walk around campus without bras under their blouses. Skirts became progressively shorter. Expressions of personal freedom like this had come into style. Simon noticed, and also noticed that political ideas could be an aphrodisiac.

Mary, an arts student he met at the Student Centre, invited him to see the film *Blow-Up*, being shown by the Film Society at the Physical Sciences Centre, and they ended up talking film over a pizza. She told him she did batik and woodcut prints and tie-dyed her own blouses, one of which she wore. They ended up at her apartment, shared with two other girls, on Lorne Crescent. Alice from Ontario, as her roommates called her, brought out a few joints while all they sat around on the floor listening to Cream, the Doors and The Chambers Brothers. It was while *Time Has Come Today* was playing that Mary passed her hand into his and pulled him away into her bedroom. It was his first time.

Adam and Simon still lived at home in NDG with their parents. Simon invited Mary to have dinner at his parents' home on a Friday night for the Sabbath.

"So you're the girl my son talks about? He tells me your name is Marion. Such a nice name." was his mother's enthusiastic greeting at the door. "Come in. Come in."

Mary gave Simon a look that said: What's with Marion?

A little later his mother asked "Would you want to *bench lecht*, Marion?"

Mary looked at Simon, perplexed. Simon looked back. "Light the candles," he explained.

"Ah, your parents must be Reform?"

Again, the look of confusion. "I'm not Jewish, and my name is Mary." she answered.

Hannah gave Simon a pained look. "So, fine, I'll light them myself."

The Sabbath meal was quiet. Mary stared at the *gefilte fish*, took a small bite, and stared some more.

"You don't like my fish, Mary?"

"Oh, it's fish. I didn't know. It's very delicious." Mary gave her most gracious smile possible, but left the rest of her plate untouched.

"So eat."

"It's an acquired taste," answered Duvid, to be polite and rescue the girl from Hannah. Duvid now queried Mary about her parents and their background, before it was Hannah's turn again. Simon squirmed as the questioning continued.

"You're a very nice girl, Mary, may I call you Marion," Hannah finally said, "but do you understand what you're getting yourself into?"

"Ma, leave her alone."

That seemed to stop her. They all sat silently now, no one sure what to say next.

"So you'll come next week, Marion? Maybe I can teach you a recipe."

"I don't know. I may be busy with school and stuff."

"On a Friday night? You shouldn't work so hard."

"I'll have to see."

"Simon, you be sure to bring her. I like this young woman."

"Okay, Ma. Thanks. I'll try."

Mary didn't come back. Hannah knew better than to ask why.

A few weeks later, Simon wandered into the McGill Daily offices to deliver his notes from an interview. One of the girls typing copy looked up.

"I know you."

"What?"

"I know you. I do. From a long time ago. It's your hair."

"Who are you?"

"You don't remember me? We've been pretty intimate in the past."

"Um?" Simon was completely perplexed.

"Think. We almost drowned together. Val Morin, the river. You can't get much more intimate than almost dying together. I saw you naked. Remember the bees?"

"Rachel, right?"

"C'est moi."

"Yes, I do remember, except you're thinking of my swollen brother."

"So, not you?"

"No, I was watching you take care of him. Inspired you, it seemed."

"That was a long time ago. I'm all grown up."

"I see that."

"And you are Simon. Or is it Adam? No, he was more serious and together. You're definitely Simon."

"What are you doing here?"

"I could ask the same thing."

"I do a few interviews for the paper. And you?"

"I type copy, proofread, take photos."

"Cool. So, we should get together. Have supper, maybe."

"Sure, I'm unencumbered for the moment. How about Friday night?"

"I'm going to my parents. I do that every Friday."

"So, okay."

"Why don't you come? I'm sure my mom would be delighted."

"Maybe another time. I think we should compare notes first, so I don't say the wrong thing. I'm good at that. So tomorrow night instead. We'll have a beer and see a film."

"A beer? Where? Women aren't allowed into taverns."

"No imagination. Come by my place. Here's my address and number."

"How about some pasta? There's this great Italian place on Peel. They serve beer, too, if you order food. I'll treat."

"Now you're talking. Great, call me tomorrow."

"So what have you been up to all these years?"

"Hard to say, really. Busy, studying fine arts, doing photography. You may have heard my parents both died."

"Sorry. I heard about your father, but not your mom."

"It was two years ago."

"But you seem okay."

"Yeah, really. I don't show my insides easily. When my mother died, I was left with a triplex near Park Avenue and a bunch of silverware—what was I supposed to do with that? Polish it every day? The triplex was more of a slum than anything of value, but the rent paid what was left on the mortgage, so for a time, I lived there. My tenants weren't easy to deal with. Maybe I was too young for that sort of thing. Anyway, an uncle helped me sell it. I made enough to buy a cottage on a small lake in Val Morin, on Lake Mimi—cute name, eh? —and my Hasselblad camera, something I'd always dreamed of. And to pay for my education. The summer cottage is a great place to get away to. Good investment, too, I think."

"Very pragmatic."

"I told you I've grown up."

"You and I have been out of touch a long time."

"How long is it now? About ten years, I guess. And your parents?"

"Both well."

So it went. After dinner, they went to see *Rosemary's Baby*. Rachel loved it. Simon wasn't impressed.

"She waddled too much."

"No, she didn't. Women really go through that when they're pregnant. You need a few lessons on real women."

"So you're going to teach me?"

"Don't be stupid. You really don't know anything about women. You need a girlfriend, but it's sure not me."

Simon felt he had hit a wall. He really didn't know much about the female half of the species, but wouldn't admit it.

"So are you coming to my parents' tomorrow?"

"No. I don't think it's a good idea."

He was disappointed. He had hoped to bring a Jewish girl home this time, just to impress his parents. He wasn't sure he liked Rachel that much, really. She was so contentious.

"So what do we do now?"

"You could walk me home."

So he did. She invited him up for coffee, but her roommates were all sitting around, munching on cookies and playing Risk in the central room of the apartment. Rachel introduced them all. There was Sara, a nursing student, Michael, who was going for a commerce degree, and Arnold, a math major. They each glanced up from the game, mouthed a quick "hi". Simon felt awkward. He followed Rachel into her room. Rachel had a bottle of wine and two glasses next to the bed.

"Here, open this. Pour us each a glass."

"I'm going to get comfortable," she said, and returned from the bathroom a few minutes later wrapped in a bathrobe.

"That's better," she said. "Let's light a candle and turn off the light."

They sat on the bed and sipped the wine.

"Do you play any games?" she asked.

"Not really."

"Do you dance?"

"Some."

"Here, listen to this." Rachel stood up and put an LP onto the turntable. "*White Rabbit* by the Jefferson Airplane. Come on, do this girl a favour. Dance with me."

She pulled Simon upright and leaned into him, sliding her hands down his back. Simon and Rachel swayed slowly to the music. He could feel himself becoming aroused. He leaned down and, to his surprise, her lips touched his and her tongue slipped past them.

"Oh, I'm getting dizzy," she whispered. Rachel leaned back, pulling him down on top of her on the bed. She ran her fingers across his lips. He gasped. He was ejaculating in his pants. He didn't know what to do.

"Hey, what do you think you're doing? My God, did you just come?"

"Well, you got undressed. You got me too excited."

"So this is my fault? Because you can't hold yourself back for more than a few seconds?"

"Maybe I'd better go."

"Good idea. You're pretty useless to me now, you know." She smirked.

"Can I call you?"

"Not just yet. Try practicing a bit first. Let me call you."

It took a while. Three months later, Rachel called him and left a message for him with his mother. It was almost summer.

"This girl Rachel called."

"Oh. Rachel."

"So excited you are? Who is she?"

"A friend."

"Oh, a friend. A girl who is your friend. Such a thing can be? She wants you to call her. Is that what girls do these days, call boys?"

Simon didn't want to get into that conversation, but his mother was not one to let go.

"Who is she, already? Another *shikse*?"

"No, she's Jewish, Ma. You know her."

"I do? Not Rachel from the cottage? The daughter of Dora?"

"Yeah, that's her."

"Oy, I don't like her."

"What?"

"She's not a good girl. She has a reputation. I heard people talk about her."

"What are you talking about? You haven't seen her in years. What do they say?"

"Never mind."

Simon was nervous. He had difficulty with rejection. He still felt uneasy about what had happened. But she had called him. That meant she wanted him, not the other way around.

"Hello?"

"Hi, it's me, Simon. I'm returning your call."

"Oh, hi. I'm glad you called back. Thanks. Okay, wait, don't get the wrong idea. This is strictly business. Listen, my roommate Michael is going away to school in Toronto in a month and we're going to need a replacement to take over his room."

"I don't have any money."

"It's not expensive, split four ways. Look, I have connections. I can find you a job at the library, reshelving books. I have a friend who works there. They always need someone."

Simon, knowing his mother would object, agreed to move in with Rachel and her friends.

"You're doing what?"

"Moving downtown. It'll be easier to get to school."

"With what money will you pay the rent?"

"I found a part-time job at the library."

"Oh, so now Mr. Showoff has a job. Duvid!"

Duvid didn't object, though.

"He spends all his time there at the university, anyway. He comes home after we're asleep. He wakes up after we leave for work. We never see him anyway. You'll still come home for Friday nights, right, Simon?"

"And bring me his wash, too?" complained his mother. "So where are you moving?"

"Rachel lives in an apartment with three others, another girl and a guy. They need a fourth. Don't worry, we'll each have our own room."

"Boys and girls living together? What is happening in the world? What will my friends think?" Hannah complained again.

"Hannah, it'll do him good to live with women. He never had a sister. Anyway, Adam is staying put. At least that."

"So I have one good son."

"Hannah, don't talk like you prefer one son over the other. You'll give him, how do they say it on Ed Sullivan, yes, a complex. You know, like the twins, Jacob and Esau."

"So, since when is my husband such a Torah scholar?"

So Simon moved in June, long before the beginning of his next year. Things were relaxed while the weather was hot. There were no school pressures. Sara was off with her boyfriend most of the time. Simon rarely saw her. Arnold was an asshole. He rarely spoke, and rarely cleaned up after himself, leaving dishes piled in the sink for days. He didn't seem to get it when the others asked him to clean up. In the end, they gave up and washed his dishes too. Arnold never said thank you.

On Fridays, Rachel's group of friends often drove up to her summer cottage. Their parents would let them have the car keys, trusting they would do nothing more than drink a few too many beers. Rachel invited Simon from time to time, telling him she felt sorry for him, stuck in the heat of the apartment with Arnold.

Simon's parents felt betrayed again. "You're not coming for *shabbos* dinner again? You go with your *goyische* friends instead? What's happening to my son?"

"Ma, most of my friends are Jewish. Stop bugging me."

Simon spent two weekends at the cottage. It was agreeable to be back in the country. A bit of nostalgia was good for his soul. Lazy mornings were reserved for languorous hours of unproductive fishing, and for fighting off the persistent horseflies darting silently around them, waiting to take a bite of flesh. Late evenings while the sky was still light enough to see were for skinny-dipping in the lake.

"Close your eyes, guys," the girls yelled, when they ran into the water squealing. They dove when bats swooped down to swallow the insects flitting just above their heads. Rachel dove under water, swimming between Simon's legs and came up laughing in front of him.

The nights were for melting marshmallows and cheap Romanian wine, the sudden burst of orange sparks from the campfire blotting out the stars, searing the skin of their faces as they hung close to it and to each other for warmth against the early summer chill. High above them in the black, clear sky, a passenger plane passed silently, on its way to Europe on a Great Circle route, its white tail light flashing rhythmically. The second weekend, they concocted a treasure hunt through the woods. There were three teams, he and Rachel, Sara and Mindy, and David and Ron. They weren't sure what they were looking for, mostly finding quartz crystals and spent shotgun shells. Mindy followed a trail of shed porcupine quills down a slope into the woods.

The others heard her scream. "Hey, over here. Quick."

They all gathered about. Mindy was pointing at something rounded and white under a fallen tree trunk. A human skull. She and Sara became very agitated. She wanted to call the police right away. Rachel pulled out her camera and took a photo.

"Who wants to hold it for a picture?" she asked.

"Disgusting," Mindy said.

"That's sick," said Sara. There was an awkward silence.

"I'll do it." Simon stepped forward and held the skull at stomach height, without looking at it. "I just hope no small critter crawls out of the eye socket. It feels kind of crumbly."

Rachel snapped the photo.

"What's that?" Simon had felt something. He pulled his hands away and the skull tumbled, disappearing under a shady bush.

"Good, it's gone," Mindy spouted, and shook her hands vigorously.

"Hey, I didn't get a good shot. You're not even in the picture."

"I didn't want to be," Simon said. The treasure hunt stopped there and the group made their way back to the cottage.

"We'll call the police when we get back to town," Rachel volunteered, once back at the cottage.

"I don't want my parents to hear about this," was Robert's comment. That seemed to sum up the group's feelings.

Mindy responded. "We could get in trouble."

"Bunch of cowards, you guys. Well, at least I got the shot," Rachel proclaimed. "Anyway, I don't remember where we found that thing. Can anyone?"

"Not me."

"Me neither."

There seemed to be a collaborative consensus around that. Sara was the last to comment.

"Let's not go into the woods again. It gave me the creeps."

That night, Rachel climbed into bed with Simon, on the pretext she was cold and needed to snuggle up. Rachel pulled herself close. Simon didn't complain.

"I'm glad I got the picture today, but to tell you the truth, I don't want to sleep alone. Sara's right, it's really creepy. Hold me tight."

"Okay." he smiled.

"Knock it off, this is not what you imagine. I really am scared."

"Okay, I'll try to control myself."

"Good boy." They went quiet for a moment.

"Do you agree with the others that we shouldn't report this?" Rachel asked.

"There's too much to explain, and the others don't want to get involved. Me neither, really."

"Scaredy cats."

"And you're not?"

"Sure I am. Where do you think it came from?"

"Maybe someone got murdered."

"You're making my skin crawl."

"Sorry. There can't be any other explanation, you know. And if it is a murder, the killer doesn't want to have the body found."

"You're so morbid. Relax." Rachel slid her fingertips along Simon's back, tickling him.

"Hey!"

"A beautiful girl just climbed into bed with you and you're complaining."

With that she kissed him on the mouth.

"Rachel, maybe we shouldn't do this."

"Are you kidding?"

"Why do you want this? I mean, really. Can't I just hold you–so you're not scared?"

"You talk like a girl. What's wrong?"

"Look, I can't do this on and off thing. If we're going to live in the same apartment, I don't want to feel jealous every time you're out with another guy. And you will be, I know it. I'm afraid I'll fall in love with you, and then what? I'll be too much of a mess."

"Such a serious guy. Well, too bad, you lost your chance. I'm really not scared any more. Good night."

Rachel slipped out of Simon's bed.

"Listen, Simon, I don't fall in love. It doesn't happen to me. I was nervous and cold, and I felt sorry for you."

"Sorry for me?"

"Yes. You looked so lonely. I thought I should help you out."

"Thank you so much! I thought I was helping you."

"We were helping each other. Look, I truly feel very sisterly towards you."

"It's a good thing you don't have a brother. You'd really screw him up."

He spent the rest of the summer in the city with Arnold, and didn't miss any more *shabbos* dinners with his parents.

"How's your new apartment?"

"Hot."

They didn't ask him what he meant. They bought him an air conditioner for his bedroom.

When summer retreated, relationships in the apartment stayed platonic. No touching on Simon's part. That was the stipulation at the beginning when Rachel and her friend Sara let him move in. Despite this restriction, Rachel saw nothing wrong in casually wandering around in a towel after a bath. Sara did too, but she looked uncomfortable, like she was just trying to be "cool". Rachel walked in to pee while Simon was taking a shower, calling out to let him know she was there. Sara was more restrained, but said it was cool to be "liberated" when Simon said anything about Rachel's behaviour.

Arnold was laconic. Besides, he had a girlfriend, Gloria.

Rachel continued to walk in on Simon while he showered. He wasn't sure any more if he should protest or act "cool" like Sara. Simon tried hard to adapt, even tried to be friendly with Arnold, but

Arnold wasn't sociable, except with his fish. Arnold always whispered to his fish in their tank while he fed them every day.

"So you like fish?"

"They're okay, I guess."

"You talk to them?"

"You think I'm crazy?"

"Okay, forget it."

Silence.

"So, you're into sports, Arnold?"

"Yeah."

"You play any sports?"

"Nah."

"Not even hockey?"

"Nah. I can't skate."

"I can but I never enjoyed it."

"Yeah?"

"Yeah. When I was a kid..."

"I really don't want to know."

"Okay."

Arnold was taller and heavier than Simon. Not a great talker. Simon asked the girls how he had gotten a girlfriend, but they didn't understand it either. So the two guys didn't talk much at all.

They competed for the television when the girls were out, but otherwise avoided each other. Simon enjoyed getting Arnold's goat. His goat was very vulnerable. If Arnold was watching a hockey game when Simon came in, Simon clicked the TV knob over to something else. Inexplicably, Arnold did and said nothing. At 11:00, Simon always insisted on watching the news. Any report about the U.S. space program or the Middle East grabbed his attention. When the sports news came on, he would click over to any late night movie. Arnold wouldn't react.

Finally, Simon found the chink in Arnold's armour. Arnold kept his fish tank in the common room, and whenever a fish died, floating upside down at the surface, Simon would stick a cut-out paper fish on the tank, with a cross for an eye. Arnold finally lost it. He beat on Simon's closed door, and threatened to move out. The girls, being practical, intervened so the conflict would stop.

All this did nothing to allay Simon's urges. At night, while studying in his room, he was distracted, to say the least, by the girls in the apartment building across the street who had never bothered to put up curtains. He desperately needed a girlfriend. His room wasn't the best place to study. The library might be a better choice. It would also get him away from Arnold and Rachel. Meanwhile,

Adam was always studying hard, hoping he could get into medical school. His parents encouraged him by buying him a fancy leather briefcase.

"Was it a briefcase of many colours," Simon asked when Adam dropped by to tell him about it.

"What are you talking about?"

It was not yet cool in the full sunshine of early autumn, the red leaves still clinging to their branches, reluctant to release their grip. The closeness of winter worried them. Simon would roam the McGill campus during the day. There were few women in his science courses. Between classes, he surveyed the small clutches of girls, and enjoyed their imagined company. They smiled seductively, gesticulating frenetically, chattering about yesterday's date, which young professors they found dreamy, the frat party next weekend. They sat in the grass on the field in front of the Arts building in small groups, actively disregarding him. His best spot became the main library, since he had a part-time job there.

Simon was thin, not quite handsome, his expression usually dour. He didn't attract girls like some of his friends did. He was neither tall nor short. His muscles didn't bulge, although he filled out his shirts well enough. His bright red hair stood out, though, like a fire engine on the street. Some girls did notice him in the library as he collected the carts of books already read and wheeled them off to be shelved. He spotted them glancing at him out of the corners of their eyes. Invariably, though, their eyes darted back to their books when he approached them, spooked by the frown that he wasn't aware he generally wore.

He sat in the library one day, not working, a book in his hand, something to glance down at between staring at one particular girl sitting in an armchair nearby. He hadn't noticed the name of his book when he pulled it from the shelf—something like *English Village Hierarchies in Post-Crusader England*. Not a course assignment. The tome upside down. The girl saw this and smiled cautiously, before she returned to her work. While she studied, she looked up at the ceiling, one hand gripping a pencil nervously, plunging it between the fingers of her other hand over and over. When she noticed Simon's eyes focussing on her hands, her face flushed. A fleeting smile crossed her face. Her eyes flitted away. Tossing her head of hair to one side, she rose and left, leaving her tie-dyed book bag on the arm of the chair. While he was really studying a little while later, she returned and sat down.

The girl wore a long flowered dress, a slit down the skirt front. It was draped securely over her upper body, highlighting her breasts and her narrow waist. She sat sideways, her legs bent in front of her at the knee. Their shape was obscured and emphasized by the looseness of the material that gravity had distributed around them in deep folds and hinting shadows. Her toes curled lightly into the chair's material. As she shifted her legs, the slit rode up. He stared furtively at a beckoning field of lightly sun-tanned skin.

He lit a cigarette and the smoke floated into his eyes, surprising him and forcing him to inhale. He coughed suddenly. She smiled at his oafishness and looked up, unable to ignore him. Their eyes met for a moment before hers dropped, but not before he saw the interest behind them flash through her mind.

Catherine was aware of him looking her over. She liked the sensation. She was caught between her attraction to this boy and fear of the same. A smile was fighting to grow on her face. Despite herself, her discomfort, she liked his look, the hunger in his eyes. His awkwardness was cute. She liked the thought of his thought of her. While she looked away, speaking in body language in place of words, shifting, looking to one side, picking at her many pencils, he wrote her a note, and flew it over in the form of a paper airplane. Then another. She smiled off to one side to hide her interest, rose, turning away from him to gather her things, and walked off, trying not to turn her head back in his direction, but the effort was obvious. She feigned tripping, bent down to adjust her sandal, and picked up one of the airplanes, and scurried away.

She was back a day later, again willing to distract him. She was still afraid and still attracted. He seemed too serious, too intense. He had a dark look to him. Although at first hesitant, his rough charm, like a vine in a lush forest, grew over her silent objections after several of these meetings in the library. His tendrils insinuated themselves into the skin of her thoughts.

Over a period of two weeks he kept flying poems written on slips of paper over to her. One day he plunged down on his knees next to her, begging her to go out with him. She declined, but importantly, didn't get angry and tell him to leave her alone. To him this was encouragement. He placed other notes in the books he knew she was consulting, guarding them so no one else got to them first.

I cannot but think
How the world would seem kinder

If you lay here beside me
And let me listen to you

Breathe

The leaves were now yellow—most had already fluttered to earth.

He would not be deterred. There were mock swooping attacks on the lawns of the campus, running down at her, whooping like a banshee, and flopping down next to her while she tanned in the last rays of a cooling world and pretended to study. His rough charm at last won her over. After a few minutes of this, one hand up to shield her eyes from the sun, she finally gave in and spoke.

"Do you imagine that I'm interested?" Her accent was French. Intriguing.

"Yes, I have a great imagination."

"Not enough."

"What's your name?"

"Catherine."

"Aah. Now you can't ignore me. I'll speak your name and you'll turn your face to me."

"And your name?"

"Simon."

"I like that."

"You'll like it more, Catherine."

"You're too intense."

"You already like that. Catherine."

"Suppose we go see a film?"

"Um, okay, we could do that. When?"

"Tonight."

"Too fast. I have to study. I have a project due after tomorrow."

"Friday?"

"Okay, so Friday night."

"That's really great. I'll need your address."

He called his mother and told her he couldn't make it or *shabbos* that Friday evening.

"Why not?"

"Not enough laundry."

"So, another *shikse*? Maybe you'll bring her to us another week."

"Ma, I'm not ready for that. I have to give you a chance to think of ways to torment her."

"Someday. Simon, you will regret how you speak to me."

"Ma, you know I'm joking."

"Jokes like this kill mothers."

"You're not dying."

"Not yet."

He picked Catherine up at her apartment a little off campus, in the student ghetto. He had the nerve to take her to a softly pornographic film which was in fashion with the university crowd, and she hadn't objected. After it was over, they sipped increasingly cold and bitter coffee at The Yellow Door, a student-run coffee house just east of campus.

"I've never been here before."

"No? You're missing something. This is the worst coffee you'll ever taste in Montreal."

"So, something to look forward to, at least."

"Sure, you can bask in the sun-filled rays of my adulation. The muffins aren't so bad, though."

"You'll make me fat."

"Impossible."

She smiled. "If only you knew."

He tried to describe his dreams of a life as a journalist. "Really, that's what you plan to do?"

"I scare you, don't I."

"Terrify."

"So I'm that fascinating?"

"Yes." She leaned forward and gave him a peck on the cheek.

"Is that all?"

"Later." She smiled again and took a sip of her coffee. "Tell me where you come from."

"Really?"

"I'm interested."

"Really?"

"Really. Okay, enough. Let me read you this poem I wrote for you."

"A love poem. Just for me. I'm flattered."

"Maybe not."

I cannot but wish
You'd put your head in a zipper
And pull it up quickly
So that I could hear you

Scream

"So you really do like me."

He smiled and put one hand at the back of her neck and eased her face towards him. She kissed him, and he tickled her at the waist. She giggled.

He walked her home, and she let him kiss her again at the door. She let him touch her breast and then the firm mound lower down.

"Wait," she whispered.

His eyes were closing, his heart thumping in his chest. She turned and fished intently in her small purse for her key, unlocked her door and pulled him in. The place was dark. It was neat and smelled of clean dishes and starched bedding. Simon noticed. It was quite a contrast with his own place.

She slipped into bed and he tried to follow. The bed seemed to be covered in a multitude of layers of sheets. He slipped under a sheet, the wrong one, and was unable to touch her. There were several more layers of sheet below which she huddled, too warm. The covers on the bed kept getting in his way as he tried to engage himself in her body, while she laughed hysterically, urging him on. His legs became tangled, as he tried to shift position. He desperately pushed the bed sheets away, throwing them over his head onto the floor fold by fold. He didn't know why she needed so many sheets. She laughed at his annoyance. It was hours later that they fell asleep next to each other, facing each other's hypnotized eyes. The apartment was hot, the radiators blasting heat into the air. The pair slept without bedcovers.

During that night, the heat woke Simon. Simon rose and opened a window, had a glass of cold water, and came back to bed. He looked over Catherine's sleeping body, her small, edible toes, her perfect feet, her smoothly curved legs, now undone equally with the rest of her, inviting as they had been before when they alone had beckoned his attention. Her nose was so delicate, her closed eyelids smiling to themselves. He imagined he had always been here, and always would remain here, next to this girl. As the room cooled, he pulled a sheet over the two of them. Catherine rolled and moulded herself against him. Simon was filled with desire, but he restrained himself and let her sleep. Eventually, so did he.

The sheets were all over the floor in the morning, surrounding the bed, a sea of bedding, as if waters had arisen during the night and carried them off like effluvial detritus. They woke up to the sound of the phone ringing. They hadn't slept much–the coffee had been strong and their robust appetites for each other had kept them awake. Catherine's mother was on the phone. She would be coming by in a few minutes to pick her up and bring her and her dirty clothes home for the weekend. She asked Catherine if she had a boy with her–there was something in her voice that gave his presence away.

"*Bien non, maman.*" Catherine denied it.

While she spoke to her mother, Catherine twisted herself into a bathrobe. After she had hung up, Simon sat on the bed, watching fascinated as Catherine showered and dressed.

"You've got to go. That was my mother."

"You have a mother?"

"She's coming over in a few minutes."

"So I can't meet her?"

"Ha! Not yet. She's a force of nature. You'll have to run or she'll eat you alive."

"Why didn't you say so?"

Simon threw the bed sheets around, wildly trying to unbury his clothes, almost tripping in the process. He couldn't find his underwear, and clawed on the clothes he did find. Catherine physically pressed him towards the doorway and out the door. Simon was about to ask when he could see her again when he heard the main door downstairs bang shut. It wasn't the time to be inquisitive. As he was hopping down the stairs towards the front door of the apartment building, an older woman with a small crucifix dangling conspicuously around her neck came up the stairs, breathing a little deeply. He wondered if this was Catherine's mother.

She seemed to eye him suspiciously, before her eyes clouded with indifference and she proceeded up the stairs.

As Simon pushed open the front door of the building, he heard Catherine's voice echoing in the stairwell.

"*Maman, je t'ai beaucoup manquée.*"

"*Ah, oui, je suis certain de ça. Alors, où est ton jeune homme?*"

Simon marched out the front door of the building and waited a few steps away. He leaned back against the ornate cast iron railing of an exterior stairway, and waited. Catherine and her mother walked past him twenty minutes later, chatting and looking like they were both ignoring his presence. He followed Catherine with his eyes as she walked down towards her mother's car.

He called her that night, but she wasn't home yet. On Monday night she was, agreeing to see him again the following Friday.

"My mother found your underwear in the wash. She went completely nuts over a little thing like that. Imagine. She's going to kill you, you know."

"You're kidding, I hope."

"She did and she will. Next time she sees you. You'll see."

She laughed and he did too, but very uneasily.

She surprised him with a gift on the Friday night he came by to pick her up. It was a new shirt and a pair of jeans, something new to him, with a brand name, Wrangler. He'd never worn a pair before.

This time, after the movie, they went to his place. None of his room-mates seemed to be home. When she saw his room, Catherine spent a half hour cleaning it up, putting his dirty clothes into a plastic garbage bag and making his bed. She gave the dishes in the kitchen sink a thorough washing.

"Those aren't mine," he protested

"The cockroaches don't care whose they are."

Simon sat waiting on his bed, bemused by the excessiveness of her need to clean, sucking on a cigarette that she wouldn't let him light. He hoped that his other roommates wouldn't see this activity. He would be the butt of their jokes for weeks. After Catherine was finished, she prepared for bed. She went to the bathroom, showered, and brushed her teeth with the toothbrush she always carried with her. She was back soon, her wet hair wrapped in a towel.

When Catherine got back to Simon's room, he was in his bed, undressed, his bare back against the wall.

"There's critters about. I ran into someone on the way back. She was waiting to get into the bathroom and only wearing a towel."

"Oh, that would be Rachel. Sara wouldn't do that sort of thing."

"Rachel? Sara?"

"Roommates."

Catherine gave him a twisted smile.

"Completely platonic. Really."

"Okay, mister. *Debout.* Up. Get dressed. We're going over to my place. There, the only woman walking around half-naked will be me. Besides, I don't want any cockroaches crawling across my face during the night."

Simon grumbled a bit but dressed quickly enough. As they walked out his front door, Catherine noticed the brass bar bearing three Hebrew letters nailed at a slant on the right doorpost. He saw her curious look.

"I've seen one of these before, but what is it?"

He tried to explain it to her.

"It's called a *mezuzah*. Some sort of protection. I'm Jewish. All of us here are."

"Protection against what?"

"I'm not sure. Maybe you."

"Sounds like what my dad would have said when I asked a question about the faith."

"The Catholic faith?"

"Yeah, that one."

"Well, my dad would know why it's there."

Catherine didn't question him any more. She was quite indifferent. Simon found her attitude refreshing, but still in some way puzzling.

It was late spring. It was several months they'd been together now. Catherine called him on the morning of her final exam. He had been asleep when the phone rang. His mind felt muddy. She asked him to wish her luck.

"Good luck."

"Simon, is that all?"

"Um?"

"What about 'I love you'? Simon, I'll call you when I've finished the exam. We can talk after. By the way, I love you."

Simon was speechless.

"See you later," he repeated. While he heard the phone disconnecting, he mumbled "I love you, too." Too late for anyone but the air around him to hear. After he hung up, Simon tried to get back to sleep. He was too aroused, though, and sleep eluded him. He felt blurry.

Catherine insisted later that Simon take her out that evening, to celebrate the end of her final exams. They went to a spaghetti house, the same one he'd been to with Mary at another time. They both had pasta, his with tomato sauce with shrimp, a taste acquired in rebellion against the kosher state his mother maintained at home. Simon ordered a half-bottle of red, just the house wine, but it went well with the food.

Catherine was ebullient. She wouldn't stop talking, and Simon allowed her to carry on while he took small sips of wine. The carafe was soon empty. He ordered another. He was delighted to see her again. They sat at right angles to each other, so they could lean their faces close to each other easily. She kissed him to lick bits of sauce that he had allowed to escape from the corners of his lips. He leaned back and laughed.

After the next glass of wine, things became quiet. Over the glowing centrepiece candle, Catherine's mood turned sombre and inquisitive.

"You told me you were Jewish. I don't know anything about your religion."

"I don't know that much either, like I said. What I do remember is that we're supposed to be a stiff-necked people, and that everyone hates us."

Catherine had a quizzical look on her face, like she wasn't sure how to respond.

"What are you talking about?"

"My mother always told me to be careful, not to expose the fact that I'm Jewish to non-Jews. That would include you, but it's too late for that now."

"So what is being Jewish really all about?"

"That's hard to explain. It's a religion that's really old, thousands of years. It has a slew of commandments—rules. Six hundred plus. Also unnumbered books and commentaries about them."

"I thought there were ten."

"Those are the first ten, the best-known. Yeah, I know, there's a lot. Anyway, bear with me. In the Old Testament, God calls us a stiff-necked people over and over. I think that meant we were a pain in the neck."

"Like you are now?"

"It really means we're stubborn. I was making a joke."

"What about the New Testament?"

"No, not included. So, Lady Catherine, I guess you're not big on religion."

"No, but I was baptized as a little girl."

"Okay."

"Look, Simon, I don't believe any of those things I learned as a child."

"So we're alike, you and I. But my mother would kill me if she knew I was seeing a non-Jewish girl."

"Why?"

"My parents had a hard life living with Catholics. Brutal would be the right word for it. Europe was a barbaric place not very long ago. It's hard to explain some things. Have you ever heard of the Holocaust?"

"Sorry, no. What is that?"

"Now's not a good time to explain."

"Because we're enjoying the evening?"

"Yes, enjoying things. Can we do that? My parents can't. With them, life has to be serious all the time. And you know, whatever I do is never good enough for them."

"*Pauvre* Simon."

"You're make fun of me, but it's true. My parents like my brother better. I know that sounds like something out of a Freudian story, but it's really like that. He's perfect. And he's going to be a doctor. It's the top of the heap as far as a Jewish parent is concerned."

"I think you have a complex. Enough with your parents."

"It's true. Listen, here's a story. It goes like this: A young Jew tries to do well but is never able to live up to his father's ambitions for him. He does well in school, but his grades aren't in the nineties. His father is disappointed in him. He's accepted to a good college, but not Harvard. Again, a failure. He graduates *cum laude*, not *magna cum laude*. Same story. He studies for his Ph.D., because he doesn't make the cut for medical school. He does research on cancer, and discovers a cure. Deservedly, he gets the Nobel Prize. So, the son brings the news home to his father, thinking he's finally hit the mark. So the old man mutters, 'Cancer? I have heart disease. What good are you to me?' So, you see, you can't win."

"I'm sure that father smiled proudly even though he said those words." Catherine took a sip of her wine. "Anyway, you just said your brother was going to be a doctor and your parents are so proud of that. Maybe you're just a little jealous. Anyway, if you brought home the Nobel Prize, your father would be proud."

"Maybe so, but he would still complain to his rabbi that his illustrious son couldn't read the Hebrew prayers properly. Anyway, I never will. Reporters don't get Nobel Prizes."

"So the Pulitzer. Look, Simon, you're here with me. Your parents aren't watching us. Take a deep breath. Relax. Anyway, everyone's parents are problematic. We don't get to choose them."

"So, about yours?"

"Hm, so, *mon père* was a hard worker, a tough guy, *un col bleu*, a blue collar worker, they call them. Never complained about life. He just did what he thought he was supposed to. Brought us all up. I was the youngest for a long while."

"Us?"

"*Mes soeurs, mes frères.* We were six, just counting his children. There were the others, too."

"Others?"

"My parents were Catholics. It was expected they have large families. My parents decided to adopt two, a boy and a girl. They weren't rich, but they were good Catholics."

"Boy."

"Yes. He died when I was seventeen. *Trop de cigarettes*. Too many children to raise. But he was in the union. He had a good insurance policy. That's how I can afford college."

"And your mother?"

"I think she had an affair while my father was alive. I'm pretty sure that's where one of the adopted kids came from. Maybe both. They look too much like us. She was gone for a couple of years when I was young. My father said she was working in France. Anyway, *ma maman et moi*, we're not close. I see her every few months."

"*Pauvre bébé.*"

"*C'est malheureusement vrai.*"

"So, you're not scared of me."

"You know I am. I don't know if anyone can be really faithful in a relationship."

"Yeah, your parents' mess can affect you. Mine have, in many ways. My parents have never strayed. So it is possible."

"So we're both traumatized by our parents' lives, Simon? I suppose everyone is. I hope I don't scare you too much."

"Not yet. How about you me?"

"A lot."

It was a wet night. Rain had fallen while they were in the restaurant, and now, as they made their way along, the street shone through the dark, a mirror to the bright headlights of the passing cars and the street lamps overhead. Catherine held his hand and smiled into his gleaming eyes. They swung their arms back and forth to the loud rhythm of the stereo of a passing car.

As they walked briskly to her apartment, the rain started again, at first a few drops that they could feel cool on the backs of their hands. It started to pour, and they ran, holding their hands over their heads, Catherine squealing and Simon roaring through the blasting rainstorm. They threw their heads back, drinking the rain as it poured into their open mouths, their eyes illuminated by the lightning blasting above in the wild sky. At the door of her apartment, they stopped to kiss, their drenched clothes conformed tightly against their skins. Water dribbled down their foreheads and into their eyes, the rainwater that they allowed into their mouths slipped out again, mixing together and pouring off the lines of their jaws in small cascades. They could feel their bodies below their wet clothing, cold, and below that, warm, pressing urgently into each other.

Much fumbling with the key got them entry into the apartment. Once in, they pulled their soaked clothes off, facing each other, matching piece for piece, the clammy clothing stuck to their skins and coming off reluctantly. Simon helped Catherine pull off her tight wet jeans, after she despaired of not being able to do it by herself.

Catherine pulled off her moist underwear and bra and threw them into the pile of her other clothes next to the bathroom door. "*Je suis vraiment bourrée.* I'll never eat so much again. I must be an extra size now." She paused. "Do you think I'm fat?"

Simon surveyed her body, face to toe, slowly, stopping intermittently along the way to relish her curves, the arcs of her breasts, her smooth belly, the slight mound below, the dip into her sexual parts, where the soft hairs still glistened wet and barely hid the long narrow line where he wanted to spend the rest of his life.

"Fat? Ya, you sure are." He smiled leeringly, quickly regretting the comment when he saw the sudden glazed look in her eyes.

"I don't mean that. You're beautiful. You have a great body."

"Don't try. Well, yours is not so great."

"What do you mean?"

"Yours is no record breaker, you know."

"What?" Simon was taken aback.

"My mother told me Jews had large penises."

"She probably said noses."

"No, really, she said penises."

"How would she know that?"

"Hearsay, I'm sure. Obviously she was wrong. My cousin's was bigger."

"I'm sure there's a story there, but I don't want to know."

"I'm not talking."

"Does this mean it's all over between us?"

"Not so fast, you. You've already taken advantage of my honour. You're not getting off so easily."

Catherine reached behind her onto the bed and grabbed a pillow. She swung it loosely, until it collided lightly with his head. Pushing him over, she fell on top of him, sucking on his lower lip.

Her wet skin stuck to his as he entered her, as she slipped over him, slowly, while he became progressively harder by the second. As he reached his deepest penetration, as he felt her core reaching out for him, he came suddenly, as a burst of air groaned out of his excited chest. He must have had tears, or the remnants of the rain, in his eyes, for Catherine now leaned down and delicately licked his closed eyelids, swallowing away a strange sadness that bubbled out of him.

He was still hard, still inside her, when she stopped moving and drew him out of her body. She wandered into the bathroom to shower, stopping along the way to pick up her discarded clothing and throw them into the bathroom hamper. 'Women!' he thought, slightly apprehensive. She was a bit too neat.

When she came out later, wrapped in a towel, he was already asleep. She shook her head back and forth and thought: 'Men!'

Here he was, instantly asleep after coming, while she felt full of energy. She was horny and felt ready to jog up the mountain. One look out the window at the weather made her shake her head. Maybe not just now. She smiled with pleasure and instead cuddled in next to him.

A year later Simon graduated and began to work at his first real job. It was at the Montreal Star, one of the city's two major English-language newspapers. Later, in the autumn, they decided to marry.

Simon made the announcement at Sabbath dinner, without Catherine present. He had been too nervous to invite her.

"If I had the nerve in my day to marry a gentile girl, my own father, your grandfather, would have sat *shiva* for me. He would have considered me to be dead to him. You have the nerve to ask for my blessing?"

"Ta, please stop." Simon pleaded, "Why couldn't you leave these old-fashioned ideas behind when you left Europe?"

"Because I left my family behind in Europe, dead, dead because of the gentiles. If I had known before you were born about this Catherine, maybe you wouldn't be in this world."

"Ta?"

Duvid left the table in a huff. Simon looked at his mother.

"Your father's right. You're making a mistake. A big mistake."

17 Eli's Journal

I have just come across my journal and have been reading through some of my earlier entries. Things have changed so much for me. It has been such a long time since I wrote anything here, although I don't know why–I haven't been even a little bit busy, and my life has settled into a monotony. Perhaps that is it. I'm content, no longer so driven by the troubles in my life. Surprising, when I think back to how stressful and full of trepidation the passage was. My memories are not fading, but the urgency I once felt has calmed. I did not date my earlier entries and now regret that oversight, but it is too late now, and so, even though each occurrence in isolation seems to have clarity, I am confused about dates, years, seasons, and the confluence and overlap of events, and whether some things really happened as I remember them or are refined or polluted by my imaginings. Too much time has passed for me to hold it all clearly in my head. I will now try to bring it up to date.

After first arrival following my escape from the East, I lived in the hostel for a number of months, learning the town, meeting locals at the coffee houses near the university, and reading, trying to catch up on all that I had missed. When my money ran out, I had to find work. The West remained such an enigma. It was not all as I was told it would be, but in some ways it was. Decadence, true, all around, but an attractive sort of decadence, easy to like–irreverent, artistic, creative, self-indulgent, vibrant, yet at times ugly. A self-centred freedom, each man in his own universe, defining the self for oneself. It confused me, for I had been defined by others, and I searched for who I was, and despite the freedom, I chafed. I felt detached from this world of material things and rapid change. I was a conundrum, a confused interior looking out at a confused exterior. Who was I? An easterner, an orphan, a chemical worker, and, according to my mother, a Jew. I had little understanding of what it all meant, and there was no longer anyone to tell me.

I wanted to feel useful, to work, and yet with my limited training as a technician in the chemical industries, my talents were sorely inadequate. The money I brought with me disappeared surprisingly fast. If I was to make my way, it would be in some other aspect than the work I knew. I felt crippled, like my hands had been shackled or cut off. I found small jobs to feed myself, first with a moving company, but I grew tired of the insults and the backaches. In the hostel's cafeteria and at the restaurant down the block, I cleaned tables and washed dishes. For a while, I found a measure of serenity in this sort of work. The simplicity allowed my mind to wander, but it soon felt aimless and dreary.

I started to write some poetry, even a few songs. I am my mother's son, after all. I think often about my mother. Sometimes I dream I could go back for her, to rescue her from the labour camps and bring her with me. They are the wishes of a naive child. In this universe, I know it to be impossible.

At least I have my papers, so maybe I can move on to somewhere else. I feel an increasing emptiness, a restlessness, as if my feet itch and the only way to scratch them is to walk.

One day, Lina, one of the girls at the centre, suggested I could use new clothes. Lina was blonde, with shiny eyes and very fine hair on her upper lip. She had small breasts, and her narrow waist begged to be held, and when she smiled at me, it brought tears to my eyes. I had to turn towards the washroom so that she would not notice them. Looking at myself there in the mirror, I saw that Lina was right. My clothes were shabby, shapeless and dull. One afternoon, Lina invited me to accompany her and her friend Steffi to the flea market. Steffi was looking for a camera, and I tagged along eagerly. Along the way, with their help, I found some clothes: shirts, pants, a leather jacket. Steffi held each one up to me while Lina looked on and decided if it fit. As she pulled the clothing against me, I turned red. The girls tittered and stared. I turned redder still. Finally, they turned away and allowed me to relax. I paid the old woman who ran the stall. She looked me over and shook her head, mouthing some obscenity which I didn't understand but made the girls laugh.

Lina commented, too loudly, "That lady must never have been young."

The old woman directed an obscenity at Lina. More giggles. This time, I laughed too.

On the way back, Lina and Steffi and I, their arms passed around mine, marched by a stand of musical instruments. A guitar attracted my eye. It was a little worn, but when I tried it, its sound was warm and smooth. Its strings looked in good condition.

"You play?" Lina asked.

"Yes."

I saw a glow in her eye, and while I was paying, I heard the two girls giggle again.

"Will you give us a concert tonight?" Lina shouted, and grabbed my hand.

"I don't play very well." More giggling.

That evening after supper, with nothing much else to do, I took the instrument down to the dining room. While I tuned my new guitar, Lina waved at me from the couch, where she was talking with Erika, a redheaded girl with freckles on her nose, quite pretty. Erika turned towards me, then whispered something in Lina's ear. Lina pushed her friend's shoulder, smiled, and returned to their conversation.

I began to practice quietly in a corner of the hall. I sang a few of my mother's songs. When I looked up from my guitar, I was surprised to see I had attracted a small audience. Lina and Erika were sitting in the front row.

Lina came up to me afterwards and asked if I would join them for a beer. The two girls talked and talked, and I mostly listened, until the conversation drifted to my origins. I learned that I had a certain notoriety in the centre. I was hesitant to talk but a beer or two made my tongue more mobile. The girls marvelled at my story about crossing the minefield into the West. They touched at their hair. They patted at my forearm or my shoulder.

Erika asked, "Where is your family?"

"I don't know."

"Are they dead?"

The stark question felt like a blow to my chest. I recoiled. "Yes. Maybe. Dead? I really don't know."

At this they seemed to melt. Lina smiled in sympathy, while sipping at her beer.

"I'm so sorry. I didn't mean to upset you," whispered Erika. A sadness darkened her face.

With her voice soft, Lina asked, "You're not sure about your parents' fates?"

"No, I'm not. I don't know what's become of them." I shuddered visibly, and Lina gripped my forearm reassuringly, but her questions continued.

"No idea?"

I was squirming now. I had to escape, and yet, I had to continue to answer, as if I was held by a spell. "My mother probably is dead. She may still be alive in a labour camp inside Russia."

Lina sighed. "Russia? I heard that you're from Poland."

"Yes, but I wasn't born there, I was born in the labour camp in Russia."

"Oh, my." She paused for a moment. "So how is it you're from Poland?"

"She was born Polish. I was separated from my mother when I was a boy and sent back to Poland, to my 'home'. To the orphanage. That's what makes me an orphan."

"I also heard that you're a Jew."

"Yes."

"So your mother was Jewish. We learned in school what our country did to your people during the war." I answered with silence. Lina stopped questioning me.

Erika smiled, trying to reassure me. "What about your father? Where is he?"

"My father may be alive."

"Where? Also in a labour camp?"

"Somewhere. Or dead. I can't know."

"What do you mean?"

"My parents are hidden from me. They reside in a box in my head. Until I can open that box, they are both dead and alive."

"So they might both be alive. You may not be an orphan at all, isn't this so?"

"If you put it that way. Yes, it may be so."

Lina started in again. She seemed eager to help me in some way. "Why don't you try to find out. Look for them."

"But if I find out, I may be condemning them both to death. As long as I don't know, they may yet be alive. I don't think if I have the heart to know the truth."

"If it was my mother, or my father, I would look. I would not stop until I knew for sure."

"Lina, you are only guessing at your thoughts. You can't know such things if you have not lived them."

"I do know. Maybe I'm braver than you, even though you crossed the barbed wire to get here."

"That was not bravery. It was a happenstance. I was never brave."

"I don't believe you. You are courageous. I know you will search."

"Where could I look?"

"Why don't you go to Israel? Maybe he's there. Or she."

"Not all Jews live in Israel, you know. The world is large."

"You must start by looking somewhere. And the world is small."

My father? How could I even begin to find him? My mother once told me he died during the war, and another time that he didn't. A Jew captured by the Germans would not survive for long. She might have invented this possibility of survival to make me feel better, as she might write a song plucked from the air. She was a smart woman, wily and strong. Always protecting me, and maybe in telling this lie, doing just that. And probably she was starved or frozen or beaten to death by now. There could truly be no one to find.

And yet, something stirred in me. It tugged at me to move forward, along the road that would carry me along to these distant spaces I have passed through in my thoughts.

18 Complications

Catherine's water had broken earlier than she had expected. It was a late Saturday evening and the two had fallen asleep while watching a rented film. She leaned over Simon, shaking him lightly to prepare him. The contractions had started and already were three minutes apart. Simon reacted quickly, pulling on his jacket and nervously searching the pockets for the car keys. Simon rushed the bag of things she had prepared for the hospital down to the car and came back up for Catherine. He found her in the shower.

"Hey, we've got to go! You're not going to deliver here or in the car!"

Catherine pushed her head out from behind the shower curtain. "*Vraiment*! I'm not going to the hospital with dirty hair, Simon. Now just go down and wait for me. I won't be long. Relax."

Simon fumed quietly. Catherine would not be rushed by anything he would say. He had to give her his advice anyway. "Just be careful not to fall in the shower."

"Do go downstairs, Simon. Just wait. I'll be right there."

That night, lightning flashed during a light summer rainstorm. Simon held her hand until she raged at him for causing all her agony and threw him out. Matthew was born after Catherine had screamed in pain for hours. She had at first insisted on a natural delivery, but after six hours finally asked for an epidural.

Simon was out in the waiting room through all this, smoking next to several other expectant dads. He called his parents, who arrived much faster than he expected.

"*Mazel tov*, my son," his mother uttered as she entered the room, waving her hand at the smoke. "So, soon I'll be a bubby. How is Catherine?"

"It's very painful. It's hard for her."

"Poor girl. Imagine when I had you and Adam. Talk about pain. Twins!"

"Yeah. Thanks for asking about her. Where's Ta?"

"Parking the car. The hospital parking is too expensive."

It wasn't long, though, before Duvid marched into the room and ran forward, grabbing Simon in a bear hug. "Wonderful. So, Simon, how does it feel to soon be a father?"

"I'm terrified."

"So you should be. Now you're a grown man. A *mensch*. You hold your son's life in your hands."

"If it's a boy we'll have to order for the *bris*. We'll have it at our house."

"Hannah, don't go so fast. The baby's not born yet."

"Ah, Duvid, you don't remember the *bris* for your two sons? That we had to prepare quickly."

"It was a different time, not like today. Simon, here, I brought two cigars, one for each of us. We'll celebrate after Catherine has finished giving birth."

"Do you know this is the most important moment of your life, Simon? The birth of your first child."

"I know, Ma. That's what scares me, but I feel, I don't know, filled with happiness."

"A blessing, Simon. A real blessing."

"Thanks, Ma. I'm going back in now."

"Come out to tell us when it's over. We'll wait here."

"It could be a long time."

"I won't smoke the cigars without you."

Matthew was born with neonatal jaundice. He had to remain in the hospital for a few days under bright lights, his eyes blindfolded, until his liver cleared.

Catherine blamed Simon for this, something to do with antibodies and blood types, which her doctors had explained and he remembered vaguely from a genetics course. He would ask Adam to elaborate later. Catherine's mother somehow heard of the birth from an aunt and came to see her grandson at the hospital.

"*Ah, bon, un petit fils pour moi. On aura un baptême bientôt.*"

"*Non, Maman.* No baptism."

That was that. Catherine refused any further discussion.

A few days later, Matthew was circumcised at the hospital. Simon had managed to find a doctor to perform the service according to Jewish law, as no *mohel* would perform such a ceremony. After all, Catherine wasn't Jewish, and so neither, according to Jewish custom, was Matthew. After the ceremony, the family and friends gathered at Simon's home. Simon's mother had ordered an enormous buffet, "big enough to feed a herd of elephants", his father muttered under his breath. His father drank a toast from a bottle of cognac that he had saved for years for just such an occasion. Simon was a little tipsy. He leaned heavily on the dining room table while he spoke to his cousin Sharon, who had driven into town from Ottawa to see his son welcomed into the tribe. She had been one of the women who turned away as the doctor made his cut. Catherine also had been unable to endure the sight, and the two had huddled in a far corner for the few moments that Matthew cried, before he was pacified by sucking on a small piece of linen soaked in sweet wine.

Catherine wasn't in view at first when the real party began. She was in the bedroom, suckling Matthew, and when she did arrive, she appeared disturbed and agitated, and soon excused herself again.

Sharon's husband Barry came over to talk to Simon after refilling his glass with wine. He had spent a number of minutes in intense discussion with Adam in one corner of the room. Adam had finally been rescued by his wife, Lyssa, after he had sent her some desperate glances, and she had deftly led him away to the kitchen.

"*Mazel tov*, Simon. Hot day. This wine really makes me sweat."

Sharon snapped at him. "Barry, I hope you're not going to get drunk today. You know I don't like driving on the highway."

"Don't worry, dear. This is the only glass I'm going to drink. Really. Hey, I think Ann is calling to you over there." Sharon turned, saw Ann, who wasn't waving, and slipped away in her direction. It didn't take much to separate the couple any more.

"Boy, women, I tell you. A guy can't even celebrate his favourite cousin's son's *bris*." He dropped the contents of his glass into his mouth and grabbed another glass full of wine off the table.

"Maybe Sharon's right, Barry. Maybe you should go a little easy."

"You're only saying that because now you have a son and are suddenly a responsible adult. I don't have any children, Simon. That's why I can still drink."

Simon sighed an *'oy veh'* to himself and shook his head a little. "How long have you two been married?"

"Ten years, Simon, and still no kids. My mother-in-law is going nuts, already."

"Yeah, I'll bet. So how are you and Sharon doing in Ottawa, Barry?"

"Can't complain. It's nice to be near to the seats of power. Sometimes its like the seats have come off, though, and we're looking at the underwear. Do you get it, seats...underwear? What the hell, drink up. Still lots of money being spent up there, even if the hospitals are such a mess here in the big city. Computer software is the best game of all to be in these days. There's still room for you to invest, if you want. The company's growing and you could make a bundle."

"No thanks, Barry. I'm not so good at taking risks, you know. Especially now, what with the baby and the house and the job market for journalists not being the steadiest in the world."

"Well, you'll regret it someday. You know that."

"Yeah, I know that."

"How's your dad, Simon?"

"Oh, he's okay, I guess. Always depressed, you know. He's had too much shit in his life."

"Does he ever talk to you about it?"

"He's mostly avoided that."

"I would be depressed too, if that had happened to me."

"I don't have many details, but my mother told me that whatever happened in Europe, they couldn't let the Germans win. They had to have children and live an ordinary life, like other people. That way, the Jews would have won."

"Nice sentiment. Was he in the concentration camps?"

"I'm not sure. Probably, but like I said, he didn't talk. Something happened in Israel that I sort of remember, though."

"What was it?"

"There was a war before we came to Canada. He came home silent. He didn't speak for months. Nothing. Just screamed at night. It was scary. And when he finally did talk, we left for Canada."

"So?"

"I don't know more than that."

"You know, I ran into this guy at the synagogue in Ottawa. Son of a guy who was in the Canadian army during the war. Really intense fellow. He was looking to do interviews with holocaust survivors, said he's writing a book about their experiences. I wondered if maybe your parents might want to speak to him. I was talking to Adam about it, but he was completely against me giving this man your parents' names. What do you think, Simon?"

"Look, Barry, I know you want to do the right thing, but this isn't it. I only know some my parents' stories, but I've interviewed others. I'm really careful about how I ask; these people are very fragile. Someone like that friend of yours could push them right over the edge. Look at my father. Do you know how many pills he has to take every day just to keep on going, and how little sleep he gets in a night? No, no way, Barry. Your friend is going to have to find other fish."

"Fish. Sure. You just told me you've done this questioning yourself. Sounds to me like you want exclusive rights, no competition. You're an astute fisherman yourself."

"Fuck you, Barry. If he wants interviews, how many hundreds of thousands of people are there that he can question? He doesn't need everyone that's still alive."

"Well, he says he does. The survivors are dying off already; in a few years there won't be anyone left to interview. He says this is a debt people have to history, to the truth."

"Truth. Sure. Shit, Barry, the answer is still no."

Barry slunk away to bother someone else, and Simon continued to circulate. The phone rang. One of Catherine's sisters answered and waved to get his attention. He held the receiver against his ear, shielding the other against the din of a few dozen people talking all at once.

"Simon, hi! I just got into town. I heard you had a son. Mazel tov." It was Rachel. She was living in New York. How had she gotten the news, he wondered?

"Read it in the Births Announcements in the Montreal Star. I get the paper mailed to me. I'm in Montreal. I'm hopping in a cab in a minute. I just want to be sure that I've got the right address."

He confirmed the address and hung up. He hadn't seen his old roomie for some years. He wondered what outrages she was getting into now.

The party was beginning to wind down by the time the cab dropped Rachel at the door. Adam's wife, Lyssa, who had never met Rachel before, answered and led her to Simon. He turned red as Rachel fell on him and gave him a slobbery kiss. Lyssa stared.

Rachel looked around her and admired the house. "Hmm, nice place. You have good taste, Simon. But no, it must be Catherine's. I know what your taste is like: yard sale eclectic." Rachel paused for a moment. "Pleased to meet you, Catherine." she said, "You look so good, considering you gave birth only eight days ago. I'm Rachel, Simon's erstwhile roommate."

"Rachel, this is actually Lyssa, Adam's wife. Catherine isn't feeling well. She went to lie down for bit. They don't call it labour for nothing."

"Oh, I'm sorry, I hope she feels better soon. You know, Lyssa, I don't know anything about giving birth, and I don't intend to know any time soon."

While Rachel awkwardly tried to pull out of her several blunders, Simon wandered away to get her something to drink.

"Lyssa. Sorry about the mistake. I should have known better."

"That's okay, it was a natural conclusion to jump to."

"So I finally meet Adam's wife."

"Yes, that's right. Do you know him, too?"

"Of course I do. I knew both brothers when we were young, and Adam dropped by often at our communal pad while they were in school."

"Oh, did he?"

"Yes, but don't worry. We were just friends. Anyway, I haven't seen him for years. Not since I moved to New York."

"New York must be an interesting place to live."

"Interesting is hardly the word, Lyssa. It's fascinating, vibrant, exciting, and invigorating. And crazy and irritating. And that's just scratching its edges, really."

"What do you do there?"

"I'm a freelance photographer."

"Oh, I should have known with that fancy-looking camera over your shoulder. Everyone else has one of those little ones that cost twelve dollars. And that's Canadian funds."

"I never go anywhere without it. You never know what might go down."

"My, you do sound so American."

"The doctor's life must be exciting for both of you."

"Not so exciting for me, really. Adam spends almost every minute at the hospital, except when he's sleeping, and even some of that time. He's just finishing his specialty training."

"So he still keeps those wild hours?"

"Yes. I stay home with our daughter."

"You have a little girl?" She cooed.

"Yes, that's right. Her name is Lara. She's one year old now."

"Lara. After *Dr. Zhivago*?"

"No, not really. Just like that."

"Oh, my. One year old. So you've been married how long?"

"Well, we aren't officially married yet. We plan to have the ceremony once Adam finishes his training and finds a position somewhere."

"Oh. How adventurously romantic. I wouldn't have thought Adam was that kind of guy."

"What kind is that?"

"Oh, when I knew Adam, he seemed boringly staid, really. I always thought he was the straight man extraordinaire."

Simon chose just that moment to reappear with Rachel's drink. Rachel looked relieved, as if she was hoping this would extricate her from another mess she was about to dig herself into.

"Thanks, Simon."

"Sorry, I got delayed a bit. I just popped upstairs to check on her. She's resting. She's really very tired."

"Rachel and I were just discussing history."

"Oh? What era?"

"Recent history. Like when Adam and I first met."

"Oh, yeah. Well, let's see, isn't it almost four years for you two?"

"Three."

"Rachel, I feel like I know you already. Adam's mentioned you a lot. Don't worry, nothing too scandalous."

"That's a relief."

"Or if it was, he's not telling. Simon, I'm going to check on Lara. I left her upstairs asleep. Maybe Adam and I will get going soon."

"I haven't had a chance to see Adam yet."

"Rachel, Adam's on call. We really do have to go."

Lyssa shifted away from them and cut through what was still a throng of people.

"Wow! I wonder what Adam told her! She looked a little iffy about me, don't you think?"

"Yeah, but that's you being yourself, Rachel."

"Well, maybe I do come on a little strong. It's the New York in me."

"I'm sure that explains it."

"Simon, I didn't want to ask while Lyssa was there, but I can't help myself. What's with the *bris*? You were never religious. And Catherine, did she convert?"

Simon was watching Lyssa as she slid through a doorway into an adjoining room. A moment later she was dragging Adam after her up the stairs to the bedrooms.

"Young lady, this is not your business. It's Rachel, if I'm not mistaken." It was Hannah, who had just come up behind Simon to greet his visitor. Calling out to one of the other guests, she walked off, but not before whispering something in Simon's ear. He turned red.

"God, Simon, I'm always getting myself into trouble whenever I open my mouth."

"Seems to be one of your God-given talents, Rachel."

"Well, at least I know when it's time to retreat. I'm going to go. Here, I brought you this for the baby." Rachel drew a small package out of her bag.

"That's sweet of you. Thanks for dropping by. It really is a surprise. Too bad you didn't get to see Adam."

"Yeah, too bad. Anyway, if you're in New York, drop by. Don't lose touch. I can't afford to lose too many more friends." She gave him a peck on the cheek.

"Two pecks, Rachel. This is Montreal, remember?"

"Well, from this New Yorker, you'll have to settle for that. And, hey, you're a married man. Bye."

"Okay, Rachel, take care."

With that, Simon turned away to mind the rest of his guests. Once again, Rachel's presence had him feeling as if no time at all had passed. He still felt an unnameable attraction, the one he dared not show. He hoped he was pulling that off.

He noticed his cousin Barry was downing another glass off in the corner next to a large plant and veered to avoid him. Rachel was letting herself out the front door, while Lyssa and Adam, carrying Lara, were picking their way past couples jabbering on the stairs. Adam didn't seem to have noticed anything. He was too busy checking his pager. His jaw was busily chewing gum.

The phone rang. Simon picked up the receiver.

"Simon, it's me, Rachel."

"Oh, hi! It's been a few months now. How are you? What's up?"

"Simon, the reason I'm calling is that I'm going to be in Montreal for a photo show and I thought I might drop by."

"Catherine's right here. I'll ask her."

"Yes, maybe you'd better."

"Hey, Catherine, this old college friend is coming to town and wants to drop by. Is that okay?"

"Simon, you know very well I don't interfere between you and your friends."

Simon turned back to the phone. "Catherine is fine with that. Hey, why don't you stay with us? It'll save you a hotel bill and we'll be able to catch up a little better on old times. We didn't get much of a chance at my son's party."

"Are you sure Catherine won't mind?"

Catherine's eyes had gone wide at Simon's suggestion. She didn't like surprise visitors but wanted to please. A fleeting frown visited her face, but engrossed, Simon didn't notice. When he turned back towards her with a quizzical look on his face and a thumbs up, she nodded. Not vigorously, but she did nod. That was enough for Simon.

"It's my old friend Rachel." Catherine's eyes opened even wider at this news. Simon turned back to the phone.

"It'll give you a chance to see Matthew. He's seven months old now. He's sitting up and smiling and everything. Catherine remembers you from college, but only from meeting you in the dark. She wants to get to know you better."

Catherine placed her index finger upright in front of her lips and made a shushing noise, but Simon waved a hand at her dismissively.

"That's wonderful. Thanks."

"So when will we see you?"

"Next Friday. I'll be in for the weekend. Thanks so much."

"Not at all. I insist."

"Does Catherine also insist?"

"Sure she does." Catherine glared at him.

"That's really nice of you, Simon. I'd love that. I don't get the homebody thing much any more."

"Okay. See you then."

"Bye, Simon." Simon hung up.

"That was a sneaky thing to do. You didn't qualify the 'old friend' as a woman, did you?"

"Oh, don't get all tiffy. You'll love Rachel."

"Like you said, we've met. The girl in the towel."

"That's all you know about her. The girl in the towel. A comprehensive character study. Write 500 words."

"Oh, fiddle, Simon."

She's not like what you think. You really will like her."

"Like you do?"

"Relax, okay? She's just an old friend."

"Let's hope that's all she is. For your sake."

"And for yours too."

"What does that mean?"

"It means that you're more concerned than it's worth."

"You think I'm exaggerating?"

"Yes, you are."

Catherine stood in front of the sideboard. Two Sabbath candles in the *menorah* waited to be kindled. She lit a match, passed its fiery head across the wicks and their warm light bathed her face. Catherine lifted her hands to cover her face and recited the prayer.

"What are you doing?" Rachel's questioning voice rattled her.

"It's Sabbath."

"And?"

"I'm doing this for my family. You're supposed to light candles for the Sabbath. You know that."

"My mother never did. I never did."

"It's the Jewish thing to do."

"Are you Jewish?"

"I haven't converted, no. Not yet."

"So you're not Jewish. Why are you doing this? Did Simon ever say he required that you do this?"

"Well, no."

"You said you're doing this for him. What gives?"

"It's a tradition."

"Yours?"

"No." Catherine paused before she reacted. "I want to be polite because you're a guest in our home, but this is not your business. Do I have to remind you that I didn't invite you, Simon did? Why don't you just go to some hotel instead of annoying me like this?"

"I apologize. I do have a big mouth sometimes. I thought you had invited me too, or I wouldn't have come."

Simon chose that moment to come home. "Hi, ladies. What's for supper, Cath? Why all quiet, you two? Hey, is something happening?"

"Rachel is going to a hotel, Simon. She's not comfortable in our home."

"Why?"

"Simon, I really think it's better if I stay somewhere else. I can afford it and I won't interfere in your lives that way."

"Hey, Rachel. No. I was looking forward to talking over old times. Cathy has always been interested in sitting down and chatting with my old friends. Isn't that right, Catherine? Besides, you brought that bottle of expensive wine and I'm looking forward to tasting it. Catherine, tell her you want her to stay."

"Yes, of course I do." Catherine turned away, beet red. "We'll talk later over supper. I hear Matthew whimpering. I'll go feed him."

Still turned away, she mumbled on. "I'm sorry, Rachel. Stay. It's Sabbath. Please accept the hospitality of our home. Simon, I'm going to get Matthew in his crib. I'll serve supper in about a half hour, after I've finished feeding him. Maybe you two could set the table?"

After Catherine had disappeared up the stairs, Rachel muttered to Simon, "What did you do to that poor woman, Simon? She sounds more Jewish than your mother. And that's saying a lot."

"I don't know what's going on between you two, but if I were you, I'd tone down the liberated New York valkyrie role. It's not working here."

"There I go putting my tongue in the wrong gear again. Sorry. You know how I am sometime, Simon. Look, I can do this job of setting the table myself. Why don't you go relax?"

"I'll go take a shower. It's been a long day. Long week. See you at supper."

Rachel looked over at the Sabbath candles and sighed. It was going to be a tough weekend for her. She put her tongue in her cheek and pretended to bite through it.

Once finished setting the cutlery down on the place mats, Rachel had the urge to pee very badly. Soon standing outside the locked bathroom door, she could hear the shower running. It only served to make her more desperate to get in. After a few more minutes of this, necessity overcame delicacy, and she tapped lightly but desperately on the door. She hoped she would be heard.

The bathroom door opened a crack. Simon's head poked out, wrapped tightly in the shower curtain. He asked what she wanted.

She kept her voice down. "If you must know, I have to pee. How long are you going to be in there? Your skin is going to melt off."

Simon had water dripping from his nose and chin. He had difficulty keeping his eyes open. His reflex was to close the door on her, but her need was so pathetic. For a half-second he debated whether he should be letting her in. Catherine would be outraged if she found out. But then again, she might be equally angry if she found urine stains on the hall rug. He relented.

"Where's Catherine?" he asked nervously.

"In the kitchen. Feeding Matthew."

"Okay, Rachel. I'll let you in, but just don't flush the toilet when you're finished, okay?"

Rachel nodded tentatively. Simon was pulling his wet head back behind the shower curtain.

"I promise I won't look. All right?"

"Do you think I care, Simon? I'm more worried about your wife walking in on us."

"Just do it and get out." Simon's head disappeared back into the shower's stream of water drops. The room was full of steam, the mirror covered with a dense mist divided by the courses of the few single drops that had coalesced and slid down its face. Rachel hesitantly slipped down her shorts and underwear and sat down on the toilet. The pee burst out of her. It was such a relief. She had been afraid that she wouldn't be able to hold herself in much longer.

"I really needed that," she yelled out over the sound of the torrent on the other side of the curtain.

"Don't yell, Rachel. Catherine might hear you. "

"Oops, sorry. I wouldn't want you to get into trouble over little old me."

"Just cut the cutes and try to get out of here, okay?"

"Okay."

Finished, Rachel rose. Without thinking, she pressed down on the handle of the toilet as she stood up. As the bowl filled with a rush of swirling water and slurped to empty, there was a muffled scream from behind the shower curtain, and she realized her mistake. But it was too late.

Simon bellowed loudly as the hot water hit him and he scrambled wildly to get out of its way. In less than a second, he landed on the bathroom floor, facing Rachel. He was dripping wet, water flowing down his sides into puddles on the bathroom floor. Rachel was partially bent forward, one hand still on the toilet handle, her panties held by her other hand. She had raised them to just below her knees when Simon exited the shower in a frenzy. In her distress, she let them fall back around her ankles.

Both froze. Simon wanted to retreat back behind the shower curtain, but the water would still be too hot—the toilet bowl was always slow to fill. So he reached for the only towel, which hung on the towel bar just behind Rachel. She grabbed for the towel too, giggling nervously.

A tug of war followed. One end of the towel slipped over Simon, the other over Rachel. The middle stayed on the towel bar. The tension they both applied bounced their bodies toward each other and they touched before either could react. They were flustered. That's when they heard Catherine calling to Simon from the hallway.

"Are you in the shower, Simon? My breast milk leaked and I need the spray cleaner. Is the door open? Hurry up. I can't leave Matthew by himself."

While Catherine turned the door handle, not waiting for an answer, Rachel and Simon were already in the shower. Rachel had managed to drag her dropped shorts and panties with her as she hobbled in. They tried to half face away from each other. Rachel's tee shirt was quickly dripping wet. Her foot landed squarely on a soap patch. To keep from slipping, she grabbed Simon's arm. Despite the rush of water across her face, she kept her eyes open, pleading silently with him not to let her fall.

"Did you find it?" Simon called out.

"Yes, I did. You know, Simon, you should lock this door when you're in here. Your visitor would be really embarrassed if she came in and found you drying yourself. Or maybe not."

"You're right. Sorry," he called out above the hiss of the shower. Rachel was now trying to turn her face out of the stream of water without looking directly at him.

"What's this mess of water on the floor?"

"I had to pee."

"Next time just pee in the shower. That's what I do. Okay, see you in a little while. I'm going back to the kitchen. Supper is almost ready. You'd better clean up in here when you get out. After that, find your bitchy little friend and tell her to come down to dinner."

"I will, dear. Do try to be civil, will you?"

Rachel giggled despite herself but her laughter was blessedly muffled by the white noise of the shower.

"Did you say something, Simon?"

"Yeah, I said: 'yes, dear'."

"Don't you 'yes, dear' me, you dick."

Catherine left the bathroom, and closed the door behind her. Simon quickly reached out and slid the door latch shut. "Good boy!" Catherine called out to him as she walked away.

Rachel shivered. Simon's skin was becoming goose-bumped too. The warm water had just run out.

Catherine rose during the night. She wasn't sure what it was that woke her—Matthew might have cried out momentarily, or it may have been the cracking sound of the floorboards shifting as the house settled with the night's cooling. Whatever it was, her eyes opened to darkness. She was thirsty. Simon lay snoring next to her. For a moment, the cruel thought that she should wake him up so he could get her a cold drink tinkled in her head, but her sensible self rejected it, despite the anger she felt about the intruder sleeping in their house.

Had Matthew been crying, she would have roused Simon by now to take care of him. That was the agreement between them. She was the active parent by day and he was on duty by night. She glided her fingers gently across her husband's forehead and smiled. He was just too easy a guy. He couldn't bring himself to say no. There was a good and a bad side to that trait, but for this brief moment, the good aspects of it prevailed in her mind. She eased herself out of bed and slipped on a silky robe. It wouldn't do to be in a state of undress and come across Rachel on the stairs. Hopefully, her putative rival wouldn't be sporting a towel and nothing else. Catherine sighed. Her home felt like it was in a state of invasion since Rachel had walked in.

The house was cool and very quiet. Catherine opened the bedroom door and stepped out into the silence of the hallway. She peeked into Matthew's room as she passed it, assuring herself that her son was still breathing, still alive and healthy. The carpet under her bare feet was heartening in its softness. The darkness slid around her frame, warm and fragrant.

The stairs to the downstairs hall responded to her footfalls with small groans and cracks. She had been after Simon to fix these noises but he had demurred, claiming that he would have to replace each individual stair for this to work. It wasn't normal for the stairs to crack, she had told him, not even in a house this old, but he hadn't considered her argument solid. Anyway, he said, what's the big deal? No one can hear the noise but you. To hell with him, she sighed deeply.

Catherine pulled a glass out of the kitchen cupboard and leaned into the open refrigerator. As she turned, the fridge light showed she wasn't alone. Rachel sat at the table, holding a half-full glass. Wearing a towel. Catherine dropped her glass, startled. It shattered in the sink. Rachel gasped.

Catherine felt she had to get out of the space she owned, her kitchen, pushed out by this invader who was usurping her space and also, she was sure, her man. She rushed back to the bedroom, leaving the door open so that it would be very visible to Rachel as she passed. The couple were a unit, impregnable. She clicked on the light switch in their *en suite* bathroom and left the door of the bathroom open so that their bed was bathed in a dim but unmistakably expressive light. She dropped her robe and slipped into bed, berthing herself against Simon's body, lifting the blanket away from him and slipping her fingers over his groin. He was hers, only hers.

And there she lay, her eyes shut, until she heard Rachel's muffled footsteps pad closer, stop, and a sharp intake of breath. Catherine opened one eye and saw Rachel's silhouette framed by the doorway. Catherine, by now exhausted, couldn't maintain her vigil long. Sleep's cloud was darkening over her.

Numbness stretched and squeezed the passing moments. Rachel must have gone by now. Catherine released Simon. He moaned and turned toward her in his sleep. One hand fell heavily on her breast. She pushed it back across his chest and down so he touched himself. He moaned again and began to move rhythmically. Catherine turned away, drifting deeper. Simon rotated towards her. As sleep blurred her, she heard Simon's rumbled gasp as he came against her buttocks. A feeling of disgust melted thickly into dream and her jealousies disappeared until morning.

Rachel padded back to her room and shut the door firmly.

When Catherine woke up to feed Matthew, Rachel had gone. Simon was press-ganged into cleaning up the broken glass.

Catherine told him that Rachel had caused it, not really so far off the mark.

With the Rachel incident becoming more remote, life settled into its dually arduous and dull routine. The baby needed her, day and night. Catherine was exhausted. Simon helped, a little, during the nights, but it could never be enough.

Catherine kept delaying getting back to work. Anxious and guilt-ridden, she was reluctant to leave Matthew in the care of a stranger. She used words like 'abandon' and 'desert' when she talked about it. Simon told her she was being needlessly melodramatic. She, feeling herself belittled and patronized, accused him of being fully capable of abandoning and deserting them. She became moodier and more melancholic by the day. The couple's sex life deteriorated. During these long monotonous days, Catherine was overwhelmed by being stuck at home, constantly enslaved to the needs of a young child, away from any friends she still had, in this unfamiliar neighbourhood they had moved to, and of having given birth to this chimeric child, neither English nor French, neither Catholic nor Jewish, neither here nor there.

Simon spent more of his time at work, plunging into his projects. His articles were getting some recognition. At home he was met with a wall of cold, and especially so in bed. His wife blamed it on her hormones. He couldn't fathom what was happening. He was away too much for that to be possible. Now his latest assignments meant more travel too, often to New York City. Catherine was suspicious that there was another woman. Likely it would be Rachel.

Their son Matthew was now ten months old. When he arrived home from work, Simon often found Catherine sipping a glass of wine in the kitchen, while Matthew, in the grip of a colic attack, cried in his crib. On these occasions he carried his son out to the car and drove him around for an hour or two before he calmed and dropped into sleep. He would eat while Catherine bathed in the whirlpool bath she had asked for to soothe her back, which hurt from lifting and carrying Matthew all day.

"My mother said it would be like this."

"What would?"

"My life would be a mess."

"A mess? You're not happy being a mother?"

"It's being the mixed-up *mère d'un enfant mélangé*. She told me that's what would happen if I married a Jew."

"Your mother has always interfered."

"Don't go saying things like that about my mother. Your parents aren't so wonderful, either."

"What is all this about, for God's sake?"

"Look Simon, let's stop fooling ourselves. Your parents have never accepted me. I should ignore them, too?"

"Catherine, maybe it's time you got away a bit. Or went back to work. And found someone to look after Matthew during the day."

Simon regarded her in silence, not knowing what to say next. He realized his parents weren't making the marriage easier by their constant niggling to him about Catherine not being Jewish.

"Why can't she convert? Rabbi Gorensky will do it. It'll only take a year. Easy."

Too much of a goy for their kosher boy. His parents were driving him nuts. Couldn't he talk her into converting? Simon had argued to his parents that they had tried, tried hard, but been too discouraged by the rabbi to continue. It was his job, the man had told them, to make sure that conversion was taken seriously. It couldn't be made too easy.

"But it is easy," insisted Hannah.

"You learnt when you were a child. You didn't know anything else. Of course it was easy for you, Ma."

"It was not easy for me. Learning to be a Jew is easy, but being a Jew never is."

"Sure, Ma."

It was more than Simon could deal with. He didn't know how to help Catherine out. He didn't know enough about being Jewish himself to know where to begin.

19 Gravity

Simon glared up at the large letters of the Children's Hospital sign above its front door, afraid to go in. Simon shook his head, trying to negate what Catherine had told him over the phone. Simon's son was deathly ill.

Catherine's voice had been alarming when she called, shrill, spoken through fixed teeth. Beyond the usual edginess of her voice, it was a mix of cloudy exhaustion and the sharp, cold edge of fear. Their son Matthew, only three, had just been admitted by the hospital's emergency staff. Arriving later, Simon was confused and terrified. What could have happened to his son? How was this possible? Simon tried not to run, not to scurry about like a rat discovered. He asked at the information desk where his son was. He was directed pleasantly down to the left to the Emergency Department.

Catherine filled him in once he arrived bedside. She had found Matthew lying unresponsive in his room on the floor, drool and vomit streaking the path he had taken out of bed. It was lucky that Duvid and Hannah had been visiting. Duvid had driven the car through any number of stop signs and red lights to the hospital. If his car could have flown, it wouldn't have arrived any faster.

While Catherine blamed Simon, he sipped absentmindedly at a can of Coke she had left next to the bed. Had he checked on Matt during the night when she was out for her once-a-week art class and visiting her sisters? He was so irresponsible. Was he so absolutely sure he had had no fever, that his behaviour was not just a little odd? Was Matthew unusually lethargic, or excited, or distracted? Simon should have been home more–why was he always away on assignments, always bringing trouble home with him, why, in heaven's name couldn't he have a different job closer to home, regular, unfettered by unusual hours and intrusive obligations.

He should have known–couldn't he see it with his eyes, was his mind always obscured by thinking of other places, other people, maybe even, even, yes, other women. He should have brought Matthew for his medical exams on schedule–or did he even know when that should be, what vaccinations were due, or that he had that cold from being at the nursery school that Catherine had tried so hard to save her son from by staying home, and being a good mother by simply being there? On and on. Simon stood there, shoulders hunched, soda can in hand, straw gurgling. What was happening? There or not, it was his fault. Catherine's logic was impervious to anything that he might say.

He didn't have the psychic will to argue it with her. He gave in silently. He wondered why he had stayed with her so long, although he knew the answer. It had begun with the ties that held them together, the marriage, the shared objects, the house, their child, the many difficult times that complicated their shared simplicity. Each difficult time produced clash and argument, recrimination and guilt. She suspected him of some crime, but his only crime was fantasy. He convinced himself that their shared history was strong enough to overcome his doubts.

A short time after Matthew was admitted to a room on the neurology ward, a lumbar puncture was done to test for bleeding into the brain, and following that, he was heavily sedated for a CT scan of his skull. Simon stayed with Matthew through the whole unpleasant procedure. Catherine had left for a few moments of respite and a bowl of soup. He angrily wondered aloud why the puncture wasn't scheduled after the scan, while the sedation was still in effect, but the resident just shrugged his shoulders. There was no need for local anaesthesia, he insisted, since young children of Matthew's age were unable to feel pain the same as an adult did. Their nervous system was too immature. Such a stupid man. Simon knew better and insisted. The resident complied grudgingly. He was inexperienced. The needle bent during several tries in which he continued to hit bone. The anaesthesia was a failure. Matthew screamed through it all. Such a stupid and incompetent man.

Jarred by the time the procedure was over, Simon accompanied his sleeping son back to his ward. A debilitated child lay in the bed next to Matthew's. The child's weak sounds and flailing limbs disturbed Simon, and he had to retreat from the room. He needed a cigarette. As the orderly who had brought the bed left the hospital room, Catherine's mother arrived. She had brought along a Catholic priest. He stood there garbed in black, a benign smile on his face, out of place among all the dour men walking past him wearing their white coats. Catherine's mother had in her hand a small plastic container filled with water. Matthew moaned in the room while Simon held the two back.

"Edythe, what are you doing here? Matt's had enough today without this barbaric nonsense. Let him sleep."

"It's holy water, Simon. Where's your respect? This is a good father of the Holy Church."

"Look, get out of here. Take that water away."

"Heresy! You may be an unbeliever, Simon, but don't get in the way of what will heal your son."

The priest looked uneasy. Simon protested that his son was Jewish, that the priest had no jurisdiction over his soul, but Edythe repelled his arguments.

"According to what Catherine tells me, he is not a true Jew. So what you say is nonsense. This priest can only do him good."

Simon's face told the whole of his feelings. At that moment, Catherine arrived and greeted her mother with a kiss on the cheek. Putting her arm around her mother's shoulder, she ferried her and the priest past Simon's protests into the room. She gave a half-smile to Simon. Simon glared back. He stayed outside. The priest carried out the duties Catherine's mother had asked him there to perform.

Simon half-listened through the closed door to his son's frail whimpers and the mutter of soft prayers being said. Simon, repelled, fled the scene. When he came back later, his mother-in-law and the priest were both gone. Catherine sat reclined in an armchair next to his son's bed, her head propped against a pillow, asleep. Matthew was still unconscious and moaning. On the window sill was the plastic container, now half-empty. Next to it lay a tiny gold crucifix fixed to a fine chain. Simon lifted the chain into the light streaming in through the window. It glinted, dangling back and forth. He blinked at it, uneasy. He had the odd feeling of staring through a narrow window into another space. Simon took the plastic jar, sniffed it, and emptied its contents into the washroom sink, before returning to his son's side.

Something had changed. The little boy looked at peace now, sleeping quietly at last. His chest rose and fell, rose and fell. His neck seemed so very fragile. Simon started when he heard Catherine shift in her chair. He quickly replaced the cross on the window sill and slipped out of the room.

An hour later, Simon's parents arrived. They commiserated with him in the hallway, in deference to the sleeping mother and son. He held the door open so they could peek into the room.

"Simon, he looks like he doesn't eat. I can see his bones through the skin. Maybe you would want I should bring him something later?"

"No, Ma. It's okay. He has an intravenous, and he can't eat until he wakes up. The doctors don't know when that's going to happen."

"Did you maybe think to ask your brother Adam to look at him?"

"Ta, Adam is working in the emergency room at the Jewish. He really doesn't have time to come over here. And besides, this isn't his area of expertise."

"Simon, all these great doctors in this specialized ward, do they have even a small clue so far? Could it hurt for you for once to ask a little favour of your brother?"

"Listen, it's okay. The doctors here will take care of him."

He wished that he really believed that. He wished his brother could arrive in a cloud of smoke and make the diagnosis and pronounce the miraculous cure. Simon turned his head slightly to follow the figure of a pretty nurse passing by quickly, behind his parents. His mother noticed.

"You take care, Simon. You take care."

"Yeah, Ma." Despite himself, he was so horny. All the stress he had been under since this all happened seemed to make it worse.

For the two weeks that followed, Simon and Catherine took turns sleeping in a cot next to Matthew's bed at the hospital, taking the car home by turns. After a few days, the boy had regained consciousness. Matthew's head was bundled in bandages, enveloping tens of thin electrodes glued to his partly shaved scalp. He was kept awake to test his brain waves, then allowed to sleep to accomplish the same goal. By day, when Catherine was there, the neurologists tried to decide what had gone wrong. Nurses walked in and out of his room throughout the night. The clattering of stainless steel instruments and glass containers and the light of the flashlights used to check on his son's condition unsettled even more Simon's already disturbed sleep.

He finally gave up trying to sleep and got up. He had expected to spend the night in the cot next to his young son but he felt suffocated. He needed a change of air. In his sleeping son, breathing softly in the cot, he saw the nocturnal darkness of his own youth, the real chasm he now walked through. It was truly the valley of the shadow.

Simon dressed and paced through the wards. After an hour watching soundless television talk shows in the lounge attached to his son's ward, he wandered down into the cafeteria for a cup of dispensing machine hot chocolate.

One of his son's nurses walked behind him, carrying a cup of coffee to the next table. He heard her before he saw her. He felt the tug of her gravity pulling lightly on the skin of his neck as she passed and sat at a nearby table. She saw him as he turned towards her and waved him over with a half-smile. She mentioned his son. Fumbling for words, he thanked her for her concern and found the courage to sit down.

"I'm just being a human being."

"Thanks, human being."

She smiled at that. "My name is Patricia. Patty."

"Simon."

"I know."

"I really don't know what's happening to my son. Just tests and more tests. Nobody tells me anything. Even my brother, the important doctor, doesn't duck in. Thank you for looking after him."

"You'll see, it's mostly over with. Your boy seems to be getting better. He ate very well today. Especially that chocolate bar you smuggled in. Oh, good, I see you're able to smile. He's in the best hands, you know. You're very worried, I know. It'll work out. It will."

"When I was a boy, my father saved my life. My brother and I were wading across a small river in the country and we were pulled away downstream. It was lucky my father was there that day—he usually worked in the city. Jumped in, just like that, and saved us. I can't be like my father. I can't save my son."

"It's not the same sort of situation."

"I know, I know, but deep inside, my soul tells me I should be able to. It doesn't make sense, but who ever said the heart made sense?" Simon stared off into space, quiet now.

"I told you, it'll be fine. In a little while, you'll be playing ball with him again. Have faith."

"Thanks for saying that." He cracked another small smile in response to her encouragement.

Faith! The sound of the word exasperated him. He patted his sides looking for his cigarette pack. He was about to place one in his mouth, but she stopped him. She grabbed it, and held the index finger of one hand lightly against his lips. He found her soft touch enticing. He had the urge to taste her finger with his tongue.

"You shouldn't smoke in here. Even if it's still allowed, it soon won't be. This is a hospital, remember. Come."

He had known that. She rose and took him by the elbow. She was so terribly attractive, gliding slowly next to him, shifting and turning, hot and cold. She ignited his breath. She turned his skin to fire when her fingers touched softly behind his elbow. He felt the rising damp heat in his crotch, the fluttering of his heartbeat. She tugged lightly on his wrist to point the way to the hospital entrance. There, he reached into his pack again, this time offering her one. She shrugged it away and her laughter tinkled gently, a bell in the shapeless darkness. He lit his own and took a long drag before exhaling.

Patty told him it was the end of her shift in a few minutes, and asked if he wanted to tag along as she walked to her lodgings nearby. It was late and dark. She would value the feeling of protection, she said. Simon said he couldn't. He had to get back to his son's room.

"Too bad," she breathed, as he turned away.

He felt both frightened and vaguely guilty. He sensed that another woman wouldn't help him. He wasn't really sure what it was that would. Still, he found it hard not to think about her later as he lay sleepless on the cot at his son's bedside. She hovered just behind the curtain that was his visible world, undulating back and forth, flying in an elliptical orbit.

Meteors consort with the Earth, their fire brightening the night sky as they disintegrate. They burn through the air; they scorch the ground. Comets approach the sun, their gaseous ices and stony cores copulating, their glowing tails serving as the punctuation marks of history. Even the distant galaxies, their enormities invisible to the unaided eye, hover in the blackest void, before colliding, displaying their sexual yearnings, passing back and forth through each other in billion-year oscillations, certain of their slow desires. Gravitational fields drive the thrusting of this cosmic intercourse.

Simon had his own limited gravity. He could accept the orbit of another body, and himself orbit as the satellite of another. His free-falls, though, couldn't accommodate the loops and ellipses, the small tugs and orbital distortions, that pulled at him from so many different directions, from the satellites, the many moons, that swung wildly and desperately around his life. Their attractive forces disrupted him.

Now he was again swinging closer to the sun. Staring at the dark ceiling, he became increasingly agitated. He at last decided he couldn't sleep at all. He would walk home, a good hour away. Matthew would be all right by himself, with all his nurses and doctors hovering a breath's duration away, with all these machines with their wiggly lines, sweetly blipping away. He was stable. Nothing was happening and there was nothing that Simon was capable of doing for him.

Simon dressed, and started walking home. He would drive Catherine here for her bedside shift in the morning. To blow off steam, he turned his long walk into a run in the park close to his house. He jogged for over an hour, until he was exhausted. His mind was a frenzy of thoughts. The police, on a routine drive through the park, came upon him as he was doing a last slow lap, cooling down. A short blast of the siren brought him to a halt and he turned to stare into the bright headlights of the police car. The car door opened and a burly cop dangling a night stick climbed out.

"What are you doing here? The park is closed."

"Nothing. Running." Simon had one hand up shielding his eyes.

"Running? From what?"

"Nothing. Just running."

"People around here are afraid of thieves."

"I'm not a thief. I'm not doing anything to scare anyone."

The policeman pulled out his ticket book. "Do you have some ID?"

"I didn't do anything wrong. What is this about?"

"Maybe you'd like to come down to the station with us?"

"You mean I'm being arrested? For what?"

"ID. Please."

"Look, why aren't you going after real criminals instead of a guy jogging in the park? That's what we pay you for."

"Okay, so no ID. Come with me."

"Wait a minute, I do have ID. Here."

"This is a parking pass. Where's the rest?"

"I left it in my car."

"Which is where?"

"At home."

"Okay, keep walking to the squad car."

Simon, in his adrenalin-induced state of agitation, pushed the cop, and ran deeper into the park. The police car's siren sounded again and they came after him. A half hour later he was sitting on a bench at the station, waiting to be processed. His back hurt where the truncheon had hit and brought him down. Simon stared at a pair of handcuffs on his wrists.

The officer at the desk had allowed him to call Catherine, who, unamused, came down to the station to pick him up. She explained about their son. Simon was allowed home in his wife's care and a warning to stay away from the park. Whatever his story was, Catherine didn't want to hear it. He set up a bed on the couch, wondering if he was an idiot to have walked away from Patty the nurse.

The next morning, at six, the phone rang. He was pulled awake by Catherine. They had to get back to the hospital. Matthew had had a convulsion early that morning and had deteriorated after it. Simon dressed on his way to the door.

When they arrived at Matthew's floor, one of Matthew's doctors was standing next to the elevator waiting for them. Her face dark, Catherine dissolved and she dropped against him, repeating the word 'baby'. Simon was silent. His gaze focused narrower, and he realized Catherine was beating her hands against his face but he felt nothing of the blows. At last she dropped, and a doctor and nurse leaned over Catherine, trying to pull her upright. Simon looked at the nurse. She wasn't Patty.

"You weren't with him like you were supposed to be. You left him alone to get yourself arrested, and he died."

Simon had no defence. "Catherine, I'm going in."

He gestured to the nurse to stay with his wife, and went into Matt's room. The little boy lay there, seemingly at peace, his eyes shut, a serene look on his face. Simon's body shook when he reached forward and touched his son's soft face. Simon's sobbing funnelled away when Catherine, escaping from the nurse, burst into the room.

"I want to see my son," she cried, and dropped onto her son's tiny body, her wailing filling the room.

Simon left the room. To see his son dead, his family broken, his wife overcome by this deluge of anguish, was more than he could bear. He paced the hallway until Catherine, after what seemed forever, exited Matthew's room, and buried herself in Simon's arms. The couple melted together for a brief moment of shared grief.

"Can we please leave now?" he asked bitterly, "There's nothing more to do." He turned towards the elevators. Catherine walked a few paces behind him, for the moment compliant.

He did feel grateful for one thing: he could have been in bed with Pat the nurse while Matt was dying. He would have felt guilty for the rest of his life.

By Jewish custom, the funeral took place the following day. As he abandoned his son to the darkness of the soil, Simon felt crushed, by guilt, by loss, by despair. Today it was his turn for legs to fail, gravity to drag him down. He howled his grief into the sky and the earth. Adam, alarmed, slipped an arm under Simon's shoulders. Their parents were by now seated in the limousine, ready to leave, and gestured urgently for their sons to join them. Adam pulled his brother up, out of the muddy earth.

Catherine wouldn't leave the graveside either. She knelt at the edge of the hole, while Edythe briskly circled the grave and mouthed the Hail Mary. As the first shovelfuls of loose soil spilled over the casket, a gold chain dropped into the hole, clattering against the hard polished wood below. Catherine's mother stopped pacing and slid her hand across the back of her daughter's now-unadorned neck.

20 After Shiva

The days of *shiva* followed–the mourners, the low chairs, the prayers each evening at seven, the silent condolences. With that ended, Catherine and Simon were now home together and apart, two separate voids. In the days and weeks which followed, they became ever more distant, their planets spiralling off from each other's pull. Conversation stopped. They walked past each other in their home as if the other was an invisible ghost.

21 Candles

Eight months since the funeral. Simon arrived late from work to find the house in darkness. As Simon got out of his car, a lone fire truck parked on the street pulled away. A few neighbours standing in tight groups on the sidewalk across the street from his house jabbered and nodded to each other as he walked by. Inside his front door, the odour of candle wax and acrid smoke permeated the air. The rugs were soaked with water.

Catherine sat in the kitchen, sipping a glass of wine in partial darkness, her feet on the wet floor. One lit memorial candle sat next to her. Arrayed around Catherine's feet was a lake of dead candles, their flames doused. The windows were wide open.

Catherine looked up as Simon came in. Next to her elbow was a two-inch hole in the centre of the kitchen table, the hole's wooden edges blackened.

"You're late. You missed all the fun."

"What happened?"

"The power went out."

A patch of matte blackness, dark smudges overlaid on each other, coated the back wall and the ceiling above the table, where flames had almost reached before being doused. Simon scanned the path of the now-dead fire.

Again: "What happened?"

"Simon, I can't live like this. I miss Matt. I'm always by myself."

"I understand, Cath. But it's eight months now. You have to stop this."

"No, you don't understand. All you know is that sophomoric world with women like that Rachel in it."

"Why are you bringing her up? You haven't seen her for at least a year."

"That friend of yours made quite an impression on me. She's evil."

"What?"

"Look, she wouldn't even let me light candles. So now I'm free of her. Matthew is dead and I can light all the candles I ever fucking want to.

"Oh, my poor Catherine."

"Don't try. You won't soften me up like that, not now, not when my angel is gone."

"Cathy, what do you want?"

"What do I want? Are you blind? I'm so, so tired. You expect the perfect woman waiting for you every day when you arrive home, offering you a glass of wine. Here, so take this." Catherine gestured her wine glass towards Simon.

Simon took the glass, if only to stop her from drinking more from it. "I don't expect anything."

"That is what is wrong with you. You have nothing to do with what happens here in this house anymore. It could come this close to burning down," Catherine swept her arm dramatically across the dark panorama, "and you would just say 'Cathy, be careful.' I'm right and you know it."

"No."

"Well, yes, and you're still bringing trouble into this home. You let Matthew die, but before that you let everything go crazy with your magazine articles. You put Matt and me at risk, and you just went ahead as if we weren't important. They almost kidnapped Matthew, as if you cared."

"You're right, I should have been more careful with my stories."

"Yes, you really should have. You didn't think at all about the good of your family. All you cared about was the good of the world, not us. I would go out for a stroll and came back to find those scrawls all over the front door. And I saw them, coming at us, big men carrying baseball bats. It was terrifying. It was your father who saved us, as usual.

"He was driving by, about to come in and see his grandson. You should have seen him, fierce, with the tire iron whipping through the air in his hand, and him yelling like a spirit out of hell. Those men dropped their bats and just ran. It was just stunning. And your father is an older man."

"He's only 58. Not so old."

"Your dad always seems to show up when he's needed. He was here when Matt had his first convulsion. He drove us to the hospital faster than any ambulance could have. He was here to drive us to Matt's appointments with his doctor. He was so strong. I don't know what I could have done if he hadn't been there. He helped us. Not like you. You were in New York, on an assignment, you said, maybe with that crazy Rachel girl."

"I haven't seen her since the last time she was here."

"So there was some other crazy woman. Who knows with you running around all over the world all the time."

Simon knew better than to respond to the comment. "I'm sorry, Catherine, the last thing I expected or wanted was to do anything that would hurt you again."

"Well, so isn't it strange that that's the way it's turned out."

"What does all that have to do with this fire?"

"You have so many of those Jewish candles around. I lit one after another after another. It was so lovely, a lake of lights, shining like goodness through the dark of the world. I couldn't stop myself. One after the other after the other, and again more. A gift from God and back to God. I need light, Simon. All this is darkness and grief." She waved her arm again to encompass the whole sorry mess of the house.

"Catherine, I'm in mourning, too."

"You don't act like it. You get up every day and go to work. You come home and work some more. Nothing is different for you. Where is the mourning? You're just sorry for yourself."

"Look at you. You drink too much wine. You're self-indulgent. It's time to stop lighting all these candles."

"If I could light them every week like Jewish women do, there wouldn't have been so many left tonight."

"You can."

"No, I can't. That's what everyone says to me. That I shouldn't be doing that. Only Jewish women do it. It's not my place."

"Who told you that?"

"Rachel did, for one."

"Rachel is your guru on things Jewish? That's nuts."

"And your mother."

"My mother said that?"

"No, she didn't, but I saw her looking at me like I don't belong. And your cousins whisper it all the time. So would you, if you spoke the truth, but you're a liar."

"No, Catherine, I'm not."

"A liar and a hypocrite."

"Catherine."

"A liar and a hypocrite and a devil."

"That's your mother talking."

"My mother makes a lot of sense."

22 Magic

Only five years had passed since Simon and Catherine had married. It was a long sentence, written in the grammar of time. Passing so quickly, that time was full of punctuation marks: temporal commas and apostrophes and semi-colons. It had had its share of exclamation and question marks, but now started to acquire a number of periods. There were the first hints of finalities.

To mask the reality that Matthew was truly gone from their lives, they returned to acting out their routines, as if life might really go on.

The simmering anger came to the surface at a baby shower for one of Simon's cousins. Catherine overheard whispered remarks about her family. Rumours. Derision. Conspiratorial laughter. Quick retreats of the eyes when she looked at the gathered clutch of tittering women. Furious, she broke into hot tears, wailing.

Duvid intervened, quickly separating her away from the others to avoid a scene, explaining that she had a migraine. Simon followed, mute. She was livid in the car, angry at all those colluding in belittling her, at Duvid for making excuses as cover for her fully justifiable anger.

Simon should have taken her side, not stayed quiet. She was his wife, after all.

He should be more committed to her, to her honour, than to these relatives of his. He owed her that, at least that. She had wanted to confront, to finally give vent to her disguised feelings, and he had the nerve to block her. Her rage accrued and pressed in on the true cause of it all: Simon, who had dragged her away with a lie, after he had dragged her into this damnable family. Catherine focussed her frustrations on Duvid, who hadn't said anything, because his was the guilt of being Simon's father, progenitor of this dysphoric downpour, generator of her humiliation, instigator of her rejection by the Jewish rabbis. They were the ones who spewed luxuriant trellises of possibilities, lured her along, before they put stumbling blocks in her path. And finally, this entire community of rats and bloodsuckers–guilty, guilty, guilty. Simon drove, afraid to look sideways at her.

When she got home, Catherine cursed Duvid, again and again. She wished him dead, invoking the name of God in her appeal.

Simon was taken aback at the vehemence of Catherine's invective, and quickly dismissed it. It would pass, he thought. It always did.

Only two weeks later Duvid suddenly became very ill. He went through a period of difficult breathing, heavy coughing. Adam tried to get him to see a specialist. He arranged the appointment, but Duvid refused to go at the last minute.

"I am fine. You can see I am as strong as a horse. My son is a big doctor, but he cannot even tell when his father is healthy."

Adam was annoyed, but knew he wouldn't win this fight. One morning, though, Hannah called him with news that she had found blood on Duvid's pillow. She complained that Duvid still refused to see a doctor. Adam's insistence finally got Duvid to go for a medical exam. Adam drove him to make sure he carried through.

In the car, Duvid kept muttering.

"It's a shame a son should treat his father like a child."

"If you would act like an adult, I wouldn't have to."

"You are telling me how to act?" Adam kept his eyes on the road and shut up.

The physician arranged for an immediate set of tests, and Adam took him there directly, ignoring Duvid's efforts at delay. The test results, when they came back, showed lung cancer. There were already metastases to his spine and liver. It was almost certainly too late. At the insistence of his wife, Duvid hadn't smoked since Adam's bar mitzvah, over two decades earlier.

"Another injustice against a man who has seen too much of it in his lifetime," his wife Hannah would later declare, when it was too late for anything but protest.

After hearing the news, there were torrents of words over the phone between Simon and Adam.

He isn't an old man, they said. He hasn't even turned sixty yet. He just got back from his visit to his home town in Poland. He was expecting to retire later this year, early. He looked so vigorous, so healthy, just a few months ago. He was planning to travel again with Hannah.

They couldn't accept it.

Hannah always wore her emotions like a bright red dress. Her sons and husband had always been the focus of a life in which she had already lost too much. She was not ready to lose more. She held on to her sons more tightly as her husband was drawn slowly away from her.

Catherine was both upset and secretly vindicated when she heard about Duvid's sudden illness. Catherine had never been comfortable in Duvid and Hannah's presence. They had never welcomed her into the family. Hannah and she had managed to live an uneasy, ignitable peace of sorts.

Simon's parents had lived through terrible times, victim to the hostility of the deadly gentile; Catherine was just one more of those. They felt betrayed by their son's choice of wife.

Simon recalled Catherine's maledictive attack when he got the news about his father's cancer only weeks after she cursed him. Some particle within him was crushed by the association. He couldn't take the power of the curse seriously. He had been educated in the culture of science. He didn't believe in witchcraft. He was neither superstitious nor religious. But the archaic beliefs born of an ignorant age long past touched deep inside him where his rational self didn't rule. In that place was located a conspiracy between nature and thought. The couple's relationship could never again return to love.

Catherine's definition of a man was in reference to her own father. He had been a man of tradition, a hard worker. He had also done most of the domestic work. Her mother was a melancholic, her degree of depression measurable by lethargy and the decibel level of her voice. She had found another man, confused that with finding God, left the family's home, and came back pregnant a few months later. Shortly after that, Catherine's father died. Catherine was left to take care of everything.

Catherine expected of men what she had seen in her father, like men of his generation: a seeming indifference to hurt, uncomplaining faithfulness, spartan strength. He never brought another woman into the house. Catherine didn't know the pain he never let her see. Catherine expected Simon to be like her father, giving, never taking. And without the messy despair Simon was prone to. Simon had his own definition of father—also grand, heroic, impossible to emulate, a definition based in childhood. It condensed as the moment his father had saved him one day from drowning. To Simon, his father had at that moment been like the Gideon and Samson he had learned about in the Talmud Torah classes he had attended after school. Even when he was battling his father, and his father was belittling him, he knew that he could never achieve his father's power. Yet it was strength that gradually receded as Simon grew up.

Simon had never known Duvid other than knowing him to be his father. He couldn't. There was no outward sign to echo the seismic movements, the grand collision of tectonic plates floating on the magma of this man. Or of the lava that would someday become Simon's, congeal into his island. Simon could never fill the large shoes of his own father. or the role that Catherine expected of him either. These men were of a different generation, had lived in a time of heroes, of myth, a time when the demands of life required stoicism and sacrifices which Simon could never make. He was not strong enough. He had no clear vision of what life required of him. He only knew that he was not up to the challenge.

But getting back to Catherine's curse: it was indeed magical. It was secular magic, unlinked to the idea of deity. In a cynical world, none of us of course would ever admit considering that such a thing could exist. Without the balancing force of God in our thoughts, it's an embarrassment to admit that we can believe in the existence of such intangible things as enchantment and curses. Yet in the dark of night, we lie in our beds and think of the blankness which waits for us after the moment of death. We pull our hands and feet, (yes, we adults) under the covers away from the demons we refuse to acknowledge in the day. The sour tightness that we feel in our bellies when we contemplate all this, the sudden fear of this void without dimension, brings us to wish, yes, wish that we could acknowledge the possibility of a god of any kind, of an afterlife of any sort.

Perhaps not all of us confront these demons. For some, this transforms into belief, which perhaps was always there, hidden. For others, the reality of the loneliness of death transcribes itself into a love of life. For still others, it translates into depression and anger. All these reactions can be seen as reasonable outcomes of an impossible situation. Perhaps they are valid ways of dealing with this mystery. Yet who is to say what is the best way to live? So when an event that defies logic happens, we open our eyes wide, yet remain silent, fearing that to acknowledge it will be to accept the incoherence of our lives and the universe which we inhabit so fleetingly, our moorings lost, and we washed away into the rushing surf.

Duvid was certainly not blameless regarding Catherine. He had never been able to accept Catherine as his son's choice of wife. Even at the celebration of the birth of his grandson, he could not stop himself from speaking against Catherine and her weakness, her religion, even though Catherine professed to have none. "How can a person not have a religion?" he asked, even though he held the same idea in his own head. She was tainted.

What should have been a joyful occasion for her became like the bitter taste of ashes in her mouth, in the biblical idiom of her adopted family. Recently Duvid had made a sort of peace with

Catherine, but she had been unable to forgive the pain of the rejection. So, at dinner, when Simon came in late from work one day after the first curse, she again uttered a malediction against his father while cutting lettuce for a salad. "*Je voudrais qu'il soit mort*. I wish him dead," she had muttered over and over, while ripping the head of lettuce to shreds. To Simon, it was voodoo. Unbelievable nonsense.

A few weeks on, Simon remembered the curse when the news of Duvid's illness came. Simon never reminded her of her words. It would have been pointless. She had not forgotten it either, but mentioning it would only have brought a protest of denial from her.

"You're Mr. Scientist—that's your training. How can you believe in such junk?" would have been her words. She would have blamed him. What she would base his guilt on this time he could not imagine, but this was her talent. He had endured it many times. He couldn't understand this ability to reject the truth, to twist it around so credibly.

Simon was well aware that it was not possible that her words could really have had any such lethality. He was a modern man, skeptical, educated in the scientific tradition. In his soul, though, somewhere in the recesses close to the base of his skull, or hovering in a thin layer of electrogenic air, microns outside the realm of his skin, he also knew that it had produced precisely that result. Better to be away from such a malicious person, who could devastate a life so easily. This he accepted as he simultaneously denied the possibility of such power. Contradictions could live comfortably side by side in these deeper parts of his being.

For the cosmos, the real effect of Catherine's words was nil. In the terms familiar to Simon's inner mind, some spiritual cosmic wormhole had caught her words and spilled out a reactive radiation of death over Duvid. It was beyond possible that she could have summoned forth the cosmic rays—flying at light speed from a pre-galactic primordium so very far away in time, space and energy—that penetrated Duvid's skin and sinew and destroyed his already-injured cells' chemistry, producing this disease. Words, thoughts, turned into physical event, the answer to prayer or curse—was this a force of nature, as integral a component as the four known fundamental forces that held the parts of the universe together in their dance away from the moment of the Creation? Of course it was impossible. Absurd.

23 Particles

I see only you.
Turning, dancing, your body smiling.
Closing on me, holding so far away.

At the limits of vision and imagining, a diffuse elementary particle slides through time. Alone. It spreads infinitely, from the centre of the expanding universe where time begins, to its unseen edges red-shifted beyond any detectable wavelength, occupying a single dimensionless point in a space manifested yet distorted by its own presence.

Here is paradox. Matter creates the space it occupies, and yet its presence produces its distortion. Can undistorted space, a space where light flies unhindered by this curvature, exist? Matter affects space. Space affects light, curving its path. Light by the inherent limit to its rate of travel, by traversing this curved space, must affect the progression of time in that space. How can it be otherwise?

Overwhelmed by emotion, this particle falls into orbit about a cluster of distant protons, expectant. In its own way it waits for affection.

This particle is everywhere, spread out like haze in an absolute vacuum, an oily coating on the exposed surfaces of time. on the curled threads of chance. It sails above waves of improbability, condensing, thicker here, thinner there, following fastidious prescripts which regulate its capriciousness. It is lonely. It waits hopefully to be transformed.

Where are you, where do you go, between the moment of before and that of after?

It observes its partners as they all dance together in sticky random orbits around central clusters of fundamental particles a breath away from nullity. Their like charges repel and yet hold. They brood over the brevity of their lives.

You are my breath, my inspiration. Where are you gone, from the end of one infinite moment to the start of the next? Where are you, my love, my world? I feel you around me, inside me.

Something is about to happen. A wave of unrequited desire coalesces. It becomes particulate, meanwhile recalling its birthplace along the ancient rim of the universe, thrust out by the death of a star billions of years away on the edge of expansion. After a humbling journey, it flirts clumsily with the competing nuclei of a passing molecule. In its adolescent thrusting, it discharges prematurely, its passion dooming it to dissolution. Bursts of material energy emerge, speaking in a language without syntax. Massless, uncharged ghost-particle neutrinos flail about, defending this tetherless territory.

Embryonic quarks, orphaned, escape the nuclear forces grasping for them. They fly from these islands of dysfunctional uncertainty, betrayed by their dying parents. They have short minutes of objective time before disintegrating into pure energy. From within, from the point of view of their own internal clocks, they will live almost forever. They feel indestructible. With a joy derived from motion, they pass into and collide with atoms held together as water, degrading their electron clouds. Fresh ions kiss others strung together like pearls on a spiral string. A romantic tragedy is enacted, for as their strength dies, the bonds of attraction in a molecule of genetic memory are broken. This living molecule is only a small part of a small part of a cell in the depths of a human lung. It recoils in pain, summoning help. Enzymes evolved for the one purpose of repairing this damage slide along the helical molecule, sniffing out the injury, but they are distracted that day. Something else gathers their attention, perhaps the shudder of an unhappy woman's tears, or the disdain of an angry man.

They fail to heal the damage. The break won't be undone. A tumour snarls out its terrible cry of birth.

Chance, randomness, following the precise regulations of time and space, breaks through the lifeline of one man. He is the father of Simon and Adam. None of them, neither father nor sons, knows the intimate secrets of the myriad particles within himself that whirl their dervish dance in the blackness of fundamentality. Each of these indiscrete wave-particles is as ephemeral as the light dancing in the web of forces between them. Suspended forever and an instant in the hush, it is entertained by the music of the stars in their forever orbits, by the intangible lacework that connects the galaxies. It is one universe. One. And forever alone.

Look at the man. He seems so solid, so present, so real. It seems he could live forever, but from moment to moment his unravelling is more and more certain. Every bit of matter that occupies the human body is a guest, there for a few moments of time, soon to be lost, to be exchanged for another equivalent. Every one of these particles, atoms, molecules, organelles, and cells will remain intact and unchanged within the confines of this body for only moments, minutes, days, or weeks, before being seamlessly replaced. Each molecule of water has only recently been swallowed, entered the blood, slipped through the membranes of cells, then is lost again by evaporation, in the exhaled breath, in sweat, or by excretion, only hours or days later. Each hard calcific crystal in his bones will be dissolved by remodeller cells, as the body's supporting structures are modified and reconstructed again and again, over the course of weeks and months and years, unnoticed by the person whose weight they support. The man reaches out unconsciously, his electric fields crossing those of others, mapping the space between.

The man is just a shell, a frame, for this dance. It is as if he doesn't exist. As he was before birth and will be again after death. An anthill for the ants, a cloud for the raindrops, a sea for the sharks within. Even the galaxies are such. Transient. Ever-changing. Ghost. Perhaps he is only a thought in the imaginings of the world, an idea projected and sustained from moment to moment by the mind of God. Or is he a thought of his own thought, creating himself unknowingly, purposively or otherwise? Or unknowingly creating God?

Goodbye, my love. I must go.

Simon and Adam took as much time as they could to visit with Duvid at the hospital. The therapy had only just started, and already it had taken its toll. He lay heavy in his bed at home. He was a little tired, he said. It would pass soon. He would confront them in a kindly way, suggesting that they might come more often, or at least call. It would put their mother more at ease.

"And when I'm gone, you should take care of her. It's a son's duty."

"Don't talk like that, Ta. You'll get through this."

"I want to die," he stated categorically, as if death was not something to be feared.

Simon wanted to argue with him, shout at him: "Live. Clutch life. Cherish it. Hold it tight." Simon wanted to argue that the universe would go on forever, so it would not miss him too much if he died a bit later. But he didn't say these words. He couldn't talk to his father about his impending death. He couldn't bring his mind into focus, to eat and swallow the idea.

Only Adam was able to do this. He was more familiar with death. It was a companion every week, sometimes every day. He could refer to it casually, welcome it in, dismiss it when he could, walk with it when he had to. He was its witness and its interpreter.

"Eat," they told Duvid when he complained of the nausea. "You need to preserve your strength."

"Have some more."

"Drink the Ensure."

"Eat." They glossed over his complaints that he could taste nothing, since the radiation and the chemotherapy had started. They repeated the mantra their mother had spoken over and over when they were infants:

"Eat."

One Sunday morning, Duvid's eyes brimmed. His hands, suddenly frail, trembled. He looked away, pointing past their heads at the door.

"The Nazi is there, coming to take you. Run away, boys. Run fast. To the forest." He paused, his teeth chewing at air, while looks of distress passed across his sons' faces. He calmed after the outburst. His sons smiled at this, his raving done. They could get back to their mission, to get him to eat.

"How can I eat when I have killed the fisherman. I have killed the fisherman..." His voice trailed off. Simon stared quizzically at Adam, who simply shrugged his shoulders. It was the chemo talking. They remained hushed.

Duvid finished the visit that day by placing his hands on their heads, blessing them. They were embarrassed but accepted the gesture.

They went home to their mother's kitchen and sat with her, allowed her to feed and fuss over her two sons. During the meal, the men hesitatingly mentioned the comments about the fisherman. While not wanting to distress her, they urgently needed this knowledge of who their father was, things he had never described before, personal history that would forever fall away from their hands and disappear into oblivion with his death. If she knew anything about it, Hannah didn't share that knowledge. On their way home, Adam dismissed it all. Their father's medication sometimes caused hallucinations. Simon took this opinion in without comment, but there was an authenticity to his father's crazed words that he couldn't shake away.

Duvid's illness tore Simon's heart more than he could ever have known. The two had not apparently been close. They rarely spoke of much. Duvid had spent the last few years of his life, before his sickness, in depression. He recently had spoken of his lost youth, lost family, lost possibilities. Under the care of a psychiatrist, he had been taking a variety of antidepressants and sleeping pills to try to hold his darkness away.

Several weeks after his diagnosis, after the first sessions of chemotherapy had begun, after he had blessed his sons, Duvid was discharged home from the hospital. He was booked to return for further sessions as an outpatient.

Hannah insisted he lie down on the sofa in the living room. She turned on the television, and once sure that he was comfortable enough, she sat in an armchair, relieved momentarily, and quickly fell asleep, exhausted from the weeks of worry and rushing to the hospital. When he saw that Hannah was asleep, Duvid got up quietly and made his way to his workroom. Good, the closet door was shut. He carefully eased the door open and examined his hidden papers, his record of the hidden past. Here, certainly, were the ones which he had recovered during the last hours of the death camp in Poland, and which he still feared could bring down a storm of troubles on his family if that German ever stole them back.

Who knew when the German might be back? Who knew? Duvid hadn't heard from him since leaving him behind in the forest, but he was sure the man would have been able to set himself free. He had been terrified of his return. Now that he was ill, how could he protect his family if he died and the Nazi returned afterwards?

But there were also his other mysteries, his deepest secrets. They were still kept hidden within his heart. Why had he left Israel? Hannah might know, but his sons must never find out. And his first love, gone and yet not gone, dead and yet not dead, still burned inside him, haunting his mind like a ghost. He could not consider talking to Hannah or his children about her, even if he survived his terrible disease.

On the one hand he could not bear to part with these documents, this jumble of writings, poems, correspondence, all these varied pieces of paper and fabric that hid the contents of a past world so dear to his heart, but on the other, he wanted to be sure that his wife and his sons would never see any of these, even after he was dead. He looked down and there they were, tied in neat bundles with strips of fabric, carefully arranged. He let out an audible sigh to find them undisturbed. Here too was where he kept his legal and financial records–his will, his discharged mortgage, the keys to his safety deposit box, his bank book. This bunch he set aside, sliding them into a large brown envelope.

He hastily pulled out the suitcase that held his patterns. He opened it, used his shears to carefully cut a slit in the lining so that it remained almost invisible, and, except for those pertaining to money, stuffed the documents in the cavity, replaced his cutting patterns, and eased the suitcase back into its place. That was all he could do. In his depleted state, there were no other hiding places he could find that might be safer. He was so tired—tired of these old fears that had kept him awake at night. Maybe that was what had made him sick. He returned to the sofa and lay down. He waited for Hannah to wake up and prepare supper.

The evening meal was quiet.

"Is the food to your liking, Duvid?"

"Hannah, I can't taste anything."

Both were quiet after that.

Later Adam came by to see how Duvid was doing.

"You don't have to worry so much about me. I'm dying but I'm fine."

"Ta, don't talk like that."

"There's no need to be so sentimental. It's true, no? I'm dying."

"Ta."

"Wait here."

Duvid walked off heavily and came back with the brown Kraft envelope. He pulled out the folded papers inside and handed them to Adam. Adam stared at the will with alarm and dropped it onto the table.

"Ta, you'll be back to normal after the chemotherapy sessions have done their work. You really should be planning a vacation with Ma. It's thirty-three years you're married. When have you ever gone away together besides that cottage in the country when Simon and I were boys? Buy a new car. Live a little."

"What are you talking about?"

"You're not going to die, Ta. You're going to beat this."

Duvid stared at his son. He stood and stepped forward. He put his arms around his son and kissed him on the cheek.

"I love you," was all he said.

Adam was thrown off balance by this show of affection. His father had never hugged him before. He had certainly never told Adam he loved him. Adam stood there limp.

"What's going on?" Adam asked.

"What do you think, I've gone crazy now? I just feel tired, my smart son. Don't worry, I won't kiss you again."

Duvid released his hold, and shuffled off to the bedroom.

Duvid had made up his mind. He emptied his bottles of pills into his hand that night, after Hannah was asleep, one bottle at a time, and swallowed them all. He went back to bed. At three in the morning, Hannah awoke and found him gasping in his sleep. Unable to awaken him, she panicked and called Adam, her son the doctor. He was not there.

Simon she knew was off somewhere on an assignment. After considering what to do for a short moment, she called Catherine. Despite their mutual antipathy, she had to rely on someone, even if it had to be her *shiksa* daughter-in-law.

Catherine was compelled to act. She called 9-1-1, then hastily drove over to Duvid and Hannah's house. The ambulance was there when she arrived, its lights flashing into the night, announcements in French crackling out of its radio every few seconds into the dark air. She could see the attendants wheeling Duvid out the door and onto the walk, while pumping his chest. She went in and held Hannah in her arms, trying to comfort her, then drove her to the hospital.

When they arrived, Duvid lay unconscious on a stretcher in Emergency, waiting for admission into the Intensive Care ward. Catherine took Hannah down to the registration office to sign some forms. They found Duvid's stretcher assigned to a hallway because of the crowding, and sat next to him for a few hours until an orderly arrived to take the stretcher to one of the wards. Now satisfied that her husband was at last being cared for properly, Hannah agreed to let Catherine drive her home. Catherine came in with her, then convinced Hannah to swallow a sedative tablet and made sure the older woman went to bed.

Catherine called Adam, leaving a message on his pager, and phoned Simon. He was in London, covering some international conference. It was by now four in the morning in Montreal, and nine in London. She caught him at his hotel, just as he was coming back from breakfast. Simon sounded shocked when the pills were mentioned. He would arrange for a flight home that day, if he could, and asked her to please look after his mother and contact Adam to give him the news. He said he was happy that she didn't sound angry any more. Catherine made no comment, just muttering a goodbye. She hung up, then drove home. There she went into what had been Matt's room, lay down on his bed, and fell asleep quickly.

She woke up what seemed only minutes later. Half-asleep, she looked around, confused, and realized she was in her son's room, that Matt wasn't there, that he couldn't be there.

It was like a splash of cold water. She pulled herself up suddenly with a start. The phone was ringing in the hall. Catherine pushed herself out of the bed, almost tripping on a toy on the floor as she ran to answer.

It was Adam at the hospital. Duvid was still in a coma, but he had been moved to a semi-private room. Adam wanted to know when Simon would be coming back. She didn't know—she hadn't yet heard from him about the arrival time of his flight. She hung up and looked at her watch: it was five-thirty in the morning. She turned back to her own bedroom and lay down, but was unable to sleep. In a few minutes, if he had lived, Matt would have been waking up, wanting her to come and play with him. She began to sob.

Later, while she was taking a bite of toast and a coffee, Simon called. His plane would arrive at six that evening, and he would take a cab directly to the hospital. She got up, dressed, and drove back there.

It was late afternoon. Hannah was standing next to the bed, both hands firmly holding the bed rail, her hands white from the pressure. Adam burst into the hospital room, locked eyes with Catherine and his mother, then quickly shifted his gaze to his father's still form. There was a frantic look on Adam's face, as if the ground was moving below his feet. It was.

There was nothing outward to indicate his father's state except the monitors arrayed on carts behind and above him. His heart was beating; a respirator was making sure that his body received its necessary ration of oxygen. Fluids dripped in, oozed out. The blood in his veins, the cells lining his gut, the spicules of bone in his marrow were oblivious to all this. They felt no sensation at all.

Adam was standing with his right hand on Duvid's chest. He had seen this situation many times, had always been detached, cool, always supportive. Now it was too real—he could not barricade himself away as he did with his patients. Catherine watched him as he rearranged his thoughts, made peace with his father. The pace of Duvid's breathing was increasing. He was gasping. It would not be long. Adam slid an arm around his mother's shoulders and guided her out of the room to a bench just outside. He didn't want her to see this happen.

Catherine couldn't bear to stay. She went out into the hallway for a breath of fresh air, but the odours of dirty linens and adult diapers were overpowering. Hannah sat there, looking lost. Catherine retreated back to Duvid's room to wait for Simon to get back and sat down next to Duvid's bed. After a few minutes, she fell asleep.

Simon walked through the large entrance doors into the main hall of the hospital, past the information desk and the flower shop, his eyes passing across portraits of long-dead staff and shiny brass plaques dedicated to old benefactors, the size and ornateness of each plaque proportional to its age. He followed the signs directing him through a labyrinth of corridors to the hospital pavilion where his father lay dying. The elevators were old, their doors painted over many times. After a wait which seemed to last forever, their doors finally opened. He glanced quickly into the eyes of two other visitors, they looking as solemn as he thought he must. One balding man dressed only in a loose hospital gown and slippers stood among them, connected by a tube to a bag of clear fluid, his face unreadable. He stared at Simon.

The elevator stopped again, this time to let two men dressed in blue wheel a large hospital bed into the car. The passengers all pressed themselves against one wall of the conveyance, letting the bed enter. The body in the bed seemed asleep, the cheekbones thin, the skin pulled tight into the hollow cheeks, the neck extended sharply. The mouth was open and toothless. The two attendants joked with each other about the weekend never seeming to end. The elevator cranked upwards, finally opening on Duvid's floor. Simon squeezed his way between the man with the metal stand and the side of the bed, rattling its bars, and out the door before it could close on him. He almost sprinted down the hall to his father's room, slowing just outside it. Hannah sat on a bench outside the room, her two hands working one another. He bent to kiss her on the cheek.

"Adam won't let me stay with my own husband, imagine." she complained.

"Stay here, just a little while. I'll come out soon."

He stood upright, staring at the closed door, afraid to go in, afraid he was too late. He opened the door, saw Duvid, the pump still working, and its action induced Simon to gasp his own breath. Catherine was sleeping in a chair next to Duvid's bed. What was she doing there after all the acrimony?

Adam was bending over his father's face, listening for his breath. He turned to face Simon's awkward advance into the room.

"How bad is it?" Simon asked in a whisper, hesitating, afraid to receive the answer.

"It won't be much longer." Adam whispered, "You were far away. It was hard to reach you."

Adam knew him well, could read his various anxious states so accurately, and knew how to dig into them. He didn't mention how he himself had been unavailable, despite being so close by. Simon turned his head slightly and passed his eyes over Catherine's sleeping form.

He came close to his father's inert form and gently rolled his father's limp fingers between his own. They were blue and cold to the touch. Death was entering him through his fingers.

24 Devoid of Thought

Something pulling me, there, over that edge, saying come, come closer, come to me, I have been waiting, longer than you can know.
...it is the voice of my mother...

From a forbidden place, Death now stared at Duvid, silent and devoid of thought. Death had been waiting a long time for this moment, since Duvid had walked away from Him alive from the death camp. He was still waiting for Duvid to make Him laugh, to cut the bleakness He was so used to. He was waiting patiently for His payment. His grip held all who had lived before him. All that would live after him were there too. Time is endless, the universe finite. All that ever happens or can happen will, in a higher dimension, always have happened.

Is the past really there, or is it instantly gone, a shadow burnt away by the sun, of no value except in memory? Does the future truly exist? Does it have substance? Is it only moments that may happen, strung on a liquid thread like intangible beads, like raindrops gliding along the spider's web after a summer shower? Does it congeal as past slips away and the present instant becomes time? Can it be created ahead of itself, by effort or by luck?

The strings of chance, interacting with each other while the principle of uncertainty held them apart, came together at the nodes of life, at birth and at death. Time is and was the intervener. It flowed, like a stream, in only one direction. It was this stream that now bubbled in front of Duvid, calling him to enter its waters, join that great journey toward the infinite. Duvid's mother took his hand and walked him slowly away from this world.

25 Laws

There is another story, one that has long been told. It begins, as all good stories should, at the beginning. It is a familiar story. It has many ways of being told.

At the beginning...
...the four basic forces of nature were one, in the seething expansion of a single point becoming a writhing nascent universe. As the great energy levels and density of the infant world dissipated, as time and distances became themselves, these emerging forces separated, defining their roles at their different levels of existence. So, it can be asked, were there other forces, fused with these we know, waiting for that one moment when the temperature, the gravitational pull, the vibrational frequency of strings, the volume of the invisible dark matter, and so many other unknowable factors, added together to reach just the right set of conditions? Could they come apart, become immanent, insinuate into the lives of people, things, events? Was God a force of Nature? Was Nature a force of God? Chicken and egg. Yin and yang. Sense and nonsense.

At the beginning God was free. There was no Earth, no Heaven. No Laws had been promulgated. God had no constraints, no limits to His freedom. Everywhere was chaos, a universe of indifference. Life could never populate its crevices and pools. One creature could not care for another, nor hate either. There could be no love, and so, no anger.

God felt the bitterness of this absence. Against the indifference He determined to build a fence, one which would limit Him in the same ways it limited the chaos. And with this act of creation, His own act of faith, God felt the dwindling of His power, the loss of His control. The constraints He had placed on the realm of matter and energy, time and distance, now applied to Him also, and as the edges of His universe, ever expanding and evolving, became remote from His influence, He could only look on in utter silence and hope that this great work would not one day bring Him regret.

Duvid's life ebbed out slowly, like the dark water before him. There was no better path, no other path.

Catherine slept. She dreamed she was standing at her father's open grave but he stood next to her and touched her hand. She was crying and her father was comforting her. She was wrenched awake. Adam and Simon were both standing over Duvid's form, and she could hear the muttering of the *Shema*.

Shema Yisrael, Adonai Elochainu, Adonai Ehad.
Hear, O Israel, the Lord our God, the Lord is One.

Duvid was dead, this fierce man she had fought with, been angry with, this man who had endured so much, this kind, gentle man who had so loved her son Matthew, whose joy was to see him run and laugh. Emotions pulled at her, tore into her. She remembered the death of her own father. She rose, walked over to the bed, crossed herself, and silently mouthed an *Ave Maria*. How could one know whose words would rise, and to where, if anywhere? She placed one hand on Simon's shoulder and began to cry.

Simon knew that he would be the one to tell his mother, who now sat on a bench just outside the room. He did not know how he would do it, what words he could use, and also knew that no words would be needed or ever adequate. Hannah was a religious woman. Her beliefs gave her life structure. What could he say that would mean more to her than the images that already filled her mind. She had prayed for her husband's life and yet had lost him. Hannah was embittered, angry at the doctors who had promised so much with their optimism, angry with God for his inadequacy.

She had muttered over and over again: "They told me he would be cured. Your husband will be cured, they said!"

It would not be easy.

26 Emergency Room

The dream was nearing its climax. Lyssa. Her eyes were wide, her lips wet, her clothing dropped to the floor. She climbed on him, placed herself directly over him, bore down. The pleasure was exquisite, soft and rhythmic. Just to his left, the pager signalled. His wife smiled sweetly and waved goodbye as he tried to clutch at her. She dissolved away as his eyes opened. The pager kept beeping cheerfully. For seconds, Adam stared at it, confused. Were they calling him because his father was on the verge of dying? No, that was months ago. Months ago, his head repeated. Your father is dead. You're on duty. Duty. He felt like flinging the thing against the wall, but he didn't. Duty. He recognized the number–the Emergency Room. He dialled the phone next to the bed.

"Dr. Gryn here. What? Yeah, I'll be right down." Adam put down the phone and rubbed the back of his head, tired. He put the pager back on his belt and turned his head toward the window of the cubicle where he slept. His watch said 4:06 a.m. The hour of oblivion.

Adam, covering emergencies that long weekend, had only had this one snatch of sleep in eighteen hours. He had been at the Jewish General Hospital a few years now. Before that, he had been a new staff member at some of the staidly English hospitals, among which he had rotated before he was pressured to leave. He had been lucky he was on very good relations with the head of Emergency Services at the Jewish. The Emergency Service was not his first choice, but he wanted to stay in Montreal, close to his parents, and that was what he had been offered.

Simon had caused Adam much grief with his sensationalist articles about almost comic incompetence by veteran staff, not trainees. Medical cases botched, senior staff bailing each other out, betraying the younger, more vulnerable staff and residents.

Slips, these were called, when he brought them up to staff, but his naive remarks were met by a solid wall of silence. There was a long list of errors and omissions, easily obscured unless one knew there was a pattern to them. Adam now realized he shouldn't have stirred the pot, but he had been outraged. "Better stay quiet about this," he was told. Stupidly, he had spilled these to his journalist brother, trusting Simon would keep the information to himself.

Simon had snooped around and written a series of shocking articles, independent of what his brother had told him, but anyone affected would still be suspicious. Adam had been taken aside one day and told to find other pastures to shit in, as if these fields didn't smell bad enough. Now he found himself on call, fighting fatigue, where he could have had a kinder life.

Damned brother! Why couldn't he just keep quiet? Adam should have stipulated that this was off the record, Simon had answered. Adam felt betrayed both by his professional colleagues and by Simon. It was only his mother, invoking some sort of power of the ancestors, that had imposed peace between them, a cold sort of peace, but peace nonetheless. In a few hours, Adam thought bitterly, he would be sharing a hotel room with his brother in New York. Another concession forced by their mother. *Shalom bayit*, she declared. Peace in the home! She was the matriarch, the one who ruled over the family's well-being. Only half a year ago the family had been shattered by Duvid's death.

Only Lyssa softened his life, and just now she wasn't there. Hell wasn't something that came after death, it was all around him. Adam had been wakened to attend to the inmates of this nether world.

The next case on his roster was a teenaged boy who had been in a fight, kicked in the head, side, and legs. He had staggered into the emergency room on his own after crawling a quarter mile to the hospital. Only then did he allow himself to give up to shock and lose consciousness. The young punk, green and pink hair tufted together in rough bundles, wore torn black pants and a pair of black-laced high leather boots, a safety pin through one ear. Ornamentation was now enhanced by pathology: the dark red patch on the left side of his face, the frayed lip, the chin deviated to one side by the fracture of his jaw. The face was horribly swollen and distorted, the skin covering the left chest a livid purple. All added to his already bizarre look.

Adam exited the staff locker room in his hospital blues. He had left every adornment that served to identify him as an ordinary human being in his locker. Only his dangling I.D. badge spoke for who he was. He drew in a long slow breath before he rushed down the hallway and passed through the sliding doors into the trauma room. The young patient was surrounded by several green-garbed bodies, indistinguishable one from the other. The members of the team were made equal by the uniform banality of their costume. They were priests readying for some purification ceremony, participants in a religion called disease.

There was the danger of a lacerated liver, of internal bleeding. X-ray films covered the wall-mounted viewer. Adam noted the splintered ribs and the cracked jaw. The patient needed to be stabilized before he was moved to the operating theatre. The monitors chirped, tracing a set of wiggling lines. They displayed the state of the young man's vital signs. There would be difficulty starting the I.V. The anesthetist would need to intubate around the facial trauma in order to place the boy in an induced state of paralyzed unconsciousness, a whisper away from death.

Adam paused. A radio was playing quietly in the corner, distracting the team from the routine grimness of its work. Light classical music wafted through the space, ephemeral and distracting. He winced. The beauty distressed him. It made no sense.

"Hey, Michel," he blurted out to the orthopedic surgeon from behind a surgical mask, "guess what? It's my birthday tomorrow."

"Gee, what are you doing here, then?"

Someone laughed. The area went silent for a long disconnected moment. One by one, the team joined spontaneously in singing "Happy Birthday". Adam's face, the little of it not obscured by his surgical mask, reddened, while they all went on with their tasks. Nurses and orderlies walked by. The young patient was wheeled away for surgery. A worker from housekeeping mopped the floor of the empty cubicle. Someone turned off the radio.

The thought of sleep was now almost irrelevant. Adam turned to check the charts at the front desk. It was another day, another night. He had to keep moving. Routine chaos, the ordinary horror of other people's lives was spilling over his lap. He saw the last patient's blood had left a vermilion stain on his fresh uniform. Adam turned back towards the locker room and there slipped out of the outfit, letting it fall to the floor. He didn't bother to pick it up and throw it into the wheeled laundry hamper standing against the wall next to the window.

The emergency department team was swamped with new arrivals.

'Welcome to Montreal, welcome to Quebec,' Adam thought, 'welcome to health care purgatory.'

Adam splashed some cold water on his face at the small sink next to the locker room. He squeezed his eyes shut at the sight of his own wraith-like face staring back at him in the mirror. Where had the years gone? There was no time to think about that.

Adam paused and pushed a stick of gum into his mouth, chewing vigorously. He had to get back to work. Another four hours on duty. He inhaled deeply and pushed back into the emergency ward. He scanned the bedlam around him. His jaw muscles kept working on the gum. The waiting room was packed. The hallways were full, stretchers in rows along both walls. The nurse at the front desk looked up from the pile of waiting charts.

"Here, Adam," she muttered, and pushed one into his hands. She was still on the phone, arguing with someone.

"Thanks," Adam responded in a less than enthusiastic voice. Adam noted the deep vee-neck of her blouse, and kept chewing.

"Did you hear about Dr. Berryman?"

"The anesthetist?"

"The one and lonely."

"No. What about Joyce?"

"She was mugged. In the parking lot."

"What?"

"Yeah. Last night. She was on her way in for an emergency."

"You would think that doing this sort of work should give you a carte blanche in the world."

"I know what you mean. It's so unfair."

"God. Poor Joyce. Is she okay?"

"Just a little shook up, really, the way she tells it. But she's got one hell of a bruise."

"She sure is a tough bird."

"Sure is. Anyway, enough gab. Get back to work."

Adam had never liked Joyce, who always seemed to pour herself into her work to compensate for a lack of a social life. Or maybe that explained the lack. Not like him. No, not like Adam, the party animal. Adam tightened his mind. Personal issues like this would colour his thoughts and make him miss something important in a diagnosis. He had to stay clear. He glanced at the chart in his hand and called the man's name.

The patient had been in before, never with anything serious. He was seventy-seven years old. The man rose and followed him into an examination room, hunched over to one side and limping as he walked, nothing unusual for a man his age. Adam questioned him, before doing a cursory exam. He seemed fine. No pain or other symptoms, except a mild cold. Nothing else seemed abnormal in any way. The man's pressure was a bit elevated, but nothing alarming. His heart was fine.

The old man in front of Adam needed something, but it wasn't medical care. Another lost soul pleading from loneliness. It was sad that he had to get it here.

Adam didn't have much time. The ward was more than full, cases arriving faster than the staff could handle them. He had to move on. Adam told the old man there was nothing he could find wrong with him, no medicine to prescribe. Adam walked him out of the emergency area and waited with him for a moment. The old fellow persisted.

"But you didn't take an x-ray. How can you know there's nothing wrong without an x-ray?"

"I'm sorry, but there's nothing more that I can do for you. All the tests in the world aren't going to find what's wrong with you. Look, are you married? Do you have any children?"

"Married? I was married for forty-seven years. Ethel, she was my wife, we had to bring her here after she got the stroke that night, but they couldn't help her. Never learned to talk again. I had to push her around in her wheel chair, give her baths, feed her, worse things even, everything. She lasted for a few months, before she had another stroke. That one killed her. And do you think my son and daughter-in-law helped? Even once? Ah, too busy, always rushing around. I know, they have a child, always in a hurry to get her to piano class, ballet, every day busy, and when she had an appointment with the orthodontist, while they were working, who do you think they asked to take her? Me, of course. I was not too busy. Not with my Ethel to take care of. And now that she's gone, do I ever get a phone call? Never. I have to call them to tell them that I'm still alive. Not even one phone call."

The man's speech sputtered to an end as a younger man came up the hallway and greeted him. The young man nodded to Adam, who nodded back, and with one hand on his (Adam surmised) father's shoulder, he directed him out of the emergency area towards the doors. Adam watched the two walk off. He wondered how much of the old man's complaints of neglect and ingratitude were real. The fact that he cared surprised him again. He didn't know this man, except for the notes he had read in the man's chart. He really should be a cipher to him, a number on a folder, not a name. He didn't understand why he put himself out when he should really be protecting his own emotions.

What the hell, stop it, he thought. Adam walked over to the main desk for the topmost chart and scanned it quickly, taking in the details of what had been written by the triage nurse and the resident.

As he was reaching for the charts, the pager sang to him again. This time it was his young friend, Mark E, who needed his attention. He was in intensive care again. Adam would have to go to him.

Mark had been Adam's patient since being diagnosed with muscular dystrophy, but still able, despite his gradually weakening muscles, to move his body around with his own strength.

Mark had passed through the emergency ward countless times. The prediction was that he would die in his mid-teens. His strength had steadily waned. Wasting muscles, fighting one another, drooped, no longer able to act as slings for his bones. His chest muscles succumbing, he was now in a battery-powered pneumatic device wrapped around his abdomen to help his chest to rise and fall. Yet there seemed to be other than the usual isotope of oxygen in his lungs, one that sustained those around him. Always bright, open, gentle, even generous, he was fully knowledgeable and accepting of his fate. He had struggled on.

While sharing a few words over bad coffee, Adam would hear that this or that patient of his had died recently. Another had been admitted for surgery, or pneumonia, a weakened heart, or kidneys that had shut down. Each time he heard of the death of one of his patients, Adam nodded, noted the passing of one more. The universe became colder. It was Mark's turn now.

Mark had been in intensive care for a few days. He was complaining of a toothache, among other things. It seemed such a minor thing, when stacked up against everything else that he had endured. Adam knew better than to dismiss it, though. In Mark's fragile state, he was in danger from any infection.

Adam entered the intensive care unit. His head turned from one side to the other, scanning each patient, until he saw Mark in the giant motorized wheelchair. The air propelled by the external chest pump whooshed in and out.

"Hey Mark, how's my best patient?"

"Just fine. I'm going to walk out of here any minute."

"I believe you, Mark. Let's just fix you up a bit first."

"Hurry up. I've got a date tonight."

"Who's the lucky girl?"

"That nurse over yonder." Mark answered with his usual big grin.

Mark's assisted breathing was laboured, and when Adam placed his stethoscope in position, he heard the effects of the liquid building up in Mark's chest. One tube snaked out of the skin of his chest, another thinner pair from his nose. A bottle of clear fluid hung next to him on a pole, its contents flowing slowly into Mark through a fine tube and needle taped to the back of his wrist. Adam looked in Mark's mouth. A lower front tooth had a large red swelling around it. He summoned the dental resident.

Adam checked through the thick chart, seeing the note that carried the letters DNR. He closed the chart, took a quick deep breath and turned back towards Mark and smiled.

"Going to the disco tonight?"

Mark answered, but Adam didn't hear the answer. No need to listen. He knew what it was. There was something else he wanted to hear, but it never came, no matter how hard he leaned into the howling wind to listen for the sounds. Words shaken free of desperation, free of lingering death, free of lives doomed to end, those words rarely came, no matter what he tried. At Adam's bidding, the medical resident on the ward came over and started to leaf through the chart. He stopped suddenly when he read the medical orders. While they waited for the dental resident to arrive, Adam invited him for a short walk down the hall.

"It must be rare that you need a dentist in this ward," the resident remarked.

"True."

"This guy's in pretty bad shape."

"Yeah, he doesn't have much more time."

"So what's the point?"

"The point?"

"Of keeping him going. Of making him comfortable? Especially with all those people waiting for a bed downstairs. He can't exactly be grateful for your efforts. He probably would rather be dead right now."

Adam felt his gall rising, something unexpected again. He eased himself back to flat calm before he answered.

"Would you choose that in his place?"

"Yes, I would."

Adam let his voice rise. "You have all the answers."

"Look at him." the resident protested. "How can he want to continue living."

"Once we're dead, we'll be dead forever."

"So what?"

"You have a hard head. Some day, you'll be there yourself."

"I wouldn't fight if I was him."

"Maybe you chose the wrong profession."

"That's not fair. I'm here to help people."

"So why give up so easily?"

"Everyone dies."

"Everyone dies, but before they do, they live."

"Come on."

"Okay, Dr. Tough Guy. One day you'll be sick. Would you want you as your doctor that day?"

"Sure." The medical resident, tired of the seemingly pointless argument, started to walk away.

Adam was upset now. He paused and sucked in a long breath. "Don't, whatever you do, doctor, ignore me and pretend I'm not here, or you'll face the fucking consequences!"

The medical resident responded to the threat by turning around and staring at Adam. He muttered something derogatory under his breath and turned back to the chart. They had both been on call too long.

The dental resident had the awkward grace to show up at that point. He looked out of place amid the rows of beds with their ventilators, suctions, and bottles of fluid hanging from shiny metal poles with narrow tubes plugged into all these inert, quietly groaning bodies. Banks of monitors, their wiggling lines gliding across a multitude of oscilloscopes, were beeping rhythmically. Adam quickly rattled off the patient's history to the dentist, giving him more information than he really needed or wanted.

The two discussed the case briefly. The dental resident didn't question the philosophical underpinnings of his work. He simply went ahead, anesthetizing and removing the tooth, then made a note in the chart. With a quick nod to Mark, he walked off briskly. The medical resident had stood quietly watching all this.

"I hope he didn't hear our little discussion."

"I know." Pause. "Doctor Gryn, have you ever had to turn off the power?"

"Pull the plug?" Adam sighed. "Twice."

"You were able to?"

"It wasn't easy."

"Look, I'm sorry about being so cynical. I understand what you're saying. I just don't want to. My mom died young from cancer. She fought, we all did, but in the end it was too much for her. Always in pain, and the doctor intervened at the end and helped her. He didn't say that's what he was doing, but that's what it was. It was peaceful at the very end, once they had pushed enough drugs into her. It was tough for us all when we knew she was about to go, especially for my father. I was too young to really understand. All I remember is how much it hurt to lose her. I know now that it was better for her that way. For my dad, too, really. He had spent all his time next to her. He was exhausted. That's why I think some patients should be helped to die."

"I'm really sorry about your mom. I think I understand."

Adam backed away. He hadn't mentioned his own father. The medical resident shook his head, then walked off quickly until he was gone from view. Adam felt like he had failed as a teacher, that he had allowed things to get too emotional, but somehow he felt better. He went back to bid Mark goodbye, knowing that he wouldn't see him again. Mark lurched and struggled to move his arm between inflations of his breathing aid. Holding Simon's gaze with a shaky eye, he reached into a leather bag hanging from the side of his chair and pulled out a tiny metal-cased flashlight. Wheezing and puffing between words and phrases, Mark croaked out "I heard you have a son. Could you give this to him for me. I won't need it anymore."

Adam hesitated, turning the small object in his hand. "Daughter. A bit too young for this, but I'll save it for her, Mark. Thanks. Don't worry. You'll be okay." Mark looked back at him serenely, releasing him from responsibility for the lie. Adam gave Mark a pat on the shoulder and walked away. He could feel Mark's presence behind him, falling into the abyss.

Adam left a message at the ICU desk to call him with any change in Mark's condition. He quickly hiked back to the emergency area to pick up the next chart. The pile wasn't getting any shorter, and some of the charts were weight-lifter's dreams, hefty items full of past history. Some of these people had been in a multitude of times; often it was their only contact with the medical system. They relied on the emergency ward for their regular care. The next patient was a five-year old boy.

Adam poked his head into the waiting area in the hallway and invited the boy and his mother in, asking them to follow him into an examination cubicle. The boy was wheezing. His inhalations were rough and difficult. He was fighting his body, and it was fighting him. It was asthma. A half hour on a mist ventilator in the asthma room would do the trick. He explained the diagnosis and the recommended treatment to the boy's mother.

"Hey, buddy, not feeling so well? Soon you'll be as good as new." Adam looked up and saw that the look of exhaustion and concern on the mother's face had been transformed into one of thread-thin relief. Adam reached into his pocket.

"Hey, buddy, I bet you like to read in bed at night after your mother puts out the lights. I sure did when I was your age." The boy gave a careful nod, looking at Adam, then hesitantly at his mother.

"Well, look what I've got here in my pocket." Adam pulled out the tiny flashlight and pushed it into the boy's hands. "You read a lot, fellow. That's an order. Someday you help someone who's sick, too, when you've read enough." The boy's mother came forward to thank him, but Adam was already out of the room. A nurse was coming in to guide the boy to the asthma suite.

Adam's shift was almost over. He asked about Mark. As Adam had expected, his young patient had died. The nurse at the front desk, the one with the fascinating v-neck blouse, had passed on the message. Adam silently said the first few words of the *kaddish*, the prayer for the dead. Someone else had shut off Mark's pump. Adam was grateful that he had been relieved of the need to take his light away himself. Adam forced thoughts of Mark deep inside himself, where other similar memories crowded together. Here he could ignore them, at least for a while.

He was quite fatigued, badly needing rest and comfort. He needed to release his emotions. The dreams were ever more vivid, his desires more repressed. He missed Lyssa so much when he was on these protracted on-calls. Adam looked forward to the weekend coming up soon, even if he would have to be with Simon. At least he would soon be away from Montreal, away from the emergency room. He would be in Brooklyn, away from this bleak landscape. He hadn't seen his brother for a while. Maybe they could talk things out. He needed that. After the conversation about Mark, he felt that something had changed inside him. He didn't know why. Besides, regarding Simon, he was tired of the bile. Maybe it really was time for peace.

Adam walked into the washroom and looked at his face in the mirror. After his sleep deficit, it looked especially haggard. There were bags under the eyes, the beginning of lines on his forehead and at the corners of his mouth. His eyes were wet. He wondered at this, at the dangerous emotion gathered about Mark's passing. He shivered the thought away. He touched the empty place inside his pocket, where Mark's flashlight had been. He had needed to get rid of it. Some things had to stay separate.

Soon he could walk out the doors of the hospital, to be greeted by the early morning sun, and breathe the fresh air. For now, though, he still had an hour on duty.

27 Mystery

I slip through the rushing waters of your stream. You stand on the bank and smile as I float past. You stretch out your hand. I touch your fingers; I believe you can save me. You pull back your arm, still smiling. "I am not for you," you shout over the roar of the waters. The stream pulls on me. The water is cold. I look back, and, water filling my mouth, I cry out to you. You turn serenely and walk away.

Lyssa was mystery. Enigma.

Adam had met her at a party, a birthday party for a mutual woman friend. It was her fortieth, and it was festive. Everyone had brought some treat for the birthday girl- fancy cakes decorated with threads of spun chocolate or edible flowers, carved fruit in the shapes of animals and plants, small balls of sweet paste wrapped in a foil of real silver.

Almost everyone came with an escort. But not Adam, who was always too busy for anything resembling a social life. If anyone asked him why, or suggested they knew a wonderful woman he would hesitate or defer. His dates were seldom productive, that is, rarely did the women he took out agree to see him again, if indeed he called back. Not that he wasn't interested, or that, 'God forbid', as his mother said, he was queer, or socially inept. He was simply married to his work, so much so that he had little energy, emotional or physical, or even the imagination, for anything else.

But Lyssa, well, she was there, waiting for him. Not consciously, not knowing he would be there, but still, waiting. As if she had always known him. She was drawn across the room the moment he entered. Like a cat, patient, about to pounce, yet independent. Adam felt instantly attracted to her, but couldn't explain it. He didn't even want to try.

Lyssa. Lyssa. Adam closed his eyes, that night after the party, with only this one thought. Lyssa. Lyssa. But still, even that thought wasn't clear. She was mysterious. A question. Unknowable, except those small parts she let him own or take or touch.

Even now, after he had already known her for a few years, after they had lived together for this long, much of her was hidden. Even now, after they had had a child together, who she had named Lara, after someone, he didn't know who, perhaps it really was Lara of *Dr. Zhivago*, perhaps someone else in her past, or out of her imagination, or out of another book she may have read, even now, he didn't know her. She was hidden, behind a parasol, behind a wall of Japanese rice paper, thin, easily penetrated, easily torn. But opaque.

He had found a beer in the fridge. The other men there each held a half-full wineglass in one hand and a clean napkin in the other. Lyssa sipped on a wine, more or less a champagne, a vertical column of fine bubbles rising, exploding elegantly at the surface, delicately wetting her upper lip and the tip of her nose as she drank. She was next to Adam when he offered her a napkin. She was momentarily puzzled, but when he gestured towards her lip and nose, she smiled, patted herself dry, and burst into a provocative laugh. He responded with the same, enjoying her.

"Always drink your beer straight from the bottle?"

"You don't like that?"

She purred. "What did you bring?"

She continuing to stand next to him. Embarrassed, he pointed to the bowl of potato salad that he had hurriedly managed to buy at the corner deli near his apartment just before it closed.

"My favourite," she smiled, said to make him feel at ease.

"You're very nervous, aren't you?" she remarked as he repeatedly looked at his watch and checked his pager to make sure it was still active and that he had received no messages from the hospital switchboard. "But nervous, in a charming way."

He felt encouraged.

"And what did you bring?" As he expected, her choice was much more interesting, more cosmopolitan.

"Stuffed vine leaves, flavoured with cardamom and lemon. I made them myself. Try them."

"My favourite," he had answered, smiling again, then laughing again.

They had sat together with their buffet plates balanced on their knees. She was lithe and cat-like; he had an air of solidity. He remained wordless, listening as she spoke. He didn't want to argue. He had enough of that at the hospital. She claimed that cats knew when their owners were about to arrive, while they were still distant, beyond its sight, its hearing, or its sense of smell. The cat would be there, at the door, scratching, purring, stretching out on its belly, running its tail against the door, long before its owner was close, had taken a key out, or touched the doorknob.

She had expected an argument on this. The endemic contentiousness of men made her shudder. It was as if they questioned her right to live. Adam wasn't like that, she was finding. It pleased her. "Don't you believe me? Don't argue!" she was ready to say. He hadn't challenged her, though, putting the wisdom down to some female sense, that form of knowing that he couldn't fathom.

That night he had fallen asleep thinking of her. Thinking of her name. She was already sleeping, lying there next to him, this person he didn't yet know and perhaps never would.

She had told him, later, on another night, not there at the party, that she wanted his child. Lara, that was to be her name. She knew it would be a girl. There was no question in her mind. She had not yet become pregnant, not yet undergone a sonogram or any other type of test. With his medical expertise he was skeptical, but she was right. Lara she was, born when they had known each other for two years.

She had wanted that child even then at that party, as they stood looking at each other, had wanted it since he had entered the house with his friends Trisha and James, and had seen her standing against one wall, looking over the crowd and waiting, it seemed, for him to come closer.

He came home late one night. Lyssa was already asleep. He took his shoes off before he got to the door, held his breath, and let the key glide into the lock. As he opened the door, the cat was there, looking up at him with its bright, other-worldly eyes, purring. Her animal spirit, floating free, greeted him. It turned and led him up the stairs to her bed, then retreated to its own.

Lyssa was mystery. And her cat was there now, testifying for her and luring him, again, into its realm, into Lyssa's realm.

Lara was not really his, only hers. He had only contributed his semen, felt that this was in essence all she had desired from him, that act of procreation. Somehow, although she loved him, her daughter was in her mind apart, in a separate place, a place he could not penetrate, despite having penetrated her for this purpose. Love was what they made, often, even when they weren't making Lara.

Love was what Adam was thinking of now, as he left the hospital for home. He was thinking of Lyssa, of his dreams and his needs.　　　It　　　was　　　his　　　birthday.

28 Birthdays

His spirit was island. A mapped island, mapped in contour lines, layers piled one upon the other, stacked desires and regrets, some larger, some less urgent, sitting here in the middle of this dark cold turbulent ocean, froth and dark green cast all about.

His was a volcanic isle, jutting sharply above the noisy water, sinking deep to its origin on a deep sea fissure, a ridge in mid-ocean, the crust of the earth rolling out here, being born in pain and heat. An island which was, where water gave way to air, corroding, eroding, the construct of dense basalt, glassy obsidian, and effervescent pumice. A contradiction facing itself and enfolded within itself. His was an island of ice and fire, bathed in fogs, neither a child of winter nor of summer, roiling hot pool and frozen, slow-moving glacier.

In that cold ocean, just beyond the point where the breakers start their roll towards the crumbling shore, there, biding its time, circling, it seems forever, was the shark.

Late afternoon. Menacing clouds gathered overhead, thickening, the sky darkening. The air was fresh, waiting to be inhaled. Simon breathed it in, wavering, soon to take leave of his city. It was also his birthday. No matter.

As a gift to himself, he had left work early. He felt his past, before life became so complicated, pulling at him. His birthday had given him an excuse to play hooky. He drove down to his old stomping grounds, roamed around the small European specialty shops and cheap clothing stores on St. Lawrence, and picked up a bargain tie and a plastic raincoat for his trip. After buying the bagels on Fairmount, he stopped in at the Bancroft Snack Bar at the corner of Mount Royal and St. Urban for coffee and cheese cake. It would have spoiled his appetite for supper, except there would be no supper. Outside the restaurant, workers were on a scaffold, exchanging the sign over the door for a new one. *Beauty's*, it said. Simon scratched his head. 'What's that about?' he wondered. The old sign had been fine with him.

Coming out, he glanced north towards the brown brick cube of Bancroft, his elementary school. Nostalgia, thick and juicy, rushed over him like a stream in flood. Like a spawning salmon returning to the stream where it had been raised, he felt compelled to walk over to the ancient courtyard apartments on Esplanade where he had lived as a boy. Looking around, though, there was unfamiliarity about the place, a change of definition in his head, as if the poles had shifted and he was looking north when his inner lodestone said east.

Before entering the restaurant, he had left his car along Mount Royal, next to the park, in the single parking spot still available, but most of the parked cars had cleared out by now. He checked the parking signs again to make sure he wouldn't be ticketed. He still had another 20 minutes, plenty of time to take a quick look at his old home. He wandered over towards the front door that had been his when he was a boy.

Simon knew there would be no birthday party for him tonight. His brother was already at the airport, flying separately. Adam and Lyssa would have celebrated the previous night, but no, he remembered that his brother had been on call overnight. No party for him either. It didn't make Simon happier to know that.

Catherine hadn't celebrated Simon's birthday for several years. He no longer pretended that shared events mattered. That morning when he had wandered into the kitchen, she was already gone for the day. Shopping. Anything to get out of the house. Anything to get away from him.

Simon had made himself a toast and smeared some chocolate hazelnut spread over it. Looking at it, he impulsively reached into the junk drawer and pulled out the Hanukkah candles. He pushed one through the spread and lit it. When he blew on it, it tipped sideways and down into the Nutella.

"Happy birthday, Simon," he muttered with disappointment in his voice.

Simon ventured into the same courtyard he had grown up in but had never returned to since. He expected the same slum-like conditions he remembered. To his surprise, the apartment building had been repaired and upgraded, and turned into condominiums. It looked beautiful, although a little put on, artificial. He drew a bagel from a large paper bag and took a huge chewy bite. He heard singing coming from the direction of his childhood apartment.

Curious, he approached the living room window of the ground floor flat where he once lived. There was a party going on inside. A woman was carrying a large cake covered in a sea of light, too many candles to count. Men and women about his age, in their thirties and early forties, stood around, plastic wineglasses in their hands. Ranged along one wall was a table covered in a cloth, heaped with food–salads, bread and rolls, sliced meat and bread, and mixtures of exotic-looking foods. The ceiling was covered in helium balloons.

A man came forward, flushed with emotion, and blew out his candles. He was instantly smothered by women kissing him, some on the cheek, others full on the lips. The window was slightly ajar, and he heard the birthday song being sung for "André". Simon couldn't help himself. Who were these people? He had to get closer. Filled with envy, he wanted so very badly to exchange places with the man on the other side of the window glass. Fascinated, his usual guard down, he approached and put his face against the glass. He should have known better–he was spotted by a woman at the party. She pointed one wineglass-bearing hand at him, yelled out loudly, and promptly spilled her wine. It sprayed across the window.

Simon backed away, aghast and ran back to the street. Was this rightly his party, he wondered, one he would have had in this place, had he never moved, never met Catherine, never veered from the life his parents had wanted for him? Simon bit into his cheek and felt an oddly satisfying crunch of pain explode between his molars. He dropped the remains of the bagel to the ground. From a tree nearby, a squirrel rushed forward and retrieved it. Rubbing his injured cheek, he returned to his car, reached into his bag, and pulled out another bagel. He bit his cheek again and muttered under his breath. He tasted blood.

There was a parking ticket on the windshield. Thirty-five dollars. "For God's sake, not again," he muttered, and got into his car and headed home. It was getting late and he had that flight to New York to catch.

Once home, he had only enough time to gather up his valise. The old yellow one had been his father's when he had arrived in Canada years ago. It was old and quite useless, but Catherine had, without asking him, lent his other bag to her sister Marie for her trip to Paris. He strained on the old bandaged handle, hoping it would last the trip. He mumbled goodbye to Catherine as he passed behind her on his way out the door. She didn't turn away from the television set. He returned to his car and drove away.

Towards the west, the sun was just now dipping below the base of the dark blanket of clouds, preparing itself for the trip below the horizon, and its brilliant glow pervaded the air around him. His eyes closed reflexively. Red flickers through closed eyelids gave evidence both of the outside world and the stuff of his own body. Simon's teeth clenched together as his jaw muscles contracted. He still tasted blood.

The day was sagging, getting old. Simon gripped the wheel with one hand, the fingers of the other drumming the steering wheel in time with the music of the radio. A raindrop fell against the windshield. Simon drove east. This coming September, Matthew would have gone to the elementary school he had just passed, if only he was still alive. Simon let out a deep moan, almost a howl. He was still grieving. For his son, for his father. Could it really be almost three years that Matt was gone? Duvid too, not so very long ago. How many months? His vision blurred as his eyes filled and spilled over.

The day was rapidly clouding over now. It was ending. Sabbath eve was coming. The air started to carry the odour of burning wax, the sum of candles by thousands burning separately and together to herald the coming of the newest Sabbath. For Simon this was not to be a window in the solid wall of the week as it had always been for his parents. He was not persuaded. He had left his mother's simple beliefs behind years ago.

A fine rain started to fall, almost a fog, and drifted against the windshield. A pretty young woman, her daughter's hand held tightly, ran by. Their feet struck the pavement with a harmonious rhythm, throwing up broken sheets of water from quickly forming puddles. An old man at the corner shuffled forward. Simon turned on the wipers, and left him behind. He drove past the traffic light at the main street intersection and turned left, north along Decarie towards the Metropolitan. He was finally on his way to the airport.

As he passed over the sunken expressway, he saw the tangle of traffic moving slowly, trying to get home, away from the week's traumas to others more intimate. He muttered a bit, knowing that he should have left earlier, or maybe taken the 20 instead of the 40, but a glance in the opposite direction told him that he would face the same challenge going either way. The traffic guessing game was like the lottery, impossible to forecast. The slowness of the traffic would give him even more time to think, something he wanted to avoid. His jaws clenched as the car in front of him came to a sudden halt, in response to another to his right sliding across two lanes in front of it and muscling off in the express lane.

He hadn't told Catherine where he was headed. They didn't speak to each other anymore. Their son Matthew had remained their tenuous glue, while he was alive. No longer. There were too many other things gone wrong. He had once hoped having a family would tie up his loose ends, in some fashion cushion him, but in the end the effect had been the opposite. Things just happened. Or didn't. Why should he be the one who had to feel guilty?

Simon focussed back on the road ahead. It was still clogged, but the cars seemed to be moving a littler faster than before. Maybe it wouldn't be so bad after all.

He had spoken to Adam just before the weekend. His brother was still chafing. Adam hadn't forgiven what Simon had done to him. They would have to endure each other, while sharing a single hotel room. Simon now wondered why he had proposed that, but it was too late to back out.

Neither brother really wanted to go to the wedding in New York, but, after all, they had so little family. They felt obligated to maintain the links. More important, their mother had insisted they go.

The wedding was happening late tomorrow, Saturday night, after the sun had set and the Sabbath was over. He grabbed another bagel and bit down into his cheek again.

The rain had stopped by the time Simon reached the airport and boarded the aircraft. As it gained altitude, the water receded from Simon's mind. The fragile fuselage became simply an airplane, and he simply on a short flight to New York City.

He didn't visit New York often. In the past it had served him only as a transfer point for flights to somewhere else. Traveling for pleasure, as the customs agents put it, was unusual for him. He had flown most often on assignment since starting out as an investigative journalist. He didn't like flying.

"Something to drink, sir?" He accepted a small bag of peanuts and a tiny bottle of Coke from the female flight attendant.

He tossed a few nuts into his mouth, chewing them slowly. Simon sipped at his drink. He should have eaten before leaving home. Two bagels, one shared with an enterprising squirrel, hadn't been enough. He scanned around him, saw no one he found interesting enough to gaze at, and again looked out the small window at the red clouds and the dimming sunshine. Sitting next to him in the aisle seat was a young man, a little rumpled, in jeans and a t-shirt, reading a magazine. He looked up from the page, checked his watch, and glanced out the oblong glass pane at the dark sky speeding past.

"Can't be very far from New York now." The young man looked excited, a water drop in a hot frying pan, skittering around just before it could mercifully be allowed to evaporate.

"First time flying?"

"Yeah. And my first time in New York."

"Glory be. Double milestone!"

The boy giggled in a childish way. "My girlfriend's studying at Columbia. We've only talked on the phone the last two months."

"You must really miss her. Sorry."

"Yeah."

Neither spoke for a few minutes.

"You've been to New York a lot, haven't you, sir?"

Simon winced at the word 'sir.'

"Many times."

"Going on business?"

"No, not this time. One of my cousins is getting married."

"What line are you in, sir? I hope you don't mind me asking."

"I'm a journalist. Please don't call me sir. Makes me feel old."

"Um, sorry. Wow, that sounds exciting. How did you get started?" The young man was interested.

"Oh, school newspaper. The Montreal Star after graduation. I started out as a science reporter, and then did a column on religion."

"That's weird."

"Yeah, made no sense. A conflict of interest, really. I freelance now. Hard to get a full-time job in the news business these days."

The boy looked puzzled.

"Newspaper folded. Lost my job."

"Write for the tabloids? It seems like you could just make things up these days."

"You're right, but I don't do that. I have standards. Sometimes it's tempting to scoop a story no one else has, but I try to stay ethical. Like all of us, though, I have to eat. Some of us like to eat more than others."

Simon thought about the story Adam had told him. Truth was sacred, he had told himself, even if it hurt someone. Like Adam. Now he regretted it.

"You sound jaded. Doesn't your profession have a mission? You know, free speech, first amendment, all that."

"It doesn't always work out that way. Not even usually, unfortunately. Truth can be elusive. Ethics can be elastic."

The boy went silent, maybe not sure what to make of Simon's evasive comment. Simon settled back into his own thoughts, back to his college days, so long ago, when he wasn't yet a little old, not yet called "sir" by a novice, still free.

Well, now he was again. He looked forward to looking up Rachel again when he got to New York. He had called her from Dorval Airport while waiting to board. She had seemed eager to reconnect. They could throw a few stones into the water that had passed under their bridge.

"What's your name? I'm Alex."

"Well, Alex, my name is Simon, Simon Gryn. What are you studying?"

"Philosophy and Religion."

"Interesting. Where?"

"At Concordia."

"That used to be Sir George Williams in my day. I went to McGill."

"I think I've heard of that place." The boy grinned. He craned his head past Simon to see out the window. The sky was a deep red by now, almost purple.

"Eager, I see. Would you like to switch seats? You'll have a better view."

"No, that's okay."

Simon was touched and a bit terrified to hear the boy's interest in his work. He gave Alex a long glance. The boy probably thought Simon was 'cool'. In his own youth, when he was about this age, things had been wild, maybe wilder. It was a while back, when he had been a student journalist.

When Simon arrived at McGill University, there were dramatic shifts going on in Quebec society. He recalled standing in the cold of January on de Maisonneuve, looking up, as computer tapes and punch cards rained down from the upper windows of the Hall Building. These were the Sir George Williams College computer riots. A group of students, accusing a professor of racism, occupied and ultimately destroyed the computer labs. Research records were destroyed, years of work lost in a flutter of punch card confetti thrown out the windows.

At the *McGill Français* march during autumn of the same year, he had slipped in among the marchers. Police from around the province had been brought in to ring the university's downtown campus shoulder to shoulder. When the march had, inevitably become violent, one policeman landed a truncheon on his skull. Hannah was horrified when she saw his face caked in blood once he had arrived home. For Simon, though, it was an epiphany. He felt transformed, elevated, as if his taking part had mattered in some way.

Bombs had been going off in Montreal for some years, in mailboxes in Westmount, in the stock exchange, at city hall, in an armoury. These targets were extensions of the English and capitalist presence, as seen by extremists of the Quebec separatist movement. The city was ultimately locked down by the Canadian Army in 1970, after the kidnappings: of James Cross, the British trade commissioner, and a Quebec cabinet minister, Pierre Laporte, who was ultimately murdered. Plans had also been made to kidnap the Israeli and American consul-generals, but the arrests of the murderers aborted these actions.

Smaller events also cemented the feelings of distress. One day, as Simon sat in the Student Union building on McTavish, Radio McGill broadcast a fake announcement that the U.S. had dropped an atomic bomb on Hanoi. The war in Viet Nam was a burning issue, and Simon, taken in by the false news, was sure the world was about to be end. Only later, walking through downtown, looking for televised newscasts of the attack, or horror in people's eyes, did he realize it had all been a sham and how gullible he was.

Adam had a summer job in the McGill Genetics Department mouse lab alongside an Jewish-American draft dodger, Jacob Stein. He invited Jacob home for Shabbat dinner. The twins' parents were welcoming, but uncertain what to make of it all. It seemed that the turmoil of Europe that they thought they had escaped was returning. Yet it was a heady time for Simon, a crazy time, full of hope and disappointments. He missed its energy.

'I've seen it all.' he thought. The young man next to him seemed so young and innocent, ignorant of all the damage the world could do to him but hadn't, at least, not yet. The boy was still looking past him, staring out the window at the clouds, an unreadable look on his face. Through the airplane window, Simon could see the last remnants of the dwindling dusk. At the end of the darkened wing, the rhythmic flashing of the red light danced up and down with the wind and changing air flow. The movement worried Simon a little, even though he knew that aircraft were engineered to flex.

Yes, Simon the journalist here, reporting on his experience as the plane plummets at hundreds of miles per hour into the ground. He hears his mother asking why he needs to fly so much.

Can't my son take the train, or drive?

They're more dangerous, Ma. It's been proven. His mother gives him a knowing look. The ground rushes closer.

You'll see. I'm right. You will regret, my smart-ass over-educated son, for not listening to your mother.

Shut up. Ma, he whispered under his breath. He was sweating. His breathing quickened. His flight phobia was kicking in again.

Okay Ma, you're right. He realized that he was terrified. Simon shut his eyes. Maybe this simple act would make the plane vanish, as if he were a two-year-old making a distressing sight disappear. He took another deep breath, willing himself to be somewhere far away. Another deep breath, filling his lungs, slowly, so very slowly. Okay, he was starting to calm down a bit. He concentrated on his world of journalism. Why was he still doing this, why hadn't he settled on something more durable, something that paid better?

His parents had handed off to him one problem that had always stirred him. They and their generation had been through the greatest of turmoils, the Nazi terror and its debris. That war had placed brackets around one period of time, fenced it off like a cage in a zoo, where unspeakably cruel things could be done without reference to anything outside the bars of that enclosure. Many of his parents' friends and family were among its survivors.

But his dilemma was that without these barbaric times that killed so many that he never came to know, he would not have been born. Simon's parents had met because of the upheaval of the war. He was born bewildered, a Jewish phoenix rising from the ashes of his people, not sure if he should fly or not. So for a time he donned the feathers of the birds around him, a cuckoo raised in the nest of avian strangers.

Simon had once nurtured a romanticized image of journalism when he was a then-naïve student reporter. He had truly believed he would distil uncomfortable ideas into a clear liquid called truth. Now, older, more cynical, he saw himself more as a scavenger, and lately, turned full circle, even more like prey. The image of himself as the hyena, with its sharp teeth, its hunkered back, the hunger in its eyes, tearing callously into dying prey, was perversely satisfying. But the refugee stories he had worked on so hard had made him feel more like a bottom feeder. He took the risks, and the story had bitten him back. He was swimming awkwardly below the surface, his breath held. Other people were drowning in this history. He himself had barely reached the air-rich surface above these waters.

The series of articles he had written about refugees had gotten him into so much trouble. The world was full of nomads from so many troubled lands. Like Simon's parents had once, these exiles tried to enter this country, their lives often in danger. For the most part they were unwelcome in their new homes. The courage and determination they had needed to get here went unrecognized.

Simon saw immigration as a right, not a privilege. It was a simplistic belief, based partly on his own family's history, and Simon understood that the child's limited experiences did that, functioning as axioms for the adult's assumptions. The seeming validity of ideas was thus born from logic distorted by sentiment. And so developed political consciousness. Right wing, left wing, middle of the road, all were valid, all were fervently believed. All were flawed in each their own way by the paths that had been taken to them.

And so this idea: The whole world was one open space. People should be able to choose where to go without being restricted by those lucky enough to have gotten there first. The movements of people, individuals sliding along the surface of a globe, brought new ideas and energy, revitalized the stagnant culture and economy of their adoptive homelands. In many minds, though, these were marauders, as they had been for centuries and millennia, come to devastate the lands they entered, supplant those who had come before. Immigrant or invader?

People fleeing from almost-certain danger had to be sorted from the menace and corruption that a few among them could bring to their new home. How to distinguish the false ones, who had committed terrible crimes in their homelands, and were ready to commit more, disguised in the veil of refugee?

He'd come close to trouble with that story. Why the editor chose him to research the story he well understood. He was a Jew, after all. Just the one to look into this story about war criminals living the quiet life in some suburb of Vancouver, or Regina, or Montreal. These weren't the Nazi war criminals who had fled Europe after the War, though. It was largely too late for that story. Many of those were now old men. They were no longer much of a threat to anyone.

He protested to his editor that he couldn't be objective. Secretly, though, he relished the assignment.

They had come from Asia, Latin America, Africa. They had stolen funds, raised armies of mercenaries, culled their minorities, and struck deals with a West willing to overlook such details in their appetite for profit. They moved into the drug trade and slavery. Free enterprise, they called it, which they also called freedom, or even democracy, but it was far from any of that. They had escaped when they could no longer hold on to power, but their funds had gone before them, and their connections kept them in the game. There were bodies along the way, dead children and grandmothers, but business was business. Nothing personal.

They had entered the country through actions and inactions by members of vast bureaucracies. Some came via mistakes, some by bribes, meanwhile keeping details of involvement in such sad and terrible crimes out of the public eye.

He had done the story perhaps a little too well, and the wealth of detail had become a book. He had done well with it. He could for a time choose the stories he would investigate. He should have been more afraid, though. Former masters of atrocity didn't welcome exposure with serenity. They still had a mesh of supporters, duly paid and ready to act. Danger could be opaque. He had lived with it. It could also be blatant. This he had lived with too.

He had lived easily with the messages on his answering machine, electronic noises on a loop of plastic film, or so he told himself. He lived less peacefully with the notes scrawled on scraps of paper, slipped under the windshield wiper of his car, or scratched in the paint on his car door. The drive home, with glaring, brutish-looking men in cars next to or behind him made him uneasy, but these men didn't wear badges displaying their affiliations–they could just have had a bad day at the office. He shrugged his fears away. The screaming swastikas and hate messages felt-markered or spray-painted on his front door or across his driveway threw Catherine into hysterics.

One day, they had openly come for his son and wife in daylight. It was only through fortune that his father was there and fended them off. That was when he had stopped his enquiries, after Catherine had met him at the door, screaming, the day of the attempt on her and their son. She was holding Matthew in her arms. His parents were both there.

"My too smart son acts like a child. He doesn't understand simple mathematics. One man and one woman makes three, and that's as far as a man should take his responsibility." That was his mother's comment as they walked out the door.

"You shouldn't have had a family! I'll leave you and take Matthew with me, because you won't protect us. This story is more important to you than we are."

But the newspaper articles had already been published, the names named. The public inquiry followed. Little changed. Too many cozy arrangements with politician's assistants had been constructed. And Simon, stubborn, determined to act on what he called principle, still held the same opinion–the world, all of it, belonged to each and every one who lived in it. Duvid called him ridiculous and stupid. A fool.

Simon received a journalism award for his trouble, but as he walked off the dais, the looks in the eyes of his applauding confreres told him that he had been too zealous, not cold-blooded enough. They were all jealous, he argued in his head. He did question himself, though.

In this amoral age, was anyone motivated by right and wrong anymore? The fear of losing what they had weighed more than ethics in keeping people out of trouble. Karl Marx knew this. It was an overlooked factor in class struggle. Those with more to lose than gain would try harder to live their established "moral" life. Those with less could overturn rules they had no part in writing. All, pushed far enough, would descend to callousness. Self-interest was a property of life in society as much as density or elasticity were properties of the materials of the structured world.

Simon again looked out the airplane window at the now almost-blackened clouds below. The airplane's air had an odour of something stale overlaid with an artificial freshness. The plastic of the seat backs was visibly aged and cracked. Cosmic radiation streaming through the body of the craft during all these years of cruising at these high altitudes had accelerated the damage. Simon suddenly felt fragile and exposed. He looked around, drawing on a silent camaraderie of weakness with the others on board. The boy beside him turned towards the aisle, looked forward and aft, hoping the flight attendant would bring him another snack. He evidently hadn't had much supper either.

"What story are you investigating now?"

No answer.

"Am I being too nosy?"

"No, no. Nosy is what I do. I don't mind your interest. I'd rather that than indifference. The story I'm working on now is no secret, really. I'm going to Israel to interview some former Soviet bloc immigrants. They're having a hard time adjusting, and so is Israel in adjusting to them. Should be interesting."

The boy's face lit up. "Israel, eh? You're Jewish, right?"

Simon nodded, said nothing.

"I once wanted to visit Israel, but my girlfriend thought it would be too dangerous."

"Just because Israel is always at war?"

"You're trying to be funny."

"Yes, but it's not funny at all."

"You're not wearing one of those round little hats?"

"Most Jews don't. But we're still Jews."

"Okay." The boy went silent.

Religion, Simon thought, a hard concept. It took effort to have faith. The Cro-Magnon or Neanderthal soul in him prayed, though Simon the Westerner didn't. It was part of his genetic makeup, built into the architecture of his mind. Sometimes he thought he believed. Sometimes he just wanted to.

Questions like this were essentially a waste of time, he had decided long ago. His father's camouflaged silences, his mother's dread, had restricted his questions by tests of necessity and fear.

How to forgive God for allowing it all to happen, his uncertain, indifferent God, betraying His own people. Hadn't He chosen them, after all? Or had they really chosen Him?

Such betrayal. The Holocaust had decimated the Jewish people, his people. There had been a multitude of pogroms, wars, crusades, inquisitions, and other human disasters that had come about during these last few thousand years, but none could compare with this. It was not the cruelty of the killers and torturers. There had always been plenty of that. It was not the size of the destruction. Scale was not a measure of evil. It was the industrial, detached, mechanistic approach that had been taken by the Nazis. Blueprints, efficiency analyses, factories, industrial contracts, train schedules, assigned workers, research on the technology of mass murder, attempts at the economic uses of the by-products of the destruction—the hair, body fat, eyeglasses, clothing, gold teeth, and so on and on. It had all been so well-planned, so rational. Pseudoscientific medical experiments, the degradation of people to the point where they didn't see death as worse than the horrors of this life.

The inhuman factor, then. The Nietzschean *ubermensch*—these 'supermen'—consoled themselves that they needed, for the sake of the future world they strived to create, to do terrible things, justify the atrocities as necessary work done by brave people overcoming their own human weaknesses. This wasn't only and purely hatred, of only following orders. It came from a different plane of existence.

They could rationalize. They would go home in the evenings, detached, unstained, bounce their children on their knees, savour their suppers. What were once human beings were now seen as vermin, differentiated only by their numbered tattoos, fit for nothing but work or death.

They had been transformed into *homunculi*, *golems*, shape-shifted creatures, now spiritless, waiting only to be destroyed by the hand pointed left or right. The ritual writing on the skin of their forearms, encrypted them as a sequence of digits, identities from which all meaning had been withdrawn. Those branded in this manner received the questionable favour of a few days or weeks extension of life as slave labour. Those not labelled died immediately on arrival, anonymous, unacknowledged, in abundance.

Human beings totally dehumanized—bits of protoplasm waiting to be squashed, skittering like beetles beneath a dark, starless sky. This holocaust had left a scratched line across the terrible sliding surface of history. It was as much a revolution in human thought as the great western religious movements of the first millennium. The world was such a different, diminished place after it was over, a gouged excoriation filled with this moral scar tissue. The evil had tainted us all, all now become transient flesh, without soul or value.

Guilt. To have survived when others whom one loved—children, or parents, a wife, or a sister—had not, how could a person forgive himself or herself? This poisoned the lives of the survivors. Like his parents. Like himself, their son.

And yet these people, despising themselves for living on, felt obligated to continue. They had been given the burden of remembrance, the burden to rebuild, to repopulate. Why were they still here? Raw luck? Character? Ability? Some survived, others died. The living carried within themselves memories of a world erased.

There were many stories, a multitude, too many. There were too many tales to tell, to record, to read. And what of the orphan stories, the stories known only by ghosts, where there were no survivors, whole families and whole towns destroyed to the last soul? And would the knowledge of these stories cripple the children and grand-children of the survivors? Were they better not knowing, living strong and fearless, untouched by the past?

Where were the mathematical laws that made one person live, another die? Could the smallest act make a difference? There were no simple cause-and-effect reasons why things turned out the way they had, no simple correlations.

But there must be reasons. There must. Must! Otherwise what? How to maintain faith in a disordered universe? How to believe in his own reality, to understand?

Too difficult, the determining factors fading away into wafts of smoke, the gentle sprinkle of butterfly's scales, invisible in the wind, the thinnest dust, gleaming in the brightness of the sun. The finely structured fabric of disorder. The parallax of curse and blessing passing each other in a fog.

Fog. Simon stared out the window, deep in thought. Wisps of vapour raced by, illuminated by the lights on the wings. The plane bumped up and down a bit. Turbulence. Simon grabbed the arm rests, his fears suddenly returning. The plane was beginning to glide lower and had entered the cloud cover. He was again back in his surroundings.

The young man next to him had his eyes closed. The seat back in front of him was tipped back and he could see the bald head of the man in that seat. He too seemed asleep. He realized he had to use the washroom, but not so badly that he would disturb all around him to get there. He would wait. It shouldn't be much longer before they landed. He glanced at his watch. Twenty minutes, not more.

He let his thoughts wander again. Thoughts of history, science and superstition. Despite hatred and fear in twisted minds over centuries, human thought had also deduced the basic structure of our universe.

The principle of uncertainty had been derived in the first decades of this century. One could measure either the position or the velocity of a subatomic particle, but not simultaneously. The observation of an event changed that event, so that it could never be fully described.

Did this apply to humanity? Trying to discover both the position and speed of an electron in its cloud around an atom, of a person in this crowd around a planet shifting–predictions were possible, but could be right or wrong, or both at once. The indeterminate nature of nature seemed so durable at our level of reality, but under it all, subatomic, it was insubstantial. As fragile as the love that shaped it. For nothing can be known for sure, and ultimately, perhaps nothing can be known at all.

The observer changes that which is observed, converting the unpredictable into the irredeemable. Such outcomes need no purpose, are acts without meaning or motive. But their message is: by our presence, we change what we see and it changes us. In that, perhaps, there is hope. For Simon, it was the journalist's motivating factor.

If we set circumstances in motion, how do they impinge on our lives later? The stone is thrown into the pond, the ripples follow. The stone is thrown into the sea, skipping once, twice, gone. Does its impact add to the waves, create the storm, touch our wayward boat, steering that fearful sea? Where is its effect, where does it touch land again, climb the shore, creep up while we walk the sands in the dark night? What of the shark that watches the stone's slow twisting dance to the sea's bottom? Does he turn away, or does he know–there is my food, there my lust will be fulfilled.

Can we alter the future? Throw that stone more to the left? Push more on the tiller, lean harder into the wind. Can we walk faster along the transient, sliding sand dune? Avoid the shore that day? Does the act of decision have any validity, or do random events finally bury most efforts we make to control our lives? Can we defeat entropy? Is chaos tangible, showing itself as a fractal landscape, event within event, mirroring itself endlessly in opposing looking-glasses. History repeats itself, chaotically, from scale to scale, small to large, an endless shoreline. Each scale is spiralling ever downwards, dislodged from a butterfly's lightly beating wing. Torn from the sandpaper skin of the undulating shark.

Simon was wrenched from his reverie. The tenor of the airplane engines had changed. They were louder, fighting the flaps that were rising on the plane's wings, working it lower toward the ground. Simon focussed suddenly on now. The boy next to him was staring out the window. The great city was spread out below, its white sea of lights seductive, waiting for them to enter.

Simon anticipated the dreaded overseas flight to Tel Aviv that would follow after the wedding he was going to tomorrow. Today, though, the destination was New York City. Just a family wedding, his second cousin's son getting married. Morton. Such a name. He had never met the boy, but family was important, at least some of the time. Duty (and his mother's insistence) had forced him to come. After the wedding, he would be off again. He had been assigned the new story. Maybe that would help him with his questions.

Awareness of gravity and inertia came back overwhelmingly as the plane banked to the left on its approach to LaGuardia. Simon's stomach tightened and he squeezed the armrests with both hands, as if, he thought self-mockingly, this useless action would somehow save him if something really did go terribly wrong. All this time he looked out the window at the crazily changing tilt that the ground kept making. He again pictured the airplane around him invisible. He was floating in air, floating rapidly, the hard ground seconds away. He was not enjoying this. The engines of the plane sounded groaningly old, battling the air and gravity.

Simon's face went through colour changes from white to whiter to flushed heat. He hated flying. And it was getting worse each time. Fear was at its worst now. Then came the loud rush of air banging against the fully raised flaps, the bump as the wheels bounced against the runway, the screaming roar of the engines going into reverse to brake the plane's rush toward the airport buildings, and finally the slow taxiing up to the apron. Some of the less-jaded, more superstitious passengers applauded the landing. On the other side of the aisle, he noticed an older woman crossing herself. Oh yeah, pray, Simon thought to himself. At his age, barely into his fourth decade, the fear of death had a long way to go before it would translate itself into faith. Maybe it never would. The boy next to him let out a long rush of breath as he stared out the window. Simon smiled in sympathy.

29 Old Valise

Happily, the hotel room Simon had reserved was near the airport. Less effort required. He was feeling low on energy, and New York was not a city he enjoyed being in any more.

At the front desk, the clerk told Simon that he could go right up and issued him a room key. He found the elevator, tapped at the correct floor number, and waited for the doors to open. He cantilevered open the door to the hotel room. His brother Adam had already arrived. He looked up and grunted. He was still angry, it seemed. It would take time before he would forgive the trouble Simon had caused him. But then he turned and smiled. Maybe Simon was wrong in his first impression.

They rarely stayed together anyway, not since their marriages. The last time Simon could remember had been at Isla dos Mujeres off the Yucatan, years earlier, just before the start of university classes. He shuddered at the memory of the giant cockroach attacking him in the bathroom of their hotel room.

"Well, greetings, welcome to New York. And happy belated birthday. How was the flight?" Adam had flown in earlier from Toronto and was putting his things away in the top drawers of the dresser, going over a check list in his mind. He had carefully brought only enough for the weekend. He seemed friendly enough, or at least neutral.

"Not too bad, except for the turbulence and the lack of food and leg room. Happy belated birthday to you too. Feel like an old man yet, like me." Simon responded. He was too tired to carry on a conversation at that moment, only wanting to put his clothes away and get to bed, despite his hunger.

"You should have flown first class, like me."

"We're not all millionaires, Adam."

"Sensitive today?" Adam eyed Simon's suitcase. "You could do with a luggage update too. Yours is pretty beat up."

"It's the one Ma gave me after Ta died. Catherine gave my good bag away to her sister Claire for her trip without asking me. I wanted to get a new one, but who ever has the time?"

As his suitcase emptied, Adam abruptly realized that he'd forgotten something.

"Damn! Do you have an extra tie? It looks like I forgot to bring one."

"Sorry, Adam. Only one."

"Okay, I'll have to go out tomorrow morning and buy one. Want to come along?"

"Uh, no, I can't. I'm meeting someone tomorrow before the wedding."

"Oh?" Adam stopped talking. "How is Catherine, by the way?"

"Just meeting an old friend, Adam. You're just like Ma. Stop making a mountain out of Mohammed."

Adam shook his head at Simon's screwed-up nostrum. "That's the head of a camel on a pin you're talking about."

"Ha-ha."

"I saved the bottom drawers for you. I hope you don't mind bending a bit."

Simon began to unpack now, methodically putting each of his things away. He had really brought too much, except for the tie. But that was because this was only the first leg of his journey. He hadn't told his brother about that yet.

He leaned low and his back complained. Travelling was a heavy task, especially handling a large old valise without wheels. He was running out of drawers before he got close to the bottom of his suitcase. Simon looked around for more space to stash his things, and saw the bedside cabinet where the Gideon Bible lay. Out it came to make room. He shovelled a few things in, but it wasn't enough.

"You don't really need to empty that thing completely, do you? Can't you just leave them inside it?"

"I like my clothes unwrinkled."

"You're such a neurotic."

"You would know."

"Meaning what, that I have special training or that I'm like that too?"

"Take your pick. I'm too tired to argue."

"Looks like you brought your whole house, Simon. Catherine might wonder if you're planning to go back."

Simon ignored his brother's teasing. "No problem, brother. Mock me all you want, but I didn't forget to bring a tie."

A good portion of the contents of the old suitcase were still where they had been.

"Too many clothes. Doesn't look like clothes for New York City, either."

"None of your business. Shut up."

"Very nice. So be a shit, I don't care. I don't think you'll be unpacked by morning and I'm too tired to stay up late."

Simon continued to take everything out of the suitcase, piling it carefully on the floor between the two beds. He just didn't like leaving them any longer than necessary in this crummy, smelly old suitcase. Adam was right. He'd brought a lot. He would need them, though, once he was in Israel. Maybe he would have the time to buy a new bag tomorrow, before his "date."

"Now what? Are you just going to leave it there? You'll trip getting out of bed during the night."

Simon picked up each pile and carried it over to the top of the desk-dresser. Two drawers were empty and that took care of most of the smaller items. He carried his suit and sports jacket to the closet, and added his five shirts. When he was finally finished and was closing the old valise, he noticed a loose edge at the inside corner. He pulled on it and saw that there was something secreted there, a few old manila envelopes. One envelope came away as he gave it a light tug. He teased it open. It felt brittle. Inside the flap he could make out the edges of old paper and bits of stained cloth. They seemed fragile. The faintly musty odour irritated his nose.

Must be his father's old sewing patterns. He looked over toward Adam, who was sleepily watching a rerun of part of a hockey game.

"Look what I found here." Simon fingered the suitcase handle. Adam glanced up and the look on his face came alive as he noticed the flustered look on Simon's face.

"What's up?"

"I found something under the lining of this suitcase."

"Oh ya, what?"

"I don't know. A big yellow envelope."

"Probably Ta's old cutting patterns. Junk. Like that bag. Who needs it?

"Why do you think it was hidden?"

"Maybe it's private stuff that Ta wouldn't have wanted us looking at."

"You're such a romantic."

"You think?"

"No. You wouldn't know romance if it hit you in the face. So I shouldn't look at it?"

"Exactly. Good night. And I'm at least as romantic as you are. Ask Lyssa sometime." Adam abruptly clicked the television off with the remote and flopped his head down on his pillow. "Flip off the light, will you?"

Within minutes, he was snoring lightly.

Simon flipped off the light. He stared at his brother in the illuminated dark and sighed. How did Lyssa put up with the guy, he wondered? Women's motives always eluded him.

Sometime later, a stream of expletives burrowed hazily through Simon's dream as his brother, walking to the bathroom in the dark unfamiliarity of the hotel room, walked into Simon's open suitcase, and almost tripped. Within the dream, his father sat on the corner of the bed and laughed, to Simon's great satisfaction. He was glad to see the old man could have fun, even if only posthumously.

Simon hadn't slept very well but had finally given up and gotten out of bed. He was ravenous. He could hear other early-risers, baths running, the sounds of rushing water vibrating through the complex of pipes that made up part of the hotel's skeleton. He sat in the room's armchair in his underwear. He waited for Adam to wake up, and remembered his discovery of the night before. He was about to get up to look at the contents of the envelopes when Adam woke up, stretching and suddenly farting loudly.

"Oh God, Adam."

"Just physiology. Everyone does it."

"Okay. Let's get out of here and let it air out. I'm hungry."

"Give me a few minutes to lie here. I don't usually get the luxury to do that." He closed his eyes for a few minutes, while Simon headed for the bathroom.

A little later they were waiting for their eggs and toast to arrive at a deli across the road from their hotel. Adam asked Simon about his find.

"I haven't looked yet."

"Well, on second thought, there might be something important there. You never know. Maybe we should have a look later this afternoon before the wedding."

"There may not be time."

"Why's that?"

"I'm meeting someone."

"Who?"

"Researching a story."

Their breakfast arrived and the brothers dug in hungrily.

"How's work going with the trauma team?"

Adam's face sagged haggardly. His weariness bubbled outwards through his skin, trying to escape into air. Simon's world was forgotten.

"Thirty hours at a pop, yeah, it isn't easy. It's hard to think straight. I worry about making the right decisions and I'm tired of having to care all the time. Why am I doing this? Maybe I'm trying to atone for something."

"Maybe you are, for something that happened before you were born. Maybe you're in the wrong profession."

"Not like your carefree job, eh? Just kidding, Simon."

"Maybe it is easier than yours. I don't really have to deal with people as individuals most of the time. It's more abstract than that. The event, the issue, the motive, that's what really matters to me. I don't think I could do what you do, deal with pain one person at a time. And I don't have to make those judgments. You deal with keeping people alive, and, I guess, have to decide sometimes when not to. I don't think anyone has ever died because of something I wrote, or didn't. Not yet, anyway."

"What about me after what you wrote?"

"You didn't die."

"My life didn't get better, that's for sure."

"I'm sorry. Truly. My life hasn't been a happy time either, you know."

"You're right. I shouldn't *kvetch*. You lost Matthew and Ta. It's been harder for you."

"And Catherine as my wife. Yeah, harder. You know, Ma wanted you to come look at Matthew when he was sick, but I kept telling her you were too busy. Thanks for coming by anyway."

"There was nothing I knew to do besides what was already being done. I came every few nights and looked at his chart."

"Well, you left me the notes."

"I'm sorry I couldn't help more than that."

"It helped me."

There was a look of relief, the whisper of a smile, on Simon's face.

"It must have been hard for you, working two shifts at your hospital half way across town and dropping by to see Matthew, too. You really must have been dead tired."

"And I still am. And I will die, if I have to keep this hospital schedule for too much longer."

"Well, maybe you should try something else. You could open your own office and spend all your time hiring and firing secretaries, keeping the books straight, and worrying about paying the rent."

Adam laughed at this. "Could be worse, you're right. Come to think of it, though, what about your dangerous immigrants articles? Somebody really could have died."

"Yeah, well, that's true. Me."

"You were foolish, putting your family in danger. Catherine was pretty upset."

"It scared her, but that type of story is what I do best, Adam. It's my job and I try not to get into trouble. I'm really a very happy coward. And you, killed any of your patients lately?"

Adam dropped the discussion. He still hadn't digested his thoughts after Mark's death and he didn't want to display these messy feelings to his brother. Or himself. He shrugged. "Only the ones who haven't paid their bills."

"Lucky we have universal medicare. Keeps you from wanting to kill anyone."

"Yeah, I'd be a real menace if I was a doctor down here in America."

After breakfast, Adam went out to shop for his tie. Simon didn't feel like shopping for a travel bag and went back to the hotel room. Simon was feeling paunchy. He was still too sleepy to go for a walk. He felt he ought to go down for a swim, but he decided to snoop instead. He came back to the room and gently pulled out the envelope he'd found in his father's valise. He gingerly teased out the thick packets with paper and cloth inside.

Within were several envelopes of different sizes and colours, as if saved after prior uses. There was also a dark blue cloth bag with a gold braid drawstring, which had once held a bottle of Seagram's whiskey. Inside this bag were a number of hand-written notes, some in minute Hebrew script, scrawled bits of rags. It looked like Yiddish, and although Simon could read it very haltingly, the writing was small, spidery, and quite faded. He could barely make them out. A few onionskin sheets held printed words in what seemed to be Polish. These were quite clear but Simon could have no idea what they said.

Inside a squarish, thick paper envelope, there was an official-looking document, folded over four times, with a photo attached. Simon unfolded it gingerly, spreading it out flat on the carpet, and inspected it. He could tell it was in German. Attached on one corner was a black and white photograph of a man in uniform. Simon recognized the regalia as belonging to the SS, the World War II elite German military branch. He didn't know why, but the face in the photo seemed vaguely familiar.

Simon decided to put it away, carefully refolding it and feeling it crackle in his fingers. He would show it to Adam later. Maybe he would remember something. He knew there was a story in the many notes. Unable to read them, though, they were still as much of a mystery as they had been the previous night. His mind gave only the dimmest of answers. There were secrets here, but what were they? They were bricks in a wall with no door.

He would find someone to translate these, but not today, no matter how exciting this find was. Simon checked his watch. Better get going. He had arranged to meet Rachel and the clock was ticking. That was exciting too.

He carefully slipped the notes back into their envelopes and returned them to the suitcase, planning on showing them to Adam later. He was pretty sure, though, that his brother wouldn't have any more of a clue what they were than he did.

30 Pictures

You are the fire of my soul. The light of day touches you and is shamed. The air around you is made electric by your movement. Your breaths cause the oceans to heave in tides. How may I merit you, your petal eyes? The smile of an angel, calm and upright, you speak to my heart. Skin soft, so soft, with the scent of lavender, smooth as polished alabaster. Purity, hold my trembling hand, and I will forever walk in silence, whispering your name in my mind.

Simon had called Rachel before the wedding, as he occasionally did when he was going to be in New York. The chance to see a smiling face in this place of frowns was appealing.

He hadn't been in this city since last autumn. The air was thick with late spring humidity. They met in a small Italian restaurant about a half-hour's taxi ride from his hotel. As he got out of the cab, he saw her smiling and waving vigorously. She looked radiant. He was again charmed by her smile. She had such perfect teeth. He walked up to her, leaned down, and kissed her on both cheeks. A Montreal kiss.

"Nice to be here with you again."

"So you missed me?" Rachel laughed.

Some muscle in his chest tugged at Simon. He discovered with a shock that he was again (or still) attracted to Rachel. As people do, he was falling back into the familiar role that he had played years before when he and Rachel were in a trapeze relationship. He would fly through the air, fleetingly trust her, let go and fall forward, and there she was, swinging from her side, seemingly ready to grab him. Too often her hands pulled away, his fingers reaching, almost there but slipping past, and he fell and fell. There was no net to catch him. He swung. He wavered. He fell. Just call me Charlie Brown, he thought.

Rachel was just fun to be with. Or maybe, he thought now, he was a masochist. Maybe that's why he had stayed in his marriage, a feeling of guilt redeemed only by suffering, the need for punishment, somehow related, he felt, to his parents, and what they wanted from him.

The realization that he was now free to act exploded in his head. He hadn't yet made the transition away from the constraints of marriage, even though, rationally, everything was over between himself and Catherine.

"I did miss you. Quite a lot, remarkably."

Rachel's smile twisted a little. "Well, I didn't miss you. Anyway, you're still married."

Simon didn't say anything. Should he tell her? He remembered only too well that Rachel had always been the initiator. When she had wanted him, many years before, before Catherine, he was there, compliant. When she didn't, he accepted, slinking off. Catherine had been so much easier to figure out. With her he could be brasher, more sure, and he got his way–at the beginning, anyway–until Matt was born. That event had refocused her, redirected her beam toward their son, drifting away from him. A darkness spread over him. His own light was drifting too.

He enjoyed talking with Rachel. Her sharpness could turn his arguments on themselves. She could be dangerous to the man lured by her charms. Dangerous to Simon, because he truly was lured. Also, strong-minded, volatile, skeptical, obstinate. Alluring, even at her frumpiest. Best to stay away, but now, here they were together.

He felt bewildered. Simon liked Rachel's spontaneity and honesty. She always seemed to be genuinely happy to hear his voice. And he enjoyed her appreciation when he picked up the tab.

"So, what will you have?" She laughed. "Let me suggest - a romaine and tomato salad with oil and lemon garlic dressing. Overly well-done *vitello parmigiano* but without cheese–gotta watch that non-kosher stuff–hey, that's veal *vesuviano*, huh? Get it, no cheese, coated with ashes. Will it be eaten by a pompeiious ass?"

Simon scanned the menu–Italian only–hard to believe. He laughed. "Why don't you order for me. You know so much more about food than I do. I'd probably order an Italian hot dog (*uno cane caldo*) and have to take it for a walk. I don't know the pumice from the *pomodoro*. Volcanic tomatoes?"

"Okay, I'll decide. I don't think you mind"

"I gave up trying to control my life a long time ago. Anyway, I don't believe we control how things work out, no matter what we decide. Choice doesn't necessarily affect outcome. I chose Montreal, you chose New York. I chose to get married. You chose not to. And we're both happy, right?"

"Simon, I don't really want to talk about this."

"So we're both having veal." Simon paused and stared off across the road at nothing.

"What's wrong, Simon?"

"I've been through hard times lately. Matthew died three years ago, and then my dad just last year. You probably heard about those."

"No, I didn't. I'm so sorry, Simon. I kept a subscription to The Montreal Star, but it closed a few years back."

"Yes, 1979. That's when I lost my job and went freelance."

"I didn't realize. How's your mom?"

"Not great. Adam and I try to look after her, but she really needed my dad. Now that he's gone, it's like part of her is missing."

"I guess it is."

"And now my marriage has crumbled."

"Oh my."

"Yes, oh my. I'm a mess."

"What are you going to do?"

"I have an assignment in Israel, so that's where I'm off to next. I'll be interviewing immigrants to Israel from behind the Iron Curtain to see how they've integrating into the country. I pitched the story to a major magazine. Now I just have to research it, sniff the ground. I plan to dig up my own past, while I'm there."

"And how are you going to do that?"

"I'm planning to visit my birthplace."

"Oh, that's right. I'd forgotten you were born there."

"I haven't been there since I was a kid. It was in a small settlement–a farm–I do remember that part."

"Well, you know how to do it. You are an investigative journalist."

"I just have to ask the right questions."

"You think you'll be able to pick up the thread now? How long has it been since you all came to Canada?"

"We arrived in 1957."

"So, 25 years. Long thread, probably a bit frayed by now."

"Hopefully not torn."

"You can do it. You have a good head."

"For someone with a good head, I've screwed up enough."

"We all do. Even me, sometimes."

"So, can we stop with all this small talk, already?"

"Funny man."

"We're supposed to be enjoying ourselves. It's such a beautiful day. We should order. Waiter!"

"I'll get his attention. I have nicer legs than you."

He smiled at that, as the waiter arrived and stared sullenly down at them through his order pad. New York! Rachel gave him their orders.

"What have you been up to since I last saw you?" He stared at her pale blue eyes surrounded by her head of black hair.

"I'm still working as a photographer. I'm putting together a book of my photos, but selling the idea to a publisher is a hard slog. But one is interested now. It's just a matter of how much money."

"Oh, if it's only that."

"But I'll do it, Simon. I will."

Simon remembered some of the photos she had taken years before.

"Remember that skull we found in the woods way back when?"

"Sure. That's one of the photos I want to include in the book. You holding the skull. Not your face, though. Only chest down. You remember that photo?"

"I never saw it."

"That night I was really scared. It was just so awkward."

"Uh, yes, it was. I was such an idiot." Simon laughed. "So, tell me more."

"Well, no man, for one thing. Happily, no children to mess up, either. I've made a few mistakes along the road, but not that one. Anyway, guys in this town don't seem to want a smart, sassy, abrasive, argumentative woman. Even if she has a great body."

"I can see how it would be hard to understand why that would be. Don't ask me to explain it, though. That's my favourite sort of woman. The great body doesn't hurt either. Cheers. *Lechaim.*"

"You're racking up points there. *Lechaim.*"

The service was fast. The first course of their order arrived steaming on their plates. They dug in.

"So what else? Not the lack of, but the full of, please. No negatives."

"The magazine work is going really well. Mostly fashion shoots, but it pays okay, even if it's all sellout. I think I've been growing up. I've accepted that I have to eat to live. I can pay my bills now, and my bank account is positive. I even buy some clothes occasionally. Do you like my outfit?"

"You look very good, Rachel. You'd look really good in anything, though. You always please my eyes. So life is good?"

"You're accumulating more points every minute. Better watch out. A girl could get ideas. And yes, life is good."

Simon saw a change in her eyes. They had a tinge of shadow now.

"So why don't I believe you?"

"About being happy? It's usually me playing devil's advocate. I'm alone, Simon. I look around at other women. Some of them have husbands, at least transiently–boy, what's wrong with our world, right? –and they have children, usually just one. Again, what's wrong with our world? As for me, I would like to have a child, at least I have this internal need to have one, part of my DNA getting ornery and wanting to move into another body before this one drops dead, and I can't connect seriously with anyone. I seem to scare them off. You're a man. You can't understand. Men are made to pump their semen into as many women as they can, to spread the goods far and wide as possible. They don't want to stick around and be happy. Women have to raise their children, give up on their life and individuality for that, and these days, still do everything a man is supposed to be able to do. It's all a crock, but it's the only crock in town, really."

"So what constitutes life for you in the Big Apple? Plenty of apple sauce, at least? Are people here more exciting than the ones back home?"

"People are pretty similar everywhere. They just seem to wear their lives more on the outside of their skin around here."

She didn't say anything for a moment or so, just paused and looked up into the sky. Non-existent clouds above were reflecting in her eyes.

"Oh, lots of activity. New York is like that. You know how I never liked the quiet life very much. But the apple sauce is a bit overcooked. Not enough vitamins, a little too much cinnamon or saccharine sometimes."

Simon remembered Rachel's disruptive effect whenever she came to Montreal. Maybe she had more scope to do that here and get away with it.

"Continuing the gene theme, we didn't evolve to be happy. It's not a trait that gives any selective advantage in the heredity wars."

"Maybe you're right, Simon. Maybe we just know too much. Were our parents any happier, you think?"

"I know the answer to that one. Look, can we not get into that?"

"I'm sorry, Simon."

"So, tell me about your book of photos."

"Oh, I'd really like to show it to you. Do you think you'd have time?"

"I told Adam I'd be back around 5:00, though the wedding doesn't start until 8:00. He likes to get ready way ahead of time. Obsessive."

"It shouldn't take that long. We'll take a cab to my place. My treat, okay?"

"Only if you let me pick up the tab for this lunch."

"Of course you're paying. I'm really old-fashioned, didn't you know?"

"So old is new."

"That's the new me, then. Old."

There was a pause as they each sipped at their wine, smiling and pensive, all at once.

"Guess what I found in my hotel room." He was going to tell her about the papers in his father's valise, ask her for her reaction.

"A dead body?"

"No, but if I did, I bet you'd probably want to come over and photograph it before the police got there. Hey, I see that sparkle in your eye. You can't fool me–you really would. Look, let's eat and, if you're sweet enough to me, I'll tell you."

He raised the glass of red wine to his lips and took a sip.

"Mmm. Not too bad for house wine. A full body with a whiff of dust and nose of smoke. Like this city."

They chatted on for a while, nibbling at what remained on their plates.

"So what was in your luggage?"

"Oh, yeah, that was a real surprise. I had to use my father's old valise, one that he used years ago to store his old dress patterns. Anyway, I was putting my things away at the hotel yesterday and noticed a bulge in the lining."

"Drugs?"

"Oh, very funny you are. My father, are you kidding? No. It's a good thing the customs guy didn't ask me to open it, though. Who knows, maybe he would have confiscated it and I'd never find out what was there."

"What was it?"

"A thick packet of letters and documents–really old-looking– like from when my father lived through the war. They're undated. I couldn't read them, because they're either in Polish, German, or Yiddish. I don't understand any of them. I can read a tiny bit of Yiddish, but it takes me forever, but the others, I don't have a clue about. Some sort of Nazi document too."

"Nazi? Really? Fascinating. So what are you going to do with them?"

"Nothing just now. I don't have time. They're really intriguing me, though. When I get to Israel, I'll find someone there to translate."

"Well, be sure to let me know what's in them. I'm curious. Have you ever been to Poland, to your dad's town?"

"No. My father went back about a year before he passed away, but he never talked much about it. Never really said much about anything that happened to him during the war, either."

"Like you say, maybe the letters will shed some light. Maybe he was a hero."

"Hardly. More likely the opposite. I don't know."

"Your mom never said anything?"

"It wasn't their way. They didn't talk."

"Mystery people."

"Exactly. Anyway, I have to know the truth. That's what I do.

"Then you'll be happier?"

"I don't know. I hope so."

"Simon, you're a pretty bright guy."

"What are you getting at?"

"Can a smart person be happy? Shouldn't she be able to figure out what makes her happy? But it doesn't seem to work that way."

"I thought you enjoyed living here. I don't really know what to tell you. Oh, I used to think I was smart too. But I decided that the smarter you are, the more you're able to realize how little you know, so that the smarter you are, the stupider you feel. I guess it's a bit of an equalizer. The stupider people think they're smart, and the smarter ones think they're stupid. If you're in the middle somewhere, it can be pretty confusing. Or reassuring. And I am in the middle. So it's hard for me to answer your question."

"You're a little too smart there. A bit pompous too, you know. I feel like I'm back in philosophy class."

"I wonder what too smart means."

"Didn't you just explain that? Look, why don't you come over to my place? I really would like to show you my work."

The apartment faced west. Full sun came in. It was tastefully decorated with a number of prints on the walls. While he was distracted by the decor, she quickly slipped away from him and stepped over to the bedroom door and pulled it shut. Rachel deftly kicked her shoes and danced back towards him, turning in a half-circle. Her arms came up to emphasize the area around her. He admired her form.

The living room area had an overstuffed sofa and a large bookcase partly filled with books and holding a couple of stone sculptures. Large pillows were thrown against one corner of the room. To the right hung a black and white photo of black arms reaching around a white tree, white arms around a black rock, bodies and faces hidden. Simon assumed that Rachel had taken them and leaned closer to inspect them, and to inspect Rachel's mind in the process.

"What do you think? Doesn't look much like Cucaracha Caverns."

She was referring to the nickname they had given the old apartment the four of them had shared, when they were still in college and low on funds. He remembered those days, her free spirit, her mode of dress, or lack of, during summer's heat.

"Rachel, great photo. I really like this one of the arms around the rock and tree. Looks like sandstone. And larch"

"Okay, professor. Too erudite."

"Hey, are you giving me a hard time for knowing something?"

"Oh, you do go on. You're trying to turn me on, like in the old days? Dazzling me with science."

"I never did."

"Oh yes you did. You just won't admit it."

"It was you turning me on, if I remember right. Who walked around in a towel? Not me."

Simon was a little tipsy from the wine he had drunk earlier.

"I'm not as smart as I sometimes think I am, unlike you, it seems. I didn't want to turn you on. Or maybe I did. Ha ha ha. I'm not telling." She giggled. "And maybe my biological clock was telling me something. Now, truth to tell, it's really screaming out loud. I'm not getting any younger, you know."

"Yes, unlike me."

"Men don't age the same way as women, you know. They get better, women sag. And I haven't been close to anyone in a while. I guess I'm just getting a bit horny. That's all."

"That's all? Well, good, so am I. So do you want to do it now?"

"Like they say back home in Montreal, at least the polite ones, get lost, creep. Here in New York, they're a lot more graphic. Anyway, I thought you guys got married so that you'd have guaranteed sex for the rest of your lives. Of course, since married life is over for you, that doesn't apply."

"Enough already. When do I get to see your photos?"

She smiled but ignored him. "Soon enough. Would you like a drink?"

He was too deeply engrossed in looking around to notice her question. He was trying to associate the photographs on the walls with her, trying to trace the path backwards to how she was when they had lived in the same apartment.

"HEY, WOULD YOU LIKE A DRINK?" This time he heard her and turned towards her face. She was smiling, amused that he was so distracted by the details of this room.

"Um, no thanks. I'm fine. Well, alright, just a little glass of something."

"Well, I think this is a special occasion." She went over to the kitchen cabinet and took down two wineglasses and a corkscrew. On the counter top she had placed a bottle of wine, red and dark.

She handed him the bottle and corkscrew, expecting him to open it. He tore off the soft metal cover over the cork, inserted the point of the spiral, and turned it until it was deep enough in, while he ran his eyes over Rachel's face and then down to her smooth rounded behind. The wine he'd had at the restaurant was still affecting him. He pulled the cork out slowly. It came out with a slight pop and a few drops of wine splashed his face. Rachel turned, laughed, and went to the linen closet for a towel. She was wobbling a bit. The wine had affected her too.

Rachel patted his face with the towel.

"That's betta, fella."

Simon handed the opened bottle back to Rachel. She half-filled the two glasses and handed one back to him.

"To New York."

"To Montreal."

They both took a sip.

"To Parma. Cheese, I mean cheers." He drank again.

"To Pompeii. Asses to ashes." Rachel drank down a quarter glass, refilled it. Giggles.

"Mmm. Not bad. Robust and seductive with a strong yet subtle nose." He laughed. He took a long draft from the glass. He was getting a little fuzzier. His earlobes were getting hot.

"Won't you show me your etchings?"

"All my metaphorical etchings are in the bedroom. Why don't you ask to see my photos?" She came close to him, leaned forward and touched the back of his hand.

The touch electrified him. Or maybe it was the wine. He imagined himself slipping his tongue between her half-opened lips, touching it to hers, running it along the edges of her beautiful teeth. He hesitatingly squeezed her hand and put down his glass on the nearest flat surface. He slipped his other hand down her neck and slowly along her shoulder, on its way to her soft warm breast. She suddenly came to attention, resisted and pulled away. The urgency quickly diminished as he tried to regain control of himself. She was smiling quizzically at him.

"Are you trying or are you trying?"

His breathing became a sigh. "Is this really happening?", he wondered to himself, and ignored his own question. Was she playing with him? He was balancing on a tightrope, wondering if he was about to fall, very softly, into her warm, feathery bed. 'I'm free,' he thought, 'I can do anything now.' And then he thought: 'If I let myself.'

"Wow, this wine is good," he mumbled.

"Um, yes. Simon, we've got to take it easy. For a minute there I was almost interested. That would have spoiled a great friendship."

"Sorry." She was probably right. He sipped the last wine in his glass.

Rachel tipped the bottle over his glass. "I know I shouldn't do this, but I hate to have an unfinished bottle of red. It doesn't taste right after it's been in the fridge."

He put his hand over his glass. "No thanks. Better not tempt fate."

She poured some wine into her own glass instead.

"So, want to see my photos?"

He could only nod.

Rachel wandered off into the bedroom, and he heard a few doors pulled open and and banged shut. She re-emerged with a thick album large enough to need support by both of her arms. "This is my *opus vitae*. I hope you like it. But be gentle. I'm very sensitive."

As she passed close, Simon reached up from his sitting position to grasp the album. She slipped down next to him while still supporting her side of it. As he opened the cover to look at the first page, her hip pressed lightly against his and she placed one hand softly on his forearm, as if to guide his movements. His skin again tingled at her touch.

The first photograph was of an old woman. She sat at a kitchen table, supporting her head with one hand. Her face was pensive, focussed on her teacup. She held a teaspoon and seemed to be stirring. Behind her stood an old man, her husband, turned slightly away from her and looking out the window.

"Tell me about this one," said Simon.

"They have had a long life together. They know each other well, beginning to end. Peering into her teacup, she sees there what the man is looking at outside, through his eyes, and he's tasting the tea she has just sipped. They share one mind. Inspecting her tea leaves, she knows their future. He, looking out the window, sees the entire world, sees all of their past. They look through time and space and one another. After a lifetime, this is intimacy: to know someone so well that you are them, you see the world through them. And when they're gone, you too are gone, or want to be."

"Makes me think of my mom."

"Yes, how is she doing, without your father?"

"Like you just described it. Not great. They were very close, lived through a lot together."

"Oh, Simon, I hope she'll get back to wanting life. It must be very difficult for her. And for you, looking after her."

"It's not easy. But, like she says all the time: 'What can you do?'"

They sat pensive again, Rachel staring at the photo album, Simon focussing on the air in front of him. The moment passed, though. Simon stared down at the next photograph.

It was of a young couple. They were lying in bed next to each other, only their faces and bare shoulders showing above the sheet, except for their hands which were pulling the sheet up to their chins, giving the appearance of two 'Kilroy's were here' snuggled together. Their bare feet were exposed by the tugging. They were laughing in a relaxed yet mildly embarrassed way. They seemed to have been surprised in bed together by the photographer.

"What about this one?"

"Oh, my friends, Josh and Marie."

"They're lovers?"

"No, they hardly knew each other. They climbed into bed together because I asked them to. I wanted them to help me compose the shot."

"Oh. It looks so real."

"Well, that's the goal."

"So they just climbed into bed together, just like that? Did they get undressed?"

"They're naked under the covers."

"No kidding."

"Pervert! No, they're partly dressed. I really got you going there."

"Well, it does make you think."

"That's what it's supposed to do–be provocative."

"Like you. Well done."

"Thanks. Anyway, they went out after that. Now they're married."

"So this is how you match up your friends: Get into bed together, kids, I'm just going to take your picture–for arts sake, of course–hey, no touching. Very sneaky. So, let's see more. What about this one of this little girl?"

On the following page, a young child, maybe three or four years old, was engrossed in making a mud pie between her open legs. A small dog leaned over her shoulder, curiously inspecting the mess.

"Oh, it looks like just something cute in the book. Pablum, to help to sell the rest, but really, this little girl is forming a *golem* out of mud."

"What?"

"A *golem*, to save the world."

"If only it were possible."

"It shows that we each have the power to change the world."

"We don't."

"Oh boy. Now you're getting serious again. I'm sorry I said such a frivolous thing. I forgot how morose you get sometime. Okay, I was only kidding. It's just a little girl. But it does show love."

"And does love save the world?"

"One person at a time, apparently. It hasn't saved me yet, though."

"Well, me neither."

"It reminded me of my childhood, before things started to go downhill."

"An idyllic moment, then. Eden, before the fall from grace."

"Yes, I suppose.'

"Well, these really are wonderful. I'm sure you'll do well."

"Hmm. Really, you think these are that good?"

"Not something most of us mortals could do."

A fourth picture caught his attention—a bus stop, a blustery day in early spring or late fall. A teenaged boy, leaning against the pole of the bus stop, his head down, hands in pockets, looking ashamed, defeated. He had done something monumentally wrong. Next to him, her face turned away from the boy so she was viewed from the side, a girl about his age. She was thin, stiff, upright, her arms thrust straight down, the fists tightly curled. Her face bore a scowl. What had happened between them? It was obvious—the aftermath of a betrayal. A perfect pose. No need for a caption.

"This is magnificent photography."

"It's an intrusion, though. Their private moment."

"You're right, but you knew you had to capture it."

"I feel guilty, though, like a voyeur."

"We're all voyeurs, then. Only our photographs stay in our heads. They have nowhere else to go."

Simon slowly looked over many of the remaining photos, while Rachel puttered about, dragging a tripod around, mounting a camera. Simon looked up, curious.

"What are you doing?"

Rachel just gave him a fleeting smile and he returned to the book.

All the photos were of people, sometimes alone, sometimes in couples or groups, in various domestic situations, all familiar and yet somehow framed in a way that made him think that the captured moments were a slice of a more involved story. They were moody, as if these people were expecting something to happen, at the moment just before it did. Some were light-filled, some dark, some sharply focussed, others hazy and washed out, but they all shared a certain sense of expectation. He found himself filling in hypothetical details, inventing lives from instants of existence. He would ask Rachel about them once he was done looking. On the last page was a brooding photo, a human skull, the bone bleached a perfect white, in the midst of a mass of wildflowers and a fern frond.

Simon looked up from the page at Rachel. She answered before he could ask.

"Oh, that last one. You remember. You had dropped it and it had rolled away. I went back the next day and found it. Everybody who sees this picture wonders where I took it. I wandered around a bit after I took that shot. It turned out that those woods were really close to the cottage my mother rented with your parents when we were young. I wonder if it was out there when we were kids picking blueberries."

"Wow. Any idea who it could have been? Anything in the papers?"

"No clue. Anyway, you're the reporter. Maybe you should look through the records. Someone missing and unaccounted for?"

"Maybe I should. Did you report it to the police?"

"No."

"I wouldn't have, either. I know none of the others wanted to get into trouble. It'd probably be too late now, though. Probably dissolved by the rain and snails or chewed up by insects by now. Could be a story, though."

"That's the keen reporter talking."

"I never said I wasn't one."

"Anyway, like you say, too late. I went back the following year and it was gone. Some burly fellow was there near the wire fence–some new neighbours had moved in across the lake, not very friendly–and asked me what I was doing there. Menacing guy. I never looked again. So we'll never know."

"You really are a strange one. You really went back? I don't know, Rachel, he or she will probably haunt you now. Or that burly guy might."

"Don't try to scare me. I'm not going to crawl into bed with you this time."

"Not like then?"

"Nothing happened. Remember? I know I shouldn't offer after you just said that, but would you like some more wine? Don't get the wrong idea, though. I just want to finish the bottle."

"No, thanks. I don't want to get back to the hotel drunk."

"Drunk? After two glasses of wine?"

"Trying to shame me, are you. Okay, you win. Pour away."

"Anyway, I don't believe in stuff like that. Haunting, I mean."

They sat quiet for a minute.

"No, neither do I."

"Simon, you really have been through a lot, lately. Your son and your father dying, and now you're separated. That's a lot to deal with."

"It's true, Rachel. It's been hard, but look what my parents went through, and they made it okay."

"You think they were okay? Really?"

"No, not really. My dad couldn't sleep. He was depressed."

"And you? Are you in competition with them?"

"Me? I ran away from home. That's why I moved downtown."

"I think your dad could have needed you to be there."

"Look, both my parents were always badgering me. I was never good enough. Not like my brother, the doctor."

"Ah, sibling rivalry. Freud would love you."

"What would you know about it? You're an only child."

"Bingo! So we're both a mess."

Simon went silent. He reached forward and filled his empty glass.

Rachel was fidgeting with the corner of the page, trying to close the book.

"That's all I have to show you. What do you think?"

"They're great. I love them. But you have to publish these. When is that going to happen? Like my father would have asked: 'With such a profession you can make a living?'"

"My mother said the same thing."

"Tell me about competing. I know what it is in journalism. You really have to make a name for yourself, keep producing, pumping it out. Maybe I could try to find you some spots to put your photos with a newsmagazine I freelance for."

She smiled and patted him on the cheek. "You're sweet, but I'm pretty busy with the fashion mag." She bent down and planted a kiss on his cheek.

"Simon, what happened between you and Catherine?"

"Life is what happened. We stopped talking. I got busy. She got lonely. Matt got sick. We were held together by wax and cobwebs until Matthew died. It all just dropped away completely."

"So that's it. Life."

"Well, I could have done more. I stopped thinking much about her at one point, and thought more about myself."

"Not a good formula for love, me first and you second."

"No."

"But maybe I shouldn't comment. I've never been married. I should know better, too. I never lasted with anyone for more than a year or so. Help!"

"I'm sorry, Rachel. I wish I could help you."

"I wish I could help you back."

"So let's get married.'

"Ha, ha, ha."

"Right. I don't know if I'd be ready for you. Or for anyone, really."

"And what's wrong with me, all of a sudden?"

"Well, let's see. You're beautiful. Intelligent. Very talented. Fun to be with. That's a lot of stuff you would have to get over so that you would qualify. But I'm still in recovery. I wouldn't wish myself on anyone right now."

"Why don't you let The Woman decide if you're right for her? Don't preclude. Some of us are much more perceptive than you might give us credit for."

"And who is this hypothetical woman who's sizing me up?"

"I'm not saying it's me, Simon, but I think I know you pretty well."

"You are much more empathetic than I remember. You used to be pretty insensitive."

"Oblivious is the more correct word, I think. I plead guilty, your honour."

"No kidding, though. You've changed, matured."

"You mean I'm an old lady now."

"No, you're not and you know it. You're closer to perfection. Men don't always prefer younger girls. Not this one, anyway."

"Nice try, but yes, it's obvious what men like. Just walk down the street behind a sweet young thing and watch what happens to

the men she passes. It's like a hot knife cutting through ice cream."
She laughed, slipped her hand down onto his knee.

"I mean it. You become better every time I see you."

"If you're not careful, Simon, I'm going to start to believe you. What will you do then?"

Simon didn't move. "I'm not afraid."

She left one hand on his knee and reached for her glass with the other. She giggled. "I'd like to take a photo of you."

"Um, sure, if you like."

"Oh, Simon, I do like. Very much."

"Maybe you've had a bit too much wine."

"I'm being serious. Art knows no bounds. Especially when it's drunk. It's like the transition between absolute quiet and frenetic action. You can see it in a face, or in a dancer flying through the air. You know he'll land, but the moment is so exquisite. It lingers, on and on, almost endless. You know—like Zeno's paradox. Suspended between heaven and earth. And it's also the superficial nature of love in our modern age—its anonymous ubiquity—do we really see each other, or do we just see the surfaces that touch? Can two people ever truly understand each other. It's as if they are invisible, or trying to see through a mask."

"Blah. Blah. Blah. Blah."

"You're right, in the end, it is all bullshit. That's the feeling I also get at times when I listen to artists describing the meaning of their art and its importance to all humanity."

"I'm sure that art does matter, Rachel, but it's not life. And life is hard, but we only have one life—it should be rewarding and meaningful. What really makes the difference is having someone to share it with. I know that, even though for me it didn't work out, and maybe you don't buy that, but it's true. It lightens the load. I know that sounds pat and cliché. It's what you and I are missing."

Rachel's face went dark. She turned away and began to sob.

"Oh shit, I've really upset you."

Rachel turned to Simon and wiped her face with her fingers. "Now look what you've made me do. My makeup is all smeared."

Simon dabbed at his cheeks. "Mine too."

Rachel smiled. "Always the charmer. You're right, though, Simon. It's something I've been fighting all my life—becoming close to someone has always scared me."

"Me too."

"I have a confession to make, Simon. I do like you. Even more than like."

"No kidding."

"Really, I mean it. For a long time. It's just been hard to say it's name."

"Me too."

"Since we were kids."

"Me too."

"Stop saying 'me too'? You should kiss me now. Before I throw you out."

Simon looked at Rachel, unsure. Before he had a chance to answer, to put his arms around her, she squealed and quickly kissed him. Her thin arms locked around his neck.

"Mmph" was all that came out of his mouth. He thought in that infinitesimal moment about how much he wanted her, and had been wanting her for so many other moments strung together back in time. But in the next fraction of a moment, desire had taken over and he stopped thinking. This was Rachel. She was going to do something unexpected, dangerous, even frightening. But he didn't care any more. He only knew that at this intangible flicker of time, he truly wanted her, truly cared for her. He couldn't bear the separation from her person. He felt confounded and confused. Both he and Rachel had reached the limits of self-control.

His hand touched her shoulder. It slid slowly down her arm to her elbow and more quickly across to her breast. It felt so delicately soft under the thin cotton top. She wasn't wearing a bra. He pushed the other hand downwards along her belly, popped the button at the waist of her skirt. Both hands now gripped her waist, and she pressed back firmly against him. He bent his head forward to kiss her ear and her neck. One hand slid lower, along her belly, lightly fingering the depression of her navel, and past it, down to the short soft hairs below. Her skin felt like fine velvet. She gasped. His heart was racing.

They tumbled sideways. They poured through the bedroom door like water and fell into the bed. The air under them seemed to firm up. The horizontal floor changed its slope towards the bed, as if gravity dictated it, the bed a zone of desire pulling them in, making falling into it irresistible. Clothes seemed to fly off by centrifugal action as they orbited the bed. In moments, and with seemingly automatic motions, Rachel had glued herself on top of him and he was manoeuvring himself so that they fitted each other, tongue in groove. The fierce thrusting lasted only a few minutes, before she twisted over him, letting out a few gurgles from deep in her throat. She fell forward with her face pressed against his neck, making a sound between a sigh and a moan. He was gasping, heated from the effort. He could feel the contraction of his heart. It was ready to explode. Her heart was pounding against his chest, the two synchronizing their different beats. He lay still now, pulling heavily against her as he felt her insides pulsating, slowly kissing his shrinking penis goodbye. He wanted this moment never to end.

Rachel started to laugh. Simon opened his eyes and looked up at her laughing mouth, her crinkled eyes with their tiny crow's feet making them look all the more sweet and charming. Her breasts dangled above his head, slowly rocking back and forth while Rachel continued to laugh her contented laugh. She tipped forward and their mouths met and they kissed softly.

"That was nice." he whispered.

"Is that all?"

"That was fantastic. Wonderful and powerful and delicious."

"Are you content now?"

"Yes, very," he whispered.

"Me too. I'm glad you came over. I love talking to you."

"Me too."

"I told you not to say that."

"No, really. I enjoyed you today. And even the sex." Rachel grinned at that. "Hey, I want to talk and talk and talk to you. I want to repeat your name forever. Rachel, Rachel, Rachel, Rachel."

"You sound like a teenager. Just come back."

"It'll be a while. Remember, I'm leaving for Israel tomorrow."

"For how long?"

"I don't know."

"Maybe I could join you some time?"

"That would be nice, but not right away."

"Chasing demons?"

"Demons and dragons, and an assignment."

"I've got a bit of that to do too."

"I've really got to go now."

"Okay. But really, stay close. Call me. I mean it."

"Parting is such sweet sorrow. Thank you, Shakespeare, for writing that line."

"That's nice, Simon. It's very nice."

Rachel got up and walked naked to the bathroom. Simon admired the rhythmic back-and-forth motion of her torso as she moved away. She had two symmetrically placed dimples on either side of her lower spine just above where the roundness of her gluteals started. He heard the shower start, got up and followed. He climbed in after her. She pulled herself against him, placed her hands on either side of his face and pulled his head low enough to plant a kiss on his forehead.

"You're sweet," she said above the sound of the rushing water, "but you'd better go now, or I won't let you leave."

"Give me a bit of time. I will get in touch when I feel I'm in shape to."

Simon climbed back out, towelled himself off, and went back to the pile of clothes on the living room floor to dress himself. After many minutes, she came out dry and still naked. She stood and stared into his eyes. She wasn't embarrassed. Neither was he.

They exchanged a few words. He excused himself uneasily, mumbling that he had to get back to his hotel to get ready for the wedding, and she walked him to the door. She said she would call him. He would call her. Soon.

"I said earlier that Cathy and I were breaking up. It's more than that. I've left her," he confided. He went silent.

"I know. I figured that out pretty fast. You're translucent, you know."

Rachel gave him back the same silence. Somehow the idea that he was free was disturbing her more than knowing that he was married. It was a threat, she realized, this possibility that he would now try to insinuate himself into her unattached life.

"So, your advice about happiness, Simon? Maybe happiness will come your way now."

"I do wish that. For you too."

"Maybe it will."

He promised to call Rachel the next time he was in New York, and she smiled when he said this. They kissed lightly, on the cheek. He turned, looked one last time at her naked body, half-hidden by her door, and walked away towards the elevator. Half-hidden. Half-naked. What he had needed was to not be hidden, to have her know everything, hear it all, see it all, and trust him enough to reciprocate. So they could be naked in all ways with each other. Honesty. He had been sure this could never happen. Until now. With lovely Rachel.

He didn't feel a bit like leaving. He wasn't going back to Montreal and Catherine; he had accepted the new assignment in Israel. He had been the natural choice—he knew the refugee experience. He hesitated now, just for an instant, wondering if he really had thought things through.

The rush and pull of the past, the tug of the future. Moment by moment, one became the other, the present a transparency, invisible, moving by in the stream of moments so fast, overwhelmed by its turbulence. He had motive enough for what he'd just done and for what he saw himself still doing. It wasn't simply lust and opportunity. Why after all this time, after all this effort, this investment of emotion and sweat and years, did this now, suddenly, make so much sense?

Because it had always made sense, had been the truth avoided. The world he inhabited, the structure he had created, was flawed, in many ways senseless. For many years he had built it, meticulously, carefully, beam by beam, post by post, but behind all that apparent solidity it was really a house of cards. He had tried to rationalize it, tried to structure it as the ancients had constructed their models of the cosmos based on the Earth being at its centre, those models of brass, with their eccentric orbits, wheels within wheels, so beautiful yet so wrong, just as flawed as the Rube Goldberg world he had produced around himself.

31 Golem

Simon checked his watch in the elevator. It was getting quite late. Adam would be waiting for him, agitated, driven by his attachment to time. Simon felt himself slipping away from control, and becoming panicky in the process. A distance was emerging, an internal division between the man he had constructed and the man he was despite this.

He was thinking of the *golem* that Rachel had referred to, the creature with a body but no soul, doing as it was told to do, unblinkingly following in the footsteps of the man who led it, until that man gave it a mission to carry out. Who or what directed Simon? His work? His father, dead but still powerful? The world?

A mission to protect the world? What world had he been able to protect? He had been intending to do that, exactly that, and in the process, his world, his own small world, had come apart, crushed by other creatures without soul. His son was gone, his father, his wife. All taken or pushed away, in one way or another. And he was the *golem* that had done it to them. He couldn't protect anyone, not one, so what gave him the idea that his efforts could have such a healing effect on the world around him?

He should look into himself, find the creature. In the legend, the *golem* is erased by the rabbi who created it when he changes the word *emet*–truth–that he had inscribed on its forehead to bring it to life, changes that word to *met*–death–by erasing one letter, the *aleph*–the beginning. Could he replace that letter, begin again, become the creature with both soul and body? If he was the *golem*, who was his creator? He had to find that root letter, the *aleph*, find where it had all started from. Delve into his father's life

Rachel shut her door as the elevator slid shut and walked back to her bedroom, then lay down on her back and stared up at the ceiling. She had surprised herself. There had been no planning here, it was truly spontaneous. It had been a long time that they had known each other. Today she had let herself see. And though she had always been in charge with Simon before, today he seemed to have taken over, overpowered her. Mulling it she realized that it had pleased her. She wondered. She had had snippets of ideas about this sort of thing when they were children at the summer cottage so long ago, acting out childish urges, or, years later, in the summer lake, swimming unfettered under a full moon.

She would probably think back on today when she was an old woman and smile. Would Simon be there next to her, smiling too? Was that such a ridiculous idea?

A feeling tugged at her. Her chest felt fluttery, almost as if she was a schoolgirl again. Oh my God, she thought. A faint smile glimmered on her face. She held her hand against her chest. Her heart indeed was fluttering. She hugged herself to keep from tipping out of bed.

32 Ceremony

Simon took a cab back to the hotel. As Simon knew he would be, Adam was long since back. He had already finished getting dressed for the wedding. He was lying on the bed, tossing the Gideon's Bible up in the air and catching it.

"Great taste. I just can't choose ties by myself."

"You're late." Adam didn't smile. "Where were you? It's almost time to go." Adam stood on the bed and trampolined up and down. He glared at his watch, as if his looking would stop the hands from moving. He adjusted his tie nervously.

"I was having lunch with Rachel. Remember we shared an apartment a long time ago when I was in school. Sorry to be so late. Couldn't be helped."

"That's your research?" Adam jumped again, lost his balance and tumbled off the bed. The Bible flew through the air, and hit the television cabinet with a loud bang.

"Sacrilege, Adam?"

Adam had jerked upright. "Nothing, just nervous energy."

"I can see that. We'll have to pay the hotel if we damage the Bible."

"Don't be ridiculous. They're free, donated by the Gideons. Even if it disappeared, no one would notice. Nobody cares about the Bible anymore."

"We would have to pay if you damaged the television or the bed."

"Sorry. So how's Rachel?"

"Rachel's just fine. Working on a photo collection for a book."

"Really? Any good?"

"Actually, quite beautiful."

"No kidding. Didn't think she had it in her."

"She's not that angry, awkward girl any more, Adam."

"You talked?"

"Yeah, we talked a bit. Look, if you don't need the bathroom, I'm going to shower and shave. Where did I put my razor?" Simon glanced over at his suitcase. "Hey, you've been going through my things."

"I was looking for that package of old papers. Where did you put them?"

"They're hidden in the suitcase, under the lining. I would never have noticed, either, but when I pulled my clothes out, it popped open. I had a look last night. They're almost all in Polish and Yiddish, except one that's in German, a Nazi document of some sort."

"What?"

"Yes, really. It had a picture and a stamp, swastika and eagle, the whole *megillah*, as they say. Well, not the Germans, of course. They wouldn't say that."

"Come on, Simon."

"Looked really official. But I couldn't understand any of it. We would need a translator."

"The family is here. A lot of them came from Europe. Maybe we should try and ask."

"Let's not upset them tonight, Adam. It's a wedding, not a funeral. Let them be happy. They don't get enough of that."

"Just trying to be helpful."

"Some other time. I just wanted to know what they were. I have a lot of questions about Ta and what he did when he was young."

"Show me the German papers."

"Sure, here." Simon pulled out the envelope and handed it gingerly to Adam, who then examined the document in silence.

"Look at this. You know who this looks like? Do you remember once, when we were young, there was a man who broke into our house?"

"Sure, the one that Ta took away to the police? Don't tell me you think that's him."

"Could be. I think. It sort of resembles the guy."

"Maybe. Anyway, the break-in was a long time ago. I think they all looked pretty much alike in their uniforms, though. Like in the old newsreels."

"You're probably right."

Simon said nothing more. He folded the papers back into the envelope they'd come in, deep in thought.

"Yes. It's funny though. Years ago while I was investigating a crime story, I had access to the records of arrests back to that time. I checked. Nothing. No reports of an arrest, a break-in, a burglary, or anything else on our street."

"How do you remember the date?"

"It was the day of the first space walk. Alexei Leonov. Voskhod 2. We watched it on TV. while we waited for Ta to come back."

"You remember that?"

"Sure I remember. I was always a news junkie. Especially when it came to space. Why do you think I became a journalist?

"So what do you think happened to the guy?"

"Leonov?"

"No, idiot, the guy in our house. Ta wouldn't just let him go."

"So, what then? He wouldn't have killed the guy."

"He wouldn't do that. He was a good man. Remember when he saved our lives, Simon? And the time he caught the mouse in the kitchen and brought it across the street to the park and let it go?"

"And a cat caught it and ran up a tree with it? Yeah, I remember that. What do you think might have happened to that guy?" Simon softened. "It's true Ta was a hero the day we almost drowned. He saved all three of us. That was only one day, though."

"Lots of days. Maybe you underestimate him. Why are you so hard on the old man? Especially now that he's gone."

"I really don't know. Why didn't he continue to save me?"

"Grow up, Simon. Be a *mensch*, like he would have said."

"I am grown up."

"Think about it."

"Maybe we should get going."

They were late. Simon dressed quickly and the two went down to the lobby to catch a cab. The wedding was not what they expected it to be. A New York affair was so much more elaborate and planned in minute detail than what they were used to in Montreal. The hors d'oeuvres, the small talk, the pictures pulled out of wallets by proud parents and grandparents of small children. The pathetic yet wonderful hope for continuity. Worldly people, seemingly fully aware of what they were doing in life, blatantly secular, reliving a ceremony grown out of the tribal, primitive past, accepting it with no observable awareness of its contradictions.

The ceremony, the chanting in Hebrew, the breaking of the glass wrapped in a napkin. The meal that followed, much too lavish, too rich. It was almost obscene and yet reassuring how much had been spent on this occasion. People seemed still to believe that such rites of passage were important and valid. Giant baskets of flowers, ice sculptures, tables full of exotic foods. Waiters and waitresses in black uniforms with white shirts, nervously moving back and forth, trying to keep each guest, no matter how demanding, happy. Dancing until 2:00 a.m. It was romanticism gelled. It was mutual mass insanity. It was a sociological event.

He had been placed at a table with young married couples, along with his brother. He could find little to talk about with them, except try in simple terms to answer naive questions about the future of the Jewish community in Quebec. They irritated him with their ethnocentric, prejudiced questions. Simon was angry. He was angry that he had failed, his plans had failed, his marriage had failed. He had started out so sure, so determined, and it had not been Catherine's fault that it had gone wrong. She had tried so hard. Maybe he hadn't. He felt miserable now.

The man next to him at their table introduced himself and his wife.

"I'm a member of this synagogue for twenty years now."

"My husband's name is above the door to the Torah School. We're very proud of our sponsorship."

"You go to services often, then?"

"Every Saturday, except when I have to work in my business."

"What do you do?"

"I'm in the meat-packing business. I just invested in a new factory, horse meat."

"Really, horse meat? Is that what we're eating?"

"It's *trayf*, but the market is just opening up. Only for the *goyim*, you know. They'll eat anything. And you, where are you from?"

"Montreal."

"Oh, yeah. I hear the French-Canadians are all antisemites."

"So they say."

"You don't agree?"

"I was married to a French-Canadian woman. Never had a hint that they disliked us. Good people."

The wife leaned to her husband's ear and whispered, "Nonsense. He said he was married to her. Why do you think they broke up? It's always antisemitism." Simon could just make out her words. She looked at Simon now.

"How interesting. Excuse us. We're going to dance. So nice to meet you. Maybe we'll see you at the sweet table."

The couple retreated, only looking back when they were halfway across the room. Despite the fact that he had broken up with Catherine, he had felt obliged to defend her to these people, liberal xenophobes trying to justify their prejudices to themselves.

Simon's thoughts broke free, roved the past now—his son, his father. The shark circling in the darkness never stops. The currents of time spill through its gills endlessly. Stones tossed from the shore spiralled downwards into its realm, wobbling back and forth as they pass into the depths, disturbing the stratified currents, waters warm, cold, warm and cold again; men and women, passing through the uncertain eddies of their time.

And so it had been for Duvid, flailing, grasping at stones falling, at bubbles rising. Trying to take one last breath. His great soul failing.

33 Poland

Duvid was gone. *Gehennem, Gan Eiden,* where would he go? Was there any small meaning to this vast convoluted structure, this religion, that had been built up over centuries and millennia, the written word based on assorted earlier unrelated and interrelated writings, in cuneiform, on papyrus, in scrolls, deriving themselves from oral traditions, legends, whose origins were forever lost, more oral traditions based on those written, commentary built on these texts, followed by commentary on the commentary: *Tanach, Talmud, Midrash, Haggadah, Kabbalah.* A pyramid of books, of books within books. Books that start out: "...at the beginning..."

At the beginning was the law. The law of the Torah and the law of physics. They were one. And then they diverged.

The Laws of the Torah that we know, inscribed on the stone tablets brought down from Mount Sinai by Moses, were by tradition, according to the Kabbalah–the book of Jewish mysticism–taken from the Tree of Good and Evil and were only a second set of laws. The laws of the original tablets of the Kabbalistic *midrashim* had been taken from the Tree of Life. They were withheld because the descendants of Jacob lost faith, built the golden calf, and were worshipping it as Moses came down from Mount Sinai. In his rage, Moses dashed them to the ground and they broke. He had to return to the mountain, to receive the second set we know. When the Messiah finally comes, the stories tell us, he will bring these original tablets with him. The Messiah bearing those mended first tablets, withheld from humankind, where was he? Would he present himself any time soon, bring his two great tablets with him?

Only Duvid, extra-corporeal, was now close to the truth. It would overwhelm him as it absorbed his essence and he absorbed it.

It was only as an older man that Duvid had summoned the courage to return to Poland again, shortly before becoming ill. He had decided to go now, while he could. Hannah wouldn't accompany him.

"You're a healthy man, look at you, you'll live forever. Why go back to that place? Go somewhere nicer, why not?" Hannah had told him. "I would come with you, if it was somewhere else, maybe Tel Aviv or New York or Miami, somewhere alive with Jews, but for me, going there is like going back to a graveyard. Worse than a graveyard. The dead, our dead, remember, have no graves there."

"Yes, of course I remember."

He was on a bus tour, organized for North American Jews to return to their roots. The other old men and women cooled themselves in a small cafe next to the bridge, sipping fruit-flavoured sodas or iced coffees. They were not from this town.

Duvid wandered back to the grounds of the old Jewish cemetery. He stood on the ruined ground, sensing a connection to it and the family who lay within it. He knelt down and picked up a few pebbles, and visited each remaining grave, placing a small stone on each one. A few bore the name Grynsztyn, but names no longer mattered. These had all been his people, the generations that had died before the war, who had an identifiable place of rest, the grandparents of his friends, his own ancient relatives, Jewish townsfolk. He placed a stone on each grave marker he saw, before standing back in silence.

It had been so many years since Duvid had been here in this town; he couldn't recall exactly how long. He walked past his old ramshackle house, where he had been threatened with death when he had tried to reclaim it soon after the war ended. He was not going to test things by knocking on the front door today. He tramped on toward the old church. The church was the same as it had been, although he could see that some repairs, here and there, had been done. Would the same priest still be there?

Yes, the old man was there, stooped now, in his garden, hoeing around a row of carrots.

"Hello, Father." The priest turned. His face was soft and it lit up when he recognized Duvid.

"Ah, it is you. It's been a long time since you last visited. How are you?"

"Old age is never an easy thing, as you know. I am glad to see you are in good health."

"Yes, yes. So far. So you have come back."

"One last time, I think."

"We never know what God has in store for us."

"True."

"God has brought you here at a propitious time. I have news for you. Well, not really news—more like stories and rumours."

"What news? It's been years since we last were together. How new can such news be?"

"Two of my parishioners have recently returned from the prison camps. They were kept behind in the labour camps long after I was permitted to return here. Times seem to have changed. But that is not the news. It is about your Miriam."

"Miriam?"

"Yes."

"Oh my God. What about her? Is she here?"

"No, she is not."

"So she is still back there?"

"Neither that. Some years ago, in the dead of winter, she disappeared. She walked out into a snow storm. Disappeared. Maybe she thought she could run. Maybe she wanted to die. Perhaps she had been driven mad."

"Don't say she has died. She can't have. She has to be alive!"

"I remember the winters. She could not have survived long. Not there. I'm deeply sorry."

"How long ago?"

"A long time. Seven years, perhaps."

"Seven years and not heard from since? Yet in my heart, I can't believe she died. I believed her dead several times in the past, and yet it was not so. Her spirit was too large—is too large—for that. But sadly, my head agrees with you—she must be dead."

"It is easier for the human spirit if we have faith. We never know what God has in store for us."

"You said that already."

"That is because I believe it. I say it every day."

"I wish I could."

"I'm very sorry to give you such news."

"I should not have come here."

"The truth is the truth. It cannot be avoided. It should not be avoided."

"I would have been thankful if you had not given it to me. Should I be thankful, now that you have?"

"You look pale. This has been a shock for you, no doubt. Here, sit down in the shade. I will bring you some water."

"My bus leaves soon. I must go."

"Go in peace. And return here in peace some day."

In his own mind, a thought went through his head—the truth can be avoided if one never speaks of it.

On his way back to the bus, Duvid knew that, despite the priest's words, he would never be back here again, nor return to

Israel, which held his secrets, secrets which he would never expose, which his sons should never know. They would not know to look, let alone where to look. And now, this blow, the certainty of Miriam's death. It was hard to bear.

The wheel of years had kept on turning in his head. In the intervening times, between then and then and then, he had married, his sons had been born, grown up and started families, in what he considered the natural order. The events of his own life had been an aberration, a break from this pattern. Memories of this town and the harsh times that followed his exodus from it would always remain fresh in his mind, as long as he still breathed.

Past, present and future, all were creations of the mind and the heart, all bits of nothing, fleeting and ephemeral. Yet they held more reality that the sacred dust that lay abandoned below his feet. He gave that dust a light kick, creating a small cloud that swirled in the wind and drifted along the road before it settled. He felt empty, cracked open. Something inside him had just broken. He turned back towards the bus. The other wandering Jews were waiting impatiently for the tour to start up again and carry them through the many *shtetls*, each of which one of them had once called home.

We can drift back now, to a time where an end and a beginning were about to separate. Duvid's body was still whole and young. He was as yet unaware of the ephemeral nature of his body, unaware that it was truly creating itself from moment to moment, pulling itself out of the immaterial. Unaware that he was projecting his spirit onto the firmament and forward into the future.

PART II – WAR AND MORE WAR

34 Marching to Jerusalem

"Duvidel, you have nothing better to do than to read all day? You're already sixteen years old. Old enough to be married and start a family, but all you do is gaze at books. Go do something useful. Your father doesn't need your help with his work? No? So, look, your brother goes to catch fish for me. Maybe you should go with him? The fresh air will do you good."

"Mama, why should I fish? I never catch anything. There's nothing to do there but sit and watch a string bob up and down in the water. Can't I chop wood, or dig a hole, do something I'm good at? Up, down, up, down, it bobs. Can anything be more useless?"

"Don't try to fool me. Here you will hide behind a tree and read those magazines from the big cities. Stories you should not know about. Poems filled with ideas that make the mind race. This is not for you, Duvid. So you'll have a conversation with your brother. He'll be standing under the *chuppah* in a few months, like his brother Avrum three years before. He'll tell you about getting married, about being a man, like Avrum did for him. I'm sure he can teach you a thing or two about life. Ah, I can't wait. Soon after I can look forward to another grandchild."

"And what is wrong with those stories, or those poems. They are modern. We can't live forever like our ancestors. Even they considered themselves to be modern in their day."

"I don't want you reading words like those written by the likes of Miriam. She was once such a good girl, *frum*, obedient to her parents. But now, suddenly, she is a poetess, and the ears of everyone in this town burns when they hear what she has written. This Miriam has brought such shame on the Jews of this village. Go with Moishe. It will be better for you."

"And what else should I do but listen to my brother talk?"

"You can gather berries for me. Or pick up firewood. Ach, you are such a man. There is always something to do, but not for men. It is obvious that God is male. He may have thought He finished creating the world, but there is always so much still to do. And what did He do once finished? He rested. Find me a woman who has the time to rest. But what would a man know about that? When they're finished their work, there's nothing else but to pray. Three times a day, even. Can a woman say her work is ever finished? Never. No wonder we're not expected to read Torah. We couldn't do as much and men would have to help us out. The whole world will shudder when such a thing happens, when men help. After the *moshiach* comes, only then will men understand a woman's life."

"Mama's right, Duvid. You come with me. Maybe you'll bring me luck and I'll catch a lot of fish today." Moishe looked impatient. Duvid cringed. He smiled defiantly, but went along. He knew better than to antagonize his oldest brother.

"Moishe, why are those hooks stuck in your sack like that? You can't find a better place to put them? They will stick in your skin, you will see."

"Ma, these are damaged. Where else could I put them that they wouldn't hurt someone?"

"Moishe, Moishe, you can't always win when you try to defend your actions to your mother. Let yourself lose sometime too. It will make me live longer. But maybe this is something you wouldn't want."

Moishe didn't respond to the bait. Instead he gave his brother Duvid a shove out the door, and quickly followed. Once outside, they oriented themselves towards the river which ran past the town on the other side of the farm fields and orchards. Moishe carried his fishing bag and his pole. Duvid grumbled as he hefted the tinplate pot that they would stuff with fish caught later.

It was a warm summer's day. The season was past its midpoint. Fruit, mostly unripened, were beginning to billow on the vines and woody greenery that bordered the path. The wind carried the waft of nectar and the fricatives of grasshopper's legs chafing, while high above, a nimbus cloud carried the promise of an early evening rain shower.

Once out of sight of their house, the young men paused. Duvid placed two cigarettes between his lips, lit them, and passed one to his brother. The two continued down the path to the river that flowed near the village for a quarter hour. Moishe coughed lightly. Duvid pulled off his shirt and let the sunshine spread across his torso. A pair of exploring flies claimed the back of Duvid's neck as their new found land. He tried to dispute their claim, but they were persistent hunters. His queasy sweating only made their quest more ardent, their appetites more sincere. As soon as Moishe and Duvid arrived at the river bank, Duvid plunged both hands into the silky water and splashed it firmly along the back of his head. His hair shivered it down onto his back. The flies fluttered off the flooded plains.

"Moishe, do you really believe such a thing as the *moshiach*?" Duvid passed his hand across the low spiny bushes that grew thick near the water, carefully plucking berries and planting them directly into his mouth. They were small but sweet. Summer sun gleamed off drying blades of bearded grass. Lovelorn squirrels called to one another with their gritty sounds. The anonymous dominion of earth, air, and vegetation was rich with squirming organisms. The air slept. It held its breath, awaiting some intervention.

"Duvid, God is listening. Be careful what you say."

"Moishe, according to the *midrashim*, any of us could be the *moshiach*, no?"

"Any one of us. You or me or Herschel the Milkman's son. No one can know."

"This is such nonsense. Herschel is an idiot. God could never choose him."

"God will choose whom God will choose. He will not ask your opinion. He may even choose you."

"Moishe, He may not ask my opinion, but I will give it anyway, whether He likes it or not. And if He wants me to be *moshiach*, I will tell Him to find someone else."

"You speak nonsense. Mama is right. Stay away from those magazines."

"Moishe?"

"What, Duvid?"

"Do you really like to fish?"

"Do I have a choice? We have to eat."

"I don't like to fish. I don't even like to kill worms. They make my skin crawl with their sliminess."

"Maybe you should learn to like it, Duvid. Worms, like everything in this world, were made by God. Maybe He made them so that we can fish. Everything is here for a purpose. That is the way God made the world. You are here for a reason and so am I."

"So, wise man, why are we here?"

"This is not something I can answer, Duvid. I am not that wise."

"Well, I will give you my opinion. You are here to give me a hard time."

"Ah, very smart. So why are you here?"

"To make you humbler. Otherwise, unperturbed, you would surely burst with conceit."

"It is clear you have been reading more than the books at *heder*. Such a marvellous vocabulary. Words that I would never think to employ. And does such reading give you wisdom, too, Duvid?"

"Wisdom is not for the young. That's what they taught me in *heder*. But I am clever enough to know that we are not here for any purpose. Maybe there is not even a God."

"Duvid, such talk will only bring you trouble."

"I prefer to live without superstition, Moishe."

"God is there whether you want to believe in Him or not. He made the world. He made you, even if He may regret that at times. What you say is blasphemy. No good can come of it. How can you say such terrible things? If father heard you, he would die of shame."

"So don't tell him."

"Duvid, you will bring the wrath of God on our house."

"Believe what you will, Moishe. Just don't ask me to do the same."

"Duvid, shut your mouth a little before you frighten all the fish with your sacrilege. Pass me a worm. It will be more useful than all your words."

Moishe took off his jacket, vest and hat, and hung them all from a low bush. His *yarmulke* he kept on his head. Under the white shirt, his *tsitsis*, the tasseled cloth, could be discerned. Duvid lay on the grass beside the bridge and idly watched. His brother fished intently, concentrating on the slight wavers of the float on the water's moving surface. Duvid let his eyes close as the heat of the rising sun touched his face. High in a tree, a wren cried out to stake its territory. The air awakened and a warm breeze shifted the leaves lightly.

Moishe smiled and let him sleep. He kept busy reeling in the fish that latched onto his hook. These he lashed along a cord passed through the gill openings and looped back out through their mouths. He left them to undulate in the cool shallows near the river's bank.

The sun was soon high enough that the fish had stopped biting. A horsefly buzzed repeatedly around Duvid's head. He opened his eyes and slapped at it in a futile attempt to drive it off. Maybe it would find other prey.

"So, awake already? I thought you would sleep all day. It's a good thing there are flies like this, to wake you up. We try to catch fish, and the fly tries to catch us. It is a type of justice, no?" Moishe chuckled.

"No, it just shows that the world is a cruel place. You laugh too much, Moishe."

"You think it is better to cry? Laugh, Duvid, laugh."

"I am. I'm laughing at you. Hey, this fly is eating me alive."

"So there is some justice in this world."

"Moishe, let's go back. We have enough fish. Mama will complain she has to cook too much."

"Mama will never complain about such a thing."

"So I will complain for her. Let's go. I have nothing to do here but provide sustenance for this miserable six-legged creature."

Moishe reached into the pouch hanging at his side and pulled out a length of carob seed, long and brown. It tasted exotic, a treat Duvid rarely had. Moishe broke off a piece and handed it to his wide-eyed brother.

"Duvid, here, a reward for your irritating behaviour. Perhaps this will sweeten your sour disposition."

Duvid snatched the treat away and stuffed it into his mouth. His jaws worked on the firm flesh. His teeth caught his cheek in a firm bite.

"Wicked fruit. Moishe, why do you give me something so difficult to eat?"

"Duvid, have you no patience? You should eat slowly, to savour the sweetness, not bolt it down like a hungry wolf. Duvid, you are truly a pest, never happy. All right, you win. We will return home. Help me get everything together. Be careful not to stick a hook through your finger."

Moishe packed up his gear, his meagre boxes of fish hooks, weights, braided line, and corks. These he placed carefully into a belted cloth bag that he draped over one shoulder. The fish he dropped into the metal pot. This he handed to Duvid, who wrinkled his nose.

It seemed longer to walk back than it had taken to reach the fishing spot. The young men's house lay on the end of town, where the Jews lived, away from the main street. The landmarks of the area were the synagogue and its associated structures, the bath house, the cemetery, the rabbi's house, the religious school, and the kosher butcher shop. Close by was the Catholic church. Twice a day, the men of the town would make their way to the synagogue for the daily prayers, once in the early morning, and again in the late afternoon, for the contiguous afternoon and evening prayers. The dividing line between them was sunset, which was the start of the next Jewish day. Friday sunset was also the dividing line between the secular and sacred parts of the week, as the holy Sabbath, God's ordained day of rest, arrived with the descent of the sun below the horizon. The meal for the Sabbath day was started some hours before sundown in the slow-cooking *chulent* pot. Special clothes were donned, and the Sabbath evening meal of *challah*, *gefilte fish*, boiled chicken and noodle soup was served, accompanied by small tumblers of red wine. Just before sunset, the Sabbath candles were lit, signifying the light of God.

As Friday approached, the bath house was especially busy as the Jews prepared for the Sabbath. Alternate days were available for its use by the opposite sexes. Women who had finished menstruating or recently given birth went there to become ritually purified, once again available for marital relations with their husbands. Here young women about to be married would also undergo a ritual cleansing prior to their first sexual relations.

Men who had been in contact with the dead and the sick, or had been contaminated in a number of other ways, also sought purification. It was a communal bath in a town where there were only primitive bathing facilities among the congregation's homes. In that way it served not only a ritual but a public health function, as did many of the Jews' multitude of rules of *kashruth*. The Jews were convinced that these laws had both a religious and a secularly cleansing character. Milk and meat would fester in the stomach, if they were there together. Pork was the flesh of the pig, an animal that flourished in mud swill. It was likely to be contaminated and cause miasmas and consumption and all manner of other diseases. Meat had to be properly slaughtered, humanely, without allowing the animal to suffer. This was surely a sign of a merciful God. Blood was a contaminant, the carrier of the living essence, to be returned to God, not eaten by man. It was to be diligently cleansed from the flesh of animals, which was first salted and then soaked in water to draw the salt out.

The men were expected by tradition to meet in prayer in groups of at least ten men of majority age, that is, over thirteen years, the age of *bar mitzvah*. Men always wore a head cover, either a *yarmulke* or a hat. The *kohanim*, descendants of the sons of Aaron, the brother of great Moses, had held the title of priest in ancient Israel, and they still carried the responsibility to maintain a special level of holiness even to this day. Special rules applied to them in particular. They were never to come in contact with the dead. They were not permitted to enter a cemetery, except when the deceased was of the man's immediate family.

On the Sabbath, no one worked. It was forbidden to light a fire, or to carry an object from one house to another. The men met in the synagogue in the morning, and spent all that morning in prayer. They wore their best clothes and wrapped themselves in the *tallis*, a large fringed cloth, during prayer. The women, if they came to the synagogue, remained at the back of the prayer hall, behind a perforated partition. They could listen and observe, but they could not participate with the men. It was the order of things, as they had always been, back to the days of the patriarchs, Abraham, Isaac, and Jacob. It would remain so in perpetuity, until the coming of the Messiah, who was expected to arrive one day, and could appear at any time. It could be tomorrow, or in ten thousand years. He would transform the world, and bring peace to all. And so a medieval society waited and held its breath for the great changes to come.

Duvid's sister Malka had, at the age of fourteen, married a man from a neighbouring village. She had by now had four children, and was pregnant again. Her husband owned the village's general store. Every other week, he spent a few days travelling with his cart from one local village to the next with a portion of his goods. In each town, he would visit the police station first. He brought gifts of a bottle of *schnapps* or several packages of cigarettes. This way, he was protected as he toured the dusty streets. It was a world of give and take, of ambiguities and hard rules. Jews were identified by a Catholic majority both as Christ-killers and as artisans and merchants. Their neighbours were also their enemies. Anger ebbed and flowed in rhythmic tides. The sluiceways of civility and law that kept the swell of troubles at a slow spill could flood over suddenly, unleashing a deluge.

On the way back from the river, the brothers passed through a clearing outside the town. It was the town's dump. Just past this was an orchard belonging to the village priest. It spread behind the church and the presbytery, where the priest lived. At the front of the church, a set of tall sprawling elm trees stood in a wide half-circle, where the road curved as it passed. Behind the church and out of sight of the priest, the boys of the hamlet hung out on Sundays after church, smoking cigarettes and exchanging adolescent chatter.

The two brothers trudged back home along their usual path. Embryonic fruit burgeoned on the priest's apple and pear trees. Interspersed within this orchard stood cherry and chestnut. The orchard was the priest's pride and his solace. Here he spent hours pruning, fertilizing, and propagating his only children. Set against the back of his residence, a small parcel of rich black earth was subdivided into rows and squares. Here grew the same vegetables as his Catholic parishioners and his Jewish neighbours—root crops of beets, cabbage, potatoes, carrots, and radishes, and vine vegetables like peas, beans, and pumpkin. A stand of corn stood as a fence towards the back, which he would give away to a neighbour as food for his cow or horse. He would use these to reward his best Sunday school pupils.

In the shadows of the trees, two older boys, almost men, lolled against a tree trunk. Two others wrestled fitfully in the grass in front of them, each trying to dominate. Into this scene wandered Moishe and Duvid, the older one carrying his sac of fishing tools on his back, the younger thrusting the pot of fish out in front of him as far as it would go.

"Look who goes there," called out Staszik, one of the Polish young men. "It appears to be a pair of pigs."

"You are mistaken, my friend," answered the other, "I think they are Jews. But I can understand how you could make such a mistake."

"How is that, Fyodor?"

"They smell as bad, and they are covered in mud."

The two friends laughed. Fyodor raised his head and studied the two Jews who had wandered into their midst, gauging their discomfort. Moishe and Duvid kept walking, trying to avoid eye contact. The two wrestlers, Wladik and Bolack, stopped grappling and looked up. As the Jews passed the larger group, a chestnut bounced off Moishe's head. He raised his free hand to rub the spot where it had landed. Duvid scowled at the Polish boys.

"Who do you call pigs? It is you who are the pigs."

"Duvid, shut your mouth. You will only have trouble."

"They have no right to insult us."

"Think more about avoiding a fight, Duvid."

Wladik called out. "Look, it's Duvid, the Jew. He is in my brother's class. You're the one so smart with languages, I hear. Good, you will need them. Soon we will throw the Jews out and you will be a foreigner in another land."

"What do you want with us?"

"What do you have in your pot? Gold, perhaps. It is well-known that you are all rich."

The four friends rose and walked quickly behind Moishe and Duvid. Wladik poked at Moishe's sack, while Staszik slipped in front of them and tapped the pot with a stick. He pulled the pot out of Moishe's hands.

"They bring us a gift. Not gold, it seems. The pot is too light. Perhaps some soup, or an apple compote. But be vigilant, that's what my father always says. A pot full of Jewish food is surely meant to poison us."

"Why don't you go away, leave us alone. We are only going home with our fish."

"Fish, is it? You have been fishing in our river?"

"It is not your river. It belongs to everyone."

"Is this not the land of Poland? Doesn't that mean it is the land of the Poles? I don't remember the teacher calling this place Jewland. Do you, Staszik?"

Duvid fended off the comment. "There is a Jewish land, the land of Palestine. I will go there one day."

"So, you see, these Jews are not Poles. They have their own land. So why don't you go there now and stop bleeding the poor Polish people?"

"But we live here. We are Poles like you."

"Poles like us. Do you hear this? Such an insult."

"Pigs wanting to be men."

"Pigs wanting to steal our food."

Bollak, one of the quartet, rammed himself against Moishe's back. Moishe flew forward onto his hands and knees, while the attacker fell back, wailing. Moishe's bag had attached itself to him by fishhooks which had been darned into the canvas and now also penetrated his skin. He thrust around wildly on the ground, clutching at the hooks but afraid to pull or even move them. His compatriots stood about, their jaws working slackly as they thought what to do. Duvid dragged Moishe to his feet, threw the pot of fish at the aggressors, and galloped away into the chest of the black-clad priest, who was standing directly in their path of retreat.

Once back on his feet, Moishe turned and knelt by his attacker. Duvid also turned around, wondering at this incomprehensible action. What could Moishe be planning, if not his own destruction? The priest now also knelt by the perforated young man.

"What is going on here?" he asked, his voice tranquil.

"These Jews are stealing our fish," answered Bollak. He clutched at the hooks imbedded in his left hand. There were spots of blood where they had entered the skin.

The priest answered. "These fish belong to no one. They come from the river. Anyone may take them. And you look much like a fish on a hook yourself. How does it feel to be caught?"

One of the other young men protested. "Father, they are Jews. We are Poles. It is our land. It is our river."

"You leave these people alone. They wish to live in peace. I am curious to see what this Jew intends to do now, though. If he is unable to help you, you will be in a fine pickle." Moishe thrust one hand deep into the cloth back and retrieved two tools from the bottom, pliers and small metal shears.

"What do you intend with those, my friend?" asked the priest.

"Hold this," said Moishe, handing him the wire cutters, while he deftly grabbed Bollak's wrist firmly in one hand and held the pliers in the other. The young man proceeded to erupt with a series of ear-offending shrieks. The priest motioned for Bollak's friends to kneel close and hold his arms and any other body part they could get a grip on.

"Be at peace," whispered the priest into Bollak's ear. "Don't move."

With that he watched as Moishe clutched each hook one at a time while the priest worked the wire cutters to snip the barbed end off the metal curlicue. Moishe carefully manoeuvred the remaining portion out of the skin. A drop of blood appeared at each entry point as he did this. Bollak's eyes protruded as he watched the operation, After the second hook had been removed, they rolled up into his forehead and he became a dead weight.

"Take him home now, you three demons. You see what comes of sin?"

Moishe added his own advice to the priest's admonition. "When you get him home, bind moistened dark bread mixed with spider webs against the wound." He reclaimed his tools and dropped them into his bag, and hefted this onto his shoulder. Duvid stared at the fish lying uselessly on the grass. Maybe he should try to recover them, he thought. His brother motioned for him to follow him away from the site of battle.

"Is this Jewish witchcraft, Father?" asked Staszik.

The priest answered. "No, this is good advice. The Jews have much knowledge of the arts of healing." He turned to Moishe and Duvid. "Perhaps it would be wise to return home. These young men are a little hot-headed today. It must be the weather."

As the two Jews rushed away while their protector still hovered between them and the four troublemakers, the priest turned to his flock and chuckled.

"So, you try to defend the honour of your country like this. It's time to grow up. One day you will have to fight against our true enemies."

"And who are they, Father?"

"The Bolsheviks, the godless oppressors of our Christian brothers in Russia. Prepare yourselves for that holy battle. These Jews are of little danger to us."

"But was it not they who killed our Saviour Jesus, and is it not they who supported the godless revolution? Isn't that what you said in your sermons?"

"Yes, that is all true, it was them. That battle, however, is in the future. For now, content yourselves with gathering these fishes, just as our Lord gathered his few fishes and fed them to His great flock at Capernaum."

The three young men crossed themselves in front of the priest, returned the fish lying on the ground to their pot, and handed it all to the priest. Bollak was just returning to his senses.

"Bless you, my sons. Now get this poor young lad home to his family before he bleeds to death." He winked. "And be sure to do as you have been instructed."

With that, he returned to his home with the pot. It seemed he would have a fish supper that evening.

The three young men busied themselves with lifting Bollak to his feet and pushing and pulling him along the path between the apple trees towards the town and his father's house.

Duvid arrived in a rush of perturbed air and sour sweat. He rushed to the pot of drinking water on the kitchen counter, ladled a glass full and gulped it down quickly.

"So, Duvid, did you bring me some fish for shabbos?" His mother was busy kneading a mound of pale dough. His sister Chaya was braiding another amorphous hunk into small rolls. Next to her elbow sat a flat hardwood board piled with an array of miniature challahs that had already faced the fury of the oven.

"The priest stole them from us."

"The priest? He would not do such a thing."

"Well, he did. You can ask Moishe." Duvid appropriated a roll, gripped one end of it between his teeth, and walked back out of the house. He pulled a cigarette from a case in his pocket and lit it. He inhaled deeply. Soon shabbos would arrive. This would be his last cigarette until after the setting of the sun the next day.

Moishe drifted serenely through the kitchen door a minute later. He paused to kiss the *mezuzah* that was nailed to the right side of the doorframe.

"Moishe, is it true what Duvid tells me? That the priest took your fish?"

"Duvid? What does Duvid know? Do priests steal? They are filled with Christian love." Moishe was removing freshly-baked breads from the flat metal platter on which they had just left the oven, and was stacking them irregularly on the sideboard. His mother was alarmed.

"No, no, Moishe, don't place them on their backs. It attracts the *eyneh hora*, the Evil Eye." She made the sounds of spitting into the air, turning her head in a half-circle.

Moishe rearranged the buns, bottom-side down, whistling softly.

"Duvid doesn't know what goes on. To him every drop of rain is an inundation. Don't listen to him." At that moment, Moishe's words took on prophetic meaning, as water drops hit the windows and Duvid came charging up the dusty wooden steps and exploded back inside through the door. Moishe glared at his younger brother's foolishness but held his tongue. In this house, admonishment was his mother's prerogative. He would stay silent for now.

"Duvid, remove your shoes!" yelled out his mother, as he left a wet trail of dirt tracking along the floor into the bedrooms on the level above. Two shoes pounded down the stairs, first one, then the second, and thudded to a stop near the bottom.

"Duvid!" His mother and sister simultaneously called his name and looked at each other, shaking their heads. There was a knock at the door, and the face of their neighbour's daughter appeared.

"Ah, it's Miriam. Come in, if you must. Come in. You will become sick standing in the rain like this."

"Thank you, Mrs. Grynsztyn."

Hearing Miriam's voice, Duvid came halfway down the stairs, still chewing on the roll. His mother pretended he wasn't there.

"Your beauty grows greater each day," she continued. "I'm sure your parents can't wait to find a suitable match."

"Don't talk to me about my parents. They will make me crazy."

"What, don't tell me there is no marriage arranged yet? A beauty like you turns every man's head."

"I don't want my parents to find a man for me."

"And what do you want? To live like in America?"

"And what is wrong with that?"

"Don't try to live higher than you are, Miriam. This is a small town. We live like always. Too much freedom is not good."

"I will leave this village one day. I will travel, but to Palestine, not to America. You will see."

"Ah, these young people. They always dream the impossible. I see that in your head you've already arrived there."

"What do you mean?"

"Everyone here knows about your poems. They are not true poems, Miriam. Those we find in the Tanach, in the Psalms of David, in the Song of Songs. What you have written is a scandal."

"My uncle says my poems are well-written. He's a writer and a scholar."

"Your uncle who lives in Krakow? He's a socialist, people say."

"Yes, he is. He encouraged me. He says the Song of Songs was itself a scandal in the time when the Tanach was being written down. There is nothing new under the sun."

"Perhaps, Miriam. Maybe that is the only thing we agree on."

"At least something."

"Yes, and that we're all Jews. So, shabbos will arrive soon. It should be a time of peace. Let's stop arguing, if only for the sake of the Sabbath."

"Of course I agree to that."

"So, good."

Miriam had seen her poem published in a left-wing Yiddish paper in Warsaw. She had submitted her work to the few Jewish literary magazines published in Warsaw or Vilna or Petach Tikvah, once even to one in New York City, in the mythic America.

"Miriam, why do you run here in this storm? Does your mother need something?"

"Yes. She asks if you might have a blue thread."

"Blue? Blue? Yes, I have blue. What kind of blue?"

"I only know that much. My sister Luba tore her dress and my mother needs to repair it."

"And for this your mother can't wait. Is it better if you get soaked in the rain and confined to your bed for a week?"

"My mother wants to mend it before shabbos arrives. And I don't get sick so easily."

"You should be careful what you say. The Evil Eye hears everything." Duvid's mother spit again, this time into a bag of vegetable cuttings that she was saving for the garden. "You'll have to excuse me, but the dough is rising and I have to attend to it. As soon as I'm finished putting it all in the oven, I will find your thread. It won't be long. Duvid will bring them over."

At this point Duvid, having finished chewing and swallowing the roll, interjected.

"I can take Miriam to the sewing room and show her the threads you have. Her mother will be upset if she returns empty-handed."

Duvid's mother conjured up the sight of Luba with her ragged torn clothes falling off her back. She looked over her own daughter Chaya, standing next to her and imagined her in the same situation. Of course, her own child had a mother and father who were both adept in the arts of tailoring, and an array of the tools and supplies of the trade right there in their home. The two were always working at something, trying to hold life together for their medium-sized family. In the community, many families had more children, few had less.

Miriam's parents were, if not rich by any man's yardstick, at least comfortable by the local standard. Miriam's father was the town's kosher butcher. He was always busy and a well-respected member of the community. He had a place of prominence in the synagogue, near the front next to the bima. So it was with some bemusement that Duvid's mother wondered to herself how such a prominent man's daughters could be dressed in what for her were rags.

Meanwhile, as Duvid's mother thought to herself about her superior ways, she realized that Duvid was in the sewing room with Miriam. Miriam the poetess, who wrote in inflamed words. They were alone. She hurried in after them so as not to have a scandal. The two young people wore serious expressions as she came in. They must be hiding something, she thought to herself. Perhaps they will be gripped by the same fever that had taken hold in our town between conservatives and liberals.

Duvid's mother had noticed Duvid furtively reading a copy of *Marching Naked to Jerusalem* behind a bush where he thought he was alone. The idea that her Duvid could be seduced by this Lilith made her shudder. With growing alarm, she thought that perhaps she had already enticed him.

A shiver went down Duvid's mother's back. Imagine such a young girl writing poetry with a title like this, *Marching Naked to Jerusalem*, one which at once inflamed both the heart and the loins. She herself would never touch such a piece of writing. Such a title would corrupt the young. This was the sort of thing to be expected from those over-educated semi-converts in the capital city, the Bundists, the socialists and anarchists and reformists, revolutionary in all things, even in such matters that pertained only to God. What did their ideas have to do with how the Jews lived their lives, in the meagre bits of time and with the paucity of resources that a person could expect to receive in life? They were dangerous concepts, wild ideas, but the young people of the town seemed provoked by some great revelation. They were wilful and argumentative. Well, she sniffed, just wait. Life will show them how immature and limited they are.

"Duvid, wouldn't it be nice if you brought these threads with you to Miriam's mother, instead of rummaging around in this dark room like frightened cats. She will choose."

Listening to his mother, Duvid and Miriam quickly gathered all the shades of blue thread that she had and dropped them into a canvas sac. The rain still poured outside but the two sprang out the door on the run for Miriam's house.

"Wait for me, Duvid."

"Hurry up."

Duvid reached back and snatched Miriam's hand, dragging her up level with him as he ran. Her hand was soft and cold, the thin fingers delicate. The sun was obscured behind thick clouds, the rains dropped as massive sheets, and the day was late enough that they were almost invisible. As they neared her house, Miriam squeezed her hand deeper into his and Duvid stopped suddenly. Miriam's body bumped against his and stayed for a moment, hugging up against his warmth, before she drew back into the cold deluge.

He shouted over the sound of the rain. "I was fascinated and charmed by your poem, Miriam, even though some of the words were not ones I would ever dare to speak."

Surprised by Duvid's confession, Miriam let go his hand, and clutched the bag away from him as he stood, ridiculously wet, on her threshold. Then she was gone. He stood fixed in place, mesmerized. Despite the violent downpour, he walked home slowly and arrived sodden.

It was a particularly warm and calm summer of opportunity. Miriam would excuse herself to pick flowers. Her mother's eyes followed her out the door with distrust, but what could she really do anymore with such an independent spirit? Duvid and Miriam enjoyed walking together in the woods near the town, talking of poetry and ideas. Sunlight filtered through florid growth and turbid air, transgressing leaf by leaf, downwards into warm turgid soil. Dapples and splashes of shade played on greenery as the light descended towards the splotchy forest floor, a mingling of shadow and shadow, plackets of vitelline light and phaeic darkness, overlaid and interwoven. Over a matter of a few weeks, fingers brushed and hands clasped. It was only natural in this landscape, verdant and richly populated with life's proud strut and organismic spasm, that their young bodies met and held and blended, a slow ballet. There was no effort, no resistance, simply a gradual conjugation of forms.

During the ebbing of a long summer, Duvid and Miriam again and again disappeared into the exuberant forest, anthracite shadows gliding through a vaguely chromatic realm. Exploring the topological expressions of this roaming landscape, here and there they paused, inhaled into their surroundings, a congealed blur of timeless wanderings.

These wild tracts were private property, the hunting domain of a distant aristocrat. As summer ripened, the sounds of intruders assailed the close stillness of this green haven. Hounds wailed. Duvid and Miriam could hear noises, hollow and distant, then closer, an aggression of brutal footfalls and loud shouts. Dry plant matter, compacted into an earthen membrane, groaned as the two dropped into the litter at the sudden report of a gun. Louder thuddings beat towards them on the aerated hollow weave of debris that made up the vibrant drum of the forest floor. They were surrounded by a rush of sounds. Moments later they were alone again. The air breathed quietly. The action travelled deeper into the trees, the sounds dwindling until an insurgent whisper of the wind was enough to overwhelm them completely.

What had they been hunting? What prey was here, besides themselves? The infusion of danger left them ignited. In the viscid stillness that followed, the reality of the incident thinned to a shivering liquid, before it slipped away. Fingers, hands, then limbs clasped, away from brooding destiny, denying the undercurrent menace of history.

Later, as Duvid lay next to a small stream, blowing smoke at the flies while Miriam plucked forest flowers for her hair, he wondered where summer would lead, where this moment hovered in the vast fingers of an immanent God, as they marched naked to Jerusalem. He waited for the hunters to return.

35 Miriam's Journal

I often visit my Uncle Herschel in Krakow. I am excited to go each time. It is not a large city, I am told, but it is the largest I have seen. My parents are unhappy about the growing discomfort in my village about my poetry. Perhaps that is why they have sent me away. It is hard to live among such a narrow-minded group of people. For my parents, these small town folk are the normal ones, but it chafes me to have to remain among them. I desire only to go to Palestine and help build the new land of the Jewish people. I know Duvid wants me to stay. I am sure he is in love with me. I am not sure of my own feelings. All I know is that if I remain there, I will shrivel up like a flower in a dry summer.

My uncle has Catholic friends. They are not like the Catholics I know in my town. They invite us into their home. I make a friend, Marya, who is their daughter. She goes to church every Sunday, and secretly, I go with her. I am overwhelmed by the beauty of the church interior. The stained glass is lovely. I have never seen anything like it. I let her teach me a few Catholic prayers. I find the Latin words fascinating. I take exception to the statues of bleeding Christs. They make my skin crawl. Such a religion of death makes no sense to me. I say nothing to Marya of my sentiments, though.

My uncle is a writer for a weekly Yiddish paper. He has occasional salons for visiting poets and writers. I sit on his divan and listen to the bright young university men argue when they meet on Sunday afternoons. Young people often gather here for clandestine meetings of the Bund. Even an occasional nihilist. These always seem so thin and wild-haired. They argue about everything.

The voices are boisterous, enraged at injustices–those against the Jews, against the poor. Voices prepared for revolution, but a revolution of oratory, not of fists and steel. I always find another exciting book to read, even by Marx and Tolstoy. I constantly glance up. I listen.

"There will never be any change in society until the masses rise and overthrow their rulers."

"But that requires violence, and violence means death for many. We Jews are pacifists. We cannot fight."

"We must fight."

"Is it really justified to kill for the cause of the people? The ends are not justified by the means. Are you prepared to kill, or to go to prison, or die on the gallows?"

"Society cannot evolve smoothly and quietly. There are too many men with vested interests who do not want to budge. They would rather go backwards than to the future. They must be pushed forward."

"And who of these are good for the Jews? The Communists? The peasants and workers? The rich? Nobody. We are without allies. Whatever we do, whoever we think to ally ourselves with, we are alone, through all history. You cannot deny this. Neither side is for us. But we must act anyway. We must heed our sage Hillel. If we are not for ourselves, who will be for us? And if we are only for ourselves, what are we? We must create our own society in Palestine. There we will be free to live as we wish in accordance with our ethical tradition. And he also said: if not now, when? The time is here to do this."

"So you quote Hillel. Very good, but the tradition of the Jews is too old for our modern age. It is outdated and unable to adapt to the times we live in. And what will happen with the Hassidim, you think? Will they come with us and bring their superstitions with them? Drag us back to our *shtetls*, even in the new land."

"We are one people. We must respect them. They preserve the essence of Judaism."

"The essence of old folktales, you mean. Better abandoned."

"Fighting among ourselves must be avoided by any means we can."

"They refuse to speak Hebrew, except as the language of prayer. In Palestine, will we be speaking Yiddish or Hebrew? And here, what should we teach our children?"

"Here we should speak the language of the land we live in: Polish, or German, or Russian."

"Yes, of course, German or Polish or Russian, but what about in our homes? Should it be Yiddish or Hebrew?"

"We must teach our young people Hebrew so that they can establish our new land."

"Perhaps the Germans will save us. The Germans are re-arming. Will they invade again soon and save the Jews from the pogroms of the Poles, and impose stability in this society?"

"Trust no gentile to be your saviour. It is a dangerous path to walk along. The Jews can never assimilate, even if they want to."

"But in Germany they do, and there they have done very well."

"You are a *luftmentsch*–a dreamer. Don't you read the news? The Jews of Germany are beset with troubles since that man Hitler came into power. First it was Austria, and now all of Czechoslovakia is taken by him. If you trust these deceivers, you are a fool. A great fool."

"*Ad hominem* arguments are invalid. You cannot prove your point by attacking me personally!"

"*Ad hominem*! Now we have to hear ideas justified in the language of those who exiled us from our land so many years ago. Speak in Hebrew, if you must use another language."

"Nonsense!"

"You speak nonsense!"

"The German Jews pretend to be true Germans. They are all assimilated and this alarms the gentile folk. They are afraid these people who call themselves Jews will infiltrate and take the reins of their society away from them."

"That is a false argument. The Jews are always accused of something, whether they try to assimilate or stay apart. Things are dangerous for us everywhere we go."

"Is it better to become like the *goyim* and disappear, after all these centuries and millennia as Jews?"

"Strangers in a strange land is what we were, are, and always will be. Perhaps it would be better for our children to become invisible."

"The only sane thing to do is to leave."

"Many of our brethren live in America and do well. It is a land of opportunity."

"And a land of forgetting. They are a land without tradition, a land of guns and the pursuit of money. Should we leave for America? They have difficulties there too. Will we ever be welcomed into any society as equals? No, I say! We must go to Palestine and begin again. It is a land without people, empty and begging to be rebuilt."

"I hear there are a few Arabs there."

"True, a few. But they will not cause us any trouble once they see how much good we bring them."

I am bedazzled by all this discussion. At that moment, I notice my aunt tugging on my shoulder. She takes me aside and whispers into my ear.

"Do not listen to all these men talking nonsense. They are men of words, not of actions, after all. They know nothing of life, only of what they read or what their rabbi tells them. Come, we will sit in the kitchen and talk over a nice cup of tea."

Reluctantly, I follow her. The hour is late. The guests are rising and going to the door. After bidding them good night, my uncle withdraws to his study with a visitor from France.

A plump-faced, tired-looking woman is sitting at the kitchen table. Her curly hair is a little unkempt, not stylish at all. A few grey hairs are woven among the others, which are a dull brown. She looks up when we enter.

"Esther, would you like some tea? Miriam?"

We both nod. "Miriam, I would like you to meet Esther Kreitman. She was born here in Poland but now lives in England. She is a writer. She would rather sit here than argue with the men in the salon."

"Hello. I have heard of you, I think."

"You are very charming, my dear girl, but I doubt that. You are more likely to have read my two famous brothers' stories."

I do not want to look unschooled, so I do not ask who those brothers might be. My aunt sees my discomfort and leans forward to whisper the names in my ear. I smile.

"Of course I have read them."

"Their stories are a delight, but they are not pleasant men, my brothers. Neither of them. I visited them a few years ago to ask for their help, before the time I published my first book. I was living in Warsaw on my own and had my young son with me. They sent me away and now they live in New York and do not answer my letters. They were very nasty! I have not spoken to them since. We are not what can be called close."

I am puzzled but do not ask more about it. I stir sugar into my tea and sip.

"Do you miss Duvid?" asks my aunt.

"Yes and no."

"What do you mean?" she asks.

"I love him. He is kind to me, generous and protective. It is sad that he has so little chance for education, because he has a good head, as smart as any of the whiplike minds that discuss their prescriptions for the world in the salon."

"But the village is the village. Duvid is poor, the son of a tailor and destined to be one himself. You know that, Miriam."

"I know this very well, Auntie. He would never be able to afford the university."

"As a Jew, of course, you know it is impossible to study in Poland. Polish Jews must go abroad to study. They go to Prague or Paris or London. This land is too harsh a place. And now, with the world turning towards war, it seems, we are becoming locked in. Worse things may happen, but not the worst."

I ask "What do you mean by the worst?"

"Ah, my dear, you will never know the answer to that question. I doubt things will ever go that far. The barbarism of the last war taught us all a lesson."

Esther has been listening attentively but now breaks in. "Watch out for young intellectual men. They have heads but no hearts. They are deceivers. If this young man is good to you, that is all you need to know. That is my advice to you, my dear girl. But educate yourself. Do not rely on a man to support you."

"One day we will both leave for Palestine, and there everything will be possible." I smile and say no more.

At night in my bed, I imagine him next to me before I fall asleep. I see his face as he gazes into my eyes. He is so handsome, and strong, not like these bookmen who speak with large vocabularies and with the knowledge of an encyclopedia, but wear ugly spectacles and are unable to lift more than a pamphlet and walk with a drooping gait, their shoulders soft and bowed. I run my fingers over my body imagining they are his hands, and gasp as his face hovers in the dark. I will be returning to Bodsanow in four weeks. I enjoy my time here but I miss him more each night.

I was staying with Uncle Hersch for two whole months. Esther was my inspiration. She looked over my early efforts, picked at this or that, and offered up suggestions. She argued that women have equal abilities to men and should therefore be awarded equal rights to learning. She encouraged me in wanting an education. For her it was like a secret food. Suddenly she was gone. She never said goodbye and I never saw her again after that.

My uncle's wife is a music teacher. I study piano with her whenever I visit. Their two daughters are romantics, immersed in a fantasy world of great stone castles inhabited by beautiful princesses and gloomy forested mountains, where dark princes battle one another. They adore reading about stormy, tragic loves, inhaling the words on the page like so much sweet mountain air. But for me, such forays into fantasy are irksome and unrealistic. I feel closer to the grit and rough edges of life. But it is not in my dear Duvid's green forest that I feel most alive, but in my uncle's parlour, when he hosts his literary and political friends. Coffee and cognac and poetry and socialist pamphlets. They politely listen to my opinion, even though I am a woman, even though I am young, even though I can see their growing impatience at my naiveté. This is the world of my poetry, a world of struggle and hardship.

36 Falling Stones

The sun clears the treetops and the long shadows begin to melt away. A stone loosens and drops into the water below it. A spume erupts from the river. A man named Avrum stands on this ancient stone bridge, looking down into the dark water that flows below it, annoyed that the fall of the stone frightens the fish he hopes to attract with his lures. The sudden violence disturbs and perplexes him. It is a bad sign. The Evil Eye, perhaps. He spits into the water, warding it off. He has rested here since before dawn, waiting patiently for his line to shiver.

Rushes grow on the water's edges, obliviously reaching for the sky, for air and sun. The day is ripe with late summer scents, the smells wafted from farmer's fields not far off, luxuriant with growth. The waters of this stream started their inexorable spill towards the sea in cool mountains far away. The flow continues on to a distant ocean the man has never seen. Again he dips his fishing line into the stream. The water's murky stain is the product of a thirsty summer. The man's great-grandfather fished here years before. This fisherman is a follower of tradition.

The bridge he stands on has been there for centuries. Its rough stones, shaped over thousands of years by the work of the water that they were later to span, have over time each been replaced. The structure speaks of permanence, though, like the ever-flowing waters below it. Like the face of the man. Change is not discernible. The sluggish stream flows on, carrying its tinge slowly downstream.

The man feels the tug on his rod and pulls in the poor creature that has nibbled his worm. The fish struggles mightily, knowledge of its portion of fate growing in its pulsing heart. It has in this way a keener measure of cleverness than the man whose rod is the agent of its death.

Before arriving at this small bridge, the dusty, sometimes muddy road that crossed it passed through a village by the name of Bodzanow, near the town of Plock. The town sits about a hundred kilometres to the north-west of Warsaw. Across the lace of years many had come this way, many a peddler, searching for his produce, or his customer. In other times, many a plunderer too had passed through, resting some days before greater battles to come further down the road. Invaders had occasionally laid the village waste. Afterwards, many years would pass before new nomadic intruders could look again upon the still-standing small bridge and the waters below it, and decide that this was where they would stop their wanderings and settle. Here had lived for many years a family, onetime nomads, too. The spelling of the family name had alternated between Gruenstein and Grynsztyn, depending on the nation of the prince who ruled the land. The man on the bridge was one of these. His name was Avrum Grynsztyn, the eldest brother of Duvid.

As time progressed, historical memory was gradually left behind, and its empty places filled in with myth and conjecture. The Grynsztyns were just one family among many. They had been in Poland for generations. They did the same things over and over again, through long hard days, through tedious weeks, and across the leap of heavy years. Ritual and prayer carried them forward. With equal quantities of effort and belief, they stayed alive in this land. It had at one time welcomed them.

In the early centuries of the second millennium of what Jews today euphemistically call the Common Era, these Jews had moved here mostly from Germany, or, as it was known by its Hebrew name, the *Ashkenaz*. At first, the Jewish influx was encouraged. Liberal, tolerant conditions favourable to their settlement were introduced and later enhanced by the rulers of Poland, but, as they always do, sometimes slowly, sometimes abruptly, conditions changed. The battle with nature alone was itself always difficult, but life's weight, like an ocean's tides, came in and went out. *Pogroms*, famine, pestilence, attacks, repressive decrees, war. All these passed. Somehow these people and their descendants endured into the twentieth century, into the last year of the fourth decade of that century. Despite the hardships, the family had become large and broad.

Things changed one more time. The stones of the bridge were again falling.

The fisherman hurried to remove the hook from the mouth of the fish. In a few hours, the sun would near the horizon and the Sabbath would begin. The fish he had caught had to be prepared by his wife. There wasn't much time left.

As the man walked home with his fish supper, he looked back. He heard a harsh roar, the engine of a heavy vehicle. He hesitated as the convoy passed, unsure of what to do, how to stand. He saluted, unsure who these warriors were, nor how they might touch his life. The rebellious curling locks of hair that hung down from his temples waved as the breeze of the trucks' passing struck him. His *yarmulke* lifted off his head and he grabbed for it. The cloud of dust kicked up by their transit obscured the insignia on the transport truck, otherwise he would have been able to discern the swastika for the brief moment he stood. In the next moment he fell, a bullet breaking through his head.

The fish in his basket, still alive, mourned the man and itself, mourned the fate of first being caught and then remaining unfulfilled in its mission. The man had no time for such reflections. No time for thoughts for his children.

In her home a half-hour's walk from where Avrum had fallen, his mother spoke to her son Duvid. "Duvidel, it is time to wash yourself. Shabbos will come soon. You should be ready." His mother wondered aloud if perhaps the new year coming, which would be the start of a new century in the Jewish calendar, could bring peace to the Jewish people. She was answered by her husband's sarcasm yelled from the sewing room.

"Why would God help us now? Aren't things now better than they ever were? They can only get worse, I tell you."

She protested.

"Don't talk too much, Shimin, *kein eyneh hora!*" and she spit into the air in three directions, right, left, and behind. "Pfst! pfst! pfst!"

She complained to her son. "Duvid, hear how your father speaks like this. Don't you become like him, an *apikoyres.*" She yelled into the back of the house "What kind of example is this for a young man?" She spit once more to chase away the Evil Eye. Her husband sat quietly at his sewing table and didn't answer. He stared out the single-paned window at a small world at peace.

He had heard the news. It was impossible not to know. There was a much greater world beyond the edges of the *shtetl* and it was stumbling into a huge conflict. A week before, the Germans had invaded Poland. The French and British governments had issued their ultimata, and when that had no effect, declared war and their intention to liberate their ally.

There had been news of this war on the crystal radios. It was bad news, and the news had even reached Bodsanow. The war was going badly for the Poles. The people of the town were agitated, waiting uncomfortably for the invaders to arrive. It was the twenty-fourth day of the month of Elul, in the final month of the last year of the fifty-eighth century of the Jewish calendar. In less than one week, it would again be Rosh Hashanah, the Jewish New Year, as the seasons turned and the calendar marched along, its pages turning, while the Earth they all lived on pursued its faithful ellipsis around the unwavering sun.

As they did every Friday before the sun went down, Duvid's father and mother and their unmarried children had again changed from their ordinary ways of doing things during the working week, put on fresh clothing, and readied for the Sabbath, which would start at the moment of sunset.

Duvid's mother and sisters had already prepared the Sabbath evening meal. They had ground the carp and whitefish for the gefilte fish, boiled the chicken broth for the noodle soup, baked the challah, the ritual braided bread of the Sabbath, and started the pot of *chulent*, which would now bubble slowly all through the Sabbath day, so they would not have to sin by lighting a fire anew during the day of rest.

As sunset approached, and with everything else ready, Avrum's mother prepared to light the two candles on the kitchen table. She, as every other week, would say a prayer over the lighting, passing her hands slowly, rhythmically, above the flames, before she placed them over her eyes, pleading with God for a good week for her family. The flicker of candlelight would bathe the room.

When the war started, Duvid, Avrum's youngest brother, was seventeen years old and living with his parents in this small town. He had been trained by his father to continue in his footsteps, shown from childhood how to hold a needle, choose thread correct for the task, make a buttonhole and sew on a button, to cut cloth smoothly. He knew how to hem so that the clothing hung properly, to draw, cut and use a pattern to fit any size. He could tell the difference between poor and good quality cloth by touch. His father taught him to use a foot-driven sewing machine. One day, he hoped, he would make enough money to buy one of the new modern machines. Who knew, though, when the village might receive a supply of electricity.

Duvid hoped to marry Miriam in the spring, once he had saved enough from the tailoring he did at home with his father, to pay for the ceremony and a few household items. The couple's needs would be simple. Children would follow. They had fallen in love over the summer. His parents had resisted this notion of love as a reason for being joined together. The idea of young people choosing their own partners was still a somewhat foreign idea for the Jews of the village. An arranged marriage would have been more to his liking, but since Miriam was from a well-off family, daughter of the *shochet*, the ritual slaughterer, this eased his discomfort. Duvid was used to ignoring his father's demands anyway, and in this matter he would have gone his own way even if Miriam had been the daughter of the town's beggar.

On the Sabbath, Duvid avoided joining his father at the village's small synagogue. He would whistle outside Miriam's home to let her know he was there. and the two would slip away into the woods surrounding the village. In these woods he had found a hut which was used for hunting by the local landlord, who owned most of the farmland of the region. In the late summer and early autumn, the landlord would go there to chase wild boar through the woods with his hunting dogs, or shoot hare nibbling on the crops of carrots and beets in the farmers' fields.

Duvid had rebelled early against his father's religious ways, refusing to pray with him in the morning. He wore neither the traditional *shtreimel*, the fur-trimmed round hat, nor the *tzitzis*, the tasselled undercloth worn below the shirt. The hat he had bunched up and thrown into a well. So on a warm summer Saturday, while his father prayed on his behalf, and his brothers showed their resentment, he sometimes escaped and led Miriam through the cooler woods to that small cottage, where they were far from the prying eyes of her mother and little sister.

Duvid had always delighted in the secrets of the forest. He pointed out this or that plant to Miriam.

"This is a fern, as you know, and it is poisonous, as you also know, but in the spring, when it first uncurls, it is edible. You eat it after it is steamed."

"Really? I didn't know that."

"So now you know. Will you cook some for your family next spring?"

"I don't think they would eat it."

"That is a shame. It is delicious. Look at this mushroom with its red top. It will strangle you with its juices even if you boil it for a day."

"This forest sounds very dangerous. You're just trying to frighten me so I get close to you."

"So, you saw right through me. But nothing is stopping you from getting close, is there?"

"No. Here, I'll let you hold my hand."

"Must I tell you more stories to make you come even closer?"
She smiled. "Go on."

"There, up in that tree, do you see the nest?"

"Where? Oh, yes, there."

"See the mother bird? It's feeding the baby, which is larger than it is."

"How is that..."

"...possible? The chick is a cuckoo. The egg it hatched from was laid by its mother in the robin's nest, and the cuckoo mother tipped the robin's eggs out of the nest. The robin doesn't know any better and she feeds these chicks as if they were her own. Meanwhile the mother cuckoo gets to rest and eat and live without having to care for her young. Come, look here on the ground. These broken eggshells are all that is left of the real babies."

"That's so sad, that the nest could be usurped like that and the mother bird not understand the deception."

"Nature is like that, cruel and unrepentant, even while it's being beautiful."

"Yet created by a loving God."

"Believe what you will, Miriam. Just come closer."

Among his friends, Duvid had acquired a reputation. They had nicknamed him 'Squirrel'. He knew the paths and the concealments the animals took to hide their presence. He had spent hours shadowing the landlord's hunters as they tracked their prey. More than once, his movements had been mistaken for those of an animal, as he crouched in the undergrowth, slipping between the trees, when a dead branch suddenly cracked. The animals of the woods around him would instantly quiet themselves, a wave of silence slapping itself down over the dark vegetation. He learnt quickly. By observing the hunters, he learnt the essentials of how to manipulate a gun.

That was a couple of months earlier, while the world was still at peace. Within weeks of the invasion, all of Poland was in the hands of the German armies, except that part annexed by the Soviet Union, by the terms of a secret treaty agreed to between Germany and the Soviets before the invasion. On this late afternoon, after a long pause in another town, two German army trucks drove up the dusty road, across the little stone bridge, and into the town's centre. Only one or two hours had passed since Avrum Grynsztyn had been shot on his way home. Twenty soldiers slipped quickly out of the vehicles, rifles in hand, and fanned out through the village, banging on doors, ordering everyone out into the street.

The Poles of the town were eager to identify their neighbour Jews. These were ordered into the town centre, where they were searched for money and any other valuables they might be carrying. Duvid and his family came out of their house when ordered. While they stood in front of the family's home, on both sides of the street they could see German soldiers banging on doors and forcing them open. Moments later he saw his friend Yacov and his family in the next house over forced out with a rifle barrel pressed into the father's back, his hands in the air. The children wailed and clutched their mother's skirt. The father was pushed forward so he fell to the ground.

Duvid stayed quiet, but a few men and women resisted, stupidly or bravely. The village's carpenter acted almost insulted that he might be mistaken for a man of wealth. Shmuel, who lived not far from the church orchard, his small horde of coins hidden in an iron pot in the root cellar, turned out his pockets. He clearly had not a penny in the world. But these two had already been exposed by Polish informers as the "rich" men in a town of poor people. Wailing and pleading, they were both shot. The German commander expressed his disgust at their cringing petulance, as he shot one still-moving body through the head, while complaining at the waste of bullets. Family members cried. The bodies were dumped into the river. One of them was Miriam's father, the kosher butcher, who had always been a prominent follower of the *rebbe*, often taking part in Torah study in his *shul*.

The German commander marched along the street, looking each person in the eye.

"This one," he yelled and Duvid's fourteen-year-old sister Chaya was pulled aside by the soldiers, to join a number of other young girls gathered in a close bunch in the centre of the street. They were ordered to strip, on the pretence that something of value might be hidden under their clothes. Duvid was livid. He tensed himself, prepared to lunge forward to his sister's defence.

"Duvidel, please, stay calm. You will only bring harm on yourself if you do something rash. And harm on all of us, too."

It was his mother's strong words, and her strong grip besides, that held Duvid back. Despite the menace of the soldiers, she marched forward, pulled Chaya out of the small throng and quickly tore her daughter's clothes off her, down to her underthings, to show the Germans how she and her family could cooperate. The soldiers laughed and pushed Chaya back and forth between them, until they tired of the game and turned their attention to the other young women. Most of these girls, for they were in many ways only girls, shrieked, tears pouring down their cheeks, and quickly complied. Three among them, more reticent, were taken and thrown into the back of a truck. They tried to scream as one soldier after another climbed in and jumped back out, their faces flushed, moments later. Later in the day, these girls disappeared with the soldiers when the trucks drove away from the town. Before the Germans left, though, Jewish homes were ransacked, windows broken, cooking meals overturned onto kitchen floors, bedclothes torn apart and pantries destroyed. Flour and sugar, any dry foods, were poured out onto the floor.

"How could you do that to Chaya?" Duvid demanded later, after the invaders were gone.

"What would you have done, *chuchem*? You think you would have chased them away, all by yourself? You would have been killed, that's what would have happened, or if not that, they would have beaten you until they chased away your *neshumah*. You would have been worse than dead. Do you think we, your family, would have survived the day if you had done that? No! We would all be floating in the river like those men, like Mintzberg, Beloff, and Schenker are now. You saw what they did to those other girls, Sureleh, Malka, and the beauty Manya? They are gone now. Did you want them to do the same to your sister? The war has come to us, Duvid. You must start to think smarter from now on. No noble acts! No more dreaming. Care for yourself first, and after that for family."

"What about my friends?"

"Forget that you have friends. They will only betray you later. I lived through a war already when I was young. It is a terrible thing. People become like animals. Promise me you will listen to your mother, Duvid. I want you to live."

Duvid's anger sputtered to a stop before his mother's logic. He knew they had to comply, but he was seventeen. His blood was boiling. Maybe he could escape to Palestine, as he had dreamed of doing for a long time?

Avrum's wife, Rivka, came by after the Germans left, searching for him. No one had seen him. She erupted in deep troubled sobs. Duvid's mother was also crying, but she now also had the task of calming Rivka down and setting her back to the task of looking after her two small children.

The Germans had left the town a few hours after they had arrived. All the Jews who had lost someone—a son, a father, a daughter—went into mourning. The chanting of the *kaddish* prayer was heard in every corner of the little town.

After dark, in every household, debates started about what to do next. The men drifted over to the synagogue to discuss the issues. Everyone had an idea, and no one had an idea. Stay. Go. Fight. Don't fight. Duvid spoke up. They should run away, leave with him, but no one seemed convinced that things could get worse than had happened that day.

"Run to where?" answered the synagogue's *gabbai*. "Do you have some idea of where you will go? The Germans are everywhere. There can be no escape. On the road, passing along like nomads, like the Jews in Sinai, what will become of our children? Of our old people? They will die. There will be no crossing of the sea this time. The Egyptians will not be drowned. Miracles we can pray for, but not expect.

"If we go, everything we bring will be stolen from us, and then what? We are already a poor enough people. We have no money, little gold or silver for bribes, and you can be sure there will be bandits along the road, and at the checkpoints, the soldiers will want payments, big payments, to let us pass. And there will be many, many checkpoints, you can be sure of that. We must stay."

The meeting descended into rancour, and after an hour of argument and counter-argument, it broke up.

Duvid visited Miriam's home later the next evening to comfort her mother. He had seen her father die, and knew that Miriam was still away visiting in Krakow. The house was far away from his, in the better section of the small town, near the synagogue and far from the church. There were flowers in the garden in front, but what had been a pretty entrance was now transformed. The front door hung at an angle, one hinge broken away from the frame. The interior was ravaged, cooking pots flung around, food fallen to the floor, furniture torn or overturned. The curtains had been ripped from the windows. Duvid imagined what might have happened to Miriam if she had been at home and was filled with anger, revulsion, and a deep fear.

A light wind that now flowed through the shattered glass. Miriam's mother was sitting in the dark, her eyes swollen. Duvid's heart filled with a sudden and profound empathy. He placed his hand softly against the side of her mother's head and cheek to comfort her, but she pushed him away brusquely. A woman was not to be touched, even with compassion. Duvid retreated.

Outside the door, he met Meir, one of Miriam's cousins. They would have to try to recover the bodies the next day, Meir muttered, even though it would be the Sabbath. Duvid volunteered to help, but the older man dismissed the gesture. Duvid was a Cohen, a descendant of Aaron, brother of the great leader Moses. He was not allowed to touch a dead body, he was told. Duvid shrugged, secretly relieved. The thought of pulling a pallid corpse from the water filled him with revulsion. He went home to think.

Things could only get worse, he decided. He would escape the following morning. Before his family members retreated to their beds for the night, he put his energies into trying to convince his brothers and sisters to come with him, but they each had reasons to balk–children, enterprises, homes.

"Come away with me before it's too late."

"It's already too late. You heard the *gabbai*."

"So you will sit here and wait? For the Germans to come back? For the *moshiach*? You saw what the Germans did here today. Who knows what's happened to Avrum? We are not safe here."

His mother spit to either side again. His father came forward, no longer quiet as he usually was. "Don't say such things. We have seen much worse in our history, Duvid. Much worse. Better to stay where you know your surroundings, where you know your friends from your enemies."

"But things could get even worse still. Come with me while you can."

"How bad can they really get? We're not in the Middle Ages any more. We Jews have seen much worse. These Germans who were here did terrible things to us, but in their souls they are a civilized people. We must simply do as they say and they will ultimately leave us alone. We Jews have lived until now, for thousands of years, despite all that we have had to overcome. We survived Egypt, Babylon, the Greeks and the Romans. The Inquisition came and went and we remain. We survived Chmielnicki and his Cossacks. We will endure as we always have. Where will you run to, Duvid, if you go? You did not answer my question."

"To Palestine. To join with other Jews. We can have our own land."

Duvid's mother responded. "Duvid, that is only a dream. You will get to the next hill, not to Palestine."

"You will see. I will get there."

"You will see, Duvid. We will stay here."

What Duvid did see was that he would have to go alone. Miriam was in Krakow. She could not know what had happened here. He had her uncle's address from her letters. All he knew was that Krakow was to the south, and that it was very far away.

Duvid rose very early in the dark. As he was about to pull the door shut, his mother grabbed his wrist.

"Duvid, I know you are doing what you have to. Go with God."

"I can't stay."

"You're right. You're young and strong and you have a chance this way. Please try to stay alive. At least, of all of us, you will live. This is my hope."

"I will come back for you."

"Don't come back. Listen to what I told you before. Think first for your own self. Please remember that. You are a young man with a soft heart. It must become hard, like the Pharaoh's. Promise me."

"I promise," Duvid answered, not sure if he knew how to become like that.

"One thing you should remember, Duvid. Your father has buried a few coins in a pot next to the crooked apple tree in our field behind the house. It will be there if you do return. For now, take this."

She passed him a cloth sack and turned and closed the door behind her. Duvid stood there for a moment, hesitating, before he turned and ran across the road towards the fields on the edge of the town. He slipped into the woods as the sky in the east was becoming pale. He was afraid the soldiers would soon return. Once in among the trees, he opened the package. Bread, some cheese, a few apples. A potato and an onion. At the bottom, four small gold coins and a few of silver, and a pair of wool socks. He whispered a thank you to his mother across the distance that separated them, then continued on his way. He continued to trek south past Nizdzin, on through the fields, gathering or stealing food where he could, trying always to keep to the safety of the woods. After a few days, he neared Wyszogrod. He knew better than to enter a large town, and moved west and south to Drwaly, where he came to a river, and slipped along its northern shore. At a set of small islands set in the river, he was able to swim and ford across, island to island to the other side. Here he rested in among the trees, avoiding the cowherds. He was shivering after he came out of the water. He burrowed into a thatch of tall grass and pulled it around himself, staying there until he was dry. He ate an apple. He was hungry but reluctant to eat more and not have for another time when he was hungrier. Exhausted, he fell asleep.

He stayed in this place for a week, tempted to go back, thinking about his parents, his brothers and sisters. A vaporous loneliness came over him. He managed to convince himself he had done the right thing in leaving, that he might yet save Miriam, and pushed south.

Then, despite his secret hiding places and his efforts to evade, his naive good nature betrayed him. From the edge of the woods, he saw a woman and her daughter struggling to traverse a fenced ditch which separated the road south of the river from an adjacent field. They seemed stuck in a section of broken down wire. He slipped down to try to help them, but the Polish woman began to scream. She suspected that Duvid was a Jew. She yelled out at a German army truck that was passing by.

"Help me, Jesus, Son of God."

The driver pulled up next to the trio. "What are you three doing?" he asked Duvid. Duvid answered in his perfect German: "We are looking to pick apples, *mein Herr*." The driver carefully looked over the woman and her fifteen-year-old daughter. Three soldiers got out of the back of the truck, their rifles slung over their shoulders. The woman tried in her native Polish to explain that she was not like Duvid, that he was a Jew, but the soldiers spoke only German and ignored her words. They laughed, taunting her, and started to unbutton the fronts of their pants.

The woman took her daughter's wrist and tried to run off. One soldier calmly raised his gun and made some joke about shooting pigs to his comrades while sighting the rifle, then shot the woman through the back. The girl wailed. Her arms shook as she raised her hands. The shooter walked forward and grabbed her by the waist.

"Who needs an old woman when we have this young flesh to play with?"

The other two laughed, and then raised their guns and forced the girl into the back of the truck. The mother's body they left off the side of the road. After they were done with the girl, one soldier after the other, they forced Duvid in. He sat on the floor, while next to him, the girl cried inconsolably.

"Stop crying!" one of the trio of soldiers yelled at her. "Be happy we didn't kill you!"

Duvid tried to comfort her. He patted her hand and showed what he thought was a compassionate smile, but she pulled her hand away and scrunched her sitting body into a ball, knees against chest, arms around legs. The sobbing continued.

Duvid gave up trying. He cursed his stupidity for trying to help these women. Why hadn't he listened to his mother's advice? He promised himself that if he ever managed to get away, he would never help anyone else again.

Duvid didn't have features which cried out 'I am a Jew' to any but the Poles, who were so familiar with them. His hair was copper, his face smooth and square. The soldiers ignored him, simply another Pole they had arrested. They had nothing to gain from beating him, only energy to lose, so they left him alone.

The truck drove on for what seemed hours. Off in the distance was the red pointed tower of a church, a cross at its top. Great trees hung their branches above the road, and then came flat farmer's fields. Finally, the truck disgorged its cargo at a large army encampment. There, the soldiers were searching a multitude of natives for the few coins they might carry. These might be hidden in the seams of their clothing, or in their boots. Duvid was made to line up outside a tent. From inside it, every few minutes, a man would stagger out, shoeless, his feet bleeding. Next a woman would limp out, crying, hands covering her face. As he was forced into the lineup, a young woman was just then being dragged inside. Duvid looked around nervously. He could see that security was lax and overconfident.

Several years earlier, his brother Moishe had briefly been in the Polish army before officials could be bribed to engineer his release. He had later told Duvid, on one of their many fishing days together, that those assigned to guard duty were always the stupid ones. There was only one guard outside the entrance to the tent now, and he was facing away. He looked more interested in seeing what was happening inside the tent than in guarding the line of yet-unbeaten prisoners. Duvid turned and walked off, joining the crooked line of prisoners who had already been in the tent. The other prisoners said nothing. He tore a strip of cloth from the hem of his shirt, wadded it up, held it to one eye, and feigned a limp. Those already interrogated were straggling slowly past the guards at the gate of the army camp. The Germans had no further use for them. Once questioned, beaten, and robbed, they were being released back onto the refugee road. The guard at the gate looked Duvid over, trying to assure himself that he had been through the same process as the others.

"You, you, limper, have you been questioned?"

"*Ja, mein Herr!*" Duvid responded and saluted, pointing to his eye. The answer was the one the German soldier expected. He shifted his glance to the other captives walking behind Duvid. Minutes later, Duvid was again on the road to the east. He soon slipped off the rutted roadway, over the fence, and through a wheat field, and headed back into the nearest set of hills. By then, Duvid hadn't eaten anything for almost a full day.

Once in the uplands, he was able to find clumps of wild berry bushes which were still rich with once-ripe fruit. Their season was finishing, and there were soon no more. The woods here were much deeper and denser than what he was used to near his home. After a few hours' trek, he finally reached a clearing in the woods where he found an empty cabin, guessing it belonged to the local landowner. In the valley below, he saw an apple orchard, its fruit ripe for picking. During his forays along the edge of the trees, he came across a noose trap holding a freshly killed hare. He surmised that it must have been set by one of the locals. He carefully extricated the body, and to hide his presence, reset the trap.

This was a food he had never eaten before, but he was too famished to quote Torah to himself. He grilled it that day in the cabin's hearth, carefully gathering dry twigs and avoiding any wet sticks that would smoke. At first, he took only small nibbles. He told himself he should eat it, even though it was not kosher, since it would keep him alive, and so was permitted.

The meat didn't last long. It was time to move on. He had stayed already far too long, although he had lost track of dates. He only knew that the weather was changing. A cool autumn was unfolding–winter would not be far behind, and with it, likely starvation. He knew that someone was bound to come by the cabin soon, and then he would be caught. He had set himself the goal of finding Miriam, but the way had been harsher than he had expected, and he had needed this interlude to reset his thoughts.

Whenever he slipped by a farmhouse during the late evening and saw by lamplight the father seated at the kitchen table, sipping tea, the children gathered near the kitchen stove for warmth, or the mother darning a sock by candlelight, the swell of loneliness fell through his heart like a rock. He missed his family. He missed Miriam greatly. He wasn't sure now which draw was the more powerful.

Occasionally, he heard an airplane flying high overhead, but otherwise it all seemed unnaturally quiet. He remained alert. He sensed that fear was his ally, as it was for the animals. He missed his mother now more than Miriam. He wondered what had become of his family, and one day, loneliness overcoming caution, he determined to go back. Packing a knapsack from the cabin with fallen apples, a partly nibbled potato that had been left on the ground, a wilted carrot that he had managed to scrounge in the fields around, he set off.

The way back to his town was much longer and harder than he could have guessed it would be. The days became wetter, the nights colder, the roads he had to traverse had more military traffic driving to the east, in the direction of new border with Russia. At times he wondered if he could continue. Concern and guilt at having left his family behind drove him on. One clear morning, he finally neared his village. He had been very careful once he had seen the German army trucks driving over the bridge into the town. He had swum through the icy water below the bridge and slipped into the tall reeds lining its bank. Stealing through the darkness of the trees, he had watched, shivering, as Jewish women and children, each wearing a yellow star on his or her clothing, were forced to climb into trucks and were then driven away. Children cried, mothers cried, babies were crying. A cacophony of tears blasted his ears. Where were the men? Duvid stared out through the vegetation, trying to make out the details of a face, a stance, a way of walking, the shape of a back. Was that his mother? His brother Moishe's wife? Did those two girls belong to his sister Chaya? He looked away, buried his eyes in the ground. It was more than he could bear. His mother's words echoed in his head: "Look out for yourself first..." Is this what she had been meaning? Had she expected this to come about?

Duvid was paralyzed with fear, unable to move, pinned to the ground by the shadows of the trees. His hands shook with his fear. He struggled not to cry, not to make a sound, not to be discovered. Only after the sounds of the truck engines had long faded and the darkness of night had dropped all around him did he dare to move.

They were gone. Everyone. He could do nothing for them. His destiny and theirs had unravelled like the braided threads of the broken *tzitzith* he had refused to wear. For the moment, he had to survive. He had by now run out of the little food he had brought with him, but in the village, in his old home, he found the remains of some food, stale bread, some stored winter vegetables in the cellars, here or there a jar of pickled beets, or a scrap of hard cheese. He felt the ghosts of his family in the cracking sounds of the floors and rafters of the house. Were they dead already? Duvid shuddered but continued to gather food. His skin crawled. He had to get out of here before the fear drove him mad.

The Polish neighbours were still out there in their homes, not so far away. He felt his way in the dark that pervaded the house, along the so familiar walls, the smooth surfaces of doors, but between the sticks of fallen or broken furniture he hesitated. He might hurt himself, true, but more perilously, the noise might rouse a neighbour. Not so long ago, months ago, he had run between or sat on them. Slowly, carefully, he reached forward. He was by now shuddering with the cold that had seeped in through the open door and the broken panes of the windows. He pulled a quilt off a bed and wrapped it around him. There, he felt better now. He pulled the blanket across a table's edge and turned quickly to catch an unlit oil lamp.

The villagers would come in tomorrow to take things left behind. He knew better than to approach any of the Polish neighbours for help. On seeing him they would be sure to denounce him. There was only one person here who might take pity and shelter him.

Duvid waited until after midnight to leave his hiding place in the trees next to the town. He slipped down to the river's edge and drank greedily, and relieved himself into the stream. He slowly slunk from tree to tree, rock to rock, barn to barn, until the church close to his house was silhouetted against the night sky. The wind had picked up. A dog barked a few times as he passed close by, but quickly settled down as he moved on. The windows of the priory were still dimly lit. Someone was inside, still awake. Duvid walked up the cinder path and knocked once, twice, a third time. He waited.

The door opened slowly, the priest dressed in his pyjamas was a shadow in front of the pale lantern behind him on the table.

"Who are you? What do you want?"

"It's me, Father. Look."

"Me? It is dark and it is dangerous to shine light on you. Someone will see. Who is this 'me'?"

"Duvid, Duvid Grynsztyn" he whispered.

"What, you are here? How is it you stand in front of me when all the other Jews are gone? Do you know how dangerous it is for me to open the door for you?"

"Father, can I come in? I am very cold. I am hungry. I will answer all your questions once inside, or I will run away right now."

"No, stay, stay. Come in." The priest closed the door behind Duvid, then led him into his study. He sighed.

"Sit. I will bring you something to eat but I can't provide much. The Germans take everything they lay eyes on."

Duvid sat and soaked in the warmth of the room. He tried to shut out what had happened that day from his mind. His mother? His brother's wife? His little nieces? Where were the men? All gone?

He shuddered, not from cold now, but from revulsion at the answers his mind was constructing to these questions. By the low light, he noticed the fireplace, and above it, an image of Jesus on the cross. Were the Jews to suffer that fate now, die like that man? Wasn't Jesus a Jew too?

Duvid suddenly wondered where the priest was. He was taking such a long time. Had he sneaked off to denounce him? Duvid jumped up, but as he did, at the end of the hallway, he could see the priest approaching slowly, carrying a well-loaded tray. Duvid took a deep breath. He returned to the chair and to inspecting his surroundings. He allowed his guard to go down. It felt good to be here. Warmth. Quiet. Pretty paintings. Soft chairs. Duvid sighed.

On the mantel rested a small green bottle of some liqueur. The gold decoration glinted faintly. Beside it rested several small glasses, of a similar style. The ceiling above him was in a complicated stucco, frozen drips of plaster hanging down in regular patterned waves across the ceiling. Small paintings hung on the walls, scenes from an ancient land. Perhaps they were scenes from the New Testament, but he didn't know those stories. He was peering at these, trying to discern their subjects. Meanwhile the priest set the tray down. It was loaded with cheese and sausage, small bread rolls, and a glass of beer, on a small low table next to Duvid.

"So, here, eat. There may not be enough to eat tomorrow."

Duvid snatched at a roll and alternated chewing it and swallowing chunks of quickly masticated sausage. He hesitated to eat the cheese at the same sitting, but then gave in. Rules! Laws! What did they matter while there was this savage war against his people?

"Ah, you were very hungry. I hope it does not offend you to receive food which your father would not consider kosher–yes, I know what that is. It is, unfortunately, all that I have."

"It does not bother me. Before, perhaps, but not now, not any more. It is quite tasty, really. Thank you, Father."

"You must be tired. Exhausted, probably. Why not stay one or two days until you are stronger?"

"You are in danger as long as I remain here."

"You also, no matter where you are. The Germans are removing all the Jews from the surrounding villages. They are shooting many. God knows where the ones they leave alive are being taken. This entire town is at risk if I help you, a Jew, but I cannot call myself a Christian if I do not. Come with me."

The two mounted the stairs to a second floor, and inside a closet, the priest showed that there was a panel which slid aside to reveal a small space which allowed only enough room to lie down. While Duvid inspected the space, the priest shuffled away and came back with a lumpy straw mattress, which he threw to the floor.

"I'm sorry for this primitive bed, but it is all that there is. This space has been here a long time. I only discovered it by chance when I was installing hooks for hanging sacks of dry food and heard the hollowness of the space behind the wall. It must have been designed in an earlier time, but I don't know why. It was empty when I came upon it."

"I'm sure I will be comfortable."

Two days later, a German army motorcycle rolled up to the church gate and an officer strode up to the door. He pounded vigorously until the priest opened it.

"Are you hiding any weapons?"

"Weapons? I am a priest."

The officer and his driver marched inside and while the officer sat in the same chair Duvid had occupied recently, the soldier pulled back a carpet and lifted a hidden trapdoor to descend into the cellar.

"There is always a trap door to the cellar in these houses. Always. And always hidden with a carpet. It seems strange to hide something which everyone knows is there, but you Poles do not have sharp minds. A German will always beat you."

Moments later, the soldier's head popped up from the cellar opening. He held out a jute sack.

"Potatoes."

"Nothing else?"

"No."

"Well, these potatoes can be used as projectiles against my troops, so I am confiscating them." The officer stood and marched out the door, followed by his driver, leaving the trap door open.

"Ah, gone. Peace." The priest crossed himself.

It was time for Duvid to go. That night, after Duvid had eaten, the priest tramped down the cellar steps with him and reached behind the bulkhead of stone that supported the chimney.

"You will need this. They say they are smarter than we Poles, but they did not find this. We are so predictable and they so smart! Hah!" He handed Duvid a package, something wrapped tightly in canvas. Duvid undid the binding.

"I hope you are capable of using that. It is quite simple, really. Just remember to unlatch this safety mechanism if you must use it. Here are enough bullets to hold off a few Germans for a while. This gun was mine when I was a soldier during the last great war, but I am a man of peace now. I have no more use for it. Now go and go quickly. If you are caught close to here, we will all suffer."

The path to Krakow, where Duvid believed Miriam to be, led him back south again, back to the forests where he had found refuge during the first glimmers of autumn. Because of the change in the weather, the barns were now occupied, but by only a few livestock. Many had been stolen by troops. The few scrawny cattle, or chickens, or sheep, expecting or hoping for feeding, mooed or clucked or baaed if he approached. Dogs outside the farm homes barked at the slightest sound he made or at the sniff of his unfamiliar odour. The hay stacks, their cut grass now fully dry, had been taken down and brought inside the barns, away from winter's rains and snows. He had to be craftier now, quieter, swifter.

At least the path was now familiar. He had come this way twice already, once leaving his town, and this last time returning. The same small roads, the same rivers with their wooden bridges, the same trees and barns, the same dogs. The same smoke hovering above the same farmhouses. There in the distance, the red-peaked church he had glimpsed from the back of the army truck. He recognized that he was now more than halfway there. It was a memory run forward and in reverse and now being run forward again. He knew the barns where corn was stored for the cows, even if less accessible now. He remembered where the odd tree might have a few wrinkled apples left on its branches, or scattered about on the ground. There was now less of a sprinkle of fallen grain in the corners of wheat fields. He was in competition with the voles of the fields, with the starlings and the crows, and the ever thicker and juicier mud. They had already taken their share. Too quickly, it was very cold now, cold enough that he saw his breath take shape in the air when he exerted himself, but still only in the evening, when there was still enough light to see it by. The days were milder than the nights, easier on the body, but detection was more likely. It took quite a lot longer this time than the first time, since there was no German army truck to carry him partway.

After several weeks of his long walk, he was back in the quiet forest again, hungry again, looking for food near the edge of a farmer's field, when he blundered across a path that a small group of partisans had scouted out. Almost instantly, Duvid was surrounded by several men and a few women, all pointing rifles at him. One man, wearing the brown jacket of a Polish army officer, with its distinctive zigzag embroidery on the collar, seemed the leader. He held one finger to his lips, pulling another across his throat. Duvid had better keep quiet. He was frisked by one of the men, who nodded to the leader, and then slipped his hand into Duvid's jacket and deftly extracted the pistol given him by the priest.

The other men were also dressed partly in ragged Polish uniforms. To keep him from running away while they decided what to do with him, they stripped off his trousers and placed them over his head like a bag, tying its legs below his chin. He was seated, his back against a tree, his hands tied behind him. The woman was left to guard him while the men continued their rounds. Duvid tried to speak through the cloth, and when there was no response, he fell silent.

"Here, I will help you. There is no need for your face to still be covered. But don't try anything, I warn you."

After his face was uncovered, Duvid looked up at the woman's face.

"You are very pretty."

She tapped her rifle butt lightly against his chest.

"Ow!" He took a sudden, deep breath.

"Don't try to distract me by charm. It won't help you."

Duvid sniffed, and asked sarcastically, "Do you think it's wise to wear your uniforms? If you are caught, you are dead."

"If we are caught we are dead anyway. What do you think, that this is a play we are acting in?"

"You have the costumes, at least, if not the brilliant dialogue."

She silently tapped her rifle against his chest to stop him from making more comments. After a few minutes of Duvid's silence, she questioned him.

"Who are you? Are you a Polish patriot? You look to me like a traitor or a spy."

He knew better than to confess to a Pole that he was a Jew. The Poles were no more lovers of Jews than were the Germans.

"I was in the army. After the German invasion, my army group was quickly overcome. I took to the woods."

"Which army?"

"7th Infantry Division, Krakow Army, in the Mountain Brigade." Duvid's brother had been a corporal in this brigade before the war. "I was a Corporal, 1st Class. I have been on the road for a long time. I hate the Germans even more than you," he fumed. His face turned a bright red and he shook his fists.

"More than me? I don't think so. This is not the worst story I have heard. I almost believe you."

Duvid fell asleep, the sounds around him muffled. He was jarred awake by the rifle barrel again tapping on his breastbone. He groaned a bit, becoming silent as the gun was pressed against the side of his head. Abruptly, he was yanked into a standing position, while the partisans debated whether they should let him live. The woman described what he had told her.

"Tell us again where you come from."

"Bodsanow, to the north. Near the city of Plock. My family lived there. Everyone I know there is gone. I saw them taken away in the backs of trucks. I was the only one able to escape."

"This makes no sense. There is a Bodsanow near here. You are not lying? You're not from there?"

"No. No. I've been travelling weeks already. I don't know this other Bodsanow."

"So why have you come so far south? Any other fool would know to go east, towards the Soviets."

"And have two armies shooting at me at once?"

"Where were you headed, then?"

"Krakow."

"Krakow! You are far off the track. And why there, of all places? Your story still makes no sense. Anyone here been to Plock?"

Most of the fighters shook their heads. One said, "I have been there. My cousin owns land nearby. I stayed with him when I was young, during the summers. I spent much time in the city."

"So ask this fellow a question about Plock."

"Plock is on a river. Which one?"

"Why, the Vistula."

"Too easy. Ask something harder."

"I rode in a boat on the river once. There's a hill with something on it. What?"

"The Cathedral."

"Again too easy. Ask again."

"What is important about that cathedral?"

"The kings of Poland are buried there."

"Correct again."

Duvid joked. "It's also a town known to be filled with many stupid Jews."

Laughter followed.

"So you are not a Jew or a communist?"

"Not a Jew, no. If you are a communist, so am I. If not, then neither am I. I know nothing of politics."

The leader of the group laughed lightly.

"So what are you doing here? Taking an afternoon stroll? Where is your uniform? We here all proudly wear what little we still have of ours. And what became of your rifle? A corporal does not carry a pistol."

"I shed my Polish army uniform before I could be captured. My rifle jammed during the fighting and I threw it away. I took the pistol from a fallen officer." Duvid tried to say nothing more to provoke them. He hadn't yet convinced their leader.

"Should we believe you? We risk all our lives this way."

"I don't work for the Germans. I'm looking for my fiancée. She fled to Krakow. This is the truth."

"Good! Something I can believe, at last. His fiancée. He's a quick and careful young man. He may even be telling the truth. Well, we have lost many of our brothers lately. He may be useful to us."

"We have to be sure he won't betray us, or say the wrong thing and endanger us if he is captured." They laughed again. "So what are your skills?"

"My friends used to call me 'Squirrel' because of how I could climb trees."

"Climb trees? This is what you think will be useful? We don't need monkeys here, we need fighters. Your first assignment will be to prove you're on our side. We're going on a little visit to some acquaintances of mine."

The next day they crept between the trees to where they became low scrub, approaching a farmhouse along the road just south of the small town of Bystra. "This place houses a small garrison of Germans. They haven't been in the area long and don't know their way around yet.

"You, *Plotzker*, you will go in first. Scout just outside in the trees next to the road. There," he whispered, "whistle when you're in place and I will catch up with you."

"What about a gun?"

"You won't need it."

"How many are there?"

"Maybe twelve."

"Maybe? You don't know?"

"Twelve. Exactly."

Duvid knew this was his test. These partisaners expected him to give them away If the Germans didn't kill him, then he might be accepted. He entered the trees, slipping along the ground and then into the low scrub across the road from the farmhouse. There they were. Seven sat in a circle, clustered together near a truck. That left five inside the house. Duvid could smell the cigarette smoke drifting towards him. One soldier rose, muttered something, and walked out to the road, next to where Duvid crouched. The man leaned his rifle against a bush and began to pee. Duvid had him by the neck within seconds. He pulled the body into the bushes and took the rifle in hand.

From the circle of men sitting on the ground someone asked "Hans? Where's Hans?"

Duvid sighted the rifle on the standing man, when he heard a whisper behind him. "You were supposed to whistle. No firing yet. The others aren't in position."

Duvid waited. Five-seconds. Ten-seconds. Fifteen-seconds. The standing soldier had been joined by two more rising. "Hans!" one yelled. They were quickly taken down by rifle shots. Duvid couldn't tell the source.

"Now."

Duvid and the group's leader fired at the other men as they tried to rise and rush for their guns. In seconds, they were all still. The farmhouse door flew open. For a fraction of a second, the silhouette of an officer stood framed in the light, his arms up, holding the doorframe, and then he too had dropped. Gunfire erupted inside the house, and seconds later, one of the fighters raised and lowered his rifle inside the front door, then came out into the light.

"It's done. Good work, *Plotzker*."

"Squirrel, if you please."

"Good work, Squirrel."

All that was left was to collect all the arms and ammunition the group could carry. They burned the truck and the house, and then they were gone, before a contingent of Germans could arrive from further up the road and pursue them.

There were other forays, every few nights, always in a different place. Duvid impressed the partisans with his ability to camouflage himself in the woods. He was slippery. His climbing skills were superior to any of them. He could make himself invisible, sneak down over the enemy as if he were fog, disappear like a leaf into a forest. The others adopted his old nickname: Squirrel.

From the insurgents he learned the proficiencies and hardness of battle and the complexities of escape. It was not like his village school. There were examinations but failure was fatal. There would be no second chances. A false move, the too early lighting of a fuse, the delay in running, these were deadly. It could be the flag of the vapour of a heavy exhalation on a cool day that would give him away, or a fit of coughing in the forest. All these mistakes, small and almost unavoidable. And then there was luck to deal with. It could be a harder adversary than error. He watched carefully, a new curriculum to be rapidly absorbed.

There were fifteen fighters in his group when he first joined them in the southern forests of the Carpathian Mountains. The numbers of the group changed with their fortunes. From Galicia's heights they would sneak at night to ambush convoys going south from Bielsko-Biala, past Zywiec and on into Slovakia. They skirted the outskirts of the small towns and cities of the region—Andrichow, Zywiec, Wadiwice—and raided the supply transports as they travelled at night along the narrow roads through the hills, between Wisla and Szczyrk, along muddy hairpin turns, with their headlight beams faint, bouncing up and down to the rhythms of the rutted roads. As winter arrived, the group retreated higher into the Tatra Mountains. There they hid the smoke from their fires, living in caves and narrow valleys, or deep in the thick forest, to keep themselves warmer than the winter air that crept into their bones and made their movements slow and clumsy. They moved as much as they were able to keep the sweat of their efforts from cooling before it could evaporate and their limbs become stiff, before a chill could penetrate their bodies to the bone. Fevers followed.

Sitting around the smokeless campfire, Duvid heard again that the Jews from nearby towns and villages were being forcibly resettled to unknown locations. The group seemed satisfied by this news, pleased that the invaders were doing at least one thing right. The city of Bialystok was mentioned, through which ran the new border between Poland and an expanded Russia. He thought of his parents, of his brothers and sisters. He was now certain that he would never see them again. They were beyond any mortal's help.

Staying alive would now be his primary goal. He cradled the pistol that had been returned to him.

37 Miriam's Journal

I am afraid. It is only weeks since the war started. The Germans hold Krakow in their tight fist. My uncle Herschel says to stay quiet. Nothing will happen to us, he says. The Germans cannot be so bad. He remembers them from the Great War. They are cultured, less brutish than the Poles or the Russians. They will not bother us if we do not bother them.

I go for a walk today with my cousin Bluma. There is a German soldier at the corner of the block. He yells at us. "*Halte! Halte! Ich werde schiessen!*" He recognizes us as Jewish. Bluma runs, trying to get home. The soldier runs after her and yells at her to stop. She does. He raises his rifle to fire.

"No, no!" I yell. I pick up a piece of broken brick on the street and throw it at him. Duvid has taught me well. The brick bounces off the soldier's helmet and he stops, turns and shoots at me. Bluma runs around the corner and disappears. I hear a second shot behind me as I rush away in the opposite direction. I run on and on. The streets are wet with rain and I try not to slip and fall. The wet cobblestones are all I see in front of me. Everything else is a blur. Finally, I stop and make my way back to my uncle's house.

He is standing at the top of the stairs when I arrive.

"Bluma told me what you did and you are never to do such a thing again. It was very foolish thing to do. Now the Germans will be looking for you everywhere. You have placed us all in danger. I have spoken with my wife about this. You must leave."

"But uncle, where will I go? I have nowhere else." I am crying with shock and grief. I am terrified. How can he throw me out when I have just saved his daughter? But I do not argue any more. He stands in front of me with his arms folded in front of him, his face tight. It is clear that he has made up his mind.

Bluma stands behind him, silent. Her lips are tightly pursed. Her eyes stay focussed on the floor. I can't tell if she is crying. What did she tell him? I have lost a friend.

Early the next morning, after the end of curfew, he tells me he will have someone drive me. He will come along as far as he feels it is safe. I thank him. He is taking a big risk for my sake. I understand this. Still, I feel he is throwing me away.

My uncle removes the yellow star that was issued to all of us from my sleeve. He slips a gold chain with a cross dangling from it around my neck.

"This Jesus will protect you, you will see."

I leave with a sack of bread and cheese and a small bag of clothing hanging over my back. We drive along a quiet street and then a quiet road into the country, on and on for two hours or more, while my uncle instructs me how to proceed.

Just before a checkpoint, at my uncle's command, I slip out of the car and in among the trees along the road. Duvid has taught me well the art of camouflage. I meet up with the car again a kilometre past the checkpoint. My uncle's driver is waiting for me. My uncle is gone. The driver says nothing, simply taking me to a nearby farm, where a man with a hay wagon collects me. I get in the back and, according to his directions, I burrow into the hay. I hear the horses' hooves plod along the soft earthen road to some other place. The wagon stops at times and I hear muffled conversations and then I feel movement again. This happens several times. I fall asleep in the hay and when I wake, it is night. The horse has stopped and is eating grass along the road.

The wagon-driver tells me I have to get out here. He points along a rise along the road.

"Follow that to the left, where the rocks have fallen, as far as it will take you. You will come upon a group of houses. Ask for a Bela Klum. There is a large German checkpoint ahead," he says, "and they are questioning everyone."

Taking my small sack of food, I get down from the wagon and drop into the tall grass next to the road. I move on my elbows and knees until I am in the trees. I look around to see that I have not been followed. There is no sign of anyone.

I sit and eat most of what I have in my parcel and lie down in a crook between the roots of a tall oak tree. Above my head a raven calls out, before it flies off in a flutter of wings. I place my sack under my head and cover myself with my coat. I fall asleep.

When I wake up, it is light. I hear birds calling in the treetops. I think of Duvid and his woods. I miss him so. After I finish what is left in my parcel of food, I walk in the direction the wagon driver told me to go. I walk all morning, then rest by a small pond. I have nothing left to eat.

I walk into a mountain community, just twenty houses set along a road. I have no idea where I am, but it seems like the place that was described to me. The villagers tell me I am in the hamlet of Binecki. I finger the crucifix around my neck. It disturbs me but I know it may save my life. The people here tell me that many of the larger towns around here have been emptied, many destroyed, but this place have not been touched, so far. Perhaps it is too unimportant to bother with. It is too dangerous for me to try to return home, if I could ever find my way. I must stay. I ask for Bela Klum and am led to a house further up the hill.

At first I don't believe them, that so many villages would be so callously destroyed. How can such a thing happen, that those peaceful places can be devastated like this? But I have seen it happen in Krakow with my own eyes.

I hear the peasants gloat to one another that in the outer world, past their protective forest, the Jews are finally being herded away. Binecki had only one Jewish family before the last war, I overhear in others' conversations. That family left for America long ago. A Catholic family now lives in what was their house. I conceal my origins. I call myself Marya, after my friend in Krakow.

In these mountains, the frivolous world I have left is banished. Singing, playing music, dance, these are time-wasting luxuries. In the woods surrounding Binecki, war thrusts its sabre from the surrounding territories. Such talents of diversion are useless here.

Bela, a farmer-woman, takes me in. Her husband was killed in the early fighting and she has an infant daughter. She needs the help. I accompany her everywhere, even to church. To allay suspicion, I take communion. The priest seems to hesitate. I think he detects something unusual about me, but he says nothing. He is a good man. I eat the wafer and drink the blood of Christ.

38 Losses

Among the insurgent group that Duvid had joined were three women, Lina, Marta, and Clara. They fought as fiercely and ran as quickly as the men. Every few weeks, it seemed, death, or worse, capture, was the fate of one or more of the group. The rest would immediately move on. Captured fighters were as good as dead, as soon they had yielded any information they might have.

Joszip and Lina were sent into a farm village at night to bring back some supplies of food and fuel. As Lina was loading sticks of corn that were a farmer's winter supply for his pigs, the man and his two sons came out with a pitchfork and a rifle and he yelled for the thieves to leave before he warned the Germans.

The farmer made the mistake of discharging his rifle into the air to frighten them and the sound attracted a nearby army patrol. The sons knew enough to hide when the Germans approached, but the farmer was slow and naive. The soldiers saw only that the farmer and the partisans were together.

The two guerrillas were found by their colleagues, nights later, frozen and bloody. The bodies hung from a tree by their necks, their throats cut, in farm wire nooses. The farmer's body had already been cut down during the first night by his sons, who carried it to the local church for burial. The corpses of the two Polish patriots wore no boots. The farmer's sons had taken them.

39 Miriam's Journal

I wonder at what has become of my family. I may never know. The world beyond this town's gates seems so far away. I have been here so very long–three years. As time passes, the inhabitants of the town of Binecki remain fortunate. Despite the war, it has been quiet here for years. I know that outside this town, there is a swirl of horror and destruction, but we seem to be protected from it. We are no threat to the Germans. Binecki has no strategic value. There are no industries in the area, only small rock-strewn farms. German war vehicles do rumble through, but they rarely stop, except for water or the occasional chicken, but there have never been any consequences for the townsfolk. They fear the Germans and always comply with their demands. Since there are few Germans about, there is also little insurgent activity. We rarely hear a sound of fighting. It is as if the world has passed us by.

Partisans wander through the town at night, obscured by the flowing night mists of these hills, but they also rarely stop, except to replenish their water, or also take a chicken. There have to this day never been any confrontations between them and the invaders anywhere near the town. It is a place at peace in the midst of the destructive swirl of war.

40 Necessity

The partisans carefully planned their revenge. There was one spot along the forest's rim where a wooden bridge crossed a stream that ran full in the spring, and became a rivulet in summer. Armored troop carriers patrolled there daily.

Piano wire, salvaged from a nearby, once-stately home damaged by bombardment, was strung between the bridge posts. Under the overhanging canopy of leaves, the wire, thin to the point of near-invisibility, disappeared from view as the eyes adjusted from sunlight to shadow.

The men watched, holding their breaths, carefully hidden in the brush. An hour passed. A German troop carrier rumbled by along the dirt road, one soldier's head extended above the turret. The vehicle slipped onto the bridge, and exited again. The head was gone. The vehicle stopped, the back opened and five troopers jumped out and fanned out along the edge of the woods. Slowly they marched along, listening, staring, sniffing at the pungent air.

Tomasz, watching from a high tree branch, began to sneeze suddenly. Duvid turned to signal him to shush. The man smiled once, embarrassed perhaps, then sneezed again. He sneezed perhaps three times in his perch before a single shot rang out. A second later, a German soldier yelled out a command.

Duvid slung his rifle over his shoulder and dropped silently to the ground from his perch. He could feel the heat of the gun barrel where it lay along his back. He burrowed his way through the underbrush to a safer hiding place before the enemy troops could find him and the others. He shook his head. There had been no choice.

Much later, Duvid returned to the bridge to examine the wire. He didn't understand why he was putting himself in danger. He just had to know if it had worked. Had he made the kill?

He could see the splatter of brownish red blood that trailed behind the tracks of the troop carrier for a short distance. The dead soldier's severed head was no longer on the road by then. Recovered by the German patrol, he supposed. Who knew why, except for some outlandish feeling of propriety. They would have put themselves in danger by exiting their armoured vehicle. How such an evil enemy could care about such niceties? How could they be less callous than he was?

When he touched the wire, it separated with a melodic ring. Maybe he had been thinking too much about the enemy's humanity, not paying enough attention to the task. One end of the wire had whipped past him, tearing into the flesh of his shoulder. He was lucky, though. The cut was through the skin, a clean slice, not deep enough to damage the muscle. Duvid tore a piece of cloth to make a compress, and held tightly against the wound for a few minutes to staunch the bleeding. When he got back among his companions, they said nothing, only nodding at the bloody dressing, then pointing him to the bottle of spirits he could use to disinfect the wound. They didn't care to hear any details of the story. His pain was his own, to be endured. His well-being was important only because he was a resource they still needed. He was of value only as long as he remained healthy and didn't become a burden. The economics of emotion allowed no more than this. They allowed him the luxury of two days to recover, and then he was out in the field again, fighting.

41 Miriam's Journal

Today a number of German troop transports pull slowly into the town centre. I stand at the well with a bucket, ready to fill it with clean water. Dogs bark. They run in and out of the dry, dust cloud trailing behind the trucks. I put down my bucket and stare. A cold fear enters me and runs down my spine. Behind the trucks, trailing behind ropes tied to the rear bumpers, I see two men and a woman. They stagger, splattered with mud, and try to stay upright behind the moving vehicles. Their faces are covered in congealing blood coming from wounds on their foreheads. They wear only buttonless shirts, hanging open at the front. The man's chest bears red and brown bruises, perhaps from recent beatings. The men's genitals dangle down limply, shrunken and ruddy, the woman's is a dark patch against her ashen skin. The muscles of their buttocks and legs seem flaccid, not up to the tasks of fighters. The older man has several days' growth of beard. His face is haggard. He looks to be in his forties, probably handsome in better days, but not so today. Streaks of white course through otherwise brown hair. The other fellow is just a youth. He looks about fifteen. The woman's hair is a dull blonde and short-cropped. She is somewhere between the two men in age. The woman's shirt is falling off her shoulders. Her breasts are not large; the nipples have wide brown zones circling them, like Eva's—she is the mother of children. What has become of them?

Before, there was the day-by-day quiet despair of waiting for the war to end. Suddenly, there is now mass confusion in the town. Shrill soldiers shout. The smell of fear infects everyone. Orders are barked out: everyone must assemble in the main square. The entire hamlet is there, the old and the young. Children cry. Dogs bark in alarm. Mothers carry children in their arms under the menacing eyes of the soldiers. They pace around in tight circles. The noise of the crowd rises with the confusion that everyone feels. Children are running excitedly back and forth, chased by their mothers. People move back and forth, not sure of where to stand, where to go. Dogs bark wildly. It is bedlam.

A soldier shoots a single round into the air to get the crowd's attention. With this, a tense quiet envelops the square. The commandant reads out a short speech. The three partisans were caught too close to this village. The officer condemns the people of the town for participating in this attempted subversion against the Teutonic nation. The speech is in German. Some understand. Many don't, and turn to their neighbours for explanation. Small knots of women and men mutter to one another. One neighbour asks the next the nature of the speech.

The captured fighters are hauled up into one of the troop trucks, and it is backed up to a large tree in the town square. Noosed ropes have already been thrown over a sturdy tree branch and hang down. Their ends are tied to the top of the truck. The nooses are looped around the necks of the three captives and tightened. The truck drives away slowly. I hold my hands over my eyes, but Eva peels them away.

"You must look," she whispers. "You must not look away."

"Why?" I ask. I take my hands away and stare into the blacks of her eyes. She knows more than she says. She has seen this coming. I am afraid now.

The three pivot out by their necks as the vehicle pulls away, their legs trying to cling to the truck bed. For a moment they hang free, then they are flying through the air. They swing slowly back and forth below the tree branch, their bodies twisting in tight half-circles. Legs dance in a jerking fashion, knees bending and thrusting out rhythmically to some unheard melody that the wind carries in from the world beyond this village. Faces turn red, then purple, bodies a stark white. I recoil as the younger man's penis momentarily stiffens, before it quickly becomes flaccid and blue like his face. The woman's bladder releases its contents down her legs and into the grass below. A pair of dogs bark wildly at the convulsing bodies, and jump high enough to nip at their bare reddened feet. A child holds up her hand, points. She giggles nervously. Her mother gives her a forceful slap on the ear. A few soldiers laugh while smoking cigarettes. The townspeople look on, their faces flat. What will come next?

Off behind me an order is shouted out. I cringe next to Eva. She holds tight to Anna, her daughter. The soldiers are herding all males, adolescent or older, at gunpoint down the road, toward the church. Twenty metres behind them, in an agitated, wailing pack, stumble the town's women, their wives, sisters, and daughters. Eva and I stand back, away from the throng. The women are kept back at rifle point by the German soldiers who form a barrier between the two groups. The women try to push forward and the soldiers push back. The whole entourage comes to a halt at the church. Four soldiers run inside. Everyone is silent now.

The sun is close to the western horizon. The villagers stand quietly, not speaking, the red glow of sunset illuminating their faces. One bumps up against the next, each jostling for a view. One woman screams and in answer, a crescendo of cries erupts. A soldier comes out of the dark church with a stack of books in his arms. Another holds a painting, while a third carries a small statue. These they deposit on the grass. Again they go back in to see what else they can salvage. The pile of articles on the grass grows and is checked by the officer. Most are transferred into the back of the truck that has just been used for the executions. The prayer books are left in the grass. The commandant, his hair blonde, but seemingly on fire from the sunset glow, bends down and picks one up, curiously sorting through its pages, a thin smile on his face. He is tall and starkly handsome. An angry look comes over his features and he tosses the small volume into the nearby ditch. One of the German soldiers standing behind him crosses himself. Two soldiers again enter the structure with several heavy containers of petrol. In a few moments they come back out. They carry the containers more easily now.

The town's men stand packed tightly together. They aren't making a sound. Oh no! One, I think it is Marek, is suddenly running off towards the woods. Three soldiers are rushing after him. I clutch Eva's hand, distressed. Unable to catch him, the soldiers are coming to a stop. They've unsling their rifles and are aiming. In the near darkness, a hundred metres short of a field of high grain, I see Marek hesitate, then he falls. The soldiers sling their rifles back across their shoulders and are walking out to where he lies. I hear a single shot and shudder.

One woman screeches. It's Renata, Marek's wife. I see her rush at the surprised soldiers. The German officer shoots, and now Renata too is motionless on the grass. The faces around me drop into a dull stare. My belly is knotting up. I feel I will come apart. I look to Eva but she is busy calming her child, hugging her tightly against herself. Eyes turn upwards to the sky or down to the earth. Children fidget and cry, clutching at a mother's hand.

My eyes focus back on the church. The gathering of men lurch stiffly forward into the church at gunpoint. From their stiff movements, I can see how terrified they are. The women are crying loudly now, milling around frantically in a turbulent circle. The soldiers seem unable to control them. I see Ludmilla overcome with madness, her hands shaking wildly in front of her. They bang the sides of her head. Two soldiers light gasoline-soaked prayer books and toss them, one after the other, through the open door of the building. The men inside call out. Ludmilla is screaming now, arms flailing in the air. Orange and yellow flames burst up like gigantic luminous flowers inside the church. Eva gasps and steps back. Anna is screeching to be picked up. I feel like my heart is breaking in my chest.

The troops surround the building. They shoot as the mass of men try to escape through the open door. One after the other, they fall back into the fire. I see my friend Jerzy writhing at the entrance, before he is engulfed in flame. Other bodies of men I no longer recognize lie just inside the entrance, while thick dark smoke wafts over them to the outside. Two soldiers run forward and force the doors shut. The screaming from inside the building is frenzied now. The wailing from the crowd gathered outside is resigned and heavy, its treble adding to the bass of the voices in the burning church. I hear wood splitting and exploding from the heat. In the near-darkness, the smoke is a luminous orange-red as fire reaches out through the door and climbs the doorframe and lintel to the overhang of the roof.

Most of the onlookers back away into the shadow of dusk. I am one of these. I pull Eva with me. A few women still stand in silent witness just outside the reach of the heat from the blaze. Their hands are stretched up to the sky. A tower of flame now engulfs the steeple, and as its structure shifts, the church bell rings once. I see one young German soldier turn away, covering his eyes with his hands.

The few women still standing just beyond the perimeter of the soldiers cross themselves ferociously. The only sound to be heard now is a blend of the deep roaring and high-pitched crackling of flames. There is a heavy thud as some large piece of the church crashes down within its burning walls. Eva, and I turn away in the darkness and creep towards the edge of the woods that surround the village. She holds tightly to her little girl. Then the shooting starts.

It is quite dark by now. I look back. The silhouette of the crowd of women highlighted against the flames of the church gets smaller as one after the other falls. Finally, all we can see is the yellow-orange inferno. Eva and I shrink further into the trees. The burning continues for a long while. The officer shouts out some order and the soldiers retreat into their vehicles. They wait there, the engines running.

I sit at the edge of the woods all night, fully awake, frozen to the spot, while Eva and her daughter sleep under bushes. While they sleep, I cry. In the early dawn, only a lingering sour-sweet odour remains, as remnants of acrid thin smoke cling close to the ground, mixing with the mists of early morning.

I hoped that it was finished, that we could escape. It seems not to be so. As the sun comes up into a strangely beautiful dawn sky, there are again shouts. The soldiers are still there. The day progresses slowly, as they march methodically from one house to the next. They carry the bodies of women and young children, a few at a time, and throw them inside this house or that, with no pattern. They are soon setting fires to those homes, until all that remains of this town are embers and ash. A grey pall obscures everything and burns my eyes. I prevent myself from coughing, taking shallow breaths. I hold leaves wet with morning dew against my face to keep out the smoke, as much as is possible. I shudder, from the cold, I think, and hide as deeply as I can in the greenery.

I wake to the loud chatter of the birds of the forest. Next to me, Eva's daughter awakens in a start, gasping. She is frightened, a small child in a fearful place. She begins to run. I rush after her but she is small and slips more easily between the trees and bushes. I am unable to grab her quickly enough and she bursts out of the shadows of the trees into the open field and rushes towards her home. I stop, too afraid to follow her any farther. In all this noisy rushing about, Eva has awakened. She jumps up and tries to overtake her running daughter. The birds have gone silent. As I look again towards the fields, I see a group of five soldiers running towards us while Eva chases after her daughter. I lose sight of them as I burrow down inside the dense brush, trying to make myself invisible. A series of rifle shots thunder from the field. Quiet returns now. The distant crying stops. I hold my breath, while a pair of soldiers come within a meter of me before passing on. Then they are gone. A few shouts, a whistle, and I hear the engines of the army trucks starting and they dwindle away into silence. The birds begin to sing again. It is an ordinary day once more. I can fall asleep.

I remember awakening near nightfall, then falling deeply asleep again. The next dawn bursts, a full day lost to me without memory. I cannot understand. My mind is filled with confused thoughts. My surroundings are like a maze. I blunder through the thick undergrowth. I have a burning thirst. I am licking the dew from leaves in a clearing when I am discovered crawling on all fours by a group of partisan fighters. I rage at them, blaming them for the destruction which has come upon my adoptive village. They seem puzzled about what to do with me. "Shoot me," I want to scream, but they gag me too quickly. My hands and feet are tied.

My words move so slowly now. They blunder about and can't reach past my lips. My forehead is tight with pain, and my belly harsh. My mouth tastes of acid. I drift back and forth at the edge of a foggy numbness. I feel like someone has beaten my head with a board and hammered nails into it. I feel to retch, but hold myself back. Then I dream again: flames, children crying, choking. A flock of doves flutters upwards, the suddenness of their flight an explosion.

42 Worthy

Duvid held firmly to the tree branch, high above the forest floor, when he heard the sounds. He was checking what might have become of Janusz, the oldest surviving member of the group, as well as Mariusz and Halina. He was also there to look into reports that the Germans were back in force in the area. He would wait until nightfall before he slipped into the nearby hamlet, to see if there were any new goings-on. He had surveyed in all directions for any sign of activity when he came across the young madwoman in the forest.

Duvid was horrified when he saw that this was Miriam, thrashing about, scrabbling on all fours, tearing clumps of grass and soil and dead leaves and dropping them on her head. How could she be here in this same area he had been in all this time? He had no time to think, or even to care. The Germans would be close, and with all the noise she was making, she was sure to attract their attention. She was a danger to herself, certainly, but also to his compatriots.

He had not recognized her at first; she had changed so much. Just as well, for if either showed they knew one another, they were in danger. Questions would be asked. Who was she? Where was she from? How was it that they knew each other? Was she a spy, and therefore, was he also? It didn't much matter what the answers to these questions would be. Suspicion and a quick death would follow for both of them. There were always suspicions. Hadn't he arrived out of nowhere himself? Now these doubts would be doubled. There was simply too much risk for the others to tolerate.

He had to think: what to do?

Duvid's eyes passed slowly across Miriam's features, trying to understand how this horrid creature and Miriam could be the same person. Mouth slack, nose wet, hair impossibly tangled, covered with crumbled foliage and caked with earth, face black with the soot from the burning village, she filled him with revulsion all the while that he wanted to take her in his arms and pull her close. As he dared climb down to the ground to come closer, she stared up at him, a faint look of distracted recognition passing across her features, a look that said come to me, hold me, save me. But it was a wordless gesture. Was she trying to protect him, or greatly overwhelmed?

Duvid thought quickly what to do. He had little choice. He whistled lightly, and within moments, others in Duvid's group were appearing out of the greenery. As they approached her, she screamed, turning in circles to confront them all, accusing them of destroying her village. At the peak of her shrillness, she screamed wildly.

"Shoot me," she yelled. Then she stopped suddenly and fell heavily to the ground. No one in the group spoke for some moments.

"Mary, Mother of God" were the first words out of her mouth when Miriam woke up the next day near their fire, her face hot. She was wrapped in a blanket, her wrists tied tightly. She looked around groggily, on the edge of fainting. The two women in the group had sent the men away and had removed her filthy clothing and washed her face and body. One began to spoon a warm thick soup into her mouth. She ate greedily, rapidly, almost choking, sucking each spoonful into her mouth as quickly as it arrived. Her face was pinched with pain. Several times she almost vomited, breathing hard in gasps, until after a while she calmed and drifted again into a foggy numbness.

When Miriam finally woke up a day later, a conversation was going on between Yuri, one of the group, and Duvid. Yuri had an aristocratic face, finely chiseled, his eyes deeply set, with dark brown irises. He was blond but had a dark moustache and eyebrows that stood out dramatically on his face. Duvid kept nervously glancing over at Miriam.

"My older brothers always fished in the rivers near my home town. Our water was always clean."

Yuri listened and pretended not to notice this. "I am a city boy. I was a teacher. I never went near a river that did not stink. Not a place to take fish from. Even with the cows and the pigs shitting next to them? I doubt it." He smiled. "When was the last time you saw your family?"

"A little after the war began. I haven't heard anything from them since."

"I hope they are well. Maybe God will protect them. We should say our prayers every day. Jesus and Mary will perhaps listen."

"It is quaint to believe as you do, Yuri, but I don't think you would throw away your rifle and pray in the midst of battle."

"Both would be good. Anyway, don't blaspheme. It is bad luck. Didn't your brothers pray?"

"Yes. too much. Thank God I'm not religious!"

"Ah, good, a funny man in the midst of war. It is good that you can still laugh. But let's not get into the philosophical. We have a war to win. If God helps, it is by guidance. It is we who do the work."

"I agree. My brothers prayed, as you said, but they were also expert fishermen. So they caught fish. They were adept at taking care of themselves."

"You are right, Squirrel, but what do you know about experts? So they know a hook from a sinker. Such experts. I also know something about fish, for what it's worth now. There aren't too many fins sticking up out of the bushes around here."

Duvid scoffed. "So, are you a Herr Doktor Professor? A member of the intelligentsia? And you know something about guns too?"

"Don't you recognize my brilliance of intellect? You couldn't tell by the way I speak? By my deliberate and careful choice of words, the breadth of my vocabulary? And yes, I know how to shoot a gun." Yuri smiled broadly at Duvid, who was throwing another quick glance at Miriam, her wrists bound in front of her. She seemed to him to drift in and out of consciousness. She had started moving a little. A moan drifted out of her.

"Ah, the Contessa is waking from her dreams. I do hope that our soup is up to her standards."

"Yes, looks like we'd better get ready for a fight."

"She will be too hungry to fight. Just have your soup ready, Squirrel."

"I'll check that her restraints are tight."

"A wise move for such an unschooled fellow."

"Ah, you are an intellectual, full of yourself and brilliant thoughts. But at bottom, you are just a fisherman, are you? So what do you know about fish that my brothers couldn't have taught me, Fisherman?"

Yuri explained that he had been a professor of marine biology and limnology at the university in Warsaw before he had joined the underground. Duvid winced at the florid academic terms but said nothing.

Yuri continued. "I never eat fish. The smell turns my stomach. Who knows what these fish ate at the bottom of the rivers. What's down there, especially in the city? All the garbage goes in, masses of raw sewage. It drops to the bottom, gets absorbed by plants and snails and clams and such. And where does it come back out? In the fish, that's where. Even in the sea it's the same. I'd rather eat a cow any day. All it ever touches is grass."

"A cow, so the Fisherman would like to eat a cow. So, let's go hunting. There are plenty of farms around here. Maybe there's one cow in all Poland that the Germans haven't plundered yet. Maybe a generous farmer will just hand his best hidden cattle over to us when he sees how hungry we look. Jesus and Mary!"

"Yes, Jesus and Mary! All right, so maybe a pig instead, or even better, a chicken. It's easier to carry. I would settle for that, even if they do walk in their own droppings."

"And cows and pigs do not?"

Miriam twisted her bound wrists, where the pain seemed to be concentrated. She muttered something that rose in volume until the two men could hear her words.

"Who are you who guard me? What do you mean to do with me?" Her eyes darted at Duvid, then quickly away.

"At least you still live," countered Yuri.

"That is something I will consider to be in your favour, if I ever escape and you become my captives."

"Look at this woman. Most women are known for the softness of their skins and the hardness of their hearts. This woman's heart is broken by the tragedy of her village, and yet it is still slippery, like the epidermis of an eel. As for her skin, it is like sandpaper, like the surface of a shark." For Duvid's benefit, Yuri began comparing cartilaginous sharks, with their rough skins, to fish with bony skeletons.

"Did you know it is unhealthy to eat shark right after catching them? They use a chemical mechanism to balance their blood against the pressure of salt in the sea water around them. Otherwise the sea would flood in and overwhelm them, like sea-stranded men dying a crazed death after drinking sea water. They do this by hoarding urea in their blood. They smell like urine. After a few days this chemical breaks down into carbon dioxide and ammonia and wafts away."

"Then they are safe to eat?"

"Yes, then they are safe."

"And so too women, Yuri? Do we have to wait to let their gases bubble away before they are safe to consume? At least they are not full of poison."

"Not most of them, but I think this woman we just captured is. She will bring us trouble if we let her stay."

"We will have to discuss it. Our numbers are low. We need all the bodies we can have."

"All the fish we can have, too, according to your thoughts. But they are not always good for us. They might be sharks, deadly when alive, noxious when dead."

"The idea that the sharks had piss for blood turns my stomach, now that I know."

"I see you are not very hungry yet. Not everyone eats shark, either. Among the Jews, there is a law that disallows such food. The Jews won't eat shark, or eels, for that matter. They are a fastidious people. Too much so."

Yuri related that he had a colleague at the university before the war, a Jew, who had described the ritual food laws to him.

"Fish without scales were disallowed, but he did not know why. Maybe this is the reason." Yuri laughed. "I do those crazy Jews one better by not touching fish at all."

Duvid laughed in response.

"Jews. Yes, all crazy. With such a multitude of laws. Unfathomable."

"The fish have been on Earth a long time, far longer than us. They will still be here when we have outlived our usefulness to the world. The waters will close over us. The surface will show no sign that we were ever here. We are all fish in a dark sea. The ocean tides tug, push, spin. What choice do we have but to swim with these powerful flows or to be carried away by the waters? Either way, the end result is the same: we drown. The difference is in the way we swim. We are either flotsam or jetsam. That is our only choice, while we are here, either to cooperate with the world, or with God, or to fight against it, or Him."

"Or Her!" Miriam interjected loudly.

"So, the Contessa is now a theologian."

"And in the meantime, whether God is masculine or feminine, we are best to avoid the sharks."

"Either way, we get very wet."

"Soaked."

Duvid heard Miriam's voice again. "My wrists! The ropes are too tight."

Duvid slipped over to her side and undid the ropes holding her. She began to yell again, but when Duvid and Yuri towered over her, she just rubbed her chin over the skin where the ropes had dug in. Then she tried to bite Duvid's hand. Yuri laughed.

"The beauty of a ctenophore."

"Another shark?"

"No, a delicate and beautiful creature that lives in the sea. Small and bejewelled. Spherical and lacy, it has a skeleton of lovely strings of tiny pearls, stitched together into a Chinese lantern, covered in a transparent thin sheet like liquefied paper. At night, it will shimmer, phosphorescent. Lovely."

"Your pretty ctenophore is hungry. And I think she really is a shark."

"We will see."

Duvid spooned the thick warm mix into Miriam's mouth. She sucked it down greedily. He could see that she knew him, despite the beard he had grown, and that she could see that he recognized her too, despite the loss of weight, the paleness and the disheveled look. Her eyes played across Duvid's face. As he fed her, her eyes showed glimmers of fire with each spoonful she swallowed. Duvid's heart pounded in his chest, but he couldn't let it hold sway. He must stay quiet so as not to endanger them both.

The coarse meal set Miriam back to herself. She spit out the description of the massacre at the village to the fighters hovering around the small fire. No one said a word to her about the three captured fighters she described.

A few weeks after her capture, the group decided that Miriam was worthy of becoming a member and issued her with a captured rifle. Duvid was assigned to train her in its use. There followed a clumsy attempt by both to avoid openly acknowledging the other. The moment Duvid stood behind Miriam and held the butt of the rifle against her shoulder, showing her how to aim, the urge to wrap himself fully around her came over him. She positioned her right hand around the stock, her index finger contacting the trigger. Her left hand brushed against Duvid's as his hand deactivated the safety mechanism. He pulled back, away from her, a low hiss of air escaping his lips.

"Stop." he whispered desperately. Miriam's face lost expression.

Months had passed since Miriam had been found. As a sliver of moon rose late at night over the mountains to the east, the group trudged down a forested path. They rarely moved by day. It would be too easy to be seen by one of their countrymen and reported, or to come across a German patrol making its way through the area. The woods were noisy. A multitude of crickets chirped in all directions, trying to find mates. A few leaves fluttered on the ground as a snake lunged for a worm or shrew in the undergrowth. Leaves and branches cracked and swished as a fox bolted from the cover of a bush. The partisans' footfalls were muffled in all this chatter.

They were under attack from the moment one of their men collapsed sideways and thudded to the ground to the sharp crack of a rifle. Other guns began to fire. The woods were now a cacophony of wretched sounds. Voices yelling German words called off to the left of the group, betraying their position to the partisans. The members of the group had all crouched or fallen onto their stomachs by now and were sliding as quietly as they could to try to encircle the enemy, while yelling out their own commands in German.

The Fisherman called out that he was circling around the "partisan" position to the left. The others were to move to the right. The German troops were confused, diligently trying to follow the movements generated by these false orders. They were quickly taken from behind. Systematically, throats were sliced open. Two, one a soldier, the other an officer, rushed at Duvid. As he was bringing his gun up into position, the Fisherman came screaming out from the trees directly at the officer. The Fisherman and the German officer fell to the ground clasped noisily in each others' arms. Duvid turned to aim at the remaining soldier when Miriam flew past him. The butt of her rifle crashed against the side of the younger man's neck. He turned, stared at her for a second, then crumpled to the ground. His arms and legs flailed as he lay there on his back, his eyes wide open. He wailed with the terror of imminent death. The rough crescent of his mouth erupted blood and sputum.

For only a second, Miriam stared at the grotesque marionette agitating in front of her. There was no time for that. She spun around and put two bullets through the German officer's head as he struggled against the Fisherman's bulk. While Yuri disentangled himself from the dead man's grip, and Duvid stared aghast, Miriam shrieked out and turned back to her first prey. She pummelled the butt of her rifle again and again against the young soldier's face.

Duvid and Yuri, aghast, managed to wrap their arms around Miriam until she was immobilized. She erupted in bellowing howls.

The battle was over. They had lost two men, while the Germans were all dead except for one young man. He could not have been much more than eighteen years old. He was bound hand and foot, with a gag stuffed tightly in his mouth. He sat slumped against a tree trunk, eyes wild.

The group couldn't take prisoners. He would have to be killed after questioning, but quietly. There almost certainly were other soldiers on patrol nearby. Miriam begged the job of dispatching the boy. The young man stared wide-eyed at the remains of Miriam's other victim.

"I own this work. It is my revenge against these monsters."

"Miriam, this is no chore for a woman."

"You think I am soft? You will see, I am harder than any of you men."

The Fisherman stared, trying to face her down, then gave way. Her eyes were stone. He turned away with the others.

"Come, Squirrel. We will wait for her to finish. Far away."

It was a distasteful job, this killing of a young man, even for hardened veterans of the hills, who had been engaged against this enemy for years. He was just a boy, really. The others deferred to Miriam. They would wait in a natural indentation in the hillside some thirty metres away.

The muffled agony from Miriam's location went on and on. Despite the cloth stuffed deep into his mouth, the boy's strangled cries were still audible. Fractured branches and dead leaves crackled furiously.

Finally, The Fisherman turned to his companions and whispered insistently to Duvid.

"It's enough now. Give me your pistol."

Pistol in hand, Yuri rose and marched out towards Miriam. Duvid followed closely. In her frenzy, she hardly noticed they were there. Yuri crouched, held the revolver to the soldier's head and shot him dead. It was over. He allowed the revolver to fall, overcome.

Miriam rose, staggering, her expression wild, confused, exhaustion written on her face. Her hands and clothes were slick with blood. Yuri handed Miriam his water bottle, so she could rinse the grisly material from her skin. She tipped it upwards and guzzled its contents, then dropped to the ground. Her eyes empty, whimpering, she crushed handfuls of dry leaves in her fists. Yuri stared at her, then rose and turned away. Miriam grasped the revolver. Duvid came closer, while she sat herself upright and pointed it at Yuri, hands shaking. Quickly, Duvid fell on her and grabbed her right wrist tightly.

Miriam began to sob, large heaving convulsions of sound pouring out of her. She was pounding Duvid's head with her free left hand when Yuri dropped to his knees next to her and gingerly picked the revolver from her hand. Duvid passed his arms around her tightly, until she quietened. Placing his mouth close to her ear, he whispered her name very softly. The sobbing slowed and after a minute it stopped. Miriam stared ahead, now silent. Yuri saw but said nothing.

By now the others had emerged, and sat in a circle around the three of them, numb and still. Each was deep in his own thoughts, exhausted and silent. Then, one by one, they allowed themselves to shut their eyes. Exhausted, they slept in heaps for one or two hours at a time, awakening in quick starts at the slightest sound, then lapsing back into turgid dreams.

At dawn, Miriam rose before the others, miserable with thirst. The newly risen sun had barely infiltrated the residual darkness of night. The moisture-laden air was cool, dew clinging to her hair and clothing. She shuddered. Her hands and clothing were caked with blood. Getting up on her knees, she crawled towards a small stream that she had heard burbling earlier. Along the way, maybe fifty metres from where the group slept, she came across the body of another dead soldier, killed early in the fighting.

This one's uniform was untouched, except for the small hole where a bullet had flown through. She struggled with the stiffness of his limbs, trying not to rouse the others, while turning the man's dense weight over and over to drag off his clothing. Rigor mortis had pulled his twisted joints tight, as if he was preparing to defend himself. He had a look of surprise on his face. Death had arrived too easily. Each of the times she shifted the corpse's centre of gravity, the body slipped away from her fingers, air exiting the dead man's throat with a groan, a hiss, or a wheeze. Her hands shook.

Miriam struggled to pull off the jacket, followed by the shirt, and finally the man's trousers. He looked pathetic lying there, pale and contorted, his skin sallow. His private parts were small and limp. Miriam spat and coughed, suppressing the desire to vomit, then turned away and crawled towards the foamy, fluttery sound of the brook, dragging the uniform along.

At the stream, Miriam dropped her head to within a centimetre of the surface, and like a hungry animal sucked at it until she was choking. The water was deep enough to bathe in. She slowly disrobed, pulling off her stained clothes and dropping them over a bush. She slipped into the water, immersing herself completely by lying flat on her back. The frigid stream woke her up. She quickly sloshed water over her skin to wash off blood and sweat until she felt clean. Her arms hurt now, and the muscles of her back ached as the cold water tightened them. She emerged slowly, painfully, intending to dress in the dead German's clothing.

"Ah, a glacial baptism. Are you converting to the religion of death?"

Miriam dropped back below the surface, before turning quickly to match the words to a face.

"That is my religion already. So, it's you, Squirrel. Can a woman not have privacy? Do you also fish like your friend Yuri, but for women?"

"It's me, Miriam, Duvid. Don't you recognize me?"

"Duvid, my Duvid. Oh how I have truly missed you, but here is not the place and now is not the time for me to inflame you. Please me by turning around. I want to come out." She sat up in the water. Her lips and fingers were blue and she was shaking with cold.

"Miriam, I remember well the splendour of your body. It beckons me."

"If you mean to sweet talk me while I freeze to death in this frigid water, you can forget that. I have no illusions. I have nothing to hide any more, no modesty left, and especially not with you. Behold a free woman."

She uncapped her hands from her breasts and stood, stepping out of the creek while Duvid stared.

She tugged at the dead soldier's shirt hanging on a bush. She covered herself with it and rubbed herself with her hands.

"Oh, that water's so, so cold! That feels better now." She paused. "Duvid, my dear Duvid, listen to me. You may remember my body, but my soul really has changed. So has yours. I'm no longer the young, sheltered, carefree poetess. Not any more. And now you're different from the ardent, naive lover of nature you once were. We've both been through too much. Can we still fit together? I don't know. You don't know either. Only once this war is over, if it ever is, and we both survive, will we know. We have to wait. For now, though, no one should know that we once knew each other."

"You're breaking my heart. Truly."

Miriam pulled off the wet shirt and passed it over the skin of her legs to towel away some of their wetness, then threw it down. She stood naked. The roundness of her breasts, the swelling of her pink nipples, the silken wetness of her hair sticking to her shoulders, all were so familiar, even though five years had passed since he'd last seen them. Duvid recalled the curve of her waist, the sparseness of the patch of black hair between her legs. After she had finished drying herself and pulled on the uniform pants and jacket, he could no longer contain his excitement.

"Miriam."

She sat down with her back against a rock, facing Duvid. She was still shivering.

"Duvid, no. We have to wait."

"Of course."

"When you found me, I saw your eye sparkle, but you said nothing, did nothing. And I understood why. Duvid! Duvid! Duvid! I too was afraid to say anything."

"It's the wise thing to do. You can't trust anyone, Miriam. Not even me. Anyone may betray you, anyone can become a monster.

Look at the Germans. They were once a people of cultivation and wit, a folk sublime and artful, the pinnacle of Western Civilization. Now look at them. Brutes, worse than wild animals. Anyone can fall, anyone can fail. Everyone has become suspect now.

"We can't let these partisaners know that we're Jews. Maybe when the war is done, we can again be who we really are. For now, only silence. Don't even look at me as if you know me. We have to act like strangers to each other, even if it's so very difficult. The world has become too large and we're all in its shadow. Love is no longer possible. Not until peace comes."

"Yes, one day, perhaps, Duvid, if peace comes before we are dead."

"We must hurry. Someone will hear us speaking like this."

"So, can we start a fire? Heat some water for tea, perhaps? During the day, surely it can be permitted."

"It would not do for us to lose our fiercest soldier to pneumonia."

"So, Duvid the partisan soldier."

"Your partisan-soldier-lover."

"Not today. Not for a long time. Will you cook my breakfast today?"

"Gladly, Miriam, but we will have to steal it first."

"Find me another outfit. This uniform is warm, but it smells bad, and its not very feminine."

"So. You haven't changed completely."

Over the last months of the war inside Polish territory, the Russians drove determinately westward against the collapsing German front. In these dark nights, the flash of far-off artillery fire reflected off the hover of low clouds, starkly illuminating the ground through the weave of the vernal forest's naked branches. The Soviets encouraged the Polish underground to rise up in anticipation of the imminent arrival of their liberators. Then they deliberately paused to allow the Germans to demolish the clandestine Polish army and political units who might otherwise later stand in the way of their control of the liberated Poland. It was perfidy of the first order.

43 Miriam's Journal

With each day that passes the Soviet armies come closer. We hear and smell the ferocity of the battle as they near. At night, the glow of artillery and the sweep of searchlights light the skies. The German army, what little we still see of it, seems to be in disarray.

I have been fighting for months now. I have become the group's specialist in interrogating captured German soldiers. The others tie the young captured Germans into immobility. I cut them slowly into pieces as I tear bits of information from them. Where is your unit? How many? Where are you headed? What are your orders? How many of us have you killed and captured? How many innocents have you killed in the villages? In my village? It doesn't matter to me if you have a good mother waiting for you at home, or a wife and young beautiful children. Tell me. Facts. Tactics. Numbers. Times. Distances. You will die anyway. Don't you see, it's logical: we can't let you live. Do you want to die slowly and in pain or, if I like what you say, how you say it, what you know, you can go quickly? Whisper it here, in my ear, or hiss it, bark it, scream it. Or sob it out. I don't care. Just tell me all of it. Every detail.

The others stand away and swig their captured vodka. I do my duty until there is nothing more to learn. It's time for the others to finish the captive.

We hope these are the last weeks of the war. Our small remnant of fighters finally lets down its guard a little. One night in the hills, our spirits lift with a few bottles of stolen plum brandy. Duvid and I slip away, far from the others. We melt into each other, laughing and crying all at the same time. In our few moments alone, we couple furiously. We claw away each other's clothing, we roughly join our starved bodies. After all those hard years and months, it is such a relief to have the luxury of this brief moment together. I have been running and fighting now for over a year, since the village was destroyed. Duvid had been in battle almost since the war began five years ago.

After our union, I take another swig from the bottle, handing it back to Duvid. We pray that the struggle is done now. Since we met again in these woods, we have not once allowed ourselves physical intimacy. Too dangerous. The others would ask questions, challenge us about our loyalty to the group. A simple touch cannot remain simple. With some bright hope for the future, my zeal for fighting, my anger, would dull. I would fear Duvid's death too much. I could never betray him, as I should, if need be, for the good of the group.

Such luxury should only to be indulged in once the war has ended, if that end ever truly comes. Yet much of the German army in this area has pulled out. I have melted a little, and tasted this brittle crumb of peace. It is such a bourgeois thing, this love. But it is too late now. It has happened.

From our interrogations, we have learned that the Germans are planning to consolidate a deeper line of defence for the hard battles to come against the Russians. I hope for them first despair and then death. We have seen some units madly make a break for it, trying to get back to their crumbling, hellish Fatherland. They are easy to ambush and undermine. Perhaps too easy.

Duvid and I are clutching one other, gasping. We cry. Our tears melt together.

The world around us explodes.

Flashlight beams and flares cast a difficult light through the trees. Long crooked shadows of tree branches divide the brightened ground. Duvid and I come numbly aware in this dissected darkness. German words yell out some distance away. I reach into my boot before putting it back on and pull out the folded piece of dirtied yellow paper. I hand it to Duvid–my Jerusalem poem. Duvid's eyes shine in the faint light. Tears well up.

"Thank you," he whispers. "So, you still have this dream of yours."

"I will see you there."

"Yes, we will be there together." Duvid pushes the folded paper into an opening in the lining of his coat.

"I hope in better shape than this poem."

We cower in the brush. We hear our confreres scream in pain. There are many shots. Duvid rolls away from me, elbowing along the ground into a nearby small clearing. "Go, that way. It'll be safer if we move separately," he whispers, indicating a direction away from the fighting. I follow his instructions and he quickly disappears towards the lights of battle. There follows a period of silence, punctuated by the shouts of the army patrol. They are moving methodically forward now, still searching the woods.

Trying to avoid crackling leaves and sticks underfoot, I slip in the opposite direction. I make my footsteps deliberately uneven in their rhythm, to not attract attention. Hours must be passing.

The first faint light of dawn washes red over the deep indigo of night. I hear a few muffled shots fired far behind me and move on warily. By now Duvid has been caught or is dead. I rest briefly. I start to cry, then to sob and to wail. My soul's contents gush out of their restraints.

44 Endurance

Duvid came awake with a rifle butt pounding his ribs. His head was gushing blood uncontrollably, blurring his vision. Why hadn't they killed him? His sight limited; he could see down but not up or sideways. He was in the back of an army truck. It had stopped its bruising movement and come to a halt with a loud screech of brakes on tires. A whistle sounded from outside the truck.

"*Schnell, mach schnell!*" More shrill whistle sounds.

Around him inside the truck were many others, men, women, a few children, all now upright, pushing, shifting, some women trying to drag children by the hand. He recognized no one. Pushed out the rear of the truck by the pressure of the mass of bodies, he jumped to the ground. Lying prone there, other's feet landing on them to the sounds of cursing, were two elderly women attempting to rise. They were trying to lift themselves with their arms pressing against the ground, while all around them, people were running, scurrying about, being herded towards a building twenty metres away. Duvid reached down to lift one of the old women, but a blow to his back propelled him forward, and next he felt himself being dragged by his shoulders through the low door of a large house, and up steep narrow stairs. Almost blind, he heard more than saw a body cartwheeling down from the top of the stairs, head over feet and again, head over feet–crash, thud, bang. The body appeared suddenly at his feet and he was manhandled past this obstruction. By now the bleeding from his forehead had stopped. He could make out the form of an officer in a grey uniform sitting in a broad armchair next to a massive bed. The man was sipping from a brandy glass. Around Duvid stood twelve or so men, downcast, silent. Fear or futility was written on their faces.

"Ah, yes, one thing these Poles do well is their schnapps. So, who do we have here? You, the Jew, step forward! Come on, reluctant? So, drag him!" For a fleeting moment, the officer smiled, then went back to a frown as he stared at a sheet of paper on his lap.

"You others, stand against the wall. Be patient, *bitte*, I will get to you all sooner than you will wish." The captain methodically lit a cigar.

"Wipe his eyes. I want him to see my rank." He paused. "Yes, so, who are you?"

"I am a farmer. Jan Volcker is my name."

"Ah, so. A German farmer among these Poles. Very unlikely. I have to leave for a new location tonight. I have no time for niceties. Who are you?"

A blow slammed his head sideways. Still Duvid didn't reply. The captain swept his hand across the top of his hair. He hadn't had it cut in some time and it had slipped down across his eyes. His face held the traces of the hard years he had been fighting. He had the look of having seen too much in that time.

"Ya, so, a farmer. A German farmer, no less. Where is your farm?"

"Not far from here, mein Herr. I was looking for my lost pig in the woods when I came upon your men. May I go back now, sir? My wife is expecting me."

"Ah, your wife. Yes, I believe that we may have found her for you. Perhaps it is your pig that we found. Hard to distinguish at times. I'm sure you must know what I mean. You are far from home. I will save you the trouble of walking. We will bring you to a better place. Just a few questions first. Answer succinctly. Look at how many others I have to question before I can leave for my next assignment. Oh, I am so overburdened, but of course we are in a war, and the German *volk* are depending on us, on me. It is my humble calling."

"Captain!"

"Yes. Yes. Let's not waste time. So, farmer, tell me, what were you really doing when you were found in the woods?"

Duvid didn't respond.

"You speak German. Answer me."

"I don't understand what you want."

"You don't understand. Perhaps you ethnic Germans have lived in Poland too long. You don't speak German well enough? Don't you speak a dialect of the language too?"

"Dialect?"

"Yes, farmer. A dialect of German. Yiddish."

"You're mistaken. Do I look Jewish to you?"

"I don't make mistakes. Looks can be deceiving, as you certainly know by now." He gestured to one of his soldiers. "His pants. Down."

The soldier next to Duvid grabbed for the hem of his pants and ripped them down roughly. Duvid stood brittle-still as the captain walked over to him and inspected his genitals.

"Ah, it seems something is missing down here. Or is it me who is missing something here? So you really are a Jew, no?"

"No, mein Herr, I had to have an operation when I was young because of a medical condition."

"Ah, yes, a medical condition, a medical condition. There are so many with such a condition. It makes one wonder at the workings of the world."

The officer pointed at the paper on his lap. "So, we found this document in your clothing. At first, I thought it was Hebrew, but no, I thought, these Poles are very sneaky. They are trying to confuse us by coding their messages in the Hebrew alphabet. But no, I'm joking. I had one of your helpful co-religionists translate it for me before he was shot. A love poem, it seems. What do you say to this, German farmer or Jew? We found a young woman friend of yours. Ah, love. Shall we kill her too?"

Duvid winced.

"Don't be afraid to show your emotion, Jew. Love is a very beautiful thing. I see so little of it lately. It is good to be able to care, but it is one of the weaker traits, and I myself cannot indulge in weakness if we are to win. But yours is a people rooted in love and morality, is it not? This is why you always lose."

Duvid said nothing.

"Enough of this! How many others were there in your group? Where was your headquarters? Where do you send your operational reports? Your supplies? Who passes you your orders? What do you know about our plans?"

"I have no group, sir."

"Come, come. Be rational. All the others are likely dead by now. Your silence protects no one. Perhaps you need an incentive. You two, take six of these village men outside and shoot them. Immediately."

There was brief scurry and commotion as the guards sprung up and forced the first six roughly down the stairs. One yelled out "I am not a Jew. Jesus, save me!" but the captain merely waved his hand, gesturing the group away.

"None of them are Jews. Ah, but they are not Aryans, either."

The captain rose and walked to the window, pulled aside the lace curtain. Moments later, the crack of rifle shots boomed just below. He tapped on the glass.

"Good, good. So, will these others be next?" He waved at the men still standing along the wall.

"Hmm. I see you feel no affinity with them." Other men were now stumbling up the stairs to augment the few remaining.

"Guards, take these to the truck downstairs. Come to the window, you." One of the soldiers tapped Duvid's back with the butt of his rifle. Duvid stumbled forward to the window.

"A little test for you. You see those three by the tree?"

There was no audible response from Duvid.

"They are from your group. Perhaps you recognize them, even though they are far away in the dark. They are about to die, unless you tell me what I need to hear. I am not a patient man. You must reply quickly. Are there others? Answer now!"

"No, no one else." Did he just see Miriam, in the darkness, under a tree, with another woman and a man, perhaps 30 metres away?

"No one else, no one else." Ropes quickly appeared, nooses slipped over necks, their bodies were rising, legs dangling, kicking wildly, then still.

Duvid fell against the window frame. He stuffed his hands over his mouth, struggling to stop any sounds from escaping.

"Ah, sadly too late. I don't believe you, anyway. How reassuring that you care, though. You have fed my romantic German soul with your ardour. Here, corporal, give this horrid piece of paper back to him. It will make him cry some more, no doubt. I feel contaminated just holding it. He looks strong and may be useful still. Bring this Jew downstairs and those other two men, too. Put German coats on them. They will shield us from the bullets of their brothers who are still out there, watching us."

Once outside, Duvid was kept standing for a few moments, waiting. The air smelled of the exhaust of diesel fuel. Trucks rumbled in the dark, their headlights out. Soldiers forced him and the other men back, as a group of perhaps thirty women, all young, were pushed or hauled up into an empty vehicle. Duvid scanned the faces of the young women, searching for Miriam—could she really have just been killed before his eyes? —but these girls were too huddled together, hidden one behind the other in a mass, milling about in the darkness too quickly. He couldn't see.

One of the young women cried out. One of the men behind Duvid raised his arms and called back. Where were they being taken? Duvid felt confused and disoriented. Too much had happened in too short a time. Duvid didn't have time to think, run, fight. When everyone had been loaded in, he was forced to mount the back of a truck that had just pulled up, and the German army coat was pulled off. The other captive men in the back of the truck pummelled him, shouting "dirty Jew" in his face. They spit at him. "Because of you. All because of you!"

At the end of the night-long drive, Duvid was rushed through a gate and judged strong enough to left alive. Head shaved. Forearm tattooed. Clothes removed. A cold shower. Striped clothing.

Days and weeks went by, on and on. Arbitrary orders were yelled, altered daily, retracted one minute, enforced the next. He was starved, beaten more, abused. He didn't care.

Duvid was at first assigned to work in the death factory. There he hefted the bodies of the dead from the gas chambers onto handcarts, and on into the ovens.

45 Work Sets One Free

The smell was overpowering: the odours of unwashed bodies, of shit and garbage, of the putrid corpses that had been too plentiful to burn right away, thrown rotting into giant pits nearby, of the stink from burning flesh–they all added and overlapped until Duvid could not distinguish one from another. He lost his sense of smell entirely.

He was alive. This gave him an advantage over those around. He had the power of life and death. He lived. Others died. Well, yes, mastery over death. That over life could come later. One miracle at a time. He could be patient. Waiting. Waiting. One more. Another. Heave. Hurl. Back again.

His influence on death slipped further from his control–he no longer shifted corpses. His hidden abilities were realized. His talents were being wasted. He was a tailor. An adept. Useful. Good, he could sew and repair uniforms. Needle. Thread. Scissors. It was simple. He needed only to follow the pattern. Cut here, along the chalked line. Slide the scissors through the fabric. Such a delight. It filled him with glee, this small bit of beauty. Think only of the stitches, one by one. Concentrate, concentrate. Slip the end of the thread into his mouth, wet it, pull it out and twist it between his teeth, slip it between his fingers, which hardly felt its power. Life. He was creating life. Part of life, these uniforms. Also death. The soldiers who wore them would be dead: within days, within weeks. Within months. He pulled the needle through the cloth, locked the stitch to anchor it, back in, out, in. Such a delight, this flow, this graceful movement.

His father working, huddled over a dress, a jacket, a shirt, in bad light, slowly going blind in the partial darkness.

"Look how this is done, Duvid. Hold the needle like this. Cut like the cloth is water. I will teach you a trade. Something useful to know."

"It won't save my life."

"Don't talk back to your father."

The needles broke. Catastrophe. Find another, thread it, start over where he had stopped. It was all he could see. The needle, the thread. The magic as pieces of cloth joined to become the shell of a man. Almost alive. A shell, but, in a way, alive. Almost alive. He had done this, was doing it. Creating. The power of life and death.

And there was the pay: the small scraps of cloth left over, that others would have wasted, but Duvid hoarded, stuffed into his pants, into his sleeves. Warmth.

Scissors dulled, then snapped. No weapons! The guards ordered him to find and collect them. No more gangrened hands for the bosses. This crawling on the floor was his work, not theirs. They were afraid to cut their own delicate fingers scrabbling in the dirt of the floor for broken needles, broken scissors. For them, no blackened, dying fingers.

Duvid had the power of life and death. He was fast, stealthy. The broken scissor tips fell to the ground, were slid and kicked and nudged into cracks and corners. The guards would see them, reflecting back the light from their flashlights. Would see most of them. The guards would miscount, lose track, forget. Duvid recovered one tip. It was enough. Wrapped in a scrap. Slipped into a seam in his pants. Hidden in a cranny between the boards of his bunk. Power over death.

His mind dulled, then focussed. The day was over. Time for his crust of bread, his bowl of tasteless soup. Not like his mother's fat chicken soup, with its golden yellow colour. His mother calling him to the table. Friday evening. The *challah*. Candles flickered. The world stopped for a day. Peace. Miriam.

"You, don't stop! Slacker!"

He hardly felt the blow. He smiled up at his tormentor. The *kapo* received an extra piece of bread for doing this. So important. He must feel stronger than Duvid. But no matter.

Another blow, harder–this time he heard it against the body of another tailor, Chaim. Then it was the turn of Herschel, the third tailor. Duvid's vision narrowed as he thought about this. He knew something the boss didn't: the boss was of no consequence. Soon this boss would be gone, replaced. Dead.

"Shit has power," Duvid muttered to Chaim. A suggestion? A philosophy?

"Aah."

The power of life and death.

Chaim, pick up a broken needle. Duvid said nothing. Think. Only think. Duvid saw him, said nothing. Herschel too said nothing. Chaim didn't ask Duvid for advice or help. He knew how this was done. The fragment was short enough to hold in cloth, long enough to break through skin. Morning. Chaim dipped it in the latrine. He concealed it in the black of the zebra stripes of his shirt. Its sharp end pointed upwards. Where the hand of the boss always fell. The next day, more blows, first Duvid, then Herschel, then Chaim was struck, until:

"What is this; a needle? You put it there? It's under my skin. Shit!" The boss was telling a joke on himself. Duvid smiled, turned away. Herschel smiled also, away. Chaim laughed. The boss pointed at Chaim, who rose when the guard came forward and roughly took hold of his arm.

"Goodbye," Chaim said. A formal bow. He winked at Duvid.

"Shit has power," he whispered. He disappeared that day.

A week passed. The boss showed the signs. Sweat on his brow, in winter's cold. His hand turning purple. Black. He stopped coming to the workshop.

"First useless, then gone."

"Where gone?" asked Herschel.

"Smoke."

The next boss was worse. Duvid didn't care. Death was waiting for him too. Death was speaking to Duvid. A buzz in his ear. A low hiss. Then a whistle. Death's message, encoded in sounds. Duvid had lost certain octaves of his hearing. Buzzes, drones, whistles, all messages in code.

I dare You to approach, Duvid said to Death. I have power over You.

He could taste nothing. The gruel he was fed tasted of nothing anyway. The loss of this sense mattered little. The world became a grey place, dull and flat, its sharp edges the black and white of his costume, the splinters of the rough boards of his bunk, the needles he poked through damaged cloth, the sharp spikes of barbed wire.

"You gave him the idea," whispered Herschel from the next bunk after the lights went out.

"I have no ideas. I have nothing to give."

"You're a smart guy. Too much smart."

The declaration over the entrance of the camp read WORK SETS ONE FREE, but standing behind the wrought iron, he saw in reverse the ironic German saying, the backwards letters. The reverse of free? Enslaved. Enclosed. Confined. Constrained. The Jews of the camp. What was the reverse of work? Ease. Idleness. Sloth. Like these guards. They were all in a sick joke together: Jews and guards, reverse free, reverse work. Together in a phrase, laughing at them all, all toys in a game. All enmeshed in this broken place. Duvid chuckled.

"You, why are you laughing? Prisoners don't laugh." One of the guards. The Ukrainian with the club. A blow to his arm.

"I do not laugh."

"I'll give you something to laugh about," the guard recited the numbers tattooed on his forearm: "1-2-3-4-5-6." An impossible number.

"*Gematria*."

"What are you saying, Jew?"

"I say nothing."

"Be careful." Another blow. His back. Hard.

"I could kill you."

"Thank you, *mein Herr*."

"Goddam Jew."

The guards wanted his services. They asked for him, his hands, his fine fingers. Protection came. Bread too. He hoarded cloth, thread, broken needles. Broken tools. Whatever he could conceal. The new boss of the tailors didn't want him any more. Too much smart. No more tailoring except for private commissions, using his small hoard or whatever supplies the guards would bring him. A frail tailor replaced him in the shop. Easier to frighten, easier to dispose of. Duvid was returned to heaving bodies again. The smells became worse, then disappeared again.

The blade tip from a broken pair of scissors. Hidden in a crack in his bunk. Black night. Duvid touched it, felt it, its hard edge. Pressed it back into the wood crack. A weapon? No. A tool? Perhaps. A trade? Also perhaps.

Duvid mocked Death. Duvid beseeched Death. He asked Him: "Do you have Miriam?"

Even if Death didn't speak, he must get bored with this place. This job, it was all too easy for Him. No skills needed of Death, no deep thought required. It took no talent to collect the souls of the dead here. So many. All the same. It had no art, no joy. So mechanical. An industry. A disassembly line, Jews taken apart piece by piece. In the end, burn the shell that remains. Henry Ford's vision reversed, backwards and yet forwards. The anti-semite in a mirror. Everything here was reversed. It was all so funny and Duvid couldn't laugh, he wasn't permitted to laugh, or even smile. But Death could smile, could laugh. Only Duvid heard Him, and spoke back.

Speak to me, Mr. Death, Duvid muttered, or are you too busy? Overworked, perhaps? No reply. Duvid thought: he should write to Death. When Death came to take him, Duvid would read Him the words, remind Him of his crimes. He would have to respond. In this place where death had become banal, expected, inevitable, Duvid must differentiate himself from all the others dying. He must not be ignored. A written record could endure. Past Death. A joke on Death. Death would like that. He could appreciate a good joke. Death could find entertainment in this.

Duvid must be secretive. It must all be hidden. Only Death should know where to find the draft. He would seek it out, float over the camp and smell for the humour, the words that would set him convulsing, his belly fluttering. Death had not lost his sense of smell. Not like Duvid had.

In darkness, with searchlights passing the only illumination, Duvid prepared to write his text. Next to him, the exhausted slept a dark sleep. If they heard or saw anything, it didn't matter. They lived only to die. Not like Duvid, who had power over Death. By mocking him, beguiling Him.

As pigment, Duvid used charcoaled bits of bone he found at his work—what else could they be good for? Dried blood scraped from clothing would help, give the words dimension, power. Wet the mixture with spit, so the ink flowed but held together. All this went into the dark organic mess. Duvid flattened the rolled cloth, pressed the bone into the mix and slid it over the cloth. It spread and was absorbed quickly, a blotch. Failure. He rubbed the bone against the wood, scraped its edge against the blade. He mixed more charcoal in, more blood. There was plenty of those. He tried again. It worked. A line, then a letter. More letters. A word.

Herschel could see in the dark too.

"Ah, a man of learning, a scribe. We have so few of those now. Are you recording your prayers? What are you writing there?" Herschel asked him this one day, as he stitched the torn pocket in a guard's coat. Extra work. A piece of bread more. Or one beating less. The arithmetic was the same: an extra day of life. Or just minutes.

"Stop watching me. Do you want my bread? Is that it? You want to kill me?"

"Truthfully, I am not your enemy. Not a friend either, but I see what I see. Should I spy on you silently, and then report you? See, I let you know that I see. I will not report you. That is my proof."

"Recording prayers? No. I have no prayers. God is not in this place. That is what I know. These marks are a record of what happens here."

"For whom? No one will find it. Dangerous and useless. A waste of energy better devoted to remaining alive."

"Yes, you are right."

"You can never take what you write out of the camp."

"I don't intend to. But if I wanted to?"

"You cannot. It is so."

"You mean, it is written? As in the Torah, which we all were taught to revere? What you cite is just scratches on paper and wishful thinking. That reverence is what has brought us here. Only what I write, with my own hand, will be written. Only Death can read it. And no one knows the future. It cannot be discerned."

"Nonetheless, it is so."

"We will see."

"No, you will see. I will die here."

"How can you be so sure, Herschel."

"This is a death camp. Everyone is here to die. For me, it is so. You, however, are lucky, my friend. You are smart. You will find a way. You will live."

Duvid tried to remember how to smile. "And why me, Herschel? Am I such a good man?"

"What is written in Torah is not about good. If you have ever read it, you know it to be so. It is written because it is written, ineffable. This there is nothing to argue about. God's will."

Duvid stared at the other man. Death. God. No difference. He was surely mad, this Herschel. They were both mad. A secret bit of relief: Herschel's prediction was exactly his own. Death was too amused by him. He would not take away the source of so much mirth, while there was so little else to entertain Him.

And God? Duvid was almost desperate enough for faith. Duvid fought the notion, his father's notion–belief. But he had been given permission to breathe. He perhaps had found a friend, almost a friend, as much as that was possible here, in this landscape of insanity. At his edges, where the sharpness had cut into him, he felt lucidity slipping back in, like pins and needles in his fingers and toes.

The war dragged on outside the world of the death camps, far away, in another world, but coming closer. Bomber flights coming alternately from east and west became more frequent. Duvid counted them, a different *gematria*, numbers of airplanes, numbers of flights, then the searchlights, the tracers fired in the night. The arithmetic was evolving, acquiring a new meaning, augmenting. Between sleep and morning, Duvid heard the far sounds of heavy combat come closer, louder. The night skies became brighter, reflecting the glow of distant battle, as armies closed in from the east. It was apparent that the war was being lost by the Germans–Duvid could feel it in the speech of the guards, a new edge to their grunts and barks and growls, the thunder in their orders. The action in the camp became more desperate, grinding, and harsh. The ruthless pace of killing and cremation picked up. More numbers. Less meaning. No trace should remain.

More work for Duvid.

Duvid lay at the edge of his bunk, shivering, crammed next to the sleeping bodies of two other inmates, sucking in their warmth. A form passed him in the dark, caught the faint glow from the searchlights scudding across the grounds outside. Herschel? A hand floated through the darkness, touched his own, held it tightly. Was it Death mocking him?

"It is my time," the shadow said.

Death was saying goodbye. Duvid was drained by fatigue, by hunger, by pain. His eyes closed. He felt nothing any more. Smell–gone. Taste–erased. Vision–narrowed. Hearing–flat, obtunded. The sense of touch was at last also slipping away. He was numb through and through.

Herschel walked away, out of the hut and towards the fence. He blinked wearily. The blaze of the searchlights cast moving ovals of bright light across the depleted ground. Herschel grasped the electrified barbed wire fence firmly in his blackened fist. He remained standing, convulsing. Others were watching. Another prisoner leapt forward, held Herschel, convulsed. Another. The mass grew, ten, twenty, all throwing themselves forward, clutching, skin burning, uniforms of stripes erupting in flames. A guard tried to drag one away from the wire, trying to stop the ghastly parade. Then he too fell, shaking. Other guards on patrol crowded around, afraid to touch any of them. The writhing horde was burning. A revolution of zombies. The superstitious guards were terrified. They argued: what to do? Shoot them? Would they stop? Possessed by fear, they called their superior officer.

"So, what have we here? Ah, yes, you Jews, so talented, so helpful. We must really hurry with our cleansing work. You, you guards, are you all too stupid to act without me issuing orders? Turn off the power. Wake those Jews who work at the ovens to take these scraps away."

The bodies smouldered now in the darkness. The searchlights shone on the fence, on the blackened, twisted cinders.

Out of black dream, Duvid was kicked awake for his work detail. He remembered he had been dreaming, something he hadn't done for all the time he was here in the camp. He had dreamed of Miriam, sitting on a tree branch high above his head, smiling. He saw then that Herschel was no longer nearby. Had he gone first?

As he stumbled about fitfully at the fence, separating the burnt bodies, he saw Herschel's remains between the wires, his face distorted, but still discernible, little trace left of the body. He dragged him onto the carts.

At the furnaces, Duvid lifted the dry flesh, so light, like air. He laid Herschel gently on the iron slab, then loaded in others, not to waste fuel, and shut the door. The fire did its job. The lightness became light, the flesh joined the air, then the sky.

Duvid surprised himself. He whispered the prayer for the dead, first softly, then silently. It was the only time he had recited it in all his time in the camp. And so Herschel could escape.

Someone else was already in Herschel's spot in the wooden bunk when Duvid returned in the evening.

For days that followed, Duvid stood for roll call, worked, defecated, pissed red blood, ate his bits of gruel.

46 Miriam's Journal

I manage to evade capture. I hide in the woods. I don't know where I am, which direction is which. The movement of the sun through the sky confuses me. Does it rise in the south? The north? The west, perhaps? I cannot remember. I do not know what day it is, what month. What does it matter? The war still continues. I hear it far away, the crashing, the thundering, I smell the smoke drifting through. The winds carry the smells of burnt explosives, of death. Airplanes crowd the sky by day. By night, searchlights dance to the continuous rumble of the aircraft engines, a music in monotone.

I wander with no purpose. The snows are melting. Spring is weaving its flowered coverlet over the forest clearings, the birds burst into joyous song in the early morning. I sense that I am free.

I am hungry. The mushrooms are beginning to grow near the corpses of broken trees. Young shoots of ferns poke up through the soil, their coiled fronds still but a promise of growth to come. Remembering Duvid's teaching, I eat them hungrily. I blunder about, my mind dark and foggy. Perhaps it is the mushrooms. Perhaps it is the years of hunger and toil eating me from within.

I realize today that I am pregnant. I feel it in the swelling of my legs, the nausea when I wake. I am becoming lucid. Hunger becomes stronger. Even after I have eaten it gnaws at me.

Within me grows Duvid's child. I must take care of myself, for its sake. I am filled with wonder at the possibility of such a miracle, life replacing death. Can such a thing still be possible?

47 Hope

Duvid's modest scraps of cloth recorded what he heard, saw, felt. He buried the texts in a corner of his bunk, deep in a wide crack in the wood, and sewed others inside his uniform. He pulled out the broken blade from where it was lodged. He slowly scraped and scratched his name into the wood of the bunk by the faint light of the searchlights, interrupted by the movement of his bedmates. This went on for a week, one letter at a time, until there was a sudden inspection during the night. His name incomplete, he quickly wrapped the blade in his scraps of cloth and shoved it back into its place between the boards. When the guards passed his bunk, one noted the letters and dragged one of his crying bunkmates away.

Duvid said and did nothing. Really, the other man was dead before he had even arrived. The date and time were abstract, arbitrary, but the endpoint–that was unquestionable.

"You, Jew, get rid of those letters scratched in the wood!"

This guard had just arrived, called by the others. He handed Duvid a rounded rasp. Duvid filed away at his name, by touch, in the dark. His surviving bunkmate slept. The guard returned an hour later and took the file back. Only a random few letters of Duvid's name were scraped away by then, but the guard seemed satisfied enough. Duvid survived, Death his accomplice.

Winter imposed itself. Every day colder. The men who slept in his pallet huddled together, drawing warmth from each other. The man in the middle snored terribly. Duvid had dug him in the ribs several times during the night to stop the noise. One night the noise stopped, Duvid awakened by its absence. He touched the man's chest. The heartbeat had stopped. Duvid huddled closer, anxious to capture the last bits of warmth from the corpse so that he could sleep until the dawn. In the morning, the man's stiff body was dragged away. A new warm body would share the bunk that night.

Not all had lost faith, or hope. One group of young women, being transported by truck to the gas chambers, sang the *Hatikvah*, the Hebrew song of hope. Duvid shook his head in disbelief, but was moved nonetheless. His dreams of Palestine, almost forgotten in this place, surged to the surface. He pushed them back down, deeper. Thoughts of Miriam and her long-crushed hopes hovered too. He pushed these away also. He would not let himself feel anything anymore. Later, he dragged the women's naked bodies from the death chamber and to the ovens.

Prayers and songs continued to go skyward around Duvid over the next few months, from a multitude of mouths, without effect. Duvid watched his hands shake and felt his fingers lose sensation. He could no longer sew. One day, the sub-commander, on a walk through his realm, accompanied by two guards and his quartermaster, came upon Duvid as he was dragging a corpse onto a barrow. He had one of the guards hold Duvid's arm by the fraying cuff of his shirt. He read off the succession of numbers tattooed on Duvid's forearm.

The sub-commander looked closer at Duvid. "Ah, yes. I remember you. I gave you this number. The 'farmer.' So, are you still such a romantic?" The sub-commandant pulled out his pistol and pointed it at Duvid. "Perhaps I should have shot you then. The time for romance is gone."

Duvid prepared himself for his own degraded death. He had survived so many iterations of this moment–teetering on the brink, about to fall. Death had become his acquaintance, a companion, a personality. He had seen so many deaths; his own no longer frightened him.

"Yes."

A blow to the back signalled Duvid that he should not speak. The sub-commandant lifted his hand and the soldier stood back. The sub-commandant returned his attention to Duvid. "So, you, a farmer but a tailor too, I hear. Such a diverse career you have. Yes, he looks strong enough. Take him."

"Yes, sir."

Another blow, and Duvid, his back filled with hot pain, fell to the ground. The sub-commandant lifted his hand again.

"Stop. I need him alive, for the moment."

"Yes, sir. *Heil!*" The guard gave the salute.

"Yes, yes, *heil.*"

He addressed his guards.

"You men, listen to me. I will take care of you. You are hungry now, I know. All the good food goes to the front. What a waste–they are all dying out there. No matter, soon it will be over. We run west. The Americans are a sentimental people. They will provide for us, good German refugees fleeing the Communists. We'll be Jewish, if we must, even if it turns my stomach to think of this. It'll be like taking a bath in shit, but better than drowning in pure water, no? Ah, well. War is war, and peace is something else entirely. We will have to make compromises, become kosher, one could say."

"Commandant, what should we do with this one?"

"Take him with the other strong ones. All these men to the repository now. They must clear out everything, all papers and documents. They will transport it all into the ovens and burn it. You will guard them and make sure that nothing gets lost before it is destroyed. We cannot afford to make mistakes."

"Yes, commandant." The quartermaster turned and looked at Duvid and several other scrawny Jews, skulking against a hill of bodies. Even though he had become accustomed by now, at such close range the smell was overpowering. He put his hand to his mouth, ready to throw up.

"What is it, man? Queasy?"

"Nothing, commandant!"

"So go ahead. Follow your orders."

"Yes, commandant!"

The sun was setting as Duvid and his fellows were being quickly escorted at a run to the records office. The clouds to the east seemed to be on fire from the explosions of artillery shells, and as darkness fell around them, the rumble of distant gunfire filled the night. In the direction of the main gate, he could faintly see camp officers running or walking out. The gate was held open for them, then rapidly shut. The rumble of a motorcycle came up behind him, and Duvid had a momentary glance at the sub-commander, seated in the sidecar of his motorcycle, being driven quickly past him. Again the gate opened, quickly shut tight.

Duvid and the other captives were forced up the stairs at a run, gun butts hammering them from behind if they hesitated in any way. At the top of the rough wooden steps, they were rushed down a hallway and through the door of a large room. Duvid was awed by the width of file cabinets and file boxes piled up along one long wall, almost ceiling-high.

"Schnell! Mach schnell!"

One of the other men, tall, very thin, his hands long and bony, clawed at the boxes, grabbed one from the top, rushed it down the stairs and heaved it onto a handcart. It landed heavily and unevenly.

"Imbecile, make it neat! Be efficient with this space!"

The man slid the box into one corner of the handcart's surface just as Duvid arrived at a run with the next. Duvid slid his neatly next to the first, and turned back upstairs as a third prisoner rushed past him with his own burden. This went on for an hour, until four carts were piled high with boxes to three levels. Two prisoners heaved and pushed to force each cart towards the furnaces. There the process went in reverse, each box unloaded and carried to the furnace doors, the contents of the box thrown into the ovens. The doors slammed shut and the burning began. By this time, Duvid's group was already on their way back for more papers.

On the fifth trip, the tall thin fellow slipped on his way down the steps and the box he was carrying fell and broke open in a strew of documents that ended up lying across steps and piled in a heap at the bottom. A blow to the head and he was quickly at the bottom of the steps himself.

"Pick it all up. Quickly! Quickly!"

Duvid, running back from depositing his latest burden on the hand cart, stopped. He couldn't climb back because of the mass of paper now obstructing the stairs.

"Help him, and be quick about it. Now! Now!"

Duvid and the others were near-exhausted by this time. Leaning down, Duvid saw that the papers he was picking up carried photos. The sub-commandant's stern face was staring at him from one. He piled the armful of paper back into the box. Turning his head, Duvid saw that the guard was concentrated on urging another of the prisoners to manhandle yet another box down the stairs past these fallen papers. Duvid quickly slipped the photo document into his shirt and up one sleeve in one quick and fluid practiced movement, where it became snagged among other bits of sewn rags already there. Duvid returned immediately to his frenzied reloading of the emptied box.

By early morning, with the sun painting the eastern sky a light rose, the task was close to being done. It would be impossible to finish, though. In the short time that remained before the Russians arrived at the camp perimeter, the guards set the storeroom on fire to destroy what was left. The prisoner who had fallen had broken a leg and was howling in pain, chunks of flaming wood and paper falling around him, while the other seven were herded back to their usual duties at the furnaces.

Duvid was still useful. There were still bodies to be cremated and evidence to destroy. Duvid was returned to his hut for a snatch of sleep. There he pushed the papers he had found into his shoe. In those last moments, Duvid pushed as many of his testamentary scraps as he could inside his uniform. Too soon, he was awake again, his eyelids glued together from exhaustion. He was quickly back to the furnaces.

Duvid and the remaining prisoners were herded at gunpoint to the gates, where the wrought iron exhortation to work themselves to freedom might be about to come true.

"Raus! Raus! Alle juden raus!"

The march away from the camp began. Prisoners next to Duvid died walking, struck down by the elements, not bullets. Winter was thick around. Snow flew from the sky. Duvid felt his fingers frosting, his toes stiffen. The wind was as merciless as the guards. It blew through him, through his flimsy outfit, but he was a little warmer than the others. He hugged his secret rags, those slid into his shirt and trousers, bearing his testimonies, close to him, not for the words held there, not anymore, but for the heat they preserved.

The march went on for four days. Some around Duvid walked barefoot, their feet red and torn open, before they dropped. He was parched, throat raw and dry, harsh from dehydration. There was no food, no water, except the bits of snow guzzled at night, slaking thirst but lowering body temperature. During those nights, prisoners huddled together in the open to preserve the little warmth they still held within them. Every morning, Duvid saw a few more, those who had been on the outside of the mass of bodies, frozen during the night. To each side of him, stragglers who had mined their last bits of energy were left along the way to die. A few were shot, but many were not and were simply left to die. Bullets had taken on a greater currency for the guards. They would need these later for their own defence. Duvid didn't dare look back when he heard the crack of a rifle. He kept walking and walking.

Finally abandoned in a farmer's field as their wardens fled, Duvid and a few others, the last surviving remnant of prisoners on the march, were left standing, uncomprehending. He had no feeling of being a free man. He thought only of his last filthy bowl of gruel, anything to fill the hollow in his belly. His hopelessness hovered beyond relief. Even his friend Death had abandoned him and drifted away in the night.

When the Russians arrived, they found Duvid's small group huddled in a barn, covered with straw for warmth. Despite the horrors that they themselves had seen and endured through the years of battle and deprivation, the Soviet soldiers were shocked. They offered food, water, blankets. It wasn't enough. Among these few of Duvid's fellow survivors of the death camp, several died over the next few days while he looked on, helpless. They were too depleted to be able to digest anything. Their tissues collapsed within them. Duvid was too nauseous to look at food. He refused it, taking only water. His friend Death had returned, but would still not touch him.

Duvid was still alive, but in the agony of the trek, threads had broken and treasured bits of cloth slipped out through the tears in his striped outfit. Most had fallen along the route the inmates had been forced to take, had been covered in mud and drifting snow, but he managed to catch a few as they slipped out of his shirt sleeves, including the one with the image of the sub-commander. He gripped these tightly when the striped uniform itself was taken away and burnt to kill any lice or other vermin it might contain. Typhus was a dreaded enemy, rampant among the released prisoners.

48 Miriam's Journal

I am discovered by a garrison of Russian soldiers. My hopes are high now, never higher. The war is certainly over. Spring has brought me renewed hope. I will be able to travel to Jerusalem now, as I intended years before.

I am questioned. While I am held, two Russian officers try to rape me after they become drunk from a store of confiscated liquor. They tear at my clothes. I fight them both off, yelling that I am pregnant. One vomits to the side, wipes his mouth with his sleeve. He laughs, while the other leers and calls for his soldiers.

I am arrested. I am accused of not being a good Communist. I must be a subversive, an enemy of the Soviet State. There is a quick trial in a tent and I am sent to a work camp, then another, and another still, far away among mountains. The air is cool, fresh. There is forest in all directions. I am confused at what is happening to me. Where is the justice of the proletariat? I despair again. Is life worth going on?

It has been many months now that I am in captivity. I give birth to Duvid's child, helped by a Polish midwife and a Jewish Russian doctor, both also prisoners.

After the birth the doctor visits me in my hut. He tells me how his luck has run out. Josef Stalin had him arrested, one of thousands, but unlike me, he will be shot soon. There is a new enemy to concern Stalin. The bourgeois capitalists of the West are sure to attack him and his country. When they no longer have Hitler to contend with, they will wish to destroy the Great Revolution of the Soviet masses, and the great Leader who stands in the way of their return to dominating the world with their ravenous colonial ethos. Eternal vigilance is more necessary than ever if the new enemy is to be resisted and vanquished.

I listen, not fully understanding, as I suckle my son at my breast and feel a softness come over me. There must be no more fighting. I yearn for peace, finally, finally. For my son, at least. It is my only hope now. I know that I will never leave this camp. Not while I live.

Another Jew in the camp helps me to circumcise the boy on the eighth day from his birth. The man tells me that he has heard rumours that the war is over. We are at peace. I look around me.

Nothing is different. I name my son Eli, after my father. He looks like him, a little. I place my finger in the palm of his hand and his little fingers close on it. It feels like heaven's touch.

49 Home

He was home. Duvid looked around his horizon, the horizon of his town, its rolling hillocks and lofting trees, its wooden fences and farmer's fields, its aging cottages, whitewashed and tidy, with their tiny windows and doors set in heavy wood frames. The shingles on their sagging roofs lay akilter, a few missing here and there, filled in with patches of sheet metal. Nothing seemed really to have changed. The trees on either side of the road looked the same as they were before, as if the war had not intervened and he had never left this place with its ghosts and memories. The houses loomed low against the sky in the same way they had before. The crows called out with their raucous voices as always from the tops of the trees. A stork still made its huge nest of twigs at the top of a dead tree near the edge of town. The same dips in the packed dirt road were filled with water and mud, as they had always been, and Duvid walked around them as he had done before the war, as he could still do with his eyes closed. Even the sun scattered its rays of light from the same direction, at the same angle. There was only one difference: there were no Jews.

The war was over. After war and war and more war. Liberation had come and now it was months later and Duvid, although he knew very well the difference between war and peace, still hadn't been able to savour the fact. Within himself, he was still battling, still running, still hiding. For Duvid, as he walked slowly across the stone bridge into the small town of Bodsanow he had left six years earlier, this was the true partition line, here and now. The war was finally over for him.

It was over. Duvid's mind flooded with relief. His heart brimmed. And yet he was also filled with fear, fear that he would soon confirm that none of his family had returned, fear of what awaited him on the other side of that bridge.

The bridge, although its base had been shaken by the rumbling of heavily laden military vehicles, still stood solid. Duvid was encouraged by its endurance. He looked down into the turgid waters flowing below and months and years dissolved away with each step he took.

Duvid had only returned once, when he had failed in his attempt at rescue. So long ago.

He stared through the space where the synagogue had stood for one hundred and seventy years. The *mikveh*, the ritual bathhouse, had stood next to it, and just steps away, the Jewish parochial school. All these had vanished. Even their rubble had been carted away or smoothed over.

When he passed their homes, some of his former Polish neighbours came out, curious to see a ghost from the past, a dead man walking.

He asked one after the other, "Have you seen any of my family?" They told him they knew nothing about his family's fate. There was no trace of them.

Some of his former neighbours called to him as he walked by, "Why did you come back here? There is nothing here for you now."

The neighbours drifted out onto the street, first a few, soon a small crowd, following him at a short distance, chattering to each other. The rhythm of their words quickened as Duvid approached his old home.

The house he had lived in before the war still stood intact. As he came close, he could see the unweathered rectangle on the doorframe shaded paler than the rest of the wood–his family's mezuzah had been there and taken down. He reached up to feel the spot he had been so used to touching before the war, a phantom object, but palpably still there in his mind.

One of the new occupants recognized him at the door. He rushed forward out of the door and waved an index finger forward into the air, almost touching Duvid's face. The crowd behind him formed a thicker semicircle and pulled closer. Their talk became louder and shriller.

"So look who's come back, one of our Jews. I remember you. You used to steal our apples. Get away or I'll make you go. You own nothing here now."

"I'm not here for property, just to find my family." Duvid's voice was shaking. He stepped back.

"Well, you will be disappointed. There is not a single one left here, but that's not all you're looking for. You're a Jew, so I know you're also looking for your father's buried gold. So, you're not so rich anymore and you won't be again. Run from here or we'll make you leave." The man now formed a fist with his other hand.

"I know nothing about any gold."

The crowd behind him muttered among themselves.

"Take yourself away from this door. My door. Do it quickly." Duvid knew that arguing with them would have been stupid, could even be lethal. He heard a female voice directed at him from inside the house.

"*Paskudniak zhyd!*" she shouted.

He turned and quickly walked away. A stone flew through the air past his head, another, two more. He quickened his steps. The crowd sped up their pace and escorted him all the way back to the bridge. There they stopped and dissipated, as he ran across it and on along the road.

Nightfall came. He had waited in the woods on the other side of the bridge. Now he sneaked back into the field behind the house. Here Duvid could smell the musty odour of the rot from a few over-wintered beets and cabbages, unharvested and gone to seed. The moist earth smelled of yearning to be planted again. Without reaching down, Duvid felt in his mind the remembered richness of the soil, its crumbling, dense texture between his fingers.

A dog, tied behind the house, smelled Duvid, and began to yelp and howl, but by the time the Polish family rose and ran out to investigate, he had already dug up the small bag of coins his father had buried years earlier next to the apple tree. He had thought to visit the priest who had once helped him, but now knew better. Too risky. He promised himself never to return to this place.

Duvid made his way to Lodz, partly on foot. He got a ride in one of the few trucks that passed him. It was manned by two men dressed in a conglomerate of army uniforms, Polish, Russian, even German. They both spoke Polish. The back of the truck was filled with an assortment of objects—furniture, clothing, tools—booty "liberated", the driver said, from local abandoned houses.

"And you, are you from around here?"

"Lodz."

"A Jew?"

"No. Do I look like a Jew?"

For the next hour, they drove on, mostly in silence, the only sound that of the noisy motor. Along the road, heavily dressed men and women were pushing and pulling carts and wagons piled high with belongings. Every twenty minutes, a Russian army vehicle drove past them at speed, quickly disappearing over the next hill. The two truckers bellowed the *Internationale* as they passed, smiling and saluting when the Russians glared at them.

"So, comrade, where are you going?" the driver asked.

"I'm on my way to check on my parents."

"In Lodz. A good son, I see. You've spent some time away. You were in the army, then?"

"Yes, I served in the West."

"The West? America? I have an uncle in Toledo, Ohio. You know it?"

"No, less west." Duvid chuckled.

"So less west. Not America, but richer than here in the East. Do you have anything to trade, then? We have food for you in exchange."

"Look at me. Do I look like I have anything?"

"You have a coat."

"My coat you can't have."

"So maybe we will leave you here on the road."

Duvid reached inside his coat and pointed his pistol at the driver. "Yes, leave me here on the road. Leave me alive."

The truck stopped. Duvid jumped out and ran and kept running until the truck disappeared around the next bend in the road. He did not intend to let himself be robbed. Or robbed and killed. He replaced his pistol in his coat pocket. Good bluff. He had found it in a pile of remains of the prison guards executed by the Russians shortly after his rescue. He smiled. He had no ammunition.

A few hours of walking and another hitch, this time on a hay wagon pulled behind a slow-moving tractor, which brought him close to Lodz. The rest he walked. Duvid made his way to the train station, where he found a few other travellers with a similar history, all Jews on the run. An agent of the Jewish Agency was handing out ration cards and train tickets. They were on their way to Munich, Germany. Duvid took a ticket, but wondered why Jews should be travelling towards Germany, of all places. It didn't smell right to him.

At a low brick building that the Agency had rented as a temporary shelter and as offices, Duvid got in a food line and slowly advanced to the front. After receiving his piece of bread, a boiled egg, a bowl of boiled turnip and carrots, and a glass of tea, he leaned against a wall and set his glass down on the windowsill. While he hungrily ate his ration, he noticed near him a young woman, on her own, staring at her food but not eating.

"If you don't eat that, someone will steal it from you."

The young woman, a girl really, looked at him and attempted a smile but didn't succeed. Her hand went up to cover her eyes.

"Okay, I'm sorry. It was a joke."

The girl nodded, then started to eat.

"That's better. You're like a scarecrow, so full of angles. You need a bit of fat on your bones, roundness, softness."

"That's no way to charm a girl, you should know."

"That's all the charm ration I'm allowed today. Maybe tomorrow, I'll have more."

"Maybe yes, tomorrow."

"Well, good, a smile."

The girl turned away, reddening.

"What's your name?"

"Hannah."

"A woman of valour. Mother of Samuel."

"Today I'm not so brave. Tomorrow I'll be better able to hide my embarrassment. Thank you for the food."

"I didn't give it to you."

"You made me eat it."

Having eaten as much as she could swallow, Hannah walked away quickly and disappeared into the crowd. Duvid returned to finishing his meal.

At the train station, small groupings of Jews ambled around, chattering, inquiring, arguing. Duvid passed from one group to another, hoping to see a familiar face. This one was hoping to go to Palestine, that one to America, where he remembered he had an uncle in Chicago. A large city, he said. Another had set his sights on Canada. Several would choose South America, or Australia, or South Africa "Anywhere else. This Europe is all a graveyard." one told Duvid. "I have lost everything here–my past, my family, my possessions. I wish only I could lose these terrible memories."

Duvid agreed with him, nodded blankly, stared into the distance, said nothing. There was little more to be said. Like Duvid, all were searching for lost relatives. There were so many gone missing. For him, as far as he knew, there was no trace left of anyone. Perhaps, if he continued onwards along the refugee road, he might find someone. Yes, perhaps.

On the trains and at the railroad station, officials of the Jewish Agency came to Duvid and the others around him, giving out rations, information, making announcements–where to go, who to speak to, what to do there. These trains, which had once carried many of them as victims, now would reverse roles and transport them to the new in-gatherings, the displaced persons camps scattered across Germany.

"Dispose of your documents," the Agency's men said, "you won't need them. You will be better off that way. Agreements have been signed between the allies. There will be no choice but to go back if they know where to send you. And you will go back to what? The bitter lives you had in those countries where so many of your families died? Stateless, the authorities won't be able to say you are a citizen of this or that country. We will issue you with a temporary laissez-passer to your final destination: our Palestine."

These visas were supposed to carry him past the borders. Duvid saw many tossing their old papers out the windows of the train, happy to be away from countries which had betrayed them. Duvid, suspicious, hung on to all his papers, all the papers he had been able to recuperate in the camp. To hell with the bureaucrats, he thought. He would take his chances and make his own way.

Duvid was directed to the DP camp in Pocking, a town a short distance away from Munich, and not far from the former concentration camp of Dachau. At the checkpoints, they were all asked to produce their documents. Everyone waved their refugee papers. No one searched Duvid's things for his papers. No one sent him back.

The train stopped at Munich, where the refugees debarked and waited for army buses to take them on to Pocking, which had been a German army barracks before the war ended. While waiting, Duvid and a few of the other men took a short walk into Munich. He needed to clear his head. Walking through Munich gave Duvid a strange satisfaction. It was for him such a bizarre irony to have come here, to this of all places on this small continent, this, the centre of the beginning of Nazism's rise. Anger moved him to feel that he could walk wherever he wanted to in this place. No Jew could have survived here just a short few months earlier. Now he could prance free among a German population humiliated by its occupation and the destruction of its ethnic dream, picking at whatever they could recover from demolished buildings, broken plans, crushed lives.

Their desperation surprised him. He had expected more from the larger than life image he had built up in his mind of this powerful enemy. Duvid saw the roads were broken by bomb craters and obscured by piles of broken bricks. A multitude of buildings lay shattered and crumbling. The smell of unburied bodies still hovered thickly in the air. Duvid knew that smell.

Thousands of homeless, numbed civilians wandered aimlessly along nameless avenues, begging for a crust of bread to eat. He was hungry too, but if he had had the bread, he wouldn't have shared it now, not with these people. Duvid felt vindicated to see all this. He hated them.

Now he finally felt truly free, even though this city filled him also with dread. Satisfied and yet mildly panicked, he made his way back to the train station and the buses, and on to Pocking.

Pocking was a troubled and turbulent place. All of humanity seemed to have crowded itself into the camp. Long lines of people stood waiting for their ration of bread and soup, grumbling.

"There are no children," one man muttered next to him. The others said nothing and just stared.

Duvid nonetheless felt invigorated by the midsummer air and the lilt of Jewish voices talking, crying, arguing, praying energetically, complaining. It was like being home again, back in the *shtetl* which no longer existed, except in memory. People were everywhere, a lucky few renewing bonds that had been severed by the war, others, the majority, questioning, pleading, and pestering in their search for relatives.

Crowds stood in front of large boards, fingers sliding down long lists, checking if maybe this one or that one had survived. Duvid knew he was only one of an enormous body of seekers, but it was clearer every day that he would never again see any of his family alive. He paused, his emotions dropping over an edge. As the augmented lists were posted every day, Duvid checked them repeatedly, for any name that sounded familiar, any name among his family, cousins, friends. For a trace of something that would tell him that he was not alone in the world. That a miracle had happened. That someone had been seen and reported. But he found nothing and no one. Not one from his town was on those lists. No brother. No sister. Not his parents. And also not Miriam. How could he expect to find Miriam's name on the lists? He had seen her die.

Duvid waited in one line after another for his ration of bread and soup, clothing, a bed, one-day jobs at manual labour inside or outside the camp, O.R.T. training courses. His small horde of coins was by now gone to bribes and food and attempts at getting information along the way from Bodsanow. Duvid's belly gnawed with hunger, but he tried to ignore it.

He went to meetings, not with enthusiasm, but to gather information, to meet up with others in similar circumstances, people who might know something that might be helpful. There were a lot of meetings to choose from. Every Jew seemed to have a different opinion and a different group. At least they served a little food.

One afternoon, he walked in on a meeting organized by the Jewish Agency, recruiting *olim* for the land of Zion. At the entrance, he was cajoled to go in.

"Do you really believe you can find some country to take you in, *bucher*? Do you want to return to Poland, then?" he was asked by the *madrich*, the Jewish Agency's man on the ground, there to encourage these Jews to immigrate to the new land.

"No." He truly had nowhere else to go. Duvid looked around for a table with food, but there was none. Duvid knew most of all that he was hungry. He hadn't had much to eat for days. That was the thing most on his mind. Politics was something that he would mull through later, once he was fed. He tried to turn and move on.

"Come to *ha'aretz*."

"What about the Arabs?" someone else asked.

The *madrich* smiled. "Arabs? There aren't so many, and they live in their own villages. There's plenty of room for both our peoples."

"What about the British embargo? They're impounding our ships and sending everyone they stop back or to camps in Cyprus. That's what I hear."

"The British will leave soon. They cannot stay forever. They just need a good reason to go and we're giving them one."

Duvid went in, stared ahead, uncertain. A talk began.

"*Chaverim*, the land of Israel has been a part of our lives and thoughts and that of our ancestors for almost four thousand years, since the patriarch Abraham first arrived there. We are the descendants of Abraham's son Isaac, and of his grandson Jacob, also known as Israel, named so because he had fought with God's angel during a long night of dream and revelation.

"Listen to me. It has been nearly two thousand years since our ancestors were driven away from Jerusalem and their Temple by the armies of Rome, which enslaved or dispersed us for trying to gain our freedom. During all that time since, we have kept alive our attachment to *ha'aretz*, our land. The last thousand years have been filled with disasters, and all of you are witnesses to what has just befallen our people.

"We need our own land. We must have our own land. We have the right to our own land. There we can live our lives as Jews, not dependent on the protection of another country's authorities. In our sovereign land, we will not see our women raped, our homes plundered, and our children killed indiscriminately. In that land we can take care of ourselves, *chaverim*! Of each other! We will make it a land of respite, a land of refuge and sanctuary, where any Jew from anywhere on earth is welcome."

Duvid turned his head to the voice of someone near him at the back of the room.

"The Arabs who live there won't treat us any differently than what we have seen here in Europe. They see us as colonialists from Europe. We arrive, we steal their land, we destroy their culture and religion. That's how they see us."

"*Chaver*, you're distorting the truth."

"They will never accept us. The Moslem armies conquered the Holy Land centuries ago. They repelled waves of Crusaders. Recently these Arabs even threw out the Ottoman Turks, with the help of those English, Lawrence, Allenby, perfidious Albion. They claim to own the same piece of ground as us, and they call it Palestine too. They want to expel us, not become our partners!"

He was loudly booed by the audience. Others standing around called out. "Where else can we go? Back to be despised, hunted, in Poland or Rumania or Hungary?"

"Or the Ukraine? Or Lithuania? Here, Germany? No."

"Or anywhere in Europe? Never!"

The *madrich* continued. "It is this attitude of fear and deference over the centuries that has brought us to this moment of tragedy. We must rise above our past and make of ourselves a new people, strong and heroic, unafraid. You will see, these Arabs will come to welcome us, once they see what we bring them. They will have equal rights, protected by law, better than they have now. We will show them the fruits of progress. We will improve their lives, educate them. They won't have to remain poor shepherds and growers of meagre crops of dates and olives on dry, hard earth, or remain wanderers living in tents, like their ancestors, and like ours, too. We have much in common, after all. They will see that. They too see themselves as tied to Abraham, through his other son, Ishmael. They too have a long history there.

"But it is our land. Our land! It was promised us, and we have lived there, many of us, for unbroken centuries. It will not retain that mistaken name, Palestine, once we are independent. Our enemies the Philistines lived there long ago, next to our people, fighting us, and now, they are gone and we are still alive and returning. It is from them that the name Palestine is derived, but it was the wicked Romans who changed the name from Judea after our rebellions, to detach the memory of the Jews from the land. They could not, however, detach the memory of the land from the Jews. No one can. Never!"

"So what will we call this new land of the Jews?" someone yelled out.

"We don't know yet. Israel, perhaps. Maybe Judea. Maybe Zion. Maybe even, yes, Palestine, if we have to. This can all be decided later. All that matters for now is that we have our own country."

The meeting ended in mild disarray, as small groups in the crowd broke off to have their own animated discussions here and there, and slowly dispersed.

Dark clouds from the past floated across Duvid's mind. His breathing quickened and he felt suddenly faint. He left the meeting room and walked briskly through the camp, trying to breathe deeply, slowly. Out of that darkness, he heard a familiar booming voice calling him.

"Squirrel! It is really you?" There before him stood the bulk of the Fisherman, the hair on his head wild and stringy, his clothes a little small for his large frame. Large arms wrapped themselves around him, and Duvid was suddenly laughing, convulsed by the telling of some cosmic joke that only he could hear. When his laughter stopped, Duvid stood dumb and confused. What was this gentile doing here among all these Jews?

With Yuri, the Fisherman, was a small knot of others. Duvid recognized one of them, Hannah, who he had recently met in Lodz. She stood back, silent. Duvid remembered her for that, her silence, which had stood her apart from all those chatterers around him. She had put on a little weight and looked better for it.

"So, Squirrel, do you recognize me?" Yuri continued, "You look like I just walked out of a grave. Well, that is exactly what happened."

"I thought you were a Pole," was all Duvid could answer. He suddenly felt giddy. 'Too much excitement,' he thought, 'it will pass.'

"I thought the same about you. It seems we both make good spies or stupid ones. Or bad Jews." His eyes were losing focus.

"You hid it well. As for being bad Jews, that is yet to be seen... Are you all right?"

Duvid felt faint now, as if the oxygen had been sucked away from the space around his head. Moaning, he dropped to his knees, and tipped forward onto his face at Yuri's feet. The Fisherman yelled out orders to others standing around. "Quick, quick, get him to the tent! To the tent."

Duvid awakened half-sitting on a cot. Hannah was spooning soup between his lips, a look of alarm on her face, as if he might die right there in front of her. Yuri propped him up, holding his lower jaw down so his mouth lolled open. He coughed once, and eagerly swallowed small and then larger spoonsful of soup. It was the best soup he had ever eaten. Just delicious.

"Who...? Where...?" was all he could manage between swallows.

"So, my friend, you're awake again. Welcome to the kingdom of the Jews. At least here we can stay alive from one day to the next. This nurse of yours is Hannah. She says very little but is very intelligent, so watch out, she may steal your heart. They say to be careful of the quiet ones."

At this, Hannah's cheeks turned a vivid pink and she turned her head towards Yuri, pleading silently for him to shush.

"So excuse me, my dear child. It's not meant as an insult."

Hannah's cheeks went from pink to beet red.

Duvid came back to life now. Speech returned. "So you're really a Jew, Yuri? You fooled me."

"Stalemate. You also fooled me."

"And how did you escape the Germans that night in the forest, Yuri?"

"I didn't. They rounded us up and made us dig a hole there between the trees. They lined us up, Marisch, Georgi, Andrzej, Arkadi, Kzenia, and me, and they shot us. We all fell in. Then they threw on us a little dirt."

"So how did you get away?"

"I was just very lucky, Squirrel. One of the first bullets must have flown astray in the darkness and glanced off one of the shovels. It hit me and I fell. Just a scratch. I pretended to be dead. The others fell on top of me. A few hours later, I dug my way out of the loose earth covering us. That's how it happened. So that would leave only you, Marya, Zoltan, and Irena. Did you see any of them?"

"All the others, yes. Hung from a tree as I was led away. You can know now that Marya's real name was Miriam."

"So she too was Jewish?"

"Yes, Yuri, and from my village."

"Ah, I see the love story forming in front of my eyes. I understand your despair now. A pity. Such a spirited woman. And what happened with you, Squirrel?"

"I was caught but they didn't kill me right away. I was what some might call lucky. I spent the next few months of the war in a death camp."

"I've heard more than I wanted to know about these places. You've been through more than anyone should."

Neither man seemed to notice that Hannah had walked away while they reminisced.

The next week, having regained some of his strength, Duvid ventured out of the camp with the Fisherman. They passed through the farming villages in the area, looking for something of value that they could trade for favours with the American soldiers who had their base close to the camp. They broke into a damaged farmhouse where the roof and the adjacent barn had collapsed. The two men skirted several bomb craters along the path leading down to it from the road. The men assumed it must have been the billet of some German troops just before the end of the war.

The place was deserted. As they entered, a dove fluttered up from the ground. Yuri grabbed for it but it flew off.

"Ah, I haven't eaten dove meat since before the war started. My parents used to own a dovecote in Warsaw. We kept some on the roof of our building. Well, you can guess the rest. The invasion came. Those Germans liked to dine well."

Duvid stepped lightly past the doorway and into the ruined cottage. In the kitchen lay a clothed skeleton, its face a desiccated mask. From its dress, he could see that it had been the farmwife. Duvid noted the fact that no one had come by to bury the body. Perhaps everyone whom she had known were also dead in the war. There was at least this bond between him and the remains that lay spread out in the rubble. Suddenly stricken by an amorphous grief, Duvid turned his head away. He was perplexed that he should mourn this woman, the enemy, someone he had never known. And yet, there it was, a perplexing empathy that Duvid had trouble resisting. Yuri broke the spell as he roughly pulled open the door of an armoire leaning against the wall. Accompanied by the crash of breaking glass, it came smashing down, engulfing the remains of the corpse. Dust billowed. Duvid gazed through the cloud at Yuri. His friend lifted his shoulders in apology.

The two settled back to inspecting the space around them. The table had been set for a meal, but the tableware had now all been scattered about. The round dining table was finely carved, with a delicate filigree of red and pale woods inlaid into a dark wood base. The legs were fluted and curved down smoothly to claw feet, now leaning outward. Its surface was splintered and indented by whatever had crashed through the hole in the roof just above it. Light flooded down through the remnants of the table and through a similar hole in the floor.

Duvid leaned forward to grab at a pair of silver candlesticks lying there, precariously close to the edge of the hole, their candles half-burnt down. He stared down into the hole and whistled. He stepped back lightly. On the wall behind him, a picture frame hung askew, its glass broken. It held the photo of a young man in German uniform, a dour look on his face, but also the hint of a smile. Duvid smiled back. On the sideboard beside his elbow, a mouse was nibbling on a brown rounded object almost as large as it. Duvid ignored the creature and reached forward. There was a jute bag leaning against the wall, holding some old but perhaps still edible potatoes next to the mouse. Duvid lifted the mouse's meal and smeared the chewed edge across the soldier's face.

The shelves of the crumbled armoire protruded into the room. Among the pile of shattered crockery and glassware lay an intact bottle of schnapps, almost full. Yuri gave out a single whoop and snatched it.

"Look at this, Squirrel. Now we will have a real meal. Potatoes and schnapps, like proper Germans." He chuckled at his own humour.

"I don't want to look any more. There is nothing else here, except for this dead woman. She makes my skin crawl. Let's go."

"I was going to take a drink right here. You are squeamish, Squirrel. From what you told me, I would not have thought that a dead body could disturb you anymore."

"Fisherman, every dead body disturbs me. Every one. I'll never be able to forget them. Besides, have you looked down through that opening in the floor?

"No. Why?"

"There's unexploded ordinance down there. It looks like a bomb dropped from the air."

"Yes, on reflection, maybe you're right. It could be wise to go now." With that, the Fisherman gave a loud whoop and flew out the door of the ruined house, waving the bottle in one hand. Duvid was directly behind him, dragging the sack of potatoes and lofting the candlesticks in the other.

"Be happy, Squirrel. We are alive. Let's get back to the camp and get very drunk. Then we can celebrate our survival as we should."

The first Sabbath celebrated since the start of the war was significant for Duvid. Hannah said the Sabbath prayers over the found candles and the group broke bread. It wasn't challah, but rather a fluffy pure white bread that the Americans had been providing. It was a wonder for them. They had never seen anything so light and seemingly indestructible.

One of the women commented in awe, "This bread remains fresh long after it becomes mouldy. And that itself takes forever." The Americans were a mystery to them, stubbornly naive and yet capable of miracles.

After the meal of boiled potatoes, Yuri and Duvid sat on the stoop outside and passed the bottle back and forth.

"It's too bad we couldn't catch that dove, Squirrel. What I would give for a taste of meat again."

"My mother was a good cook, Fisherman. On Friday nights like this, we had gefilte fish, chicken, sometimes even a little beef, cabbage borscht, and pickled beets. I thought about that often while we lay hungry in the forest. Maybe we will never taste such things again, Yuri."

"They will come back. You will see. We weren't defeated. The Germans were. We will have all what we had before."

"Fisherman, you are a dreamer."

"It made me go on. Otherwise I would have stopped living."

"Ah, do you know what made me continue?"

"No, Squirrel." Duvid took a sip from the bottle and passed it back to Yuri.

"Anger. I lived for the day that I would see these animals who tortured us brought to their knees."

"Anger. It will do for now, but do you think that will carry you forward through the rest of your life?"

"You think not, Yuri? Do you think I can live a normal life now? After all that I saw us suffer through?"

"We suffered. But it is over now. We must try to forget. Otherwise it will weigh us down. It is a burden."

"A burden that we can never throw off. It is impossible. You dream, my friend. You will suffer for it."

"I'm sure you are right, but that is all I can do."

"Life is more than dreaming. We act. We do.'

"And what will you do when you leave this camp, Squirrel?'

"I will go to Palestine."

"Palestine, eh? So, you really are an idealist. Do you want to fight some more?"

"No, I want to grow fruit trees. Citrus and bananas and dates. I don't even know what those taste like."

"I once knew what they tasted like, but I don't remember any more. So, it will be like the Garden of Eden. You will taste things for the first time. Maybe even from fruit of the Tree of Knowledge."

"Don't wish on me a curse. Adam himself was cursed in this way. You, Yuri? What do you intend to do?"

"Maybe go to Argentina, or Canada. Have lots of children. Ten, at least."

"Ten. So where is the wife who will give you so much joy?"

"I will find her in America, or wherever I go. Life is easier there. I hear that the streets are paved with gold, or at least silver."

"So now who is the dreamer?" Duvid took a long swig from the bottle. "Let's concentrate on the present. The future we know nothing about. But you are right. If we think too much of the past, we will be destroyed by it."

The Fisherman gave a long laugh, and sucked at the bottle again. "So let us think of more important things. Let us think of..." he yelled out, "...CHICKEN!!"

"Chicken!" yelled back Duvid.

The bottle was almost drained.

"Do you remember the farm we passed near the ruined cottage. I heard a rooster crow when we passed."

"Yes, and I heard a dog bark."

"Are you suddenly a coward, Squirrel? You who could hide under one leaf and the enemy couldn't find you."

"A coward? Me, a coward? You are a brave man to say such a thing to me."

"Are you threatening me?"

"No, Fisherman, I am going with you. Let us get us a ...CHICKEN!"

The two, Duvid and Yuri, were still giddy and hard on their horizons when they crawled up to the chicken coop wall. Yuri stepped on something that snapped underfoot and he brought his hand up to his face. "Oops. I mean, shh!"

Duvid held his breath, waiting to hear the dog bark. After several seconds, it still hadn't happened. He moved forward again until he found the latch of the coop door. He pulled upwards and the door swung open towards them. The smell was overpowering. Yuri began to gag. He held his shirt up over his face to stifle the smell. He hadn't bathed in weeks. Maybe his own smell could overcome that of the chickens.

Duvid whispered. "Did your doves smell this bad?"

"No, never. These aren't Jewish chickens. That's why they have such an odour."

"Yes, Yuri. Our Jewish chickens had a delightful perfumed scent. I remember it very well."

Yuri chuckled, holding a handkerchief firmly against his face with one hand, while he held the other hand out in front of him as he moved cautiously into the dark hut. Duvid could hear the fowl becoming frenzied, and the sound of their wings flapping about. The rhythm of their guttural low cackle sped up.

"Here, Miss Chicken. Take my hand. I have a beautiful gift for you. Oh, excuse me, you are married, I see. Such a lovely clutch of eggs. May I have a few, please. Oh, how kind you are. You will surely be remembered in chicken heaven."

The chicken became agitated. It clucked. Duvid, his eyes drooping from the delayed effects of the schnapps, sagged down to a sitting position.

"Ah, Duvid, look at this poor bird. She is frightened. Don't be afraid, little bird. I was only joking. I will not harm you or your lovely eggs. I will sing you a song, a lullaby, one that my mother used to sing when I was a boy."

"A song for a bird? You are a madman, Fisherman."

"Even a chicken has a right to a little happiness, my friend."

Yuri began to sing in a whisper, albeit a little out of tune, but the liquor was finally taking its effect on the men. All three, Duvid the Squirrel, Yuri the Fisherman, and Miss Chicken, fell softly asleep.

The German farmer was awake before the sun came up, as he had done since he was a boy, long before this last war and even the one before it. He had never in all that time taken a day off, except to be a soldier many years earlier. There was too much work to be done. His cows needed milking. The day would never be long enough if he indulged himself. He was proud of his heritage, the German tradition of working hard, of discipline, of attention to detail, of following rules that he had been given by his small world. War, on the other hand, that was something that had not appealed to him when he was young and in the last six years, the idea of the German folk taking over the world had found a jaundiced reception in him. He had lost two sons in the east, fighting the Russians, and one in Holland. That was enough. He was eager for the new peace. He had one more son left. He intended to hold onto him.

The farmer had finished with the milking. It was time to bring in a few eggs. It was strange that the door to the chicken coop was slightly ajar. The farmer approached carefully. Getting within ten metres, he paused and listened. There was nothing out of the ordinary. His birds were making their ordinary morning sounds.

The farmer came closer and looked inside. At first he saw nothing in the darkness. His eyes adjusted.

He almost laughed, but stopped himself, sensing that there could indeed be danger here. He hobbled back to the cottage on his war-damaged legs to waken his son. He sent him to the U.S. Army military police detachment nearby on his old bicycle, and went back to stand guard outside the chicken hut.

He had been there for an hour when the two men inside woke up, then filed out the door. Duvid held a forearm over his eyes against the glare of the sun. The Fisherman held his right hand against one temple and forehead. In each of their free hands hung a live chicken. They spotted the farmer standing guard with a pitchfork.

Yuri opened the conversation. "Farmer, are these your chickens?"

"So, intruders. The police will be here soon. I advise you to leave, and without my fowl."

The two were running before the man had time to try to convince them that his advice was good. It was too late, though. An army jeep pulled through the gates of the farm and stopped in front of the two intruders.

"Going somewhere, gentlemen?"

The Fisherman answered in impeccable English.

"We are refugees. According to the terms of the International Convention, you are required to give us your protection."

"Looks to me more that you are trespassers."

"Ah, Americans, what a naive people. Don't you see what is happening here?"

"No. Please tell me."

"This man was holding us against our will. This is called kidnapping, I believe. And worse still, he is holding my chicken."

"Oh, so I'll do everyone here a favour and rescue you. Get in. We're going back to Pocking. Here, farmer, give me these two chickens. For evidence, you understand."

"What? But this is theft. They are mine."

"I think you need a lesson in democracy and justice, sir. Who says these are yours?"

"Why, I do."

"And who says that they belong to these gentlemen?"

"We do," piped up Yuri and Duvid together, suddenly keen on the game.

"So, two to one. They win. Democracy in action."

"Al Capone must have loved democracy. What about American justice?"

"Justice, the man wants justice. In this world. You're lucky it isn't the Russians in this sector. Now they would teach you what true democracy really is. You would have no chickens left. As for justice, you would be dead."

After several hours of their absence, Hannah shyly asked around if anyone knew the whereabouts of Duvid and Yuri, and only minutes later there they were, ambling in from the gate, looking like they had slept in their clothes for a week. She looked the two men up and down as they descended from the army jeep and walked through the gates into the camp. Their clothes were stained and she could see that they were badly in need of a bath. The men shared a sheepish grin. Yuri swung a chicken by the legs from one hand. As the jeep pulled away, the head of another chicken was bobbing back and forth on its back seat. Hannah went running up to them and grasped Duvid's hand. He stared at her eager face and smiled. Hannah released Duvid's hand and touched his cheek.

She had had a dream the night before, something she couldn't recall many details of, except that Duvid had been in it. She had woken up with a feeling of need of some sort, which she quickly shook off. She wouldn't get involved with someone at this camp, no matter how handsome he might be. She wanted to settle somewhere first, have a taste of something she could rely on—some stability. Without anywhere else to go, she had chosen Israel. She would be leaving for the coast of Italy by week's end. She couldn't allow any dream to deflect her future. She was done with dreams. Duvid was just that, a dream.

50 Dreams

Children come, I will show you the magic, food in plenty, games you'll learn but never play. Dream my dreams, listen when I sing my songs. In the night, the eyelids flutter. I will put my arms around you, I will warm your cold feet. I am with you forever.

Jacob was a dreamer. He dreamt of a ladder to heaven and of battling with God Himself all through the night. He carried the reminder of his battle with God as a limp for the rest of his life. How did he view his unforgiving God, who dealt him this blow and yet opened for him and his progeny the future uncharted? Joseph, his son, was both a dreamer and an interpreter of dreams. He foretold his lordship over his brothers. He warned the pharaoh to prepare for seven years of famine. And yet he never imagined the enslavement that would come to his people. Dreams were for the ancient Jews a window into the mind of God. Their significance resonates even today.

Hannah too was a dreamer. She too was told of the future. Was she of any less value to God than Jacob or Joseph? The events that swirled around her young life were perhaps more momentous, of greater weight for the Jews and for all mankind, than those that affected the lives of the Patriarchs.

Hannah and her brother worked in an arms factory in the Soviet Union during the war. The efforts needed to produce the supplies for the war effort were enormous, involving a beleaguered hungry population of hundreds of millions. Huge sacrifices were needed and therefore demanded. To shirk this burden was equated with treason.

Hannah drifts, flotsam in a murky sea of time. Work fills the hours of light during one period, and the next period, the hours of darkness. Time has lost meaning, oozing along from the start of work to its ending. It washes around the clock's face to begin again. Exhaustion gnaws at her soul.

Hannah's brother Burach eyes her with concern and uncertainty, afraid she will starve or fall from exhaustion.

Two things fill her thoughts: food and sleep. Sparse rations are doled out in the morning and the evening, tin plates bearing coarse bread and splashes of meagre stew. Her belly is never full. Sleep time comes erratically by day or night, short and turbulent, its schedule irregular. Fragmented, fragile sleep divides pink dawns from the purple darkness of evening. Hannah drifts through states of fog and fever, between malady and delusion.

One night, Hannah wakes up in a forest. A great mist, drifting through the trees, obscures her vision. There is a strange light, without source, a glow, illuminating the thick dew congealing on the branches and leaves and the bark of the trees. Hannah walks through this mist, listening for a voice she expects to hear at any moment. Her night dress is dripping wet, it clings to her skin, it slows down her movements. She sees an old man on the other side of a low area. He is digging with a small shovel. He looks frantic. What is he digging for? Fever drifts in, fog swirls around her.

Hannah wakes up in her bed. She hardly remembers her dream. There is little time, only moments, to think about it before she has to be at her work. The next night, Hannah again wakes up in the forest. The old man is in front of her. During her day of work, he has managed to dig up his treasure. He holds it up to her.

A green bottle. A small glass bottle, shining in that dull light that comes from nowhere. What is in it? The old man starts to speak to her, but his words are inaudible. She wakes up again in her bed. This time she does remember, wonders what the dreams are about, as she splashes cold water on her face and rushes to work. She wonders who the old man is, and if she will dream again, to fleetingly escape her flat grey world.

Hannah does not dream again anything she can remember for a month or more. But one night, the old man is back again, this time an old woman stands next to him, holding his hand in hers. Hannah recognizes her mother. This man must be her father. She does not know his face; he died before she was born. She recognizes that her mother too must be dead, to be in the presence of her father. This time it is her mother that holds the green bottle up to her. It contains a liquid. Her mother speaks, telling her to drink it. Hannah always listened to her mother, so she obeys. Her parents dissolve in the mists, dropping to the ground as water, to be absorbed back into the earth in which they already lie.

Hannah wakes up in her bed, wet, covered in sweat. Her brother is working; he cannot be there to help her. Her night dress sticks to her skin. Her movements are slow. A fever hovers over her, surrounds her, enters her. She trembles. She hasn't the strength to lift herself, to dress, to go to her work. She drifts back into sleep, this time without dream. During those hours, the sounds of her factory being bombed from the air crash through her sleep, jolting her awake. The darkness of night transforms into light. The blaze ignites wild dreams. From the edge of her sepulchral forest, she sees many of her comrades dying. She is filled with joy as she sees that her brother Burach has survived the attack. Black sleep swallows her once more.

When she wakes up later, that blackness surrounds her. Again it is night. Next to her sits her brother. He gives her some medicine that he has somehow found, urging her to drink it. It tastes foul, but she swallows all of it. It is in a small green bottle. It shimmers before the one small candle that illuminates the room. She does not return to work for three days, drifting back and forth between troubled sleep and startled waking. From time to time, Burach is there, then he is gone.

Hannah at last returns to work, is confronted by the commissar, is arrested on charges of shirking her duty. No physician has certified that she was ill. Still dazed by the drift of events, she is sent north to a prison camp, in the area of the Russian port of Archangelsk. Burach, her brother, goes with her, hoping to protect her.

The train trip is long and cold. They travel in a boxcar, cramped with others, surrounded by sacks of materials. They bring what few possessions they are able to carry, from among the very few they own. Some of the others manage to bring a bit of their own food, some limp cabbage leaves, partly covered in mould, or a few darkened potatoes. Once a day the train stops to take on coal and water for the engine. The exiles are allowed to leave the train for a few minutes to relieve themselves and stretch their legs, under the eyes of guards. A thin gruel is handed out most mornings. Their small evening ration, bread and a thin warm soup, breaks the cold entering their bodies. The bit of black bread is difficult to chew, especially for those with teeth loosened by scurvy. The train trip is long, lasting two weeks. In that time, two prisoners die and are left in the fields next to the railroad track. The ground is frozen too hard to dig graves.

When they get off the train, Hannah, Burach, and the others are met by an army guard and brought to their quarters, a few tents and lean-tos at the edge of the snowy forest. The nights are the worst. The wind blows through the flimsy tent walls, and the cold ground bites upwards into their sleeping bones.

They are forced awake in the early mornings to begin their day's work. Their limbs are stiff, and they have difficulty bending to use the outdoor latrine. Over the next few months, they construct their own winter quarters, low wooden huts, with walls and floors of rough-hewn boards. In the spaces between the planks, clods of clay soil and moss keep the brisk winds from whistling through. Layers of pine boughs piled high make up the roofs. They build latrines, dig wells, and raise a communal kitchen.

The prisoners are assigned to a work detail, building facilities for the transfer of war materiel. The great Allied merchant marine armadas crossed the wide Atlantic from North America, hunted by the German U-boats, and arrived decimated at this northern port. They build the storage facilities, the distribution and loading area for the railroad, and the defence zone around the town. Food is minimal, with little variety. Potatoes and cabbage, mostly cabbage, and turnips, with the occasional carrot or beet. There is no meat, no eggs, no fruit. Bread rations were meagre. They were mostly hungry, and always cold.

Time's river flows onwards beneath the fog of Hannah's mind. Her dreams return.

Again the forest, but it is wrong. The trees are on fire, smoke chokes her. A wind blows the smoke and glowing sparks through the trees. Cinders cover the ground. Hannah feels herself lifted into the air; she drifts with the smoke. She looks through her hands - they are transparent. As she floats through the air above these trees, below her she sees a man being carried off by a group of soldiers. His face is swollen and bloody, but is somehow familiar. As she twists her head around to keep her eyes fixed on him while the heated wind pulls her along, she hears the sound of a young child crying behind her. The child's mother is hiding in the bushes, and holds her hands firmly over the child's face in an attempt to keep it quiet. The mother's face convulses with her anguish. The cries stop.

As she turns away, Hannah sees her brother Burach's familiar face next to a tree, both his hands holding its trunk firmly. He is smiling at her, but as she turns to face him and tries to approach, he starts to melt, first his fingers and progressively his arms and the rest of his body. Rivulets of water run down the tree's irregular bark and into the soil, as Burach's shrinking form collapses against the tree. The tree's foliage becomes denser, thicker, greener, as the liquid that was her brother feeds its roots.

More smoke pours out of the trees. Their leaves are a pulsating green. It becomes a more defined blue and yellow cloud that separates itself away from the tree. The forest is suddenly quiet as thousands of butterflies fly towards and then through her. On their blue wings, each has the design of a yellow six-pointed star. She can hear the whispered beatings of their delicate wings become louder and louder, becoming a roar. This laboured sound muffles the repeated words of the Hebrew *kaddish* - the prayer for the dead - "*Yisgadal veyiskadash shemei raba...*" Then Hannah is awake.

Each day is a day of hard work, it passes like a fog, the same as yesterday and tomorrow. Days and weeks slip by, turn to months. Burach becomes sick with typhus, and, within a few days, is dead. His body is taken away and burnt with that of others who have died recently of the disease. The combined ashes are dumped into a river. There is no gravesite to visit. No one left to speak to. There is only silence.

Hannah feels overwhelmingly alone. Then suddenly it is over. The war has been won. She is free. It seems impossible. With a few others, Hannah leaves for her former home in Poland. No one tries to stop her. It is like magic.

51 Seven Days

Seven days. So it is written. Six days of creation, seven days of passion and mystery. Came the seventh day, when Eve could be surgically separated from her lover so that they could be unified again. The eighth day came, when Eve through her vanity was tricked by her serpent. His only desire was not her but to continue the world through her complicit error.

No time was yet flowing in the Garden. Time stood still. There was no death, no birth, no growth. Despite the passage of days, there were no hours. One moment was and became the next, no different. God was disappointed, even bored. He regretted His act. This world was stillborn. This eighth day was to be its last.

God had created and destroyed many times before. Why should this time be any different? God was ready to create again, dissolve all this effort, to suck it back down into a formless void. And then Eve was tempted, starting the world's clock ticking towards today, secretly delighting God and saving herself and her lover, whose side still ached from the surgery which God had performed. God feigned fury, and beamed with pride and curiosity. His children were becoming interesting.

The sun rose on the ninth day, the second day of mortal time. It was the first day outside the Garden, the first day of change and death. And so Cain was born. Cain would murder Abel, his brother. And God watched, and chastised, and punished again, and secretly smiled. Centuries and millennia later, he was still smiling, hiding his face from Man. Cain was again murdering Abel.

52 Arrival

It was April 1947, a week after Passover. The night was dark, there was a new moon, that is, no moon. The slap of water against the side of the rowboat Duvid was in was the only sound. The Mediterranean Sea was calm, and the smell of the water was mixed with the odour of oily smoke coming from the land a few hundred meters away.

Agents of the *Haganah* had come to him in the DP camp. They needed experienced fighters for the nascent Jewish army. Few Jews even knew how to hold a gun, let alone shoot one, they said with derision. They needed him and others like him so the new country of the Jews would not be stillborn. The United Nations would one day vote on whether to create this land, and the Arabs and their British ally dearly wanted to prevent that from happening. The Jewish survivors of Europe needed him. Duvid didn't need much convincing.

The Fisherman had come with him, less persuaded, complaining.

"Why do I come with you, Squirrel? Tell me that. I'm not such an idealist. I am pure and simple first an academic, not a fighter. I only fight when I have to. Wars are temporary aberrations in mankind's history. And here I am walking into another war. I must be crazy."

Duvid gave him a quizzical look. "Fisherman, you're either a dreamy romantic or an educated fool. War is the only thing you can always count on happening."

"Squirrel, I know fish, not history. But I left war behind me in Poland. Enough! I don't want to be in any war again, even if I came with you to protect you from your own foolishness. Zionism! What nonsense is this? Jews haven't had a country in two thousand years. We argue too much for such an idea to work."

They had lowered themselves by ropes over the side into what pretended to be a fishing boat, laden with nets and floats and the smell of dead fish. The boat bobbed up and down with the spring waves.

"Squirrel, I'm getting seasick. I hate being on the water even more than I dislike eating fish."

"Fisherman, it's time you lived up to your name. You embarrass me in front of these men."

The two were shushed as they chattered on the small boat a half-kilometre offshore just south of Ashkelon.

A quarter hour later, the boat made a crunching sound as it hit bottom just short of the shore. There were rocks here. Every man on the boat slipped wildly over the side, splashed into the shallow water, and rushed in every direction available towards the beach and the dunes beyond. Duvid was running when he heard the sound of whistles and the barking of dogs. The British had anticipated their arrival. Duvid ran toward a pile of boulders, where he had been told to hide. Here and there rocks punctuated the soft, smooth sand. He tripped and his knee moved sideways. He felt a sharp, hard sensation in his leg. As he twisted with the pain, a dog howled in his face, followed by a blow to the back of his head. He lost consciousness.

When Duvid came to, two exquisite pains in his leg and head competed for his attention. He had no idea where he was, was happy not to care, and quickly was asleep again. He drifted. When he woke, he was on a cot in a darkened room in an unfamiliar house. The pain was easing, enough that he now could take an interest in his surroundings. Well, he thought, this isn't a jail cell and it doesn't smell like a hospital. Rescued or captured? He knew he would soon find out which, but felt strangely indifferent either way. Pleasantly calm, really. At least he hadn't drowned, nor was he in chains. Here he was, temporarily or not, in Israel or whatever other name this land would soon be given.

In the next room, he heard two women's voices. Only after a few moments did he realize that their language was Hebrew. One woman peeked in through the doorway of his room and made some apparently comical remark to her companion, because Duvid could hear a musical giggle in response. Although it seemed to be bright day outside, the windows were heavily shuttered and the room was immersed in dim light. Duvid couldn't see the woman's face. It was only when she carried a tray of food in to him did Duvid recognize her. It was Hannah, who he had last seen in Pocking. He had been surprised and a little disappointed when she left suddenly, and now here she was, his nurse.

"So, how are you feeling? Finally awake?"

"Much better, especially now that I've seen you again, my lovely nightingale. Even if your name isn't Florence, your voice is as light and lovely as a songbird's."

"If it wasn't so dark in here, you would again see that I blush easily. Or is that your intention?"

"My intention is much greater than that. I have more in mind than seeing you turning red."

"Well, too bad. That's as far as it can go between us. I won't fall for a soldier who may die tomorrow."

"Even if I die trying to win your affection?"

"I'm here to help you mend so you can go back to battle."

"And who is sending me there?"

"A colonel came by to check on you earlier. He wanted to know when you would be in form."

"What did you tell him?"

"Not for a few weeks. You can hardly stand on that leg with your bone in two pieces."

Duvid looked down at his leg to see the cast in place.

"So, what happened to me? How did I get here?"

"The jeep bringing you in also held another wounded man. He described the battle to me. According to his story, a welcoming party of Palestinian Jews had been waiting in hiding above the beach for your group to reach shore. When the British arrived to arrest you all, they were overwhelmed by Palestinian Jews dressed in British uniforms. It seems the British men were fooled and captured, but because they laid down their weapons without fighting back, the Jews were kind enough to release them, dressed in their underwear, outside a British army Taggart fort along the road."

"So these Jews brought me here?"

"Yes. They told me they found you with a dog licking your bleeding leg. Lucky you."

"It was probably not a very hungry dog."

"I think the dog had discriminating taste. Or very strange taste. You looked very unappetizing when you first arrived."

"Lucky me also to meet you again."

Hannah and Duvid both laughed lightly while she told him the story. It was not such a funny story, but it relieved the tension. Duvid found that he enjoyed being near her. Over the next few weeks, as Duvid recuperated, he helped Hannah to tend to other injured fighters in this makeshift hospital, hobbling about with his crutch, carrying her bandages and medicines for her. Emotions that he had left behind were returning, but he resisted back. There was a war going on and these feelings would have to wait.

"What happened to the other wounded man?"

"The one who came with you?"

"He left right away. He only needed a few bandages and a shot of penicillin. You would remember him. He was the tall one who you met at Pocking camp."

"The Fisherman?"

"Yes. He said he had to go fishing, then left. Yonit, the other nurse, really liked him."

"Maybe he'll be back."

"Or maybe he's already dead."

Duvid left for the battlefront when he was able to walk properly. He went back to take part in the guerrilla war against the British near Acco. He trained new arrivals in the use of guns, and spent long nights waiting silently on the shore for other Jews to leave their boats and slip into Palestine, watching for the British and the Arabs. After Israel declared itself an independent land the next year, he took part in battle after battle. Of all of them, the battle for Latrun, along the old road from Tel Aviv to Jerusalem, brought him closest to death. The Taggart fort at Latrun was manned by Jordan's Arab Legion, a tough foe trained and commanded by British officers.

The earth on the road up to Jerusalem was hardscrabble, tough and rocky, terraced around the continuous hills that surrounded its passage from the edge of the coastal plain to the heights at the gates of the ancient city. Near Latrun, their armoured bus was ambushed by an Arab unit as the early morning sun gave away their location. The fighting was tough. The sun's heat soon took its toll. Thirst slowed the group down. Swarms of small desert flies filled the soldiers' nostrils and eyes as they clung to the ground for safety. The new immigrant arrivals assigned to their group hadn't even had any time to be trained. They had simply been given a gun and driven up to the battle zone. Duvid saw several of these die as they left their armoured buses, attempting to defend their position. Some had no idea how to remove the safety catches on their rifles, and were shot down as they desperately tried to fire at their enemies. Duvid kept low, and managed to escape, but not before a bullet came almost close enough to kill him, burning across one cheek, leaving a bleeding line but no more damage than that. The same bullet caught his lieutenant in the face, killing him instantly. Duvid managed to survive the day, and eventually reached his battalion further up the road.

At long last, in 1949, the invasions were ending with armistice agreements with the various Arab states involved, and Duvid was demobilized. He returned to the small house where he had been nursed back to health, accompanying his battalion commander, who had been wounded in one of the last confrontations. Hannah was still there. This time he decided to stay near her. He could again help her with her rounds. He could drive the jeep put at the clinic's disposal into Netanya for supplies. He would make himself useful.

The hills were cloaked in green, the earth adorned with flowers, wild red poppies, yellow fennel, pink mustard, horsetails, bearded grasses, and a multitude of others. The sky was a deep blue on that afternoon of early summer. Two years had passed since he first wet his feet at the landing beach. Another Passover was over. He walked up to the door of the house and knocked, energetically, but not loud enough to frighten Hannah. He had picked a small bouquet of wild flowers.

Duvid didn't know if she had another man in her life by now. She was pretty enough to have attracted many men. When she opened the door, Duvid found the courage to ask Hannah if she would go with him to the beach. She agreed.

She brought food–challah and roasted chicken, finely chopped salad, and a bottle of sweet wine. He brought a firearm to protect against Arab marauders.

She brought the Sabbath menorah, two candles to illuminate the evening, when Man imitates God, starting His period of rest.

The shadows were long when they arrived at the beach. The sun would soon be reaching for the horizon, bringing on the sacred Sabbath. They rushed to set down their blanket, eat the picnic supper, followed by the lighting of the candles and the campfire. The wind off the water made it difficult to light the candles. Duvid slipped off his shirt and fastened it between two driftwood branches to shield them. For a moment, Hannah looked away, but then extended her arm and pulled him down next to her. The two covered themselves with a light blanket as the soft wind from the sea pulled sand and salt vapour up the beach at them. It was a warm evening. The candles flickered softly, their light gathered and reflected by his shirt. It competed with that coming from the setting sun. The beach grasses along the tops of the low dunes became radiant with gold and crimson as the sun went down. Overhead, to the east, the first stars blinked their existence. Night wrapped Hannah and Duvid in its caress.

"Beautiful evening, Hannah. The sun sets so quickly, the stars come out so early, so brightly. If only this earth was as peaceful as the sky."

"Let's swim, philosopher!" Hannah shouted over the light breeze, laughed, and ran off into the rapidly growing darkness, giggling. The power of the wind flung her empty dress back along the sand to his feet. Duvid strained against the embryonic night, shielding his vision from the glare of the campfire's brightness. He vaguely saw Hannah's unclothed form enter the foam at the water's edge. A fresh scent was blowing in on a breeze from the sea. He raised himself up and walked down to the water, searching for the sound of her splashing. He quickly undressed and joined her amid the burst of waves. It was a night of wonders. Duvid watched in awe as God opened the sky as the Sabbath night descended, as he had been told would happen when he was a child.

Hannah and Duvid made love for the first time that night. And later, as Hannah slept and Duvid sat next to her tending the fire, listening to the determined, rhythmic surge of wave on sand, she dreamed again. Duvid noticed nothing but the fluttering of her eyelids, a slight change in the rhythm of her breathing.

Dawn flows in from the east. Hannah stands in a mountain meadow filled with blue flowers as far as she can see. In the distance she sees Duvid. Pick me some flowers, she yells above the howl of the wind. Duvid bends over, and soon he has a mass of blue petals under one arm. Pick me a yellow flower, she calls out to him. Duvid stretches out at the edge of a precipice for the only yellow flower in view. Tightly clutching the flowers he already has, he finds no handhold as he reaches forward. His hand closes around the yellow bloom's stem. Pebbles come away from the crumbling cliff face, dropping into the void below. Duvid smiles broadly and offers the blossom to Hannah. He slips. A thousand blue petals fill the air, lazily spiralling down into the valley below. Hannah reaches out, but the yellow flower is also gone.

The dream is over. Hannah's eyes open. She holds Duvid's hand tightly, afraid. She will always be so.

Later that year, they will marry. War was now finished with. There would be time and the energy needed for romance, the leisure to think about the future and children. Duvid was physically intact; emotional scars were something else. These would stay with him for the rest of his life.

Life is vindictive, never forgiving the injuries that it is forced to bear at an early age. Hunger may cease. So may fear. But the fitful sleep of the injured soul goes on, embattled by archetypal imagery revisiting it in the darkness. The hard work needed for recovery is ignored for other tasks more immediate and vital.

So with Hannah and Duvid, as it was for many of those around them who had stolen from the store of luck to survive. Some injuries were visible, by appearance or by altered function. A limp, a scar, an eyepatch. Most were not so evident, were within the troubled mind. The vacant stare. The tremor in the fingers. Silence. The broken sleep, the screams of terror in the dream that came back night after night.

So it was with Duvid. Duvid, the strong lion who had built this land. Duvid, the powerful beast who had carried so many on his unyielding shoulder. Duvid, whose nights broke in pieces before the sledgehammer blows of his dying parents, brothers, sisters, screaming in fear and anguish as the great iron doors of the gas chambers closed on them and darkness surrounded their last moments of thrashing terror.

For Hannah, normal life can only be illusion. The only reality is in the tyranny of a past which still holds her in its grasp, and her dreams will come and go forever. Her moods shift, pulled by the quicksands and tides of memory. Duvid was captivated by the northern part of this land, the Galilee, that each spring in the passage of a few days and with a sprinkle of rain turned green before his eyes. He felt also an intimate attachment to the peaceful desert, the Negev to the south, with its stony emptiness, its awesome quiet, its magical changes when its spring rains came. It hid secrets between and beneath its ancient stones as surely as it hid scorpions. He came here as frequently as he was able, seeking out its hidden spaces, its carefully buried mysteries. Here he could allow his own buried anguish to climb into the light of the sun, languish in the hot desert wind, heal in the dark solitude of night beneath a sky brilliant with the numberless stars.

Duvid and Hannah married. They were ready to raise children, to build a family, to rise from the ashes. His battalion commander attended the wedding. So did Yuri, the Fisherman. A few soldiers from his platoon were there and several of the nurses who had worked with Hannah. There weren't many. There was no family. Under the *huppah*, Hannah cried with joy and with anguish, joy that they had found each other, anguish that there was so little remaining of their past lives.

After the wedding ceremony, after the prayers, after the breaking of the glass, after they had consummated their union for the satisfaction of tradition, they had returned to their guests and danced and eaten and drunk *schnapps* and wine until long after midnight.

"I am so happy, Hannah. So happy that we are together for the rest of our lives, that we can now build our home, raise children. Become normal."

"I too Duvid. I dreamed of this day from soon after we met. You were so charming. I couldn't resist you from the very beginning. Especially when you peeled off your shirt to keep the shabbos candles burning that first night on the beach."

"I was only charming because you inspired me. I love you. And I won't mention how I was moved when your dress came flying on the wind that evening on that beach."

"Duvid."

"I only mentioned."

"Yes."

"So don't blush. We're married."

"I'll always blush with you."

"Hannah."

"Yes, Duvid."

"Have I ever said what I have yearned to do?'

"Besides marrying me?"

"Yes, besides."

"Go on."

"I would like to build a house and start a farm."

"A farm. What does a Jew from Poland know about farming? And where would you do this?"

"Before I finished with the army, I was guarding a village of Yemenites who settled near Azriel, not far from Netanya. They're in a farming cooperative. Each owns his own land but they help each other."

"Yes, a *moshav*. You told me about them before. What about it?"

"They've invited me to start a farm there. It would be a dream come true for me. If you would agree."

"Duvid, I'm not a country girl. I would die of boredom there. I want to live in a big city, not a dusty settlement. Tel Aviv would be my first choice."

"Okay, so for you it's Tel Aviv then. I'll have to think what sort of work I can get there."

"You have contacts, Duvid. I'm sure you can find something."

"So no farm? You won't even consider it?"

"I'm not refusing to go, but you'll have to do a very good job of convincing me. Let's sleep on it for now. We just got married a few hours ago. Let's let our hearts be free for tonight."

"Maybe we can visit them. I know you'll love these people."

"Maybe. Good night, my love."
"Good night, Hannah."

53 Renewal

Before leaving the army, Duvid worked on laying out strategic roads and positioning new settlements that would guard the potential routes of conquest into the heart of the land. Hundreds of thousands of refugees were still arriving from Europe. These people needed homes. It had to be done. Duvid struggled to fulfil his duties, struggled too with his thoughts of the past and his fears for the future. He looked forward to peace, to a time when he could rest his mind.

Half a million Jews had just been expelled, with few possessions, from the Arab lands around Israel. These countries had a history of Jewish habitation for two thousand years and sometimes more, dating back before the time of Mohammed, before the Romans and even the Greeks, to the time of the Babylonian and Persian conquests, and to the time of Solomon and his emissaries, residing in places of fame and fable, Yemen, once known as Sheba, Tunisia, once Carthage, Morocco and Libya, lands of the Berbers, Iraq, once Babylon, and Egypt, ever known as Egypt, and the many other lands that fell to the eighth century Moslem conquests. In retaliation for their losses in battle, the Arab governments had taken their anger and frustration out on their own Jewish populations, and thrown them out. Absorbed by Israel, these people needed homes too.

Duvid's Fiat pulled off the road just past a bus stop crowded with olive-skinned men and women. A cloud of dust floated behind his car and enveloped the waiting group before drifting on. Duvid slowed and brought his car to a stop. He cranked his window open.

"Sorry! *Slicha!*" he yelled out his window at the group.

Some of the group recognized him and waved. One called out, "Welcome back, Duvid."

Duvid put the car back into gear to the grinding sounds of the gears and continued into the settlement. The old car backfired in complaint, before it quietened down.

"There's really a bus that comes out this far? I don't believe it."

"Hannah, I know that you're a city girl, and that this is not going to be Vienna or Warsaw or Paris. But for all their civilization, for all they had and still have, or may soon have again, great art and strudel and good coffee, those places are darkened by their pasts. Too many of us died there simply for who we were. We're building a new country for the Jews, and it will be great one day, maybe it will even surpass Europe. For now, though, we're all pioneers and builders, each of us in our own small way."

The brakes crunched and Duvid's car came to a stop outside a small one-storey house with stuccoed walls and a corrugated tin roof. Tied to a stake in the shade on one side of the house, a white goat with curved horns looked up at them and went back to chewing on a heap of vegetation at its feet.

"This is the Sharon Valley. Just standing here and looking north and south and east and west, I imagine King David, in love with this land and writing of it in his love poems, as he did in Song of Songs."

"That is you, Duvid, you writing your poetry to describe this land."

"Before I landed in Israel, I had the dream of being a farmer, of turning the neglected earth of Palestine into a green place called Israel. Come, I want you to meet Pesach Baranai. He led his Yemenite community to settle here, after the expulsions. He and the others established Moshav Azriel. It's a type of collective farm."

"I know, Duvid."

"So you know. Good. Come."

The interior of the house was dark, made more so by the smallness of the few windows, covered in iron shutters, and the thick cement walls. The floor was of ceramic tile, drab in colour. On a low table, an electric fan clattered within its metal basketwork, sending a faint breeze of warm air across the room.

"Sit down, sit down. So this is your lovely wife."

"Hannah."

"Yes, Hannah."

"I'm glad you could both come to visit. As you know, Hannah, Duvid was stationed here. We've invited him to live with us, to start his own farm."

"Yes, Duvid has told me."

"And how do you feel about living here with us?"

"I'd like to see what we would be getting ourselves into. If we have a family, it must be right for me, but also for my children." Hannah eyed a small lizard lazing high on the opposite wall.

"This is a wonderful place to bring up children." Pesach's eyes followed hers. "Those little reptiles help control the insects. I'll ask my wife to show you around. You'll see how lovely a place this is, our own Eden. You will have a meal with us."

"It would be my pleasure," was Duvid's response to the invitation.

"Yes, our pleasure." Hannah quickly modified his words, glancing into her husband's eyes.

"These are our citrus orchards." Esther waved her arm to show off the field of regularly placed orange trees. "Over there at the back we have lemons, and beyond, grapefruit."

"There must be hundreds of trees here."

"Many, yes, but I've never counted."

"And there, in the green houses?"

"We will be growing flowers. Carnations travel well. We will soon ship them to Europe."

"Europe?"

"Yes. By plane. We are negotiating now with flower importers in France and Belgium."

"They don't have their own flowers? They need ours? And that, what is it?" Hannah was pointing to a low metal tower on stilts, round and covered in sheet metal.

"It's a guard tower. Just beyond, there, and there, you can see the barbed wire fence. Beyond that are the Jordanians."

"So close? It's not dangerous?"

"We have learned to live with it. The whole country is never more than maybe fifteen kilometres from a border. So we are a little closer."

"Oh my God! And Duvid wants us to live here?"

Esther winced when she heard Hannah uttering the deity's name. "Hannah, we are a pious community. We don't utter the Name lightly. But I understand. You are not like us."

"I come from a large city in Europe, Warsaw. We did not take religion very seriously. I'm sorry."

"No need to be sorry. Please be aware that here we stop all work for the Sabbath."

"Tomorrow?"

"It starts at sundown tonight."

"Of course."

"You are staying with us."

"Oh, Duvid didn't say."

"I will lend you some clothes." Hannah and Duvid slept on a foam mattress bed set up in the living room. Before bed, Hannah showered by candlelight. Water that the sun had warmed during the daytime flowed from a metal drum on the roof.

"Where is the toilet?" she whispered to Duvid.

"It's in the yard."

"The city would be better, no?"

"I'll build you one indoors."

The outhouse toilet was behind the house. Hannah quickly sat and peed, carefully eying a spider building its web in one corner of the space. She had endured worse. On the way back in the dark, a jackal howled. This frightened her. Jackals could attack a child. Her own child, perhaps, one day.

"You survived?" Duvid asked when she had slipped in beside him under the covers. "Are you sure the spider didn't follow you in?"

"Duvid, you're not so funny as you think you are. There are jackals out there!"

"I'll install a light."

"You'll put the toilet inside. And put a light outside to light the path at night." After breakfast the next morning, the men went for morning prayers. Duvid didn't go along. Hannah slept in a little and ate late. Duvid waited for her on a metal chair by the front door until she was ready.

"So what do we do today?"

"Do?"

"It's *Shabbat*. We can't do much."

"We can read, we can discuss. We can pray and we can eat. What more is there in the world? It's a beautiful day. We can take a walk to the Druze village down the road."

"Arabs?"

"Yes, of a sort, but they are our friends. Okay, I see you're afraid. Don't you trust me?"

"Oh, Duvid, my love, I'm not made for this life."

"Big city girl?"

"Yes."

"I tell you what. Tel Aviv is only a half hour away by car. Haifa the same. Jerusalem an hour. Not so far. If you agree to live here with me, I promise I will buy a car as soon as I have enough money, and I will drive you anywhere you want to go. Where would you like me to take you?" The next year, the twin boys were born at Azriel and circumcised on their eighth day, the day Adam and Eve ate of the forbidden fruit and were expelled from the garden. They named one son after this Adam. Their mother named him, as was her right by tradition. The second twin was named Simon by Duvid, after his father, Shimin Lev.

Hannah worked to develop a medical clinic for the *moshav*, trying to convince anyone who would listen that they needed a nurse, a doctor, medical supplies, equipment. After much talking and cajoling, some charming and more cajoling, it came to be.

One day, Hannah opened the door and there stood the Fisherman, with a bottle of vodka in one hand.

"You," she said.

Yuri grinned and took a swig.

"I have come here to settle near you. And I am looking for a wife to bear me children."

Yuri courted and married one of the pretty Yemenite girls. The day of the wedding, people came from the whole valley. There were hundreds, much different from Hannah and Duvid's marriage day. Yuri told Duvid that evening that he still wanted to have ten children.

"Ten children, Fisherman, do you know that many names?"

"Don't worry for names, Squirrel. I will name them after the seas and the valleys, after the mountains and the rivers. There are more than enough names in this land."

"Well, don't name them after me, Fisherman. I want to live a long life."

"Let us hope so."

54 Return

The mind has its own landscape, its hills and its valleys, places hidden away, its paths largely untrodden. Landmarks are positioned here and there, unrecognized, signposts along a road woven in symbols, without ever disappearing over the fearsome horizon. A cove here provides shelter against the sudden storm, a hilltop there reveals an unexpected vista, beautiful or frightening, seen only once the peak is reached. All is in shadow.

There was the bridge again, no different than before. Duvid's hands gripped the armrest of the old taxicab tightly. Driving in had lifted so much dust that he had trouble seeing more than a few feet ahead. He strained his eyes, trying to peer through the murk and make out the landmarks which were so familiar. He felt his heart beating strongly in his chest. His mouth was dry. He realized he was afraid.

What if he met her? What if by some miracle Miriam had managed to return and was coming out of the town's fruit and vegetable store when he walked off the bus? Impossible imaginings. He dearly missed her, he suddenly realized, even though at the same moment he felt a thick opaque wall slide down in front of him, blocking the thought. He was married, had two boys now. He loved Hannah, truly, dearly. Nothing could be allowed to disrupt that, even if that possible thing came from inside him. He wouldn't allow himself to be torn, even if a miracle did happen.

He let himself be questioned. His internal prosecutor asked: Do you really believe her to be dead? And he, the witness, was compelled to answer: yes. He had seen her die. He declared it to himself again: she's dead. In this Schrödinger state, this recurring moment of doubt, something in his heart wouldn't accept that idea. The real truth was he couldn't be sure. He had never really been sure, and that unknowing had fed this obsession.

It had been four years since he and Hannah had settled on the *moshav*. Duvid was here now because he had been offered a place as a delegate to try to approach the Polish government to arrange diplomatic contacts for the first time. Whether to go was a hard decision. The past was still strong in his head. The land of Poland was still a stark, forbidding graveyard. He finally decided that he had to return, despite his earlier resolve never to do so. He didn't understand why, perhaps to answer his questions, but he needed to return to his place of birth. He had asked many times, consulted every list available, written letters to anyone he could think of, every organization that might know, but he had no trace of his family, no record even of where or how they had died.

He was, despite himself, anxious to walk up to his former home, touch its front door, pass his hand across the grass that grew along the river. Perhaps some new information was hidden there, maybe someone had tracked through and left a name, an address, a story. Hannah had been beside herself when he told her what he intended to do.

"It is too dangerous, Duvid. The Poles still hate us and the Soviets are no friends of Israel."

"I have to do this, Hannah. If I don't, how can I forgive myself for losing such a chance?"

Travel inside Poland was difficult, but money placed in the right hands in Warsaw had gotten him what he needed: a driver to take him there from Warsaw. When they passed into Bodsanow, he asked the driver to stop in the town centre. Duvid stepped out of the car and straightened himself. The dust quickly dissipated in a light breeze blowing from the west, and the beauty of the town shone forth. This was something he didn't recall, the harmony of the low houses with their surroundings, their modest brick and wood walls displaying a unity that he had never before noticed, saying: it is what it should be. The bunches of lilies growing here and there alongside neat roads, tall trees reaching into the blue sky, Duvid felt the slight breeze on his face and turned toward it, in the direction of his former home.

Duvid walked up the earthen street past the old Jewish cemetery. There was little left there to look at. It was now an overgrown field, choked with weeds, the scar of a wound within the neatness of the town. The stone wall that had once surrounded it was demolished. The stones over the graves had been scattered. Some were installed as paving stones in the road he walked on. He had no idea whose graves were where, but the remains of those he remembered in his life here—his family and friends, of Miriam, his sweetheart—their remains were somewhere far away, undignified by any formal burial, unmarked by any stone. Except for this excision, the town here didn't otherwise seem to have changed much. This part of the road was dusty and unpaved. The roof of the church next to it was still in need of repair. There it was, next to the church orchard: his home, or what once was his home. Duvid felt his lungs filling with a long deep breath. His heart was beating quickly enough that he could feel it in his throat. The house looked the same. Almost. Other people were living there. He walked up to the door of his old home. He stopped, filled with an array of emotions mixed too thoroughly to identify. A man in his early twenties, puffing on a pipe, greeted him suspiciously.

"Hello? We don't get many tourists here. No tourists, actually. Who are you?" The man took a slow puff of his pipe.

"I'm not really a tourist."

"Oh? Looking for something in particular? Perhaps I can be of help."

Duvid considered what to say.

"I once lived here."

"In this town?"

"In this house."

"This house? Really? When was that?"

"Long ago, when you were a youth."

"Before the war?"

"Yes, before the war."

"Have you come back to claim your house? You must be a Jew."

"What?"

"Yes. It was inevitable that you might show up one day. My father thought so. He talked a lot about that, until he died last year."

"Where you're standing, I once stood and looked out on a much different world. Yes, I lived here, but no, I'm not here to take back my house. I have my own property, far from here. This house, this town, they're memories for me. Long gone...and yet, here before my eyes."

The young man was silent for a moment, as if mulling over something. "Please come in, we will drink a toast."

Confused, Duvid followed the young man inside. This welcome was unexpected. The young Pole pulled a bottle of vodka spirits off a shelf in the familiar cramped kitchen. It didn't seem to have changed. The same kitchen table, a little older, stained more, stood against the far wall, under the same small-paned window. The floor was still the smooth wood that he remembered, a depressed path worn in it where the traffic of human feet, his brothers' and sisters' feet, had passed from the small salon to the kitchen pantry at its back. The ceiling seemed to have the same coat of old whitewash, and he imagined that even the spider webs in the corners of the ceiling nearest the window had been hanging there for all these decades. An electric socket, its bulb bare, was suspended by a wire from the ceiling. It was the only sign of change that Duvid could discern.

"Sit. Sit." Duvid complied and scraped his chair closer to the table. He rubbed the table's surface. He held his hand to it, unable to draw it away. There were ghosts within.

"It was yours?"

Duvid nodded, reflecting on his memories. "My mother's, really."

"Yes. Memories." The young man poured two tiny glasses half full before he lifted one into the air and yelled out "*Labriut!*" It travelled in a single sweep from the height of his arm to his lips. The Hebrew word surprised Duvid. His expression did not change. Only the almost imperceptible forward movement of his ears, and the slightest narrowing of his eyes, could have revealed that he was suddenly alert to danger. The instincts he had developed during the war were still there. He felt uneasy having his identity revealed. He followed the same motion as his host, hesitantly saying the same thing in Polish.

"*Dla zdrowia*! Where did you learn your Hebrew?"

"Ah! Hah! I was only nineteen three years ago, my father still alive. I decided to find what had happened to the Jews of our town. Gone, like that. My father hated them, even when, after the war, there were none here. Stupid old man. Drank too much. Dead now. Ah, I already said that. Maybe I drink too much, too. He was always afraid that you would come back and take this house from him. Where were these Jews, I wondered? Had they all been killed during the war?

"So, yes, I managed to get a visitor's visa to visit my crazy uncle Jerzy who was living in Holland. There, I made a little money, and took a trip to Israel. They almost didn't let me in, those damn Israelis, those crazy Jews. It was the early days, just after they had defeated the Arab armies. Not so long ago, really. I told them I wanted to visit the Catholic sites in the Galilee and Jerusalem. I crossed myself. I got down on my knees and begged. Maybe they believed me. I suppose they needed the money I would spend there.

"I ended up in a kibbutz near the Lebanese border, stayed a year, learnt Hebrew."

"The *kibbutzniks* accepted you?"

"I was willing to work hard, and they slowly changed their minds about me. I missed the taste of roast pork, but not much else. Every few weeks we ran for the shelters, when the Arabs would throw their mortar shells at us. My mother sent me word that my father had become sick. I returned home and have been here since. It's not an easy place, that land of the Jews. Even for the Jews."

"Especially not for the Jews. Well, it's been good to be here, and to meet with you. Good luck to you."

"*B'hatzlacha.*"

Duvid took his leave and walked slowly back to the car.

As he passed the church, someone called out. "Are you not the Jew, Duvid Grynsztyn?"

Duvid turned in surprise. It was the same priest he had known before the war. He was surprised that this man remembered him at all. It had been a turbulent time.

"Yes, it is me. Greetings, Father."

"Come." He gestured for Duvid to sit on a wooden bench in the shade of a chestnut tree. "So, you've come back to search for the others?"

"Yes. Do you know of anyone who returned here?"

"To my knowledge, none that have sent any news or passed through here. But I only returned here in the last year."

"And where were you?"

"I have been in the camps."

"The German camps? They are long emptied."

"Yes, in those, but I was in those of the Russians, too."

"How so?"

"The Germans took me away because I tried to hide Jews in my church. After hiding you, there were several others, but after a while, word got around and I was betrayed. In the camp I was sent to, they were too busy with the Jews to care much about me."

"I was also in such a camp. How did you survive?"

"They only made me work very hard. There were so many Jews and the Germans were in such a hurry to eliminate them. I could only watch. So I survived, but when the Russians came through, they sent me to a camp because I was a priest, so an enemy of the proletariat."

"When did you get back here?"

"Only a year ago. Ah, yes, I remember. After the Russians sent me away, I was in the same camp as a woman you probably knew before the war. Miriam from the village. Do you remember this young woman? She would really have been only a girl at the time the war began."

Duvid's face crumbled, a battle between joy and despair, more than his facial muscles could display. He felt as if a hammer was crushing him into the dirt, and that his heart had risen into the clouds.

"I'm so sorry. I didn't know this news would be such a shock for you." The priest ran to pour him a glass of vodka. He ran back, bearing the small glass. Duvid was sitting in a stupor.

"So, you knew this woman. Very well, it seems."

"She's alive, Father? How can it be? Miriam is dead. I saw it happen."

"Well, now, your eyes were poor witnesses. My poor man, this has upset you so. Sip this. It will make you feel better."

"Oh, no, not more alcohol. It's too much for me."

"Waste is a sin." The priest swigged the liquor back into his own mouth. "Cold water, then?"

"Yes, Father, thank you. I'm not a drinker." The priest trundled back inside and returned in a minute with a tall glass of cold water. Duvid drained the glass.

"You're sure it was her?"

"Yes, I'm certain. I knew everyone who lived in this village. I recognized her as soon as I laid eyes on her, although I made sure to ask her to confirm who she was. After all, she had aged, grown gaunt and stringy, I'm afraid. It is difficult for a woman to be beautiful under such conditions."

"But she was alive. I still can't believe it, Father."

"Yes, quite alive. Abundant with life, you might say. So she was your love, I see by the flush on your face. Yes, yes. Try to hold yourself steady and I will tell you what I know. I have to tell you, though, that she gave birth to a child, a boy, soon after I arrived there."

"A child?"

"Yes. It happens to young women at times, so I've heard."

"Father, your mirth has no success with me."

"I'm sure it doesn't. Would you like me to stop talking for a while?"

"No, no. If you don't tell me, I may never be able to sleep again."

"It was not an easy place to live. Not enough food, very hard work. Of course, by comparison to what those animals in the German camps did to the Jews, and even to me, it was like a vacation. At the time I was released from the camp, she was still alive. More than that I don't know."

"But she has a son? A boy? How old is he?"

"He was born a little after the war ended. A beautiful little boy. Red hair."

"The father?"

"She was not married. She wouldn't speak of the father, not to me, anyway. Whoever he was, though, he was not with them. Oh, sit, sit, please. Don't get up. You have had a big shock."

"What is the name of the town where the camp is?"

"Duvid, my ardent young man, I prefer not to say. If you try to contact her, it may make things worse for her, and you will regret what you've done. Do you have a family now?"

"Yes, a wife and two boys."

"Let me give you some advice. Go home and hug your wife, kiss your sons. Try to forget this Miriam. You may never see her again."

"Father, I appreciate your good advice, but I have to know. Where was this place?"

"So it looks like I can't dissuade you. So, the truth and nothing else. It was near the village of Mostovaya, in the Urals."

"You will write it down for me?"

"Yes. But you can never cross all the borders that stand between you and her."

"Father, I'm not such an adventurer. But a letter?"

"I don't know if a letter will reach her, either, but I suppose you can try. The days of Stalin are over now so perhaps it is possible. Conditions are a little lighter than before."

"Thank you, Father."

"Tell me something."

"Whatever you want to know."

"Do you still fish?"

"Not as much as I once did with my brothers."

"Yes, it was your older brothers who were the good fishermen. Did they survive?"

"No, no one did. I am the only one." Duvid's face displayed his thoughts.

"Ah, I'm so very sorry."

"I must go, Father. My driver is becoming impatient, I'm sure."

The priest quickly scribbled the name of the Russian town on a slip of paper and handed it to Duvid. "I only wish things could have turned out better for you. And for all the world. Don't forget this bit of paper, since you worked so hard to get it from me."

"Thank you, Father."

"I wish you an easier life from now on. I will pray for you."

"For a Jew?"

"Times change. People too."

"It seems so. And I will pray for you, too."

"Thank you. Goodbye, Duvid Grynsztyn. Perhaps you will return one day."

"I don't know the future."
"God knows."
"He doesn't speak to me."
"Perhaps not, but He hears you."

55 Miriam's Journal

Eli is a boy now, six years old, strong when he needs to be, but now he cries from hunger pains in his belly. The cook in the camp kitchen sees me and my son and takes pity. He passes me a few turnips and carrots, another time a boiled potato, some hard bread. But other days, there isn't enough to stop the hunger pangs. I am frantic. What can I do for Eli?

A miracle happens today. A letter arrives for me out of nowhere. I tear at the envelope. It has already been opened. I look at the signature at the bottom before I begin to read. It is from Duvid. How he found me, I do not know. I read it hungrily, as if it is food. Duvid tells me he is in Israel, the new name for Palestine, the Jewish homeland. My eyes fill with tears and I begin to weep. Is this possible? There is a little money for me, he says, but I don't find it in the letter. Someone has stolen it.

I rush to the commissar and begin to scream. He turns sheepishly and puts his hand in his pocket. Two American ten dollar bills come out and he places them in my hand. The rest I allow him for letting me have the letter at all. What else can I do? This money will help. I can find someone to exchange it for food. Farmers come by the camp to barter food on occasion. I already know them well. They will sell me what I need.

I reread the letter now, calmer now. Duvid has married. My heart almost stops in my chest. I read on. He has two sons, twins. I struggle to breathe. Tears well in my eyes and drop onto the thin paper. I get my emotions under control; nothing good will happen if I allow them to control me. Duvid reminds me that he expects to meet me at the Wailing Wall one day soon. Again tears fill my eyes. I know it will be a long time before I am free, if ever. I plunge into despair; I pull myself back. Eli needs me strong and healthy. Perhaps he will be the one to go to Israel one day.

I will not be allowed to send a reply, but I will keep the address. Moshav Azriel. The Hebrew words are a delight. My imagination soars as I see in my mind *ha'aretz*, the land, the green fields of the Galilee and the haze of air over the soft blue waters of the Kinneret.

The bright hills and chiseled stones of Jerusalem cry to me. I know that I will never see them.

56 Again War

Battle had continued, inexplicably turning the dream of peace after a time of horror into a recurring sleepwalk through the past recalled. Duvid's neighbour Benjamin was killed one day by a mortar attack while he was riding his tractor in his farm field. Further up the coast, near Netanya, a group of five terrorists snuck across the heavily fortified and constantly patrolled border under the control of Jordan. Three of them entered an elementary school, and killed two teachers and seven children, aged six to nine, before they were shot dead by Israeli army commandos. To the south and further north, there were intermittent attacks across the Egyptian and Syrian frontiers. No peace treaty to formally end the fighting at the end of the War of Independence had ever been signed. It had simply stopped, because the Israelis had decisively defeated the Arab forces. There was an armistice, but the Arab states would continue to try.

The telephone in the central office of the *moshav* rang many times late in the night. After perhaps thirty rings, the man in charge managed to rush over, fumbling with his keys, until he could undo the lock and answer. Out of breath, he heard the coded message. War. The citizen soldiers were to report to their reserve army units early the next morning. Duvid, Yuri, and all the able young men of the *moshav* were called up. The older ones, into their forties, were to serve in the home guard.

It was to be battle again, this time to drive the Egyptian army east of the Suez Canal. Duvid accepted it with a weary sigh. There was no choice. He kissed Hannah and the boys goodbye that morning. He promised the boys he would bring back some memento for them.

He was away a long time. Once home, his demeanour had changed. He would wake up screaming, eyes wild, frightening his young sons and alarming Hannah, then fell back into a trance. He staggered across his farm, lost, holding the branches of his trees and breaking them off, raging, casting oranges that had become grenades through the air at an imagined enemy. At night, he opened his water taps, allowing water to spill out for hours, flooding his fields, turning them into mud, and generating complaints from his neighbour. Hannah tried to hold the family together, hold them to the farm, but the neighbours were now openly hostile, and incidents kept happening. Hannah's pleaded with her husband to calm himself.

"Please, Duvid, try to hold yourself together. For the sake of the boys."

"Maybe we should leave. Maybe I was wrong to come to this country after all," he muttered. "I have an uncle in Canada. Maybe he will sponsor us. We could go there. For the sake of the boys."

"If only your friend Yuri hadn't died."

Duvid erupted again. Hannah despaired at what she could do.

The orange grove withered. Their flowers fell to the ground before they could attract bees. There was little fruit. The well he had dug himself produced a sour taste. Hannah was forced to ask neighbours for water. They looked askance and refused, hoping Duvid's family would soon go away. Hannah was left desperate and ashamed.

PART III - POLES APART

57 Landing

The grinding sounds of the extending landing gear alerted Simon, and the palms of his hands began to sweat again. The plane banked smoothly to the left and below him, out the small window, he saw the compact farm fields, like so many green postage stamps set on a brown envelope. Terraced hills appeared in the hazed distance as the airplane approached the runway of the town of Lod, outside Tel Aviv.

He had left Kennedy airport in New York at two in the afternoon, after a gruelling few hours on a bench, watching exhausted as the departures board listed line after line of cancellations because of a storm along the Eastern Seaboard. By the time his plane landed at Lod, Israel's gateway airport, it was nine o'clock on the Middle East morning. He had been on the plane for fully twelve hours and he was fitfully tired.

Border security was tight. The Israeli guards kept asking him more searching questions. They stared at his passport photo and back at him, several times, reassuring themselves that this really was Simon Gryn. They asked him, in Hebrew, "*Ma shem avicha?*– What is your father's name?" which he couldn't understand. Switching to English, the guard asked him where he was staying, but he only had the address scribbled in Hebrew on a notepad.

"No hotel reservations?"

"No."

"Are you carrying anything that someone else has given you? Is there anything you're carrying which you didn't pack yourself?"

"No."

"What will you be doing on your visit?"

"I'm researching a story."

"You're a writer?"

"A journalist?"

"Do you have press credentials?"

Simon passed them over.

"What story?"

"It's not that kind of story. It's personal."

"You're researching a personal story? You're really a reporter?"

The two guards stepped back a little and conferred loudly among themselves. One called someone on his walkie-talkie and had a conversation which Simon didn't understand. Simon was getting irritated by now. He was tired, hungry, and badly in need of a shower. One of the guards stepped forward and continued the questioning while the other stayed on the radio device.

"Do you have an affiliation with a synagogue? With a Jewish organization, perhaps?"

Simon had no affiliation. He belonged to no Jewish religious organization, served on no board of a Jewish community group, had largely divorced himself from his ethnic and religious brethren years before.

"What is your Jewish experience?"

"I had my son circumcised." Having his son Matt circumcised had been difficult enough.

"All Americans have their sons circumcised. No bar mitzvah?"

"I'm not American. You saw my passport. I didn't want a bar mitzvah. It didn't mean anything to me."

"So, Canadian. No difference."

"Much difference."

"A little advice," the burly guard smiled, "don't talk too much."

The guards asked him to open his bag. Simon had to show them that his camera really worked, that it wasn't rigged with a bomb. He had to open the camera back after rewinding the roll of film. The guards stepped back again, muttered the words 'hakol beseder' at each step and passed him along to another in the hierarchy.

He was asked the same questions again by another team of interrogators further along the route out of the arrivals area. He resented the tone, even if he appreciated the need. Airliners were being hijacked regularly, and Lod Airport had been attacked by Japanese Red Army terrorists arriving by plane ten years earlier, with the loss of 26 lives. Hard lessons had been learned. Walking out through the doors of the airport to the taxi stand felt to Simon like walking into a furnace. The air shimmered with heat and humidity, and smelled of dust. The sun's light was attenuated by clouds of fine sand which had been lifted into the sky and blown in recently on a hot hamsin wind from the southern desert.

For Simon's body clock it was two in the morning. Despite his sleepiness, he had to argue a fare with the sherut driver, who sat quietly while he waited for his car to fill with passengers for the ride out of the airport. An impatient driver behind the first in line was yelling something in Hebrew while each passenger went through the ritual dickering. "Maher, maher, tazuz kvar!" the other driver yelled with considerable force. Simon translated this as encouragement to get going.

The road trip up to Jerusalem was quick, passing by low hills covered in stunted scrub rooted in the yellow-grey earth. Here and there they passed a settlement or a monastery, where growths of diminutive olives trees dotted terraced hillsides, and the tops of date palms thrust up beyond squat hillocks. The highway was thick with the brisk flow of traffic. Then, without warning, the city opened up in the vista ahead, its buildings gleaming with white stone. Simon, astonished, was overcome with awe and wonder, suddenly enlivened, where only moments before he had been nearly exhausted.

The cab stopped in one neighbourhood after another to drop each of the riders, finally leaving him off at the Central Bus Station on Jaffa Road. From there he took another cab the short distance south along Herzl Road to the front door of a centuries-old house of a friend in Beit HaKerem. It was low, built of pale Jerusalem stone, like most buildings in the city, with thick walls and surrounded by eucalyptus trees. From the description he had read in the letters from his friend, he remembered that the house sat a short hike from Hebrew University. Simon could, if he wanted to, take a vigorous walk along the Valley of the Cross towards the Old City in the east, past the Knesset, Israel's Parliament Building, and the Israel Museum, where the famed and controversial Dead Sea Scrolls were housed in the Shrine of the Book. A little to the south of where he would be staying stood the Herzl Museum and the Military Cemetery, and just to the west, Yad VaShem, the Israeli memorial to the victims of the Holocaust. The city was dense with historical and religious sites, Jewish, Christian, and Muslim.

As Simon stood in the doorway, Jerusalem, city of hills and valleys, glowed before him, its neighbourhoods set along the crests of hills overlooking dry rocky ravines below them. Along the outskirts of the city, to the west, he could see terraced hills covered in the new pine growth of the restored Jerusalem Forest. Near the valley floor, monasteries that had stood since the early centuries of the present era awaited the second coming of their saviour. Crossing the space between one hill and the next, Simon saw a dam without water behind it. There must be a story there, he thought, but too tired to pursue the thought, promptly dismissed it.

From where Simon stood, a man used to walking can pass along stony trails, following the paths incised into the limestone of these highlands by the hooves of sheep and camel over centuries, and arrive outside the walls of the Old City within an hour. In size it is a small city, but Jerusalem is ancient, the sanctified centre of the universe. For many it is the centre of the heart.

Here David sang his songs, Solomon built his temple, and Herod raged. Here Jacob dreamt, Jesus taught, and Mohammed rose to heaven, and here, before its loss, was stored the Holy Ark that held the Tablets of the Laws given to the Jewish people at Sinai. Below every footstep, pieces of history have accumulated, been built and abandoned, and built again. It is this jumble of stone on stone on stone that the Jews yearned to enter and to pray in from the time of their exiles, first by the Babylonians, later by the Romans, during millennia of wandering in a foreign world.

Simon hadn't been able to catch any sleep on the plane, nor much the night before the flight. He pulled the drapes shut and dropped into bed, wanting only to sink into sleep, but his electric mind buzzed. Could he find the missing pieces of his story here, in this land of ancient mystery and miracle?

Simon turned and punched at a pillow. He rotated onto his back and stared up at the wall. Two small immobile lizards clung there, waiting patiently for insects skittering about in the heat. In one moment he wondered how old this house was, in the next he was asleep. What seemed a moment later, his eyes opened again. The room was dark now, a pale glow from the windows casting trapezoids of light on the dark walls opposite. It must be shortly after sunset.

He had lived in this country as a child. How old had he been when he left? Five? Maybe six? The memories were dim, untextured and imprecise, of a dusty place, people with wide smiles and exuberant voices. Red earth, scrubby grass, gnarled low trees, emaciated goats. A brilliant nocturnal fabric of stars sprang into his mind. Rapid sunsets and slow pink dawns. Shared meals and ambulating between welcoming houses on the Sabbath. Outhouses populated by crawling red and black-bodied beetles that hurried his bowel movements, feral cats roaming free. Jackals howling and dogs barking wildly at night. Shouts and whistles from lookouts waiting for the enemy to appear.

He rolled out of bed onto his feet and walked to the east window. Jerusalem sat before him, mounted on the connected crests of these heights, a wiggling splash of urban pigment, brushed on the ancient crumpled parchment of eroded ground, painted in shades of bone, ivory, eggshell, and cream, pale amber, blond, and buff. Shadows in sepia and grey divided the awakening landscape.

Regrets and doubts, came into his consciousness, taking bites of his morale. A headache started, dissolved, and he walked in to sleep again. Tomorrow he would begin the chronicles, his interviews. When he woke up, Simon was very hungry. The room was in darkness. He pulled out of his bag the letters that he had found at the hotel. He roamed out onto the cement balcony, and by the faint early morning light, opened the packets. Within minutes, darkness fell away. A cool breeze had come up as the sun touched the horizon. Afraid that he would lose some of the frail papers to the wind, he turned back inside. Sitting down on the edge of the bed, he flicked on the bedside lamp and examined them.

Many were written in the Hebrew alphabet on cloth, old and ragged. The letters were pale, brown and faded. He recognized the language as Yiddish. Another was on onion skin paper, neatly folded, the lettering sharp, careful and florid. Simon surmised it was written in Polish, from what Simon had seen at other times. It started on its first line with one name: Miriam, but Simon understood no Polish and simply stared at the carefully placed letters. A number of lines were scratched out by a smear of black ink. This must have been a first draft, he decided–his father must have been nervous, trying to be sure he wrote exactly the correct words. What could it have been about, he wondered? Simon paused. A memory jumped up from the past, the name, Miriam, vaguely familiar, but he couldn't place it. He sounded out a few words at the beginning, haltingly, but quickly gave up. He tapped his head with his knuckles, trying to reconnect an old synapse, but nothing more came to mind. He put the delicate sheet aside for the moment and went on.

In another envelope, there was a single document on a heavier paper. It was in German. The letterhead included an eagle holding a swastika in its talons. There was a photo of a man in German uniform, his features stiff, a proud look on his face. Who was this? What was this material in these three envelopes all about, he wondered? Was his father telling him the story of his life, the one he had refrained from speaking about when he was still alive, or had he been hiding it? Was Simon trespassing?

Simon was too hungry to continue the inspection. There was still one envelope unopened, but what more could it contain than more of the inscrutable same. He put the letters away, placing them carefully back into the large envelope. He wondered at the ghosts of the past emerging in the faint afterglow of sunset. He would go out and find a restaurant. He didn't even know how to order anything.

The city was waking up. A man pedalled past him with a broom and a trash bin fixed in front of him. Dusty cabs whizzed by. A *haredi* man in a black suit and fur hat rushed forward towards synagogue, draped in a large tallit. A block further, an Arab man wearing a *keffiyeh* strolled forward carrying a large shopping bag. Everything around Simon was unfamiliar, but as he walked on, he seemed to recognize each object and view as if it was endowed with a second soul, as if he carried an invisible map of the world in his mind. Socratic chatter silently clashed with the hard-edged words of the Maccabees. He was too hungry to join the argument. At the corner of the next street he saw a restaurant. Food! He slipped through the door and confronted a menu in Hebrew and strangely phrased English. The waiter nodded at his quizzical expression and brought him a meal: pita bread, *tehinah*, a salad of finely chopped vegetables, Turkish coffee.

By the time Simon got back, jet lag was still strong enough to force him quickly asleep again. Tomorrow fell towards him. Today. Simon awoke. The Tower of David, all of Jerusalem, glowed in the spreading dawn. The golden city clung to its hilltops. Stone shadows slid firmly into sheltering valleys to escape the incandescent sun. In those shadows, clinging to the terraced hills, rough stone walls protected square fields of sparse grapevines and old gnarled olive trees a thousand years old. Realities were set in tiers and lamellae. The ground bristled with mosques and churches, temples and synagogues. All the world had at one time met here. It was the centre of time and space. Simon wanted to take the next few days off to visit his father's farm. He reached for the phone but stopped. He wasn't ready. It would be better to wait until his interviews were over and he could be better prepared.

He looked again over the list of interviewees and their year of arrival in Israel. Most were of an older generation, who had arrived in the early days of the new land after the war in Europe. Only a small number did fit the profile, Jews who had landed in Israel after escaping or being released from behind the Iron Curtain. Someone at head office must have screwed up, or maybe it was a misunderstanding at this end. He had called his researcher, but had been told that there weren't enough of the recent arrivals willing to be interviewed, that they all wanted an incentive. Just like back in the old country. Simon wasn't about to pay them. He would figure out a way to make it work.

58 Stories

Simon's first interviewee, Avrumel, had come from the Soviet Union and had managed to get to Israel by boat in 1950. They sat down together at a tea shop and Simon began.

"You came to Israel in 1950?" That small detail fitted the story guidelines, but nothing else.

"Sure."

"How would you say your life here has been?"

"Who can complain? Not me. You don't know all that I had to endure during the war. For me it wasn't wonderful here when I arrived. No one could say that. It was bad, especially for those few who had a child to care for. There was more war to come also. Many hardships, I tell you. Everything rationed, food scarce, even water at times. You never knew going out to the market in the morning if you might die from a sniper's bullet or be hit by a mortar shell. We lived in tents, but when the Arabs ran away, I moved into one of their abandoned houses. Very primitive, but an American like you wouldn't understand what that means. (Simon thought 'You mean Canadian,' but shrugged the thought away so the narrative would remain unbroken.) No water indoors. No electricity. No toilet. Where you come from, you live in luxury. Big supermarkets full of every food you can imagine and more. You never know danger. So it's a little cold sometimes, from what I hear, but what is worse, really, death or snow? I have seen both snow and death. I would choose snow, if it was really so simple.

"Even the hard life we had here then was nothing compared to the war in Poland. You know, the first days of the war were very exciting for a young boy, only sixteen. Airplanes flying so fast, so very fast, overhead. Polish soldiers rode past my town at night on horseback. They banged on our door, stole our food and drink, before moving on ahead."

"I really wanted to know about Israel."

"Israel? You know everything already. I just told you."

"What about bureaucracy?"

"Of course we had to wait in line to get papers stamped. Listen, we couldn't expect to have more than one stamp in a day. If there was a second document needed, it was on the other side of town, a different department. They wouldn't have anything to do with each other, those *apparacthiks*. And always a little *protexia*, someone you know, someone you don't know, a few *agarot* here or there to moisten the way."

"What?"

"Ah, I see there is no corruption where you come from in America. (Simon protested 'Canada! inside his head.) You are an innocent. You had to know someone, maybe pay a bribe. To get this paper, that stamp, this recommendation, see that official. But not worse than war. Never! When the Germans came through my town, in their ugly grey uniforms, with them they had a few special units on motorcycles with sidecars. Those wore black leather coats. They had lightning-shaped pins on their collars. SS. The Polish villagers came out to greet them and pointed us out.

We were ordered outside. The beatings began, then the thefts, the humiliations, the condemnations, the betrayals. Some said there was even worse to come. Most didn't believe them, but I did. For me, really, at the time I thought it was a chance for adventure. I didn't think I was escaping such a big danger."

"And, bringing you back to my question, did you see much hostility from the native Jews here?"

"What kind of questions do you ask? This is something someone in America really wants to know about? Let me tell you a real story."

Simon was becoming uneasy. This was not why he had come. He wouldn't deny this man his chance to get his story off his chest, though. Simon sighed.

"Go ahead. Tell me."

"Thank you. So I will continue, yes? It was a time for me to run off, leave this town, see new places. For me and my friends, we saw it as a bit of excitement. The roads were clogged with refugees trying to get east to Bialystok on the new Russian frontier. Let me tell you, I was like quicksilver, running between the fingers of the Germans.

"Only the Poles had the talent to recognize me as a Jew. I and my friend Asher entered a small village to buy bread with the few pennies we carried. I was surrounded, beaten, and my coins taken from me. They dumped me into the forest half-dead, half-naked.

"When I woke up, I had a terrible pain in my back and a worse thirst. The taste of earth was in my mouth. My mind moved back and forth between dim and clear, dark and light. I was in a fog until my anger roused me, and I finally got to my feet. I stumbled through the edge of the forest. I came across the Asher's corpse. I was the last one left of my group. All the others were by gone–captive, tortured, dead.

"Asher had always been a brash boy and he had died because of this. As I was pummelled I saw him trying to defend his belongings, stashed in his shoes and the lining of his jacket. Asher, he lay there in front of me, all bloodied. His head was broken. I tried to ignore this as best I could. I needed to survive. It overcame my horror.

"Asher's boots fit me well. By some miracle, only his warm jacket was gone. His killers had left the boots with the body. Maybe they had been frightened by something at the last moment. Who could know? The boots allowed me to walk past the border into Russia. Asher's shirt and pants kept me warm during the next nights. I covered my friend with leaves and twigs. I didn't have more strength than that."

Simon was hooked. He wanted to get up and walk away, chalk this up as a failure, but he needed to hear how the story ended. The interview he'd originally planned fell away.

"And then?"

"I escaped to Russia at the start of the war and worked in the coal mines near Uralsk. Food was tightly rationed and I was hungry. Each day I received my piece of black bread, only enough to keep me going. I had to choose each time whether to eat it all at once and be satisfied once during the day, or to divide it up, so I would feel something less than hunger in my belly several times a day. I always chose to eat it in one shot.

"Life was so difficult then. It could be over at any time, just like that." Avrumel snapped his fingers. "How could I know, if I had eaten the bread in divided portions, if I would live out the day and come to eat it all? Who knew if someone might steal the last piece from me later?"

"It was you who was being eaten. Eaten alive."

"No, it was my parents, my brothers, my sisters, who had been eaten alive. They all died in Treblinka. I was completely alone when the war ended. I kept wondering, did they think of me on their last walk towards eternity? Then, I decided, no, they thought only about something to eat.

"I stayed on in the Soviet Union until the war ended. I kept thinking of my family all that time. Not knowing if I was the last, I was determined to go on. That thought alone was what made me live until I could leave for a new life."

"And then?"

"What and then? There is nothing more I want to remember. I had to do things to survive that I would not have done if there was no war, no danger."

"But you said you would describe your ordeal."

"Yes, as much as I need to. That's all."

"Thank you," said Simon. He rose. He felt robbed. Something was missing, like all the missing details in his own parents' story.

"What are you thanking me for? For part of the truth? It is there, but it is not something that I own, that I can give away. It is yours, what I have said, and what I haven't, no one will ever know."

"It takes courage to speak of that."

"Yes, there you are right." He paused, sipped his tea, grimaced. It was cold by now. "All right, I'll tell you more. I had two young sisters, Gizella and Ruchelleh. I heard about what happened to them from Gizella later.

"My sisters were left in the care of a farmer by my mother. Gizella said that before taking them from our home, our mother told the two that if the Germans ever came, to say nothing to them. Nothing. Then she left them with the farmer. My mother returned in the afternoon, before the curfew. Ruchelleh was four then, and Gizella was six.

"Gizella told me that the farmer had the priest come to his home and convert her and Ruchelleh. The priest taught the girls to say the Ave Maria. One neighbour remembered the girls from his visits to the town, when he would sell his cabbages and potatoes to the Jews at the market. He came with the Germans and they had him ask the questions for them. He had seen them always together, he said, following their mother like ducklings did. He was sure of it.

"The Gestapo arrived at the farmer's door. The girls were brought out and questioned. The sisters denied they were Jewish, insisting that they were the farmer's children. The neighbour shook his head: no. The Gestapo man held a gun to the younger girl's head, and spoke to the older one. "If you don't admit you are Jewish sisters, I will shoot her." They both remained silent. Even after the younger girl's head exploded in front of her, the older girl said nothing, doing just as her mother had told her. She recited the prayer she had been taught, the Ave Maria. The Gestapo man was impressed, or perhaps amused, enough to let her live.

"She was saved by the Russians. Eventually she moved here, married, and had a daughter, whom she named Ruchella. My niece. Her daughter Aviva is now serving in the Israeli army. One time when my niece was very sick, Gizella hummed the Ave Maria next to her hospital bed in Tel Aviv. I was there next to her. The doctors lifted their eyebrows at me in surprise but didn't ask any questions. They muttered between them that the Polish Jews were an odd bunch, but there were plenty of Rumanian and Ukrainian Jews, all the Jews from Europe that I have ever met, who acted strange after the war, too. How can we not? So there, that's it."

"Is there anything that you need, anything I can do for you?"

"Yes, take my memories away. That is what I need."

"Yes, I know."

"But you can't do that."

"No."

No, he couldn't do that. Through hallway doors, he had heard his father struggling with his memories, ones that kept him awake at night, or brought him dreams from which he awakened in a sweat or flailing around, fending off shadows. He hadn't had any magic dust for him either. No answers. No advice that his father would accept from a wayward son.

Moishe was the next one on the list. Simon began on his list of questions again, this time trying to be more vigilant. He didn't want the interview sidetracked again.

"How long have you lived in this country, Moishe?"

"Me, oh, almost thirty-five years."

"You came here because you're a Jew?"

"Of course, because I'm a Jew. Anyone else would have to be crazy to come here to live."

"So you don't recommend it."

"Are you a Jew?"

Simon nodded. "Yes."

"So, yes, you should come here to live. Make *aliyah*! Yes!"

"Didn't you just say it's crazy to live here?"

"Listen, son, you have to be crazy to be a Jew, but once you are, you have little choice where to live. This is the only place we're free."

"That's not true. I come from Canada, and there..."

"Canada? That country that wouldn't accept any of us before the war?"

"We came over in 1957."

"Ah."

"So, was it hard here in the beginning?"

"In the beginning, sure. Ask your father. Did he have such an easy time in Canada when he first arrived?"

"I can't ask any more. My father died not long ago."

"Oh, I'm so sorry. May you be spared further sorrow."

"Thank you. Now, when you arrived...?"

"They handed me a gun and put me on a truck. I was fighting Arabs a day after I got here. Luckily I knew how to undo the safety catch. Some didn't and they died."

"My father also fought."

"You said before, you were from Canada."

"We came to Canada from Israel."

"Oh. Your family left, so now I understand all these questions. You want me to explain to you why he left. Well, I don't know. You should have asked your father while he still lived."

"He wouldn't say, but you're still here, with all the complaints."

"I like the heat and the dry air. It's good for my lungs."

"You're joking."

"Yes. Joking. I'll tell you something. This is all God's joke. He likes to laugh, and He put us here to provide Him some mirth. That's who is joking."

"What do you mean?" Simon put his pen on his pad, ready to write again.

"When the war was finished, I passed by train to a DP camp in Germany. When we were getting off the train, I saw this man I knew, Berger, who I had spent years with during the war, but later we had become separated until that moment. He had been chased from his home, like me. We had hidden in a farm together with the help of a good farmer, who took care of us, fed us, gave us a place to sleep. We had only to help him with the tasks on the farm. His two sons had been killed in the first days of the war. They were Polish cavalry and charged tanks on horseback, he told me. So he needed our help. Then one day the Germans came. We ran away when we saw them, but the farmer had a bad leg. He couldn't run so fast. They caught up to him in their vehicle and ran him over. Like that. They took his body and tied it to a tree. We saw them use it for target practice. When his wife came running out, they threw her in the well and threw in a grenade.

"They laughed, and then Berger began to laugh, there in the trees not far from the farmhouse. He couldn't stop. On and on, while the German turned to see where the laughing was coming from. I turned to him and pounded him until he stopped. Then we ran in different directions."

"So, the train station?"

"He told me there that he laughed because God wanted him to. Because God was laughing. That God always laughed. I hit him again and he ran. He looked back at me, still laughing, and stepped off the platform right into the path of a train. And do you know what? I began to laugh. Like it was a big joke and he had known it. That's why he died laughing. I couldn't stop, not until the crowd turned on me and started to beat me up."

"What are you telling me?"

"Think a little, that's all. I'm not telling you anything you don't already know. But about your father and why he left, you're asking the wrong man. Go ask about your father of someone else."

"Where? Who?" It wasn't working. Simon was losing his detached focus.

"Where did he live?"

"Someplace. A Moshav Azriel."

"So go there. Someone will remember him. Son, I've had enough questions. I'm tired. You have to go now."

Moishe laughed, on and on. While he was laughing, he cried too. Moishe's cheeks were wet with tears. When he stared into Simon's eyes, Simon could only look away.

"I'm sorry, "Simon whispered.

"You're sorry? For what? This is what you wanted. Don't pity me now. It is too late for that."

"I needed to know."

"And now, it seems, you still know nothing. Yes, I see that you are a hungry man. So, have I helped you?"

"Yes, very much."

"You are a fool. I haven't helped at all. You need more than what I can furnish."

Simon scratched one more name off his list. Some story he would write, one that his editor would toss into the wastebasket.

Next was Gershom, who had been a barber. Again little comment on Israel, more on the war years. Simon was becoming annoyed. Whoever had set up these interviews, they were not the right choices for the story he had had assigned. His editor wouldn't be pleased with stories of war in Europe, when he expected ones about immigrants from behind the Iron Curtain. He scanned down the list. There was another name, an Eli somebody, who had arrived during the sixties. Maybe he was a better prospect. Maybe this Eli could be next, but for now, Gershom was sitting in front of Simon. It was the war again. He didn't even bother with his list of questions. He just listened.

"I hid in the sewers during the war, fighting with the rats for rotten food. The sewers were one day flooded with gasoline and lit, and it was the rats escaping that gave me the message to get away. Others were unable to get out fast enough. I escaped being shot to death, as many were as they emerged from open manholes. I woke up in a railway car, not knowing how I got there. I was packed tightly between a mass of other bodies. When we got to the camp, I must have looked strong enough for the camp doctor to point me to the line of arrivals who were not put to death right away. I saw others walking the other way, not knowing what line I was in. Then came the number tattoo, the stripes, the hard work.

"They put me to work shaving the heads of the latest arrivals. Among these, I was appalled to find my sister. She looked awful, skinny as a rake, her eyes poking out of her face, all her fat gone. Her ribs poked through her skin. I cried as I cut her beautiful dark hair with my rough razor, chopping it off in swaths. Tears streamed from her eyes because she knew that she was about to die but she stayed quiet, for me, I think. She sat there naked in front of me, her hands across her chest to hide her breasts from my eyes, until her head was bare, and then was rushed off by the camp guards to the gas. The camp fell to the Russians only weeks later.

"I saved a curl of my sister's hair and stuffed it into a set of *tefillin* after the war. I bind one to my left arm, the other on my forehead, every morning before saying my prayers."

Eli wasn't answering his phone for now. It would have to be Menachem, then. This was the last interview he would do with the older group, Simon promised himself. It was becoming more that he could bear, but he also couldn't stop listening. Somewhere in these stories was that of his father. He had to find it, even if he knew this was the wrong place to look. All these stories were connected. They formed a net that would catch the truth.

Menachem's story began. "I was a lawyer. My office in Prague had a wall of books, law texts mostly, but also my religious texts. I loved books. In 1938, came the *anschluss*. I could no longer practice. On my last day, I hid one book, my mishnah, behind a moveable panel at the back of a bookcase. I watched from the street as all my other books were thrown out the window and burned.

I ended up a slave in a factory manufacturing armaments. A bombing demolished the building and I escaped and hid outside the city until the war ended. From the arms factory I had stolen a leather coat with an embossed swastika on one shoulder. I cut it off but I still felt it there whenever I put the coat on.

"After it was over, I made my way back to Prague, and by some miracle, the building that housed my office had had only light damage from the bombing. I opened the secret panel. I was overjoyed. My *mishnah* was still there, but badly damaged. The binding had disintegrated, pages had separated. I read from it that day, praying for the first time since the war had come. I brought it with me to Israel, where it sat on a table, injured, sad, broken, like I was. Tradition said I should bury it, but I couldn't–it was all that remained from my life before the war.

"Downstairs from my apartment, there was a bookstore. I visited it whenever I could, but I didn't have any money then and couldn't afford to buy anything. I would sit on a bench between the shelves all day sometimes, reading this or that. At the end of the day, the owner came to me and told me he was closing–could I please leave?

'Don't you have any books of your own?' he asked.

'Only one, broken,' I said, and told him my story.

'Bring it to me. Maybe we can repair it."

I did.

He shook his head as he looked at it. 'A shame.'

'So, can it be fixed?'

'I have rescued others like this, but this one is easy–this you'll do yourself. I will show you.'

"I had never sewn a stitch in my life, but day by day, with needle and thread and glue, I reconstructed it, repairing the stitching across the spine, setting the cover boards in place. It took me a good six months to finish, and then I fashioned a new cover from the leather coat I still had. The swastika I threw away, but I'll tell you something. The swastika, though it's not there, stares at me every time I open that book to pray. Maybe I should have buried that book after all."

Simon spent the afternoon wandering the streets of Jerusalem. He knew he should eat but he had lost his appetite. Why was he really here, he wondered? He had no one here. He needed badly to touch home, to have some contact with a benevolent universe. Not that he had really had anyone back home, except for his moralizing brother and his mother, sinking quickly into dementia since his father's death. He juggled names in his head. He was empty.

Simon needed a hiatus. After tomorrow, he promised himself. He had one more meeting the next day, the one with some younger escapee from the East.

Back at his lodgings, he reached for the telephone, then replaced it. Could he call Adam? Would he listen? Maybe. He was his brother. He had to.

No, he was sure Adam wouldn't without becoming critical, as usual. Simon couldn't tolerate the sarcasm just now. He felt completely alone in the world. Loss and rejection were everywhere. Except maybe with one person.

He dialled Rachel's number.

59 Dr. Busy

Rachel stared absently at the photographic print suspended on the line in her darkroom. A close-up of a round stone covered by a paper bag. The anonymous world without attachment.

Simon had been on her mind a lot the last three weeks or so. He had bypassed her defences, and allowed her to break through his, in the most disarming way. Yet when he had called yesterday, he'd sounded broken. He hadn't said why he had called, only that he was still in Israel and had still to visit his birthplace. No, he hadn't called Adam. He had sounded troubled and this had worried her. He loved her, he said. The declaration seemed genuine, not merely a result of his distress. Her impulse then had been to go to him, just jump on a plane and find him in Israel.

What had really concerned her was that he had only called her. Why did he make her his touchstone? Why hadn't he called Adam? It was even more than that. She was uneasy about herself, unbalanced, not sure of which of the two was really in orbit, which the centre of the universe. She had been having difficulty sleeping for the weeks since Simon had left her apartment that Saturday afternoon, and last night, after his call, which had woken her up at 2:00, she had gone out for a walk and taken photos of doorways and building entrances.

Rachel reached for the telephone, then dialled Adam's number in Montreal. A woman answered. Lyssa. Rachel hesitated. There would have been too much to explain, and it was very early morning. She dropped the receiver back in its cradle. Rachel then tried Adam's pager number. She hoped he would call back. To her surprise she only had to wait a few minutes.

"Hi, Adam."

"Hello. Rachel?"

"Yes, Adam, it's me."

"Rachel? I'm really busy with patients."

"Adam, this isn't a social call. I'm worried about Simon."

"What about?"

"Adam, I saw Simon when the two of you were in New York a few weeks ago."

"I know. You and he weren't just talking, were you?"

"No. He told you?"

"I worked it out. You haven't changed, Rachel."

"Adam, I've grown up a bit, hard as that may be to believe. Look, aren't you worried about Simon yourself?"

"What's this all about?"

"Do you know where he is now?"

"No, I don't know."

"I just spoke with him during the night—by phone, I mean. He's in Israel. He's going down to the desert. To converse with God, he said. I think he was kidding. I hope."

"Scary. Did he say anything more? He's left Catherine, you know. He told me he was going on an assignment, but no details. I didn't ask. It sounded routine to me. I haven't spoken to him since that weekend, though."

"He said he was planning to visit some place he was born. I didn't catch the name."

"The *moshav*?"

"Yeah, that sounds like it, I think. I don't speak Hebrew, you know."

"I wonder what he wants to do there?"

"He sounded bad, Adam. Like this was the end of the world for him. I'm worried. Aren't you?"

"Why should I be?"

"Your brother has just left his life behind and hasn't contacted you in weeks. You should be worried. You really are his brother, aren't you? He's not just another patient."

"Okay, Rachel, I am worried. But he's an adult. He can make his own choices."

"I want to go there."

"You'll just get yourself into trouble, like you have before. Maybe you should just walk away."

"I can't."

"Why not?"

"I think I'm in love with him."

"So something did happen that afternoon. I had a feeling when I saw him."

"Do you think he can feel the same way about me?"

"I don't know. I don't seem to know him anymore. Maybe that's why he called you, not me."

"I'm going to find him."

"No, Rachel, think this through first."

"And who will look after him?"

"I'll go."

"You, Dr. Busy?"

"I can do it. I only have to cancel a thousand patients."

"You always were the rational brother."

"Goodbye, Rachel Thanks for letting me know."

"Maybe I'll see you in Israel."

"Take it slow, Rachel."

Adam put the phone down. He was surprised Rachel had called. Something very powerful was grinding inside her. Love. Well, maybe, but maybe not. Rachel had always been a tough bird to figure. She had meant to shame Adam and had succeeded. It was a tactic Jewish women learned from their mothers. Rachel was not one to feel shame, but she understood its application very well. Adam felt the force of it now.

Too much grief for Simon to bear. Adam nodded. Adam had seen Simon fall apart at Matthew's graveside. Then when their father had died, it had been too much for him, a lot even for Adam, the less emotional of the two. Too many endings. Too much change, even though the focus of Simon's life was just that, change—veers, shifts, alterations, modifications, evolutions and revolutions. Except he called it news, or journalism. It was about change—small, large, enormous—change. They all added together. Some shifts were bigger than they seemed. Some had little significance, even if at the time they boasted of great import, or revolved around big things. Big things. Big things and small people, that was history. Big people and small things, that was the news. It took time to pass to know the difference. Yet no amount of time would make a difference here, Adam knew. Simon had lost both his father and his son, the links that connected the past and the future.

Simon had sometimes spoken to Adam of the slow mutation that took the familiar and ripped its soft skin off and replaced it with sandpaper, gave it razor teeth and a desire for blood. He needed to understand his own self, Adam had told him. He couldn't do that by investigating the world. Being an observer wasn't enough. It was passive aggression writ large. Adam thought he knew better than Simon. He had to actively repair the damage that had been done, restore things, heal the world. This was how he could at the same time restore himself.

Brothers are never all that different, Adam knew. They just keep on fighting each other. What a mess life is.

Adam sat staring at the phone. His brother was such an idiot. He hadn't changed since they were young, with his theatrics and his flair for the dramatic gesture. So what was Simon really looking for? What was this all about, these big things—the separation from home, from his marriage, his wife and his family, the relocation to a difficult land? It might all rip him into pieces.

At the wedding in New York, Adam had advised Simon to take a happiness break. Drive to a beach, spend an evening with a friend having ice cream and coffee. Simon had agreed. What Simon had done was not what Adam had meant. Running away from home, which this was, that was for kids, Adam knew. Running off to the "Promised Land", no less. As far as Adam was concerned, Simon was acting out a fairy tale. Was he just killing himself slowly? Simon flew the world, examining the big issues. Adam worked on the small ones, each human being one at a time. Could he really help Simon?

Should he fly out to see his brother? Yes, he had to go. Even if he wasn't sure how to find him.

60 Phantoms

The Negev Desert is in constant flux. Light and colour shift and blend, day bending into evening and night stretching into dawn. The seasons reiterate, recorded in a heritage of stones. Each successive day has its distinctive character, yet echoes from one year to the next. Countless desert tribes long gone saw the same scenes, Edomites, Amalekites, Nabateans, Israelites, and on through centuries, and now Bedouin and Jew. It has stood on the rim of ensuing empires, its tented wanderers elusive.

Winter brings its cold rains, cleansing away the dust of summer. The dense soil engorges with a fleeting abundance of water. A fuzz of grass and desert flowers blooms briefly each spring on the rounded rocky hills. Nomadic flocks of goats and sheep are still led through these scrubby hills, depleting these miserly thrusts of spring growth, drinking from secret cisterns carved into the bases of the rock-strewn foothills, where dwarf desert trees stand sentinel. Year on year, hooves gouge deepening paths into the stone of these hills.

Negev summers scorch. By day the air lifts water out of leathery skin. Against this heat, desert creatures conceal themselves under stones and sand. Its people shelter in bituminous robes. The heat generates a miserly sweat, the black cloth wetted only enough to carry off the excess of the body's heat, yet not enough to dehydrate. It is a delicate balancing act, performed before a remote desert God. The act has been refined over millennia, engraved into the nomadic heritage as the herds have engraved the stones they scamper over. For them it has long been written. Simon walks in this desert. The sun rises in early morning. The only sound is the faint whir of sand grains as they quietly sigh past each other and heap together, covering the past perfectly. Shadows reach long here, where wood has become stone, petrified debris from unknown ages long gone. Stones beckon all around him, broken, crystal, cambrian, permian, cast in shadow, casts of the death that all life has known.

Simon's mood softens in the desert's quiet and solitude. Its heat instructs calm. Where is God in all this space, all this passage of time? Silence answers, silence speaks.

Stones whisper of ages past, long before the Bedouin, before Jew, before the first men traversed this forbidden landscape as they passed from the womb of Africa to populate the entire Earth. Not far away, the Dead Sea, deepest point on earth, straddles a line where the earth is splitting. Here hide the remains of Sodom and Gomorrah, burnt and crushed beyond recognition, where sulphur and fire long ago boiled up and then fell from the sky.

In a vast canyon of rock and fossil, the desert and sea are separated by time and united by space, in which they are are merged in impenetrable darkness and uncluttered silence. This is the passage the children of Israel traversed, in their transit from the desert of Sinai into the lands to the west of the Jordan River. This is where, during their long desert sojourn, they massed before their great push into these lands full with history, myth and faith, where terrible battles were to be waged. Every stone here is witness to this grand traverse. Stones are scattered all around, patient stones, sifted out from ages of erosion. They speak with silence as the sun rises to the pulsing rhythm of God's song.

The air is clear, but off towards the red hills to the east, a column of dust hints at a storm soon to come. Simon inhales deeply, savouring the small volume of air. It tastes of time and complexity. This air has passed through many creatures during the long passage of terrestrial time: the gills of giant salamander-like creatures, the tube-like respiratory channels of ancient dragonflies, their wingspan a foot across, the lungs of reptiles, tearing flesh from the bodies of other reptiles, and on to him, Simon, exchanging carbon dioxide for oxygen with trees and grasses far away. A noble and useful transaction, with such a long history.

Where did it start? How, at what moment, did that first animal creature, organizing the stuff around it, manage to extract this once-poisonous gas, oxygen, created in the furnace of some giant red star before it exploded so long ago, before it was gathered again by its gravity into the chemistry of this planet. What novel creature learned in its molecules to use this element's powerful electrons? How did it develop its ability to subvert the mission of oxygen, turn it from darkness to light, from death to life? When was it able to kick energy out of organic material and produce heat and enough usable biochemical energy to generate movement, protein synthesis, cell division: to produce life?

Was it, as it is written, on the fifth day after the cosmologists' Big Bang, when the creatures of the soil and of the air were created? The next day man was born. That man, Adam, rested the day following, on the first Sabbath, next to God, but his wife, Eve, had not yet been created. She did not experience that first Sabbath, that one authentic Sabbath, except as Adam's rib, and has not truly rested since.

But something in this sequence was missing. The plants of Genesis were made on the third day, the day before the sun and the moon were placed in the sky. What light did they use to combine carbon dioxide and water to produce sugar as their energy source and poisonous, corrosive oxygen as a by-product? Was it the mysterious first light of Creation, later overwhelmed by the exuberance deriving from our local star, the sun? That sun was now well into the sky. That faint light of creation, still arriving from the time of the Big Bang, the first moments of creation, was overwhelmed by the light of the sun.

Simon bends down, fingering stones full of past and meaning. He picks up one small stone, then another, rolls them in his fingers. He places one stone in his pocket, throws the other away, two brother rocks, now together, now apart, sharing a broken history. Long before, Moses brought two rocks from Sinai, two brother rocks, then shattered them in his rage. Where are they now, these stones, bearing their message now lost, reduced to rubble?

At last, the sun dips low, touching the western horizon, and a brisk wind blows in as the *machtesh* slips backwards through its realm of shadows. Simon shivers and stands up, watching the sun disappear and the stars quickly blink into existence in the sudden blackness of the sky overhead.

He revisits a dream of his long-dead grandfather, cutting through the silence of time and the grave to touch Simon's recoiling face with its scrawny fingers, while in his bed to one side, his brother screams in terror. His mother rushes in holding a glass of water. The thirst in his dream flows out into this darkened desert, and Simon craves water. This idea of the water seizes his mind.

In the desert, water is survival. As a child, Moses rode water. He was plucked out, to later lead his people to freedom. When he died, in his one hundred and twentieth year, he still had his moisture. This is taken to mean that he had not lost his sexual strength, was still capable of inseminating a woman. Perhaps, even at that age, he was. It was another epoch, a time of miracles. So says the Book of Exodus. Hidden from the sight of his people, he was open to that of his all-seeing God. After him, his seed continued on the paths they were to wear into the hills of history. They carried God's wetness with them.

Simon swims in that wetness, hoping that his father hasn't forgotten him. Simon waits to be plucked from the river. He wants to go home.

Simon drove his rented Fiat back from his meeting with Tzvi in Rehovoth. Orange trees hanging heavy with fruit lined both sides of the town's streets. Delightful. Tsvi worked at the Technical Institute here. He was another survivor, but Simon had not sought the man out to hear his history, but for the languages he was fluent in. English, of course. He was an academic, after all. Hebrew also, of course. The man had been in the country for over thirty years.

"The others languages?"

"Polish. Russian. Yiddish. German. French. Italian." A walking Tower of Babel, it seemed. "Like most here. We all speak several languages." Simon asked him if he would look over some papers he had with him.

"Of course. I do this all the time. I'm partly retired. I have not much else to keep me busy."

They met near the man's apartment. After most of Simon's questions were fended off, the man took the bag of scraps and rags with tiny writing on them, and pulled each one out, delicately flattening it on the kitchen table. He held each up to the light streaming through the kitchen window. Tsvi muttered, alternately scratching or shaking his half-bald head.

"These letters, they look vaguely like Yiddish, but the cloth is torn and coming apart. The ink is faded and some has flaked off, but I can read them. They talk about death, that his duty is to amuse death, crazy talk. There is nothing in these that make any sense. I'm very sorry. They may as well be blank. What are they?"

"My father hid them away while he was alive. I thought they might say something about him."

"There's no story here, I'm afraid. It's too bad. You've come a long way to learn nothing."

"That's really disappointing. I had hoped for more. There are others, different."

"Not like those scraps?"

"No. Here, look at this." Simon handed Tsvi the German document.

"This you have kept so long? Why? You should be better rid of it. This man was an officer in the *Schutzstaffel*–the S.S."

"Why would my father have had this in his possession?"

"I don't know. I don't expect anyone could answer that question now. It's too late. Take my advice. Throw it away. It's an abomination."

"What about this?" Simon took back the other documents and handed over the onionskin.

"Hmm. This is different still. This, this looks like a poem. It's in Polish. Something about walking, no, marching, let's see, to Jerusalem. And here, some biblical references. The language is quite provocative. Risqué, even. I could take it to translate it and bring it to you another time. Poetry can be quite a challenge to do properly. Anything else?"

"Yes. This."

"Ah, this is in Hebrew prose. It will be simple to translate."

"About?"

"Let's see, it starts about the telephone ringing, then some war. But it's a very long description and I have another appointment this morning. I can't finish it right now. Why don't we meet again another day and I'll describe what it says then?"

"I'm not staying near here. I'm going to be in Jerusalem for the next while."

"I tell you what, let's walk over to the post office and you can make copies there. Keep the originals with you. I can come up to Jerusalem to meet you. I have two grandchildren there that I haven't seen since Hanukkah. This will be a good excuse." Tsvi dug a photo from his wallet.

"Cute."

"What do you mean, cute? They're beautiful. You Americans, everything is cute for you."

"Of course they're beautiful. But I'm Canadian."

"Canadian, American. What's the difference?"

Simon's rented car had a manual drive. He hadn't quite gotten the knack of clutching and shifting gears simultaneously. He almost stalled heading uphill on the road to Jerusalem. Busy traffic zipped impatiently past him. A large transport truck raced up the slope behind him, forcing Simon off the road into the gravel. A stream of Hebrew expletives and the bleats of the trucker's horn shook him more. Other cars accelerated past the truck, flying from left and right, almost colliding. A set of indignant wails erupted from the truck's horn, and the intensified pitch of the its engine startled him and he steered away. His car slid a little and then he realized it was continuing to slide. A scrambled exit a second later and he stood watching as the car edged off the gravel shoulder and down the steep slope. A grind of metal against rock sounded from somewhere below. Several cars had pulled off the road and the drivers stood around him, discussing, pointing, and gesticulating. He didn't understand anything they were saying. Soon, a police car pulled up, its blue dome light flashing. Hebrew again, with a little English. Simon had some explaining to do.

Two hours later, the police car dropped him at his rented house in Jerusalem. Once back, and quite shaken, he went out on foot and bought himself a beer. He sat heavily on his cement balcony and sipped it, and decided he disliked Israeli beer. It was watery and flat, no match for the brew he knew back home, but it worked its work on him. His head cleared. Maybe he should stay put in Jerusalem for a few days, just be a tourist. He hadn't seen the city sights yet. Here he was in the city at the centre of the world and he hadn't spent even an hour exploring it. The passed most of the next day at the car rental agency, working out the insurance details.

Tsvi's assessment of the written materials had really disappointed him. He had hoped they would give some clue about his father. Well, there was still the *moshav* with its possibilities, but not yet. The man in Rehovoth had promised to bring the translations around within a day or two. That meant four days in Middle Eastern, maybe five. At the accident scene, the policeman had told him it would be best not to drive any more. Tomorrow, he had an interview already set up with a man who was living in the city. The *moshav* would have to wait.

For Adam, fresh off the plane, it was a dusty ride along the coastal highway to the north that Friday morning. When he had called the *moshav* from the airport, the tone of the manager on the phone had changed from challenging to welcoming after he explained his parents' history. He had just been asked to arrive before dusk.

The terrain had gone through considerable changes as the *sherut* travelled the highway from Lod Airport, and then north away from Tel Aviv. An ancient wrecked jalopy lay rusting along the side of the road. They had already passed a number of crumbling heaps sleeping in the dirt near the road along the way, as if their occupants had simply left them there and walked away. It was typical. Israelis didn't clean up after themselves. Adam shook his head as his taxi motored past them, appalled and mystified by the lack of concern that Israelis displayed for the land they fought so hard to hold.

A little after midday, he was dropped off at the bus stop next to Moshav Azriel. It seemed the obvious spot to begin the search for Simon. Adam felt relieved. Not knowing the road and the distances involved, Adam had worried that he might arrive in this observant community after sunset on the Sabbath. It felt like the middle of nowhere.

He removed his hat and jacket and placed them on his valise on the bus stop bench, then sat down next to it and waited. He was thirsty and sweating profusely. The hot sun hung directly overhead as if waiting for some governance from him on which direction it should travel. Adam fanned it along in its proper direction with his hat, and the sun dutifully but slowly obeyed. Amused by the simple move, he turned to fanning himself. A cloud of fine *café-au-lait* dust fluttered up behind the receding taxi.

Across the road was another seemingly neglected bus stop. Sheltered under the shade of a single tree, the twin of his low wooden bench teased him. Like everything else here–the road, the leaves of the tree, the bus stop, the valise–it was coated in dust. There could not be much coming and going here, but that suited him fine. He had called the moshav office earlier to let them know he was coming. All he had to do now was wait here.

To the side of the road next to where he had been dropped off grew a thicket of low trees, and next to them short scrubby grasses spread away to the right and left. The road itself cut through a cluster of farmer's fields. The chitter of crickets proclaimed the air temperature, if only he had the formula for figuring it out.

Another dust cloud appeared above the edge of the rise. He saw it before he heard the rumble of the tractor motor, and that before he saw the vehicle itself. In the plate-metal-reinforced cab a head and shoulders was enveloped in shadow. Being pulled behind it was a four-wheeled flatbed bearing a young woman. She was waving and exuberantly shouting his name.

"Adam! Adam!"

The tractor lurched and stopped. The dust cloud caught up and whispered past. A young man about Adam's age jumped down and grabbed his suitcase and hefted it onto the back of the trailer. His hair was a little long, in need of a barber, his face clean-shaven and deeply lined. He pumped Adam's hand energetically. "Welcome to Moshav Azriel. Come," he yelled above the noise of the engine. He seemed to have a good knowledge of English. His voice was smooth and throaty. It carried in it a murmur of authority.

"Natan," he stated simply, introducing himself and beckoning Adam onto the rear of the wagon.

Natan grasped Adam's right hand again with his own, then pushed Adam's grasp into that of the young woman and introduced her, again in a loud voice. "Kinneret, my sister." Her grasp was both delicate and powerful.

The dry dust settled on Adam's skin on the way to his destination, the farm that was once his father's.

"Ah, finally, you've arrived. The Sabbath will be here before long."

Kinneret was a little younger than Adam. Her skin was the colour of light coffee, her eyes dark whirlpools that trapped the brilliant light entering them. Her cryptic features transmuted into a gentle, shy smile that lightly decorated her lips. Her cheeks were rounded and looked polished, a fine sheen of sweat glistening in the bright sun.

"We're here," she shouted when they arrived at a house. "Come inside, it's too hot in the sun."

Adam followed Kinneret into the parlour. Her expression hard to read. The young woman looked at her brother, nodded, then left the two men alone.

"Sit, sit."

Adam sat as directed.

"Have you heard from my brother Simon, perhaps? I expected that he might have been here."

"No, not at all. You're the only one of your family here. Is he coming, too? How wonderful." He looked up and smiled. "Ah, my wife, Shoshana."

Natan's wife was carrying a siphon bottle and a variety of concentrated juices in tall glass bottles, bowls filled with citrus fruit and chocolates. A moment later, Kinneret brought a tray with a metal coffee urn. Small cups were soon filled with thick Turkish coffee and passed around. Adam sat quietly, self-conscious about his ability to speak Hebrew less well than a four-year-old, the age at which he had left Israel with his parents. The conversation lumbered along woodenly, while the afternoon quietly gathered itself for its plunge into evening. Men from the neighbouring houses came by, prepared to go to the synagogue for the afternoon and evening prayers. They fell into an animated discussion.

"Do you join us, Adam?"

"No," he answered in a hesitant tone. Natan smiled patiently. A foreign Jew could not be expected to be like him. "I understand, Adam. You must be tired from your trip. Take a shower now and then rest. We will eat when we return and then we can talk. It is wonderful that you could come for the Sabbath. I have the honour of my son Ariel's bar mitzvah tomorrow morning. Of course you will join us?"

"I don't have my suit and tie with me."

Natan translated the comment to the other men, and they all burst out laughing.

"None of us do. Don't worry, you won't need them here."

"Then you will lend me a *kippah* and a *tallit*. I didn't bring those either."

Again a translation. Again a burst of laughter.

"You are our guest. It would be our privilege to provide what you need."

"Thank you. I feel honoured."

"Adam, my friend, I have a favour to ask."

"Go ahead." Adam had taken on the local custom of speaking bluntly without fanfare or vagueness.

"I would like to call you up to the Torah tomorrow."

"I don't read Hebrew very well."

"You can say the prayer before and after the reading? It's not hard."

"Maybe, with your help. I'll have to think about it."

"We will speak later. For now, rest. Kinneret, show him to the bathroom"

The girl showed him the way and handed him a towel and some soap. "When you are finished, I can to show you around our orchards, if you will so like. The men will not have returned from prayer yet."

"I would like that."

"We don't want that you get bored at our so exciting *moshav*."

When he was ready, Kinneret took Adam out for a tour of the citrus orchard near the house. They sat in the shade of an orange tree for a few minutes, its ripe fruit hanging precariously above their heads. All around them the land was peaceful. The only sounds were the tickle of grass waving on a light breeze and the clamour of crickets complaining of heat. Kinneret passed a bottle of water to Adam. She started to say something in broken English when a roar tore the air above their heads. Adam looked up searching for its source. The harsh sound came again while his eyes were still dazzled by the sky's light. He caught the quickly disappearing silhouette of a jet flying only fifty metres above his head.

"*Pantomim*," Kinneret muttered, while another jet flew low over the orchard.

Israeli Air Force jet fighter-bombers, heading north to the Lebanese border. A dull rolling rumble strained the air for a half minute, then silence filled the air again. Somewhere in the distance the planes were already dropping their bombs, far out of earshot range.

"The Syrians have been throwing *katyushas* at the kibbutzim to the north again. This is our response. Then there will be more. It never ends." With that she got up and paced off quickly through the trees. She moved off quickly and Simon had to scramble to his feet to catch up. A minute later, she was standing close to a double barbed wire fence.

"Years ago, before the Six Days War, this is where they used to try to come through."

"The terrorists?"

"Yes."

"The border is now at the Jordan River, no?"

"True, that is where they try to cross. When they do, we find them and they are killed, but not always right away. Sometimes one or two or three will succeed to sneak in at night. They invade a school and hold the children hostage, or ambush people driving along the road, or mine the road. Then they are killed."

Kinneret turned and waved to the left. Adam followed her smile to a metal guard tower on stilts which stood only ten metres away. Whoever was in it waved back, then returned to the task of watching.

"We still watch, even if the border is now much further. You never know. Anyway, let's go back. You are hungry, yes?"

When Adam and Kinneret returned, the Sabbath candles were lit and had burnt down a quarter their lengths. Natan sat at the head of the table. Shoshana wished all there a good Sabbath. Natan handed Adam a *kippah*, and then rose and said the prayers over the wine and then the bread. Shoshana returned to bringing the evening meal to the dinner table. Outside the window, Adam saw that the sun hanging low in the sky, and then, suddenly, it was night. Adam was surprised at the speed of the sunset, the lack of twilight. The curve of the atmosphere above his head rapidly became a deep azure, and after fifteen minutes, he caught the glimmer of a star here and there.

Two children bickered at the table until Natan brusquely told them to stop.

"My wonderful children. They're not always so rude."

"That's all right. Children should be lively."

"You have children?"

"Just one. A daughter."

"Wonderful."

Conversation came to a halt for a minute, except for the liveliness of the children. Attention turned to the food. Supper was replete with meat and vegetables, challah and wine. The first course, after the prayers over the wine and the challah was patties of ground fish.

"Gefilte fish. I didn't know this was a Yemenite dish."

"It isn't. It is European, but so was my father. We have adopted it."

"Where do the fish come from? The Sea of Galil?"

"Ah, what you speak of, the Galil, is the northern half of our land, the Galilee, not the Sea. That we call the Kinneret. That is where my daughter got her name. The *notzrim*, the Christians, call it by the name you used."

"The fish are from there?"

"No. We have fish farms along the Jordan River, where the fish are raised in artificial ponds. We grow white fish, carp, tilapia, and now new varieties. We sell to Europe, even."

"The 'we' you refer to, it is not you on this farm?"

"No, we, the Jewish people, the Israelis."

"Ah. How do you know so much about fish?"

"My father trained as a biologist in Europe before the World War. His main area of study was fish. He even had the nickname 'The Fisherman.' He advised on the first fish farms near the River Jordan. I was told that he was a very funny guy."

"Only heard? Why?"

"He died when Kinneret and I were very young."

"I'm sorry."

"It was long ago. I don't remember him very well. He especially loved to talk about fish, but he didn't like fish as food. He and your father built this farm from dry earth and rocks."

"I'd like to know more about that. Where is your son Ariel?"

"He ate quickly before. He's in his room studying for tomorrow morning."

The main course of chicken arrived just then at the table. Natan stopped the discourse there. "It is time to eat now, before the food grows cold. We will talk later."

At the end of the meal, dried fruit and nuts were served with glasses of sweet tea. Afterwards, while the women cleared the table, Natan invited Simon out for a walk.

"So, my sister showed you my farm earlier?"

"Yes, it is beautiful. So is she. You should be proud to have such a beautiful family."

"Yes, of course I am."

Both Adam and Natan stared up into the stars above their heads. Adam thought about Duvid, and the effort it must have taken to found this farm community.

"Where was my father's farmland?"

"You are standing on it, Adam. My farm is large, larger than that of the others."

"Why is that?"

"Your father gave us his land when he left."

"He simply gave it away? That was a generous thing to do, no?"

"Yes. We never heard from him again after he left. Of course I was only a child then. I don't remember much. My mother's brothers helped take care of it until I was old enough to look after it myself."

"You are all one community."

"We came here when Yemen threw us out. We were offered this land on the old border with Jordan. That way we would have something of our own to defend."

"Your father was not from Yemen, though."

"No, he was your father's friend. They fought in the war in Europe together."

"When did your father die?"

"During the Sinai campaign. He and my father fought in the same unit. You don't know? No, of course you don't."

Natan told Adam what he knew of the story of Duvid parachuting behind enemy lines in the Sinai desert, along with his father, as part of a small squad of men under his command.

"When Duvid was found two days later, he was alone, sitting in a *wadi* with his back against an Egyptian tank. Something is missing from this story."

"What?"

"It's just strange. There had been a battle. There were many dead, my father included. I am told it took months for your father to be able to speak again. When he was better, or what the doctors, the psychiatrists, called better, he came back here. My mother told me that he wasn't well. He did strange things. He either didn't remember anything, or wouldn't talk about it. After a few months he said he was giving us his farm, that he could no longer stay. He left for Canada and we never heard from him again. He never said anything to you about it?"

After a long pause, Adam responded. "Nothing that made any sense."

"What about your mother?"

"No, she didn't say a thing. Maybe she never knew. Maybe she did."

"She must have known. That generation did not speak."

"No, it wasn't their way."

"Let's go back in. We have a guest here at the *moshav*. She is dropping by for tea. Perhaps you would like to meet her."

When Natan and Adam got back, Kinneret and Shoshana were sitting at the kitchen table with an older woman. Other than Adam, all were dark-complexioned, except the older woman. She seemed in her late fifties or early sixties.

"This is Miriam, our newest arrival. She came here only a few weeks ago. Miriam, meet our guest, Adam."

The still-blonde older woman turned with a ready smile, her hand firmly grasping Adam's, and looked into his eyes. There was a moment's pause. She gasped. Then she fainted, pulling Adam down with her. There was a mad scramble as everyone in the room seemed to converge on the prone body. Natan knelt and slapped her hands. There was a debate in Hebrew over what should and shouldn't be done.

"You're a doctor, no?" asked Kinneret.

Adam bent down and checked her pulse and breathing. They were normal. She had only fainted.

"She's okay. Just give her a little air. She should wake up in a minute. Do you have a flashlight?" One was quickly passed to him.

While he spoke, the woman was already beginning to recover. Adam checked her pupils. They were round and equal. With the flashlight, he saw that the pupils reacted well. A light moan issued from her, and her hands waved about. Reassured that she probably hadn't had a stroke and seemed to be recovering, Adam rose and stood back. Kinneret slipped down next to her and propped the woman's head on her lap. She held a glass of cold water to Miriam's lips and spread a wet napkin on her forehead.

The old woman opened her eyes then spoke.

Kinneret translated. "You. You. Who are you?"

Adam was confused. Why had she reacted so strongly when she saw him? What was going on?

Kinneret reached up and pulled on Adam's hand, dragging him closer to the old woman's face. "Miriam, this is Adam. From Canada."

Shoshana passed Miriam a glass of brandy and helped her to sit up. Miriam began to speak to Adam in Hebrew.

Adam asked Kinneret, "What is she saying to me? She seems to know me."

"She says you have given her a big shock. You look just like her son's father."

"Please tell her I don't know her."

"No one here knows her. She walked into the *moshav* only a month ago."

"From where?"

"She hasn't said. She says it's too long a story and no one would believe her anyway."

"What made her come here, of all places?"

Kinneret translated Adam's question.

"To find the father of her son. This is the last location she knew for him. She asks if you are a tourist?"

"She seems to know her Hebrew well, for a newcomer."

"She says she learnt it as a child."

"So did I, but I don't remember much of it. Tell her I came here looking for my brother. He and I were born here, years ago. We left with my parents when we were still young."

Miriam looked closely at Adam's face again. She asked another question.

"What is your family name?"

"Gryn."

Miriam mouthed the name. "Gryn. Gryn. Ken. *V'shem avicha?* What is your father's name?"

"His name was David."

"Was?"

"He died less than a year ago."

Miriam gasped and put her hand to her mouth. She spoke rapidly, stumbling over her words.

"She is so very sorry."

Miriam looked pensive, before another barrage of words fell out of her mouth.

"Adam, could your father have been Duvid Grynsztyn?"

"Yes." Adam said the word slowly, drawing out the letters. He eyed Miriam closely.

"And your brother is your twin, isn't he?"

"How do you know that?"

"I remember your father's letter."

Adam was silent for a moment. He needed to hear more.

Adam spent the next afternoon. Saturday, talking to Miriam. Because it was the Sabbath, he wrote nothing down. It was the day of rest, the most holy day of the week, and writing was considered work. The people of the *moshav* took it very seriously. In the evening, Miriam recalled Duvid, long gone from her life. She described memories of the Polish forests, years where she and Duvid's muted love sat silent, almost dead, while the war stormed around them.

She described their separation, her despair thinking that he was dead, her 'liberation' by Russian troops, her banishment to the Ural

Mountains, her son Eli's birth in the prison camp. Her son had been taken from her years ago, sent out to the world. Never again to be seen.

She had escaped during a winter storm and found shelter with herders who took her north, then south, then east and west, everywhere but where she wanted to go. With them, she had eventually crossed the border into Turkey, and from there found her way laboriously to Jews there, who directed her to an Israeli mission.

She had come here because of his letter to her. Her son Eli had been here years earlier, she was told. He had visited once, probably for the same reason as hers, looking for a trace of his father, but he had never come back. Where he was now, she didn't know. He could be in Israel somewhere, but could just as easily have travelled anywhere else in the world. She had reached a blank wall. Duvid and Eli had both vanished. This would be the end of her journey.

Adam listened as Miriam spoke, and then to the recollections about his father by members of the *moshav*. He really didn't understand. His memories were of a troubled man, withdrawn and silent; Adam couldn't square the circle of his father. It all seemed so wrong, that this broken man had once been a true hero, full of life, grateful for all the joys that life had brought, all its hope and its wonders. Duvid had left his sons with a bewilderingly distorted sense of who he was. The things he had accomplished were kept in the shadows. What would Simon say to all this, if Adam could ever find him?

The Sunday following was a normal workday in Israel, where the week's end was still the one ordained in Genesis, a single day of complete rest. Adam could move on now. He was in Israel to find his brother, and that brother was not here. He would have to look somewhere else. He gave Miriam the telephone number at the hotel where he would be staying. As an afterthought, he insisted she take his number in Canada, too.

"Where is your hotel?" she asked.

"Jerusalem."

Miriam exploded with joy. "Jerusalem, you will be staying in Jerusalem! I have never been there. You must take me with you!" She was so excited that Adam was afraid he would have to restart her heart if he said no.

61 Recollection

After paying his deductible for the car insurance, Simon had returned shaken to the house in Jerusalem. Feeling exhausted, he lay down and once more watched the small lizards inching so very slowly along the walls of his bedroom, then scurrying forward to nab an insect before it could jump away. He closed his eyes and slept the evening away. He woke at dawn and saw that the lizards were still there. It was strangely reassuring.

The phone rang. It was Tsvi from Rehovoth. He had read what Simon had left with him and his translations were ready.

"So fast? What time is it?"

"Too early for you? I wasn't busy last night so I worked on your items. Fascinating. Fascinating. I just drove in. I'm seeing my grandchildren later this morning. Did I say that they are beautiful? Yes, I must have. Look, I'll bring these over. There's a cafe on Emek Refaim Road in the German Colony. I'll pick you up. You can buy me breakfast."

After breakfast with Tsvi, Simon unfolded the translations in his bedroom. He reached down and opened the notes from his father's collection. Riffling through them, he came across a couple of sheets of lined paper. Below a crude drawing of a tank was a long hand-written passage in Hebrew. Several sheets stapled to the back held the translation into English. He stared at it.

I am finally remembering it all, even what I don't want to remember. We were called up, Yuri and I, by a special codeword spoken over the telephone that told us to report to our reserve unit. Battle again. The thought I had most dreaded was now true. This time we were to drive the Egyptian army west of Suez. Yuri accepted it with a weary sigh and some of the Hebrew swear words he had learnt. I had some colourful words myself, in several different languages. There was no choice, though. I kissed Hannah and the boys goodbye, and promised the boys I would bring back something for them, a desert stone perhaps, or a rifle shell.

We parachuted in behind enemy lines in the Sinai desert, as part of a small squad of men placed under my command. It was near dawn, and we would not be easily spotted. We landed in a wide wadi. Yuri, in his professor's tone, explained to us how the winter's rainwater runoff flowed through it down to the sea or into underground aquifers. Sudden torrents would flood these ravines and carry anything in them away. During the rest of the year, they would be dry as bone, their bottoms irregular and covered in worn, round stones, easily dislodged and noisy underfoot. We looked up at the sky, but there was no sign of rain, not a cloud in the darkness overhead. We were relieved that we would not face floodwaters today. At the upper end of the ravine was a wide dusty plateau, and it was in this place that we were told that a dispersed line of Egyptian tanks stood and held their ground.

Our band of men hastily retrieved their spread chutes and stowed them behind a large rock. One of the men, Yossi, had twisted his ankle in the landing. I ordered the other seven men to wait with the injured man, while I went out first, as a scout. Yuri slid quickly along the ground to my side to argue with me. The other men were spread out behind the rocks.

"You don't need seven men to guard one, Duvid. You'll need all of us in this, otherwise, why didn't you parachute down yourself?"

"I'm just going out to see what's out there, and then I'm coming back. One body will be easier to hide than eight. Yuri, you and your men will stand guard here while I'm out. The Egyptians have their own patrols all over this area and I don't want to be caught by an ambush when I come back."

"Well, maybe God will look after you, Duvid. Look behind you. You see that mountain? That is Sinai. We are as close as the Jews were who left Egypt. If God really lives here, He will help you."

"Don't waste your time waiting on God to help. Where was He when we really needed him?"

"Ah, Squirrel, let me dream a little. This is the Promised Land. Let me ask Him to fulfil a few promises."

"Look after the men, Fisherman. I'll be back soon."

"Good luck, Duvid. Do you hear that, God? Look after this man."

"Thanks, Yuri."

After a short time, crawling slowly until I could see the rim of the plain, I carefully raised my head above the level of the ground until my eyes just cleared the surface. One tank stood about fifty meters away, its gun aimed towards me and the Israeli border. I looked back for a moment, glimpsing the morning sky that was now unfurling above my home many kilometres behind me. I saw a tinge of pink at the horizon. Above my head, the sky was a deep purple darkening into a matte black, where stars still glittered faintly. It would not be long before the light of day filled the desert around me.

There was no sound except for the whistle of the desert wind. I slipped up over the edge and crawled on my elbows and knees towards the tank. From inside it, I expected to hear the radio's static crackle from the open military radio channel, but there was just silence. This was puzzling. I continued to slither slowly forward until I was next to one tank tread. Rolling against it, I listened for the slightest movement. There was none.

I was breathing as slowly and as quietly as I could. Lifting one hand above my head, I grasped the forward edge of a tank tread, and pulled myself up. I continued until I was on top of the tank turret, looking down into its dark interior. I heard a faint raspy sound—someone was snoring. I backed away a bit from the top of the opening and shouted in Arabic: 'Salaam aleikum'—peace be with you. From inside came a stirring sound, then a scream and a clambering of boots on metal rungs. A head appeared above the turret top, eyes wide, a helmet held in place by one hand. On the man's other side, the tip of a rifle barrel was poking up into the darkness of the sky.

My rifle bayonet flew forward against the man's head. In a slow-motion action the man's helmet flew off and upwards and then the rest of him dropped out of sight. The helmet clattered down the side of the tank and against the stones below. Again there was no sound from inside the tank. I pulled a small flashlight out of a pocket and peered down into the cockpit. At the bottom lay the soldier's body, surrounded by blood. At that moment, I heard the crackle of what sounded like popping soda bottles in the distance, in the direction of the wadi and knew that my men were being attacked. It was the reason the tank had been so dismally manned. The infantrymen who had been with this tank must have seen our parachutes and gone out to attack. They would be back soon. I had little time to prepare.

I had learned how to operate such a vehicle during my years of action. I leaned into the tank, locked my boots under a railing that ran along the top of the turret, and forced my hands under the dead man's armpits. The stench was overpowering. I dragged the body out of the tank and dropped it off the back, then climbed off to pull the corpse behind some rocks. A sharp memory came back to me—the similar motions of my body in the death camp during the war. I shuddered.

I wet my bandana with water from my canteen, wrapped it across my nose and mouth, and climbed down into the tank. By the

*light of my flashlight, I could see the Russian-labelled controls and
I started the tank, easing it forward towards the edge of the wadi.
Then I turned off the engine and waited.*

*The distant gunfire I had heard earlier hadn't lasted long, no
more than fifteen minutes. Someone had won. It might be my men,
but they might as easily have been discovered and ambushed, as
likely to be losers as winners. I prepared myself for either
eventuality. I peered out through the slit in the front of tank's
turret, and listened for a voice, for a language. It was still quite
dark. The pink of the sky was now more insurgent, the unseen sun
slowly rising into day in front of me. If men started to emerge out
of the wadi, that weak light would be at their backs, their
silhouettes prominent, to my advantage.*

*I had to wait only a few minutes before I heard movement, the
crunch of stones below men's boots. Then I saw them, a tight group
of perhaps fifteen men. I heard a guttural lilt, a loud gloating
laugh. It set my teeth on edge. I heard a voice. Arabic words. I
didn't hesitate anymore and started firing the machine gun until
the men in front of me were all motionless, one atop another. Then
I waited, for the sounds of pain to rise from wounded bodies, but
there was nothing. No sound, no movement.*

*I pulled myself out of the tank and carefully moved forward.
Not a sound. Not a stone displaced. Silent. I reached the mound of
bodies. There were Egyptian bodies, perhaps eight. I stopped
counting when I saw the Z'H'L insignia on the others. Israelis. And
then I saw him. Yuri. The Fisherman. I dropped to my knees.*

*All around me, the desert wind blew hot and whistled through
the patient rocks. I sat down to wait for the wind to stop blowing.
It blew on and on. It wouldn't stop, until I was deafened by it. I
screamed at that wind. Quiet! Stop! I went hoarse.*

*When men from my battalion found me, after the area had
been secured and the fighting had already passed much further to
the west, I was all alone. I was sitting in the wadi, my back to the
dead, dropping cartridge casings into an Egyptian helmet. I had
promised my sons souvenirs. I said nothing. I felt nothing. I hoped
I was dead, but I wasn't.*

*Hannah told me later that I spent the next three months
recuperating from catatonia, silent and unaware of my
surroundings. After I returned to this world and came home to the
moshav, she said that only at night did I make any sound,
screaming, my eyes wild, before I would fall back to sleep. Night
after night. After months of this, I was finally able to speak a few
words, my sentences short and laboured.*

I no longer saw my land in the same way. My earth no longer recognized me. My oranges withered. Their flowers stopped attracting bees, they produced little fruit. The well I had dug myself produced a sour taste. Ashamed, I had to ask a neighbour for water. I felt forsaken.

Simon put the notes away. He lay on the bed, watching the lizards watch the insects. Near noon, he finally sat up and went to the kitchen for a cold drink. He put his sandals on and went out for an early lunch. That final interview was in about an hour.

Looking at the food in front of him, Simon changed his mind about lunch. He had no appetite. He thought about Rachel. Just for a moment.

62 Screaming Stones

The waiter had taken the uneaten food away, mumbling something under his breath Simon couldn't understand. Probably the same thing Simon's mother would have said to him. Simon's thought of his mother was the second that afternoon. She was still mostly capable of looking after herself. If she needed help, she could call Adam or his wife, Lyssa. Maybe he should have arranged something with his brother. He sighed.

Simon was relieved to be coming to the end of these interviews. Simon had made an appointment to meet a man near the Jaffa Gate and now he had to hurry. It was inside the Old City, enclosed within the sparkling limestone walls constructed when the early Muslim conquerors first ruled this land over a thousand years before. The original city, that of David, Solomon, and later, Herod, had been destroyed by the Romans after the revolts by the Jewish zealots against their empire. The city was built on debris, layer upon layer, stone upon stone.

Simon walked past the white limestone blocks of Jerusalem's walled city. Those walls gleamed in the harshness of the sun's glow. The day was hot, a brutal day, raw light pounding him as he strode along to the rendezvous spot. Simon searched ahead of him. Somewhere in front of him was the cafe where they had agreed to meet. He was eager to get this interview over with. He marched up from the Jaffa Gate, past David's Tower, and followed the dark walkway between the Armenian and the Christian Quarters, avoiding the crowds headed towards the Church of the Holy Sepulchre. Straight ahead was the Arab *shuk*, the market.

Stumbling like a blind man, hoping to avoid the tortuous laneways that seemed to lead nowhere, he stumbled along in the direction of the Jewish quarter. Beautiful children sat on the doorsteps of a shop. Olive wood carvings of camels and crucifixes and inlaid *shesh besh* sets adorned the counters, ready for the tourists. A corrugated metal gate hung high above their heads like a portcullis. Adam held his hand across the face of the hot sun as he peered upwards at the ancient stones.

He glanced over the quickening ripeness of the exotic fruits and the vegetables, the bargaining between merchants and their customers, at the corpses of dead sheep hanging in the open air, attracting flies. As these flies buzzed and flipped belly down onto their meals, arguments about price went on below them, the ritual haggling necessary to preface a sale. The footway was narrow, covered by wide cloth awnings that allowed slits of sunlight to pass down between one and the next.

Ahead was a broadening of the way, where a group of tables and chairs sat outside a small cafe. This was the place.

Adam was hot. He ordered iced coffee in a rudimentary mix of English and Hebrew. The Arab shopkeeper knew exactly what he wanted. Ice cream. In a cup. Vanilla. A glass of ice water on the side. Simon didn't argue. He sat and spooned it up, and stared around him at a city of stone.

Stones. Jerusalem is stone. Stones that have lived. Stones that have breathed. Stones that speak. They speak in whispers. They sing. They scream.

In this chattering Jerusalem there is a silent rock. It blocks the hole where the waters that covered the earth drained away after the flood. It is the rock on which Abraham intended to sacrifice his son. That son, according to different traditions, was either Isaac or Ishmael. From here, too, Mohammed rose into heaven on a white horse. This rock is the pillow on which Jacob laid his head as he dreamt of angels going up and down a ziggurat, a ladder from heaven. Here he dreamt of his night-long struggle with God's angel before his name was changed to Israel.

Every rock, stone, grain of vitreous sand, has holiness, mission, history. In every stone thrust out by the earth are the remnants of previous life. Earth's depths teem with living organisms enduring within. The earth and its life are intimately coiled one within the other. Every plant born of earth has root, stem, seed. Every plant has earth within it, becomes earth thereafter. Isaac and Esau, brothers like rocks, had fought in their mother's womb. Simon and Adam too had issued from the same intimate darkness. For months, the red glow of their mother's blood had pulsed all around them as they took form. They had known each other's touch, each other's heart beat, had shared each particle of their existence. On a soft wind an errant butterfly is winging.

Refreshed for the moment, Simon looked up and saw another man advance towards him wearing the Austrian hunting hat the man had promised. It was distinctive, if maybe too daring, considering the locale. The man was either very bold or had a deformed sense of humour. Simon blinked. He looked down at the scribbled final name on his list–Eli. He looked remarkably like his brother, Adam. It was a bit unnerving. Calm, he told himself, probably just an illusion, distance making the heart grow fonder, the mind mushier. Try to act professional. The translation he had read earlier had thrown his usual cool off-kilter. Simon raised his arm and waved the man over.

"Ah, the Canadian reporter. We have an appointment, I believe. You look hot."

"Well, Eli, I do come from the land of ice and snow. Call me Simon."

"Simon, I also come from such a land. This looks like a comfortable place to speak."

"Are you thirsty?"

"Ice water, such would be refreshing."

"Eli, let me buy you a cold beer."

"You have not tasted Israeli beer?"

"Yes, you're right. An iced tea, then?"

A waiter, a young Palestinian man, dressed in black pants and a long-sleeved white shirt, came forward and took their orders.

"If you don't mind, Eli, let's begin the interview."

The other man sighed, as Simon set up his tape recorder and microphone. A pair of pretty Israeli women passed in army uniform, one carrying an Uzi automatic. Their skirts were too short for Simon to ignore. Both men's gaze followed them as they walked off into a shadowed laneway until they disappeared. Simon shook his head and returned his attention to Eli.

"So, when did you first arrive in Israel?"

"It's been a long time. Let me see. A year or two before the Six Day War. That would be 1965. I came here from Germany."

"A Jew from Germany? I've met quite a few here born in DP camps."

"No. Germany is not my birthplace. I was born in Russia."

"Okay, the other land of ice and snow. Many immigrants of the last few years were from there too. Before that it was close to impossible to leave. How did you get out–jump over the Berlin Wall?"

"Something like that. It's a long story."

"Anyway, this is about what happened after you got here."

"As you wish. Let's go. Questions please, sir."

"Why did you decide to come here?"

"I had a German girlfriend and she thought that I should try to find my father. We arrived together."

Simon scribbled quickly: Looking for his father.

"A German girlfriend for a Jew from Russia. Unusual. What happened to her?"

"She joined a kibbutz. She felt guilty about what the Germans did to us. Her father had served in the army, of course."

"Did he like his daughter's choice of boyfriend?"

"I think he said something like: 'Ah, my daughter is being fucked by a Jew. Wunderbar!'"

"I'll bet. How did you like the kibbutz?"

"I was not the kibbutz type. I had enough of the socialist paradise in Russia and Poland to last me a lifetime. It was a hard decision, but we both thought it was better to split up. Before the babies started jumping out. We didn't think we could be happy in the same place.

"I worked for a year or so as a technician in a chemical plant outside of Haifa. I still missed Lina, but I was busy and stupid. Then I was called up for the army. I finished my training just in time for the Six Day War. I fought here in Jerusalem. That was quite a sight, all of us praying at the Wall while the bullets were still flying. Some of the guys cried. It was an amazing feeling."

"Even for you? You hadn't been here very long, and you don't sound like you were much of a Zionist, either."

"Yes, even for me. It was something very special. I didn't know how I felt until that moment came. It was like God was carrying us forward on his shoulders."

"So you had your epiphany."

"I don't know this word."

"It means you had an experience that transformed you."

"Okay, that and more."

"And then?"

"I was in the army for another year. On leave, I went back to see Lina."

"At the kibbutz?"

"Yes. By a miracle, she still hadn't found another boyfriend. She's so beautiful."

"Let me guess: tall, blonde, blue eyes, with a perfect body."

"Yes, so you must know her."

"Most Israelis, especially the ones whose parents came from Europe after the war, don't trust Germans."

"True, but for me, this was a good thing. It kept the others back from her. She was lonely. I was lonely. I was soon in love with her again."

"Did you get married?"

"No, her mother got sick and she went back. Last I heard, she had married the son of some industrialist. Probably has half a dozen children by now. All blonde and blue-eyed."

"Well, her father is happy now. So, then? Were you comfortable here in Israel? Did you know you would be in the army so long? How did you feel about the military life? What did you think of the life in the *kibbutz*?"

"Such a barrage of questions. Where to start? It's no picnic here, no matter who you are. I left the kibbutz again–too much sharing, too much knowing everything about everybody. The army, well, not too many can enjoy that part of it. It wears you down."

"So what did you do next?"

"You know, it's amazing. I became a singer. I wrote my own songs, too. Quite successful, just not enough to be famous."

"What did you write?"

"You've heard of *Hava Nagila*? And *Jerusalem of Gold*?"

"You wrote those?"

"Well, no, of course not. But I see you've heard of them."

"So you became a comedian too, I see."

"Also, I decided to find my father. My mother received a letter from him years earlier, with a return address in Israel."

"Why did you wait until you were 20 to come here?"

"You truly are from the spoiled West. You think it would be so easy? She and I were in a work camp in Russia. Also, I was afraid he would reject me."

"So, what did he do?"

"He wasn't there when I finally came looking."

"You couldn't have been more than a child. Why were you in a prison camp? Did you steal the revolution's candy?"

"I was born there, after my mother's arrest. I was returned to Poland when I turned ten, because my mother was a Polish citizen."

"And your mother?"

"No communication with criminals was allowed. I never heard anything more."

"So, about your father, where did he go?"

"Somewhere in this big world. They told me at his *moshav* he had perhaps left for Canada. They weren't sure, though. Just a rumour."

"You were Poles apart, as they say."

"Yes, poles apart. Like the North and South Poles." He chuckled. "So clever."

"Well, we journalists love to use puns. You know, as a Canadian journalist, I might be able to help you find him."

"Where would you look?"

"Canada is not such a big country. In population, that is. Where did you try to find him here in Israel?"

"He had sent his letter from a small place called Moshav Azriel."

Simon sat back and stopped talking. Eli looked puzzled, as if he was expecting more questions, but none were coming.

"Is this another of your jokes?"

"What do you mean?" Eli gave every sign of being puzzled by the question. "Why is everything I say considered funny?"

63 The Centre of the World

Adam craned his neck back to take in the height of Herod's Wall. The shadowed borders between its stones stood out sharply in the full sun of early afternoon. Its rectangular blocks of limestone were huge at this close distance. The chiseled border was typical of each stone, and every crevice between these stones was filled to overflowing with small folded bits of paper, each a request to God to right some wrong, heal some disease, bring a blessing to a wounded soul. As much chance of that happening as came from buying a lottery ticket, Adam thought, but then, he had just bought one the night before. There was something in the air of this crazy country that seemed to obliterate the inhibitions that made a mind rational. No wonder the land had been at war for the last three thousand years or more.

All around him were scores of secular and religious Jews, praying or gawking, some in the stereotypical outfits of the Orthodox, others in shirt sleeves, all drawn here by the sense that this place was in some way special, the very centre of the world.

Adam regretted not finding Simon at the farm. It had been naive to expect that he would be there, but that was what he had expected, a miracle. The Bible had been full of them. Why not now?

Was this the rational, sane, agnostic physician he had been only a few days before? Adam shook his head. He was letting himself deteriorate from sardonic to romantic. What would Lyssa do with him if he stayed like this?

He had no idea where to search next. Maybe he'd better call Rachel again. She might know something more by now. He reached into his pocket and counted out his change. He still had enough telephone tokens to make the call. Rachel should be home now. It was seven hours earlier in New York. That would make it seven in the morning. He finally found a bank of public telephones at the back of a square not far from the Wall, but they were all in use. Calling God, he supposed. There, his old self was coming back. He felt better. Maybe it was proximity that had distorted his sarcastic persona.

It was too hot to stand there waiting. There was a cafe not far from the square. He had told Miriam he would meet her there after dropping her off earlier. He really needed a cool drink now. Miriam wasn't there when Adam got to the cafe. All the chairs were taken by tourists or young Israelis in casual outfits. Everyone ignored him as he walked into the midst of the tables and craned around, searching the square for the old woman. He shouldn't have left her. Maybe she was sick. After all, she had fainted when she had first seen him at the *moshav*. She could have a heart problem. Maybe he should have asked about that possibility.

No, there she was after all, coming towards him. She was carrying two bottles of iced coffee. She looked to be in a great mood. But then she walked right past him as if blinded by something. Adam turned and followed her trajectory. She had laid the bottles down at a cafe table. She was holding someone's hand, a younger man that looked oddly like Adam, except for the hair colour. The young man rose, then he was hugging Miriam.

And then another man at the same table was standing up too. This one did have his brother's hair. There was a good reason for that. That man was Simon, his brother.

Adam rushed forward. He couldn't believe it.

"Simon?"

"My God, Adam, what are you doing here?"

"I came looking for you, Simon."

"What? You're such a busy guy. Run out of patients? Finished healing the world?"

"Always the sarcasm, Simon. Aren't you happy to see me? I mean, really."

Simon paused a moment, the reflex response stilled in his mouth.

"I am pleased. Very pleased." Adam smiled in response. Simon turned, about to ask the next question. Who was this other man who looked so much like them?

Miriam answered before the question was asked. "Adam, this is my son, Eli, my son who I lost, who I thought I had lost. I just put a note in the Wall, asking God to help me find him. A miracle!"

Simon and Adam stared at Eli, then at each other with astonishment. Miriam meanwhile had her arms around Eli. She couldn't let go.

Later that week, Simon sat at the same cafe in the Old City of Jerusalem. He was reviewing all that had happened in the last few days: meeting Eli, meeting Miriam, finding Adam. Incredible. Yet it had happened.

Rachel had called him at his hotel. Adam must have called her and told her where he was staying. He had told her he wasn't sure what he was doing next. She was flying to Israel in two days. Would he meet her at the airport? Yes. Of course, yes. He smiled.

Simon unfolded one of the old yellowed scraps of fabric that he had found in his father's crumbling envelope. It was one of those that Tsvi had been unable to translate for him. The words had been incomprehensible to him. It was his brother Eli who had studied it and now read to him his father's poem.

I dream of her. My waking is as my sleep. She is there in the light of bright day, as much as in the darkness that shields the secrets of night from my eyes. She dances to my left and to my right, in the silence of the easy day, in the heat of midday summer. She touches the skin of my mind. She withdraws my eyes from blindness. My lips taste her taste, my nostrils take in her sweet aroma. I wrap my arms around her, I wrap myself in her. She is my sensation, my every moment. Her fingers caress my soul, her breasts feed my hunger.

I cannot forget her.

"Her? He means Miriam."

"Yes, Miriam. And it looks like he was a poet too."

Adam reached for the note. He handed it to Simon and nodded at him. "We'll keep it for Miriam. Why don't we put the others in the Wall? Ta would have wanted that."

"What about this?" Simon held up Miriam's poem, *Marching Naked to Jerusalem.*

"We'll read it together. It truly is a prayer." Eli said. Simon's eyes closed momentarily. The sloping rays of the sun glowed through his lids. He saw, long ago, his arm arching up and forward in desperation, out of the deepening river. A spume of water droplets was exploding in front of him, and suddenly, a larger arm, the hand bloody, was reaching for him.

Simon opened his eyes. The Wall was not far from where he stood. He pulled his two brothers to their feet and the three men walked off together to complete their father's journey.

64 All This Water

Duvid feels suddenly cold. Something must just have happened to stir him like this. Then he shrugs, "I should feel cold. I am dead, after all." He chuckles to himself, but the recognition makes him feel suddenly faint. A familiar face emerges out of darkness that has enveloped Duvid. A strong hand grasps Duvid firmly by the right arm, keeping him upright.

"Where have you been?"

"Busy, but that is over now. Let us fish," the man's eager face says to Duvid, "the stream awaits us."

"I thought you hated to fish."

"I do, Squirrel. I do. But there is all this water..."

65 Creation

God pulls at the large bolt of fabric lying to one side of the cutting table. The material is velvety dark and featureless. It slips silkily between His fingers, thinner than vacuum, darker than the invisible. God tugs more and more of the ephemeral cloth from a roll of invariable thickness. Its length and width, wrapped as it is around and around itself, is infinite, edgeless, deep as the world, thin as the smallest particle conceivable. Within its deep folds a litter of newly forming stars shimmers. Their glow reflects in His eyes and He smiles with satisfaction. It is a good beginning.

God inspects the mass of jumbled textile. He grips its bulges and begins to unravel its complexity, tucking its loosened threads back into the fabric, infusing it with order. Finally, it lies flat and neat, an endless field of dark material on a limitless table. God reaches for His shears and slides their tips smoothly into the weave. His hands shake slightly as He industriously cuts out the pattern for His creation, while its plan hangs as yet unfulfilled before His eyes.

One by one, the parts are extracted from the whole. The elements separate, coalesce. Vibrating threads of time unite the emerging pieces. Needles of shimmering light are born from the darkness, stellar jewels grow and mature, their energy illuminating the face of God. He is anxious to marshal and rank it all towards its proper form. He sees that He has days of work ahead of Him before He can allow Himself to rest. He has eons of time to pass through before the embryonic cloth between His fingers will be ready to speak with Him, its voice trembling in awe.

In memory of my father, also a tailor, and my mother, a sewer of furs, who together stitched the fabric that became my life.

Acknowledgements

Many thanks to the multitude of individuals who read this book and generously gave of their time over the course of its long and sometimes messy evolution: Charles Schulman, Greg LeBaron, Sharon Callaghan, Alice Petersen, Speranza Spiratos, Blossom Thom, Norm Ravvin, Tecia Werbowski, Wendy Thomas, and Sophia Wolkowicz. They were its early editors and judges, and they kept me going through moments of doubt. Their valuable suggestions nudged it along to its present form, and made me realize that it wasn't–no, not yet, it needs some more work–ready.

To my wife and love, Cheryl Everett Rajchgot, who kept reading and rereading as this novel went on and on through its multitude of iterations, while managing to still smile at me, who kept me on course and as sane as I ever get, and applied her wisdom to my ramblings, I profess my deep gratitude and respect. An enormous thanks too for applying her artistic talents to designing the cover, aptly complementing the themes of the book, a picture worth much more than a thousand words.

I especially thank my two principal editors, Susi Lovell and Sivan Slapak. On them I heap all the praise I can muster, for their diligence, patience, assiduousness, and grace.

To all of the above, thanks too for that special thing, your friendship.

As for length, this novel is as long as it is because the history it is based on is millennia long and its writing started in one millennium and finished in another. As my mother used to say, what can you do?